Miguel of the Bright Mountain

Miguel of the Bright Mountain

Raymond Otis

Introduction by Marta Weigle

A Zia Book

UNIVERSITY OF NEW MEXICO PRESS

Albuquerque

Introduction © 1977 by the University of New Mexico Press. All
rights reserved. Manufactured in the United States of America.
Library of Congress Catalog Card Number 76-57531. Interna-
tional Standard Book Number 0-8263-0447-8

This volume contains the complete text of the first edition,
published in 1930 by Victor Gollancz, Ltd., London, England.

INTRODUCTION

Raymond Otis's *Miguel of the Bright Mountain* is an exceptional novel about Hispanic village life. Although an Anglo and a newcomer to northern New Mexico, Otis learned a great deal in a short time. His protagonists are not unduly stereotyped, and their customs, particularly the rituals of the Penitente Brotherhood, are presented tastefully and with reasonable accuracy. The villagers' plight during the trying years between two world wars is neither romanticized nor minimized. The novel represents an honest attempt by a young writer to capture a complex subject with compassion and craft.

Until now, however, this book was very difficult to obtain, and its author generally ignored by chroniclers of literary activity in the Southwest. This is unfortunate; there are few "village novels" about Hispanic New Mexico and fewer still that depict the Penitente Brotherhood without sensation. Otis's picture of the town of Truchas is in many ways as skillfully drawn as Robert Bright's depiction of Talpa in the latter's excellent *The Life and Death of Little Jo* (Garden City, N.Y.: Doubleday, Doran, 1944). Both authors are Anglo outsiders who write from firsthand observation. They seemingly do not betray their local friendships, and their characters are rarely motivated

v

in strictly "Anglo" terms. These books are good, plausible portraits which supplement the bare socioeconomic record. One hopes that they will some day be joined by more fiction written by native Hispanos to express the realities of their New Mexican heritage.

Ray Otis was briefly but vitally a part of the New Mexico literary scene. Even a rough biographical sketch touches the main areas of contemporary artistic activity. In a sense, then, the novel and the author's career are equally instructive and important. The former sensitively records the rigors of the times, while the latter reveals a man eager to fit himself to express these rigors and to play a significant part in his community.

Raymond Otis made Santa Fe, New Mexico, his home from September 1927 until his untimely death, on July 13, 1938. During this short residence, he shared generously in the life of the town and the surrounding countryside while developing his nascent talents as a writer. He served Santa Fe as a member and later marshal of the volunteer fire department and as a lively participant in the flourishing arts colony there and in Taos. A champion of both the Indian and the native Hispano peoples, Otis wrote several articles and short stories in addition to three published novels. He was associated with Writers' Editions, the Santa Fe Players, and, briefly, with the Federal Writers' Project of the W.P.A. His achievements, remarkable for a lifetime let alone a single decade, deserve recognition. As friend, as neighbor, as citizen, and as writer, Raymond Otis gave unstintingly of diminishing energies during a period that was difficult for the region as well as for the nation.

Santa Fe was not Otis's first taste of New Mexico. He was born in Chicago on May 25, 1900, the fourth of five children of banker Joseph E. Otis and his wife Emily Webster Otis. As a child, he made several visits to the Cimarron area Urraca Ranch of his aunt and uncle, Anne Hohn and George H. Webster, Jr.[1] Educated at Chicago Latin School and Phillips Andover Academy, Otis graduated from Yale in 1924, with an A.B. in English. He taught Latin for a year at the Berkshire School, but New Mexico and a writing career proved more appealing.

Raymond Otis and his younger sister Emily arrived in Santa Fe during September of 1927. Soon afterward, Otis met Frances Lindon Smith. Bina, as she was called, was the daughter of archaeological painter Joseph Lindon Smith and his wife, author-feminist Corinna Putnam Smith, who wrote as Corinna Lindon-Smith. The Smiths were frequent guests at the Pfaeffley Ranch near Alcalde. The young couple were married in St. James Church, New York City, on January 21, 1928. They returned to Santa Fe and settled in a house on Camino Atalaya, where Otis began to devote considerable time to his writing.

The Joseph E. Otis family summered in northern Michigan at an estate called Birchwood Farm, in Harbor Springs. Art critic Forbes Watson was a friend and neighbor there. After Raymond Otis's death,

Watson recalled reading the young man's first novel in manuscript around 1928:

> It was another of those incredible Northern Michigan days, a light breeze, a clear sun, a blue lake, and the trees waving contentedly. Opposite me sat Raymond Otis curled up on the swing in one of his characteristic acrobatic entwinements. He was still. His well-made forehead was without a crease. Against the contrast of his evenly tanned skin his eyes were clear, merry and serious. He was the picture of a young writer silently waiting for the criticism of an older writer. He was modest, unassuming and high-spirited. Many people are merry or serious, unassuming or high-spirited. In Raymond Otis these contrasts were alive. They were striking elements in his attractiveness.

The book was apparently never published. Watson indicates that it incorporated "a testing theme, the eternal battle between idealism and materialism," and that its "autobiographical implications gave the key to a life whose sudden ending is a loss extending beyond family or friendship limits." He describes Otis's style as "quiet writing": "I do not, for instance, remember a stereotyped conclusion. There were none of those staggering finalities which often trouble young writers in the first birth struggles of their creative powers. There were no easy contrasts, no over-coloring, no flattering appeals to current prejudices." Otis's second novel, the first to be published (*Fire in the Night,* 1934), was slightly less autobiographical in that the author was only one among the many Santa Feans portrayed.

By the late 1920s, Santa Fe boasted a vigorous arts colony. Ruth Laughlin recalls the capital in the twenties as "a small friendly town where everyone knew everyone else and each individual's work was a valuable asset to the community." She remembers that "among the writers were Alice Corbin, Mary Austin, Witter Bynner, Willard Johnson, Haniel Long, Ida Raugh, Glenway Westcott, Lynn Riggs, Isabel Campbell, Elizabeth De Huff, Ruth Laughlin, Omar Barker, Roark Bradford, Earl and Marion Scott, Dorothy Hughes, John Curtis Underwood, Peggy Pond Church, Ray Otis, Phillip E. Stevenson, Thomas Wood Stevens and Helen Stevens." Elizabeth Shepley Sergeant also describes the "halcyon days of the nineteen-twenties, when one could rent two or three rooms in Santa Fe for ten dollars a month, [and] the artists and writers . . . kept their horses in the dooryard, their butter in the well (if there was a well), and heated their small adobe rooms . . . with pinon and cedar burned in small oval adobe fireplaces and air tight stoves." Even in the early 1930s, she notes that "a writer, however small his income, may here wake every day, in a setting esthetically pleasing and somewhat exotic, historical yet timeless, with perhaps too keen a sense of stimulus."[2]

Raymond Otis came to know most members of the

arts community. Perhaps his closest friend was poet-essayist Haniel Long, who first visited Santa Fe in 1924–25 and settled there permanently in 1929. Long founded a cooperative publishing venture known as Writers' Editions in 1933. Printer and book designer Walter L. Goodwin, Jr., of the J. B. Lippincott Company, who had helped establish a small, quality publishing cooperative known as Arrow Editions, was persuaded to relocate in Santa Fe and to handle the production of Writers' Editions. The first three of some seventeen volumes to bear the imprint—*The Sun Turns West* by Alice Corbin, *Foretaste* by Peggy Pond Church, and *Atlantides* by Haniel Long—were published in 1933. The associates (five in 1933, seventeen by 1938) underwrote their own books, supplied a mailing list of potential buyers, and supported each other financially or physically by gathering to mail announcements or wrap and ship new editions.[3] Raymond Otis did not publish under the Writers' Editions imprint, but he served ably as financial secretary, keeping the associates apprised of their accounts.

Haniel Long also edited "New Mexico Writers: A weekly page of prose and verse contributed to New Mexicans, at home or abroad" in *The Santa Fe New Mexico Sentinel.* He was assisted by four associate editors—Witter Bynner, Erna Fergusson, Paul Horgan, and Frieda Lawrence. In its eighteen-month history, this "page" provided a local outlet for almost two hundred established and beginning writers, artists, and photographers. Wealthy *Sentinel* editor-publisher Cyrus McCormick would not allow political matter on the Writers page, and no books were formally reviewed. However, a variable mix of short comments, sketches, essays, poems, stories, letters, and book excerpts, plus artwork and photographs, attested to a lively prewar artistic scene.

Otis contributed to the "page," and his picture appears on July 24, 1938, with the caption "To Raymond Otis—July 13, 1938. . . . good citizen, good writer, good friend." The following Sunday (July 31), "New Mexico Writers" included a brief eulogy "In Praise of Raymond Otis" by Frieda Lawrence.[4] Describing their friendship, she recalls: "At once on first meeting Ray years ago I responded to the good will in him; he belonged to that small army of men who are capable of conceiving a better world because they are better themselves than most of us. Simply and unostentatiously you felt him to be good, not sanctimoniously so, but with a sense of humor and a laugh." She emphasizes his integrity, his "fearlessness," and his sympathy for others, citing her convalescence with the Otises and how attentively he and Bina cared for her. Writing as "an elderly woman" whose younger friend has died, Frieda poignantly concludes: "I got well and sadly feel now I can never pay my debt of gratitude to Ray. . . . His wife and sister and friends tell me that he died what I consider a hero's death. He was aware of his coming end and talked about it serenely; he looked it in the eye fearlessly as he had done with life. He had the reward of dying beautifully with dignity like a man, to us he gave an example of courage! I shall always love Raymond Otis."

Another Taoseño and sometime Santa Fean, Spud (Walter Willard) Johnson, also eulogized Otis in a poetic note to his widow:

> To Ray with Love—
>
> Ray has left us forever.
>
> So quiet, sensitive and withdrawn a man that those who did not know him well might not mark that he was no longer about.
>
> Those who did know him well loved him.
>
> I saw him walking down the road to his house the day his illness became serious—finally fatal. Slender, delicate, with a peculiarly lovely line, he moved along, alone in the golden afternoon light—
>
> I did not see him again—I wish I had. I wish that he could have continued to honor our house with his presence. He was a fine friend— a gentleman.

Spud published a small literary magazine, *Laughing Horse*,[5] in which he printed a short story by Otis in 1931. Two other Otis short stories appeared in *Space,* a monthly regional literary magazine (1934–35) edited by Benjamin A. Botkin at the University of Oklahoma in Norman.

Santa Fe also enjoyed an active little theater during the 1920s and 1930s. When he was in residence, Lynn Riggs wrote plays for and directed the Santa Fe

Players. During the twenties, Laughlin identifies some "enthusiastic members including Jane Baumann, Anna V. Huey, Hazel Pond, Norman Magee [McGee], Edwin Brooks, John Evans, Jim Macmillan and Robert Brown." Otis too was a spirited actor and also tried his hand at writing for the stage. He dramatized Frank G. Applegate's short story "San Cristobal's Sheep" as a one-act play for eight characters plus villagers from Las Colonias and Cordova, New Mexico.[6]

Mary Austin was one of the more famous and certainly one of the most imposing members of the Santa Fe arts colony. After her death on August 13, 1934, her remains were temporarily interred in a prominent Santa Fe family's vault at Fairview Cemetery. Trustees of her estate could not agree about a final disposition, and the body was removed two years later and cremated. The ashes were held for another year until a decision could be made. On Friday, August 13, 1937, the following item appeared on the front page of *The Santa Fe New Mexican:*

> Mary Austin's ashes were laid to rest as she wished it, on a high, inaccessible, rocky spot in the foothills of the Sangre de Cristos, on August 11, 1937. Five saddle horses went through the center of Santa Fe Wednesday noon with Dave Steele leading the pack animals and Mr. and Mrs. Raymond Otis, her friends, accompanying the cortege as witnesses. They carried cement, sand and water to seal the ashes into the rock at

> the place chosen by Dr. Harry P. Mera, K. M. Chapman and Francis C. Wilson as trustees.
>
> There was no ceremony as Mary Austin went to her final resting place. . . . Picacho is the sharp, northernmost peak in Santa Fe canyon, south of the river. . . . On the warm last-lighted hill, Picacho, Raymond Otis scratched a name on the rock that will endure not as long as this same name in English literature.[7]

Like Austin, Raymond Otis was concerned for both the Indian and the native Hispanic peoples of New Mexico, and he too expressed this involvement in his writings and through his active support for various organizations.

Mary Austin had been instrumental in organizing interested Santa Feans to help preserve disappearing Indian arts and crafts. Initially known as the Pueblo Pottery Fund, this group sponsored the first Indian Fair in 1923. It was expanded and incorporated in 1925 as the Indian Arts Fund, and, in 1928, a permanent cooperative agreement was arranged between the fund and the Laboratory of Anthropology in Santa Fe. Otis began to work with the fund shortly after his arrival in 1927. According to a resolution in the minutes of 1938, he "gave of his time and his efforts untiringly in the advancement of the work of our organization. Serving as Trustee, member of the Executive Committee, and Secretary, his literary ability was also invaluable in the work of publicity, of which his pamphlet on The Indian Arts of the Southwest was a conspicuous example." This illustrated thirty-four-page booklet, *Indian Art of the South-west: An Exposition of Methods and Practices,* was published and distributed by the Southwestern Indian Fair from about 1931 until the late 1930s. The text is concise, comprehensive, and straightforward, relying on standard sources of the time.

Although he worked diligently for the Indian Arts Fund, Otis's deepest concern lay with the poor Hispanic peoples of New Mexico. Before the New Deal programs went into effect, the League of Spanish-Speaking Workers (La Liga Obrera de Habla Español) was the strongest organization of stricken farmers, laborers, and some mine workers. Otis apparently worked closely with this group. Liga Obrera state secretary Luz Salazar's letter to Mrs. Otis testifies to the results of this labor:

> In the name of the State Executive Committee of Liga Obrera, I am sending you our condolence in the occasion of the passing away of your husband Mr. Raymond Otis.
>
> Together with you, we mourn his death, because with his death the Spanish-American people of New Mexico have lost one of his sincere and real friends.
>
> We will never forget the interest and activity taken by him when the Spanish American farmers in the middle Rio Grande Valley were going to be evicted from their lands, and were not for his sincere help and guidance, these farmers could have been evicted long time ago.
>
> His name is alive in the hearts of 4000

> members of Liga Obrera. When final victory is
> ours, our memory and hearts will go to him, as
> one of the few who helped us, the poor people to
> make our dreams come true, the right to stay
> forever in our lands, as one who helped us to
> fight for our liberation.

Otis's experiences with the Liga doubtless helped inform his novels on Hispano villagers in northern New Mexico.

Presently available records do not detail Raymond Otis's contribution to the Federal Writers' Project of the W.P.A. in New Mexico. The undated first number of the project's mimeographed publication, *Over the Turquoise Trail,* opens with "Facts about the Writers' Project" by then State Director Ina Sizer Cassidy. The New Mexico Project was organized with fifteen workers in October 1935, expanded to sixty workers in 1936, and then "reduced to forty-two, the present [probably 1937] quota." At the end of her introduction, Cassidy notes that "Two of the workers on the Writers' Project have recently had books published, Alice Corbin's *Brothers of Light,* and Raymond Otis, *Miguel of the Bright Mountain.* Both of these books were written before they came on the Project, but are just now published." Two items initialed "R. O." appeared in Number 2 of *Over the Turquoise Trail*—a half-page note on "Three Saints" (San Ysidro, San Antonio, and Santa Inez del Campo), and a brief review of *Who's Who in the Zoo,* by the staff of the Federal Writers' Project of New York City.

Otis's job was probably to edit fieldworkers' reports and to prepare materials for the proposed State Guide.[8] A five-hundred-word manuscript by Otis on Santa Maria de Acoma, written from "personal knowledge," was submitted to editor Alice Corbin on May 5, 1937, and approved for "S-600—Points of Interest" by Ina Sizer Cassidy.

At the age of thirty-eight, Raymond Otis finally succumbed to chronic nephritis. An editorial in *The Santa Fe New Mexican* of Friday, July 15, 1938, paid tribute to his role in the community:

> In the death of Raymond Otis, Wednesday afternoon, Santa Fe lost a most valuable citizen, one whose passing will leave a deep void in the community in which he lived.
>
> While quiet and unassuming, his quick mind, ever ready smile, friendly greeting and his love for his adopted city endeared him to everyone. . . .
>
> His hobby was the fire department, and to this organization he gave unsparingly of his time and energy. He served several terms as fire marshal and assistant marshal as well as president. While serving as marshal it was due largely to his untiring work and investigations that a complete survey of the city's gas supply was made following two disastrous explosions.
>
> His interest in civic improvements was best manifest by his willingness to lay aside his own work, regardless of its importance and give of his

time and talents to the forwarding of any worthy civic project.

Although in ill health for several years, even his closest friends were unaware of it. In the shadow of death his cheerfulness continued and Raymond Otis answered the last alarm with that same gay smile that had won him so many lasting friends in life.

His remains were cremated and the ashes scattered in the Truchas area.

When Elizabeth Shepley Sergeant characterized "The Santa Fe Group" in 1934, she singled out "Raymond Otis, a young author once of Chicago, who has already published 'Fire in the Night,' the first story to deal with the Santa Fe potpourri." Noting the promise in his "forthcoming Penitente novel," she wrote that "he has some of the characteristics of the woodland creature, even to faun ears, and eyes set a little crooked in his head,—he will bear watching." Sergeant ends her sketch with a warning to

the writers of Santa Fe whom many dangers seem to confront: the danger of provincialism or homesickness for Eastern roots. . .—of becoming a prey to the near-writer and appreciative, uncritical circle that steadily grows in a place so charming to live in as this; or falling victim to the summer visitor, disrespectful of working hours; and finally of succumbing to the monumental, indifferent abundance of the land

itself, with its recurrent festivals, native or fabri-
cated, its round of balls and doings: a prey to the
sun, magical, restorative and indolent.[9]

Three years later, Raymond Otis called attention
to similar dangers in a letter to the editor of the "New
Mexico Writers" page. He proposed that "the lure of
sociability in Santa Fe is a dangerous thing." Anyone
"attempting serious work in Santa Fe" had to choose
between talking about what he planned to write, thus
dissipating his ideas, or disciplining himself to carry
through a genuine artistic creation alone. Too much
Santa Fe art was collaborative and communal. According to Otis, "if art is to be anything at all it is the
reflection of the scene and the time in the brain of one
individual capable of transmuting it"; additional
creators at best succeed in "a tour de force—mere
entertainment." He accuses himself and his friends of
socializing too much: "For it is hard to work alone in
a place where one's friends are solicitous and criticism
is non-existent. That is the great disadvantage of
attempting to make Santa Fe one's work-place. It is a
play-place, and any place like it is more or less the
same."[10]

Otis's short story "The Girl on the Piano-Stool"
(*Space,* August 1934, pp. 42–45) explores these themes
of the social and psychological aspects of the creative
process. Two poets, a novelist, and the poets' wives
play a game in which one person sits on the piano
stool and reads a phrase from a book of verse, then
times the others, who lie on the floor and scribble

compositions for three minutes. Although the talk purports to be about writing, the substance of the occasion involves gossip, concealed quarrels, and a growing "passion" between the hapless novelist and one poet's wife.

Writers, artists, and a "princess" who resembles Mary Austin join businessmen, professional men, their wives, their lovers, and a range of Hispanos in the Santa Fe of Otis's first published novel, *Fire in the Night* (New York: Farrar and Rinehart, 1934; published in England by Victor Gollancz, London, as *Fire Brigade*). The Santa Fe Volunteer Fire Department's efforts to quell a large downtown blaze in 1931 provide the vehicle for a sometimes satiric depiction of small-town interrelationships. These "side" involvements are on the whole more intriguing than the main focus of the story—a triangle involving the "Puritan" Easterner transplants, Jim and Claire Mosely, and a "pure," *rico*-descended native Hispano, Lorenzo de Baca. In fact, according to reviewer Withers Woolford, "the characters and events are mostly easily recognizable, but those who attempt to identify their friends will find it somewhat confusing because of the crossing of characteristics by the author." Woolford believes that "some of those who appear in the book are Juan Sedillo, attorney; the late Ashley Pond, capitalist; Norman Magee [McGee], merchant; Edwin Brooks, advertising; Senator Tom Catron; John Evans, writer; Mabel Lujan, capitalist; Witter Bynner, poet; Bill Roberts, mortician; and Nathan Salmon, real estate owner and theatre operator." Reviewer Esther B. Hazen notes that "the Santa Feans are not fond of the book—perhaps because they find bits of themselves in it, and also because they do not like to admit, even in a novel, that anything could possibly be wrong with Santa Fe."[11]

Otis is reported to have been an avid reader of D. H. Lawrence and to have greatly admired the writings of John Dos Passos. The influence of the former may perhaps be seen in Otis's more elemental themes of passion. It is likely that the latter's social "recordings" spurred Otis's attempts at fidelity to life in post–World War I New Mexico during drought and depression.[12]

A concern with love and passion predominates in one short story and Otis's third and last published novel. "Helen" (*Space*, July 1934, pp. 28–33) takes place at a dance in which two young adults recall a day from their adolescence when they and another boy and girl climbed a mountain together. The woman had been in love with the other boy, although she eventually married a third man. The man talking with her at the dance recalls her pain and his own, trying to understand it with well-intentioned but clumsy questions.

Passions and their consequences take on a near-epic quality in *Little Valley* (London: Cresset Press, 1937). The setting for this last novel may be Cundiyo, New Mexico, although specifics of the village are less important than the conflicts that divide certain of its families. Because of his wife Rosa's infidelities, sober, hardworking farmer Juliano Trujillo is humiliated and forced into a violent confrontation with dashing fiddler-farmer Ben Ortiz. Their uneasy truce is threatened by tensions following World War I, when returning sons defied their fathers' traditional way of life. Anxious to leave the harsh confines of Vallecito, Juliano and Rosa's war veteran son, José, eventually persuades his mother to quit the valley with him. She agrees only after a complicated series of witchcraft accusations are leveled against her. The two escape to the sordid Colorado mining towns. The third and last part of the book describes Rosa's return to Vallecito sixteen years later and Juliano's final confrontation with Ben Ortiz. Although life in the changing valley is accurately portrayed, Otis's primary interest seems to be the further exploration of a "love triangle" and its ramifications in an isolated village rather than the less remote small town of *Fire in the Night*.

Still another "passion" is the subject of "The Doll," an oddly disturbing short story published in Spud Johnson's *Laughing Horse* (no. 19, August 1931). Dolores's fascination with a china doll distresses her aging mother and perplexes their Hispano neighbors in the village. The doll is called Ramon, possibly after Dolores's lost son and his runaway, good-for-nothing father, but it is clothed in girl's dresses. Frightened that her mother will take Ramon from her and afraid lest the doll die unbaptized, Dolores finally takes it to the church, where a strange solution results.

Love and passion are certainly a part of *Miguel of the Bright Mountain* (London: Victor Gollancz, 1936), but there is a balance between the depiction of life in

Hormiga (patterned after Truchas), Borregos (Chimayo), Santa Rosa (Santa Cruz), and Gabaldon (Santa Fe), and Miguel Lopez's coming of age.[13] Too, there is the added element of the Penitente Brothers' spiritual passion. The result is a rich, integrated story, the best of Otis's novels, but one which did not have enough appeal for New York publishers. His mother-in-law, Corinna Lindon-Smith, had earlier helped him make connections with New York agents who referred *Fire in the Night* to Gollancz. Because the English firm was the only one to publish *Miguel,* the book received little notice locally or nationally.

Miguel Lopez is his mother Concepcion's favorite son, traditionally a rather difficult position in Hispanic culture. It is for her rather than for his woodsman-farmer father, Eliseo, that Miguel eventually leaves the confines of family and village. His departure is also in part precipitated by his first love, Lucinda, the daughter of village *patrón* Vicente Romero. From Don Vicente, Miguel learns the rudiments of business on a small scale, but it is not enough to fit him for commerce outside Hormiga and too much to permit him happiness running the Lopez family's tiny store. Lucinda's father's position and her schooling at the Presbyterian mission school in Borregos and the Sisters' (Loretto) Academy in Gabaldon have unfortunately made her a cheerless companion for the questioning Miguel. However, the introspective youth is also helped by the kindly but limited French priest from Santa Rosa, Father Aloysius. Inevitably, neither parent nor *patrones* nor priest can truly comprehend

Miguel's turmoil, let alone aid him in making a transition to life in town.

Miguel does not leave Hormiga for the usual reasons. There is no war. He does not seek wage labor as a miner, shepherd, or farm laborer in Colorado or Wyoming. He is not enrolled in a C.C.C. camp like his brother Pablo. Instead, he is to attend the Christian Brothers' (St. Michael's) high school–junior college, and the expected outcome of this education is never really clear to anyone involved, either in Hormiga or Gabaldon.

Otis does not give Miguel easy choices. The young Hispano's experiences in town and at school are ambivalent; his roommate Merijaldo Quintana, his Anglo employers the Fayerweathers, and especially their housemaid Maria partially offset the prejudice and unyielding incomprehension he encounters in his new life. Later, his return to the village is no less complicated, and this further transition is also accompanied by both anguish and joy.

Miguel's return is marked by his initiation into the Penitente Brotherhood, an event anticipated from the beginning of the novel. The Brotherhood of Our Father Jesus was an important lay religious society in rural northern New Mexico and southern Colorado, and Otis has tried to show its charitable and community service activities as well as its Lenten and Holy Week rituals. His descriptions, apparently based on annual visits to public services at the Truchas morada and church, are generally accurate and unsensational. Otis's fictional treatment of the Brotherhood is in many ways comparable to Alice Corbin Henderson's nonfictional impressions of rituals at Abiquiu, New Mexico, during the 1920s and 1930s. Both volumes contrast vividly with the outrageous sensationalism characteristic of most contemporary outsiders' accounts of the Brotherhood.[14]

In this novel, as in his other works of fiction, Raymond Otis is more concerned with the psychological and interpersonal than the physical. Few purely descriptive passages occur. Even Miguel's "bright mountain" is not so much an external beacon as a long-hidden center. When Miguel truly returns, not to the village but to the Pedernal (Rosario) Grant, the land he finds is as much interior and mythic as an actual place and the historic home of his fathers.

Miguel Lopez may very well have had a live prototype. The following letter came from one of Raymond Otis's many friends:

Truchas, N.M.
July 19–1938

Dear Mrs. Otis:

This is to let you know that I am very very sorry, to hear of the death of Mr. Otis. This was quite a surprise to me, as I had phone, and they tell me he was getting better.

Too bad I did not attended the services, but you know how we people live up here, when we learn the news they have passed two or three days.

I hope God has given him the best place in heaven, and that some day we will all meet again.

> With best regards, I am,
> Yours truly,
> CARPIO ARCHULETA

NOTES

This volume has been reprinted with the kind assistance of Raymond Otis's remaining family: his widow, now Mrs. William Dudley Hughes, his brother, Mr. Stuart H. Otis, and especially his sister, Mrs. Emily Otis Barnes of Santa Fe. The photograph on the cover was taken by his niece, Ms. Natalie Owings of Santa Fe. I would like to acknowledge the invaluable aid of both Mrs. Barnes and Mr. Otis in the preparation of this introduction. I also appreciate the research help I received from Mrs. Peggy Pond Church, Mr. Robert F. Kadlec, and two librarians, Mr. Orlando Romero of the Southwest Room, New Mexico State Library, and Ms. Stephany Eger of the History Library, Museum of New Mexico—all of Santa Fe.

1. Webster's contributions to Colfax County are described in Lawrence R. Murphy, *Philmont: A History of New Mexico's Cimarron Country* (Albuquerque: University of New Mexico Press, 1972). This is the area of the nineteenth-century Maxwell Land Grant, documented historically by Jim Berry Pearson in *The Maxwell Land Grant* (Norman: University of Oklahoma Press, 1961) and fictionally by Harvey Fergusson in *Grant of Kingdom* (1950; reprint ed., Albuquerque: University of New Mexico Press, 1975).

2. Ruth Laughlin, "Santa Fe in the Twenties," *New Mexico Quarterly Review* 19 (1949):60–61; Elizabeth Shepley Sergeant, "The Santa Fe Group," *Saturday Review of Literature,* December 8, 1934, p. 352. For more detailed accounts of the artists, see Van

Deren Coke, *Taos and Santa Fe: The Artist's Environment, 1882–1942* (Albuquerque: University of New Mexico Press, 1963); and Edna Robertson and Sarah Nestor, *Artists of the Canyons and Caminos: Santa Fe, the Early Years* (n.p.: Peregrine Smith, 1976). Excellent contemporary photographs of the town and its environs are in Ernest Knee, *Santa Fe, New Mexico* (New York: Hastings House, 1942).

3. Jack D. Rittenhouse, "Southwest Imprints: Writers' Editions," *Book Talk: New Mexico Book League,* December 1975, pp. 3–4. Goodwin's shop was named the Rydal Press after his family's Pennsylvania estate. He published other books, and Rydal has continued printing operations until today, although Goodwin sold it in 1941. (The last book known to bear the Writers' Editions imprint, Gustave Baumann's *Frijoles Canyon Pictographs,* 1939–40, was not printed at Rydal Press.) See also Lawrence Clark Powell's essay on Haniel Long's *Interlinear to Cabeza de Vaca* in Powell's *Southwestern Classics* (Los Angeles: Ward Ritchie Press, 1974), pp. 109–19.

4. Reprinted in E. W. Tedlock, Jr., *Frieda Lawrence: The Memoirs and Correspondence* (New York: Alfred A. Knopf, 1964), pp. 433–34. According to a recent biographer, "for Frieda, Raymond and Frances Otis represented the old pioneer spirit and idealism of America" (Robert Lucas, *Frieda Lawrence: The Story of Frieda von Richthofen and D. H. Lawrence* [New York: Viking Press, 1973], p. 268).

5. Beginning in 1922, seven numbers of *Laughing Horse* were published at the University of California, Berkeley. The fourth issue was unsuccessfully charged with obscenity for publishing an expurgated letter from D. H. Lawrence. No. 8 was put out in Guadalajara, Mexico, nos. 9–12 in Santa Fe, and a D. H. Lawrence issue, no. 13, in Ossining, New York. All the remaining numbers (except no. 17, a special issue on censorship published in Santa Fe) originated in Taos on Johnson's own Kelsey Press, now in the collection of the Museum of New Mexico, Santa Fe. See Spud Johnson, "Laughing Horse Awake from Seven Year Siesta; Ready to Trot Off the Rumbling Presses of Taos," *The Santa Fe New Mexico Sentinel,* April 24, 1938, p. 9; and Claire Morrill, *A*

Taos Mosaic: Portrait of a New Mexico Village (Albuquerque: University of New Mexico Press, 1973), pp. 133–35.

6. Laughlin, "Santa Fe in the Twenties," p. 61. See also Thomas Erhard, *Lynn Riggs: Southwest Playwright,* Southwest Writers Series 29 (Austin, Tex.: Steck-Vaughn, 1970); and Mabel Major and T. M. Pearce, *Southwest Heritage: A Literary History with Bibliography,* 3d ed. (Albuquerque: University of New Mexico Press, 1972), pp. 152–54. Applegate's story appears in his *Native Tales of New Mexico* (Philadelphia: J. B. Lippincott, 1932), pp. 239–54. A typescript of Otis's dramatization is in the collection of Zimmerman Library, University of New Mexico, Albuquerque.

7. See T. M. Pearce, *The Beloved House* (Caldwell, Idaho: Caxton Printers, 1940), pp. 216–22; and idem, *Mary Hunter Austin* (New York: Twayne Publishers, 1965), pp. 67–69.

8. *New Mexico: A Guide to the Colorful State* (New York: Hastings House, 1940) contains almost no data about the New Mexico Writers' Project. (Alice Corbin Henderson's chapter on "Literature," pp. 130–40, is valuable, however; she gives favorable mention to all three of Otis's novels.) The project files are incomplete and disorderly at present. Most materials are in Santa Fe at the History Library, Museum of New Mexico, and/or the New Mexico State Records Center and Archives. New Mexico does not figure prominently in recent histories of the project, but useful perspectives are in William F. McDonald, *Federal Relief Administration and the Arts* (Columbus: Ohio State University Press, 1969), and Jerre Mangione, *The Dream and the Deal: The Federal Writers' Project, 1935–1943* (Boston: Little, Brown, 1972).

9. Sergeant, "The Santa Fe Group," p. 354.

10. Otis's letter, dated October 16, 1937, appears as "Plight in Santa Fe," *The Santa Fe New Mexico Sentinel,* November 17, 1937, p. 7. It stimulated much local controversy and correspondence. Marina Wister Dasburg of Taos wrote to suggest Mr. Otis form an association similar to one she had helped start in Philadelphia (January 19, 1938, p. 6). Haniel Long noted his own 1925 group with Witter Bynner, Spud Johnson, Lynn Riggs, and Alice Corbin Henderson (January 19, 1938, pp. 6, 7; see also his

description in *New Mexico Quarterly Review* 19 [1949]:68–69), and claimed that "Ruth Laughlin had a group of three writers (an admirable number, in my opinion) meeting weekly in her home last winter, and Orval Ricketts wrote me some time since of a writing group in Farmington" (February 23, 1938, p. 6).

11. The Santa Fe Volunteer Fire Department was officially recognized on January 20, 1922. Ashley Pond (Ashby Warner in the novel) served as chief. Otis apparently wrote a history of the department entitled "Fireman's Follies." He is shown seated on the front fender of the fire engine in a 1933 photograph of the volunteers reproduced in *The Santa Fe New Mexican* (June 5, 1966). Two of Spud Johnson's subsequent "Santa Fe Gadfly" columns in that newspaper (June 19, 1966, and an unidentified later clipping) contain notices and reviews of the book as a good evocation of "a Santa Fe that was a small, sleepy town. . . . [with] an oddly diverse population." According to Johnson, Otis "did not spare himself. In a satiric sketch involving the several 'Yale men' who were among the first Volunteers (and he was one of that group), he tells of the organization of the Flying Heart Development Company, which, in the book is most amusingly described as 'The Winged Heel Development Corporation' in all its 'Big Business' pretentions, grandiose splendor—and ultimate failure." Woolford's review appeared in *New Mexico Magazine,* July 1934, p. 26. Hazen was a reviewer for a mimeographed publication put out for two successive years by the Department of English, New Mexico Normal (Highlands) University at Las Vegas. Largely based on materials from annual Roundtables on Literature of the Southwest, *Writers and Writings of New Mexico* was a collection of reviews and biographical data edited by Lester Raines. Notes on Otis appear in vol. 1 (1934), p. 98, and in an addendum to vol. 2 (1935). See also the review by Hester Jones in *New Mexico Quarterly* 4 (1934): 239–41.

12. For a vivid socioeconomic study of conditions in the north-central New Mexican villages in 1935, see "The Spanish-American Villages," volume 2 of the so-called Tewa Basin Study. This descriptive and statistical survey, based on fieldwork in some

forty villages, is reprinted with supplementary materials and bibliography in Marta Weigle, ed., *Hispanic Villages of Northern New Mexico* (Santa Fe: The Lightning Tree, 1975). Truchas, Chimayo, Cundiyo, and Santa Cruz are among the communities covered in the 1935 work.

13. Otis wrote two amusing "sketches," presumably about his own coming of age, for the "New Mexico Writers" page. He recounts fifteen-year-old David's "ordeal" while shopping with his mother for a bathrobe to take with him to boarding school. David is then described as he listens to an amusing lecture from Mr. Flinch, an elderly family friend, on the evils of masturbation ("David: Two Sketches," *The Santa Fe New Mexico Sentinel,* October 27, 1937, pp. 6, 10).

14. Poet Alice Corbin Henderson's invaluable eyewitness account of Brotherhood rites during Holy Week at Abiquiu, New Mexico, is in *Brothers of Light: The Penitentes of the Southwest* (New York: Harcourt, Brace, 1937), with illustrations by her artist husband William Penhallow Henderson. *Miguel of the Bright Mountain* is Otis's best attempt to present his understanding of the Brotherhood. An early short story set in Abiquiu (where he may have accompanied the Hendersons during Holy Week), "El Penitente" (*Dial* 85 [1928]: 406–13), is contrived and preachy. A brief essay, "Medievalism in America," might be termed a kind of sociological mysticism, in which Otis concludes, "There is only the soil, and a grudging desolate soil it is, upon which they [the Brothers] may work out their destinies, and that becomes monotonous. Their women are strong, a little stronger than the men. Perhaps the men have resorted to mystery, secrecy and heroics to redeem their superiority" (*New Mexico Quarterly* 6 [1936]: 90; first published in two parts in *El Artesano: A Magazine of Arts and Crafts,* Santa Fe, June and July 1933). For a comprehensive history and description of the Brotherhood, see Marta Weigle, *Brothers of Light, Brothers of Blood: The Penitentes of the Southwest* (Albuquerque: University of New Mexico Press, 1976); and idem, comp., *A Penitente Bibliography* (Albuquerque: University of New Mexico Press, 1976).

I

THEY WERE putting out the candles. After the
long Rosary service, this was the moment of reward, the
moment Miguel was waiting for. In the dim light, his
wide, dark eyes searched the room self-consciously,
fearful that others might be noticing how his heart was
beating, as if it were being squeezed by a pressure of
fingers. Other faces were intent, but not upon him, or
his heart. He felt relieved, and once more gave his
whole attention to the altar and what was happening
there. He counted the candles on the rail. Thirteen.
One was out. It was hard to see because he was so
small; he twisted his body and craned his neck in
order to peer through spaces between people's heads
and shoulders in front of him.

The two men seated at either end of the altar-rail
leaned over and pinched out a candle at the end of
each psalm, alternately; now it was the turn of the man
on the right. He acted promptly, even leaning forward
in his chair in readiness before the prayer was finished.
The other man was old and drowsy and had to be
reminded to put his candle out. To Miguel this was a
profound annoyance—he felt like kicking the old man,
or going up himself and pinching out the flame, neither
of which he would have dared to do had his life
depended on it. For he was a boy, and these were
men, serious and intent upon a mystical business. It
was none of his affair; if they even suspected his

dissatisfaction with the way things were being done, they would put him out of the church without asking him how he liked it. He trembled, shuddered, to think of the horror of it—of being put out before all these people. But he wished the old man on the left hand of the altar-rail would keep awake. How could anyone be sleepy, old or young, in the presence of such excitement, such mystery?

Ah! the third candle. The man on the right was alert. Just on time he put his candle out. Ten more. Miguel's eyes opened wider; as long as the psalm lasted, they roamed over the room, but during the response which was chanted by the people around him in supernatural, thin tones, he kept his gaze on his mother, following the movements of her lips with his, but making no sound. Some day he would learn and remember the words, but he was only thirteen now, and——

Thirteen! The same number as the candles on the altar-rail! Suddenly he didn't want them to put out any more candles. It was like extinguishing a year of his life each time. The thought filled him with a new terror—he wanted to cry out, to stop them, and his heart beat in his throat. He squirmed in the real, unreasonable agony of his fear, until his mother laid her hand on his head to quiet him. There was magic in that; his fear ebbed for a time, and the fourth candle was put out, late, by the old man on the left. Ah, the old fool! Why couldn't he stay awake? Miguel looked up at his mother in impatience.

She was passive. Too many of these services, changeless in their form and meaning, had passed before her

eyes. She knew what was coming, and her anticipation
told her no lies; she knew that when the last candle
went out she would be possessed by a vision of holiness
and terror; she would see in the blackened church, by
the inner light of her naked spirit, the night of passion,
the cross, the thieves, the thunder, and the lightning.
And she waited for it, passive, resigned, ready to let
it all flow over her again like an inrushing tide. Miguel
was restless beside her. He was too young, really, to
come to the service at all, but he had begged and
begged. And it seemed to thrill him more than anything
that happened in Hormiga, from year to year's end.
What he was actually experiencing was far from his
mother's understanding, for she was a simple woman.
Seeing him so taken in by the thing filled her with
some kind of fear for him, and it mounted now to a
flash of agony when she put out her work-hardened
hand and calmed him by laying it on the top of his
head.

Presently he took her hand away, and held it in his
own two hands, tightly in his grasp. As the fifth and
sixth candles were pinched out he squeezed it convul-
sively. The old man on the left was maddening in his
forgetfulness; they were half way through the next
psalm before he came to and realised that his candle
should be out. Then he leaned forward with a great
clatter and commotion to pinch the wick. Miguel, for
a moment, was enclosed in a flame of hatred of him,
and impatience. No one else seemed to think it was bad
—a few were amused: a faint ripple of laughter, dis-
creet, subdued, stirred the darkening air when the
old man leaned forward sleepily, minutes late. But it

was not funny to Miguel, even then; he hated those
who laughed, as much as he hated the old man. It was
his business to put out the candle, and he was spoiling
it, spoiling Miguel's illusion by being mortal and
drowsy. And this was no time or place for mortality.
As soon as the church doors were shut upon the night,
and the service begun, mortality fled, and Miguel
felt transfigured. Especially to-night, he was not mortal
because they were extinguishing a year of his life with
each candle. He was gripped by a fear again when he
realiscd that there were only six years left to him now.
They had taken away seven. When the last candle was
gone, he would surely die—or he would be nothing,
year-less, a nothingness.

He wondered. Would he be able to drift like a cloud ?
Or fly like an angel ? On white pinions ? He would rise
on the dusty air and float above these people, above
his mother, like the fluffed seed of a dandelion. How
many times he had watched them drifting in the sunlight. He would be like that, robbed of his thirteen
years. Nothingness. It would be rather fun, looking
down on the earth like a bird. Tangled—lost—in a
ravel of clouds.

Miguel prepared himself for the ordeal to come. He
fled back over the years, faster, far faster than the
deliberate extinguishing of candles on the altar-rail.
Before he was five years younger by their slow counting,
he was back almost two millenniums, walking with Our
Father Jesus to the Calvary, seeing it all with frightening clarity. He saw the mob in the streets, and, still
a boy, dared not draw near, but he followed along,
wondering what the man had done to earn his cruel

fate. Nothing he could ever see, yet men were never punished for nothing. Boys were: looking over his diminishing years, he could see how his own punishments, even those that seemed undeserved, had a kernel of wrong-doing at the bottom of them. Yet here was this Christ who was never mentioned except in praise, being punished by a load of horrors greater than any man's. It was one of the problems which he entrusted to the future to resolve for him. For the moment, it was getting very dark in the church; four candles in the big, bare place were faint enough. He moved a bit closer to his mother along the floor, until he could feel the comfort of her knees.

Probably this was the last year that he would be allowed to stay with her, on the women's side of the church; next year, and ever after, he would have to stand with the men, on the other side. He looked over there. Some boys not much bigger than himself stood along the wall. They had scared, drawn faces, but they stood up like men, on the men's side. He felt a little ashamed for a time, and then forgot about it. The unnatural, sing-song voice of the *Hermano Mayor* droned through the prayer, which, after the response, would darken the tenth candle. Miguel watched the four thin flames burning in the middle of the rail; they contained all the light of the world; all the light of the sun was in them, and something clutched his heart at the thought of their going. The end of the world—and of him—reduced from thirteen years to nothing. Adrift. As the recipient of all this he cringed, for it seemed suddenly that the whole thing was being directed upon him, like the sun under a glass, and he would be consumed in the tiny, intense point of fire. He didn't know what it meant, or why it was done, but it frightened him, terrified him and curdled his blood, lifted him to the high heaven and flung him down again, cringing against his mother's knees.

There was no escape, once the ancient, panelled doors of the church were closed. Still, he liked it for its grim and terrible progress; he was fiercely fascinated by the very fear which marched up to him and took him in its gigantic arms and bore him off, a shrinking thing, over the horizon of the world. If he closed his eyes, especially while they were singing the sad, wailing responses, enough of which he understood to know that they contained all the mystery and sorrow of the mother of Christ—if he closed his eyes then, it all came rushing: his fear marched upon him with outstretched arms, grimacing. Dark clouds gathered on the hill and lightning revealed the crosses starkly, white against the purple night. It was better to keep his eyes open, better to see the tense faces around, the tired lines of men kneeling in the centre of the church, while there was light to see by.

Three candles were left burning. Miguel's heart contracted with fear. Why didn't he cry out like the three-year-old he was? And bury his head against his mother's knee?

Then in the growing dark, the lines of men in the centre became the souls of the damned, and their squeaky voices in the responses were the damned, bleating; he cringed, and flattened himself into the rough planks of the floor. There was a musty smell in the boards, low down, and a smell of many people breathing, above. And just under the floor was the earth—he could smell it coming through the cracks— dry earth, for hundreds of years unknown to rain. The thought distracted him. Think of the poor earth under all the aged houses of Hormiga, dry for so long. Starved. The skeleton of earth, it must be, dead, the spark of life gone out of it.

The eleventh candle! Two faint fingers of flame bravely holding off the dark. Heroic light! Saving him from nothingness, from dissolution. Oh, if he might stop them now! Stop their relentless, deliberate darkening of the light of the world!

He crept closer to his mother; he was young enough still to shrink instinctively to her as the ultimate refuge. The sanctuary of her nearness had never failed him yet, while he still had no life of his own, apart from her. He was only beginning to suspect half-consciously, tremulously, like the growth of a seed in him, that there could be a life apart from her. He shrank against her until his lips were close enough to whisper: " It's getting pretty dark in here."

She heard, but her own thoughts excluded him. At a time of such excitement, Concepcion was unable to approach anything outside herself, not even Miguel, her best-loved son. She put out her hand again, and he took it between both his own. Ah, these men! the mother was thinking; shabbily putting on this service of theirs in poverty and meanness—yet, in spite of all, something of divinity came through the patches, straight from the grandeur of their immortal souls! And it took her in its stride, lifted her up and sat her on a cloud, within sight of heaven. She felt it without understanding, felt that she was witnessing something strangely and inexpressibly holy, although to-morrow she would remember it all with unbelief and a slightly apologetic hang of her head as if she had been duped. For she knew how holy the men were, every other day in the year, and yet this ceremony—performed with a few candles, a handful of *matracas* and a ten-cent sparker or two, chains for thunder, yells, whistles, stamping of feet—transformed them into archangels in the service of God. Of her it made a trembling spirit, ushered to the very presence of her Maker. Of her son, Miguel——

She looked down at Miguel. She saw that he was frightened and spoke to him in a loud whisper without much tenderness in it.

" What did you come for, then ? You knew it would be like this."

Miguel nodded and released her hand. As he did so, the old man at the left end of the altar-rail pinched out the twelfth candle—promptly; and the boy, caught between relief at the man's alertness and the expectancy of what would follow, suspended breathing. His whole being was focused upon the single point of light which now poised between himself and the void of darkness. The long psalms separating the death of candles had seemed endless; this last one rushed along with the speed of the wind. Breathless he heard the *Hermano Mayor* finish it, heard the people around him speak the last response, and in the ensuing silence his heart bounded, for the last prayer was done. He watched the three men who had been before the altar, while they, by the light, now, of one electric torch, puttered there, moving dead candles on the altar, replaced this and that, put chairs back against the wall, and Miguel, impatient, wondered how they could be so deliberate with hell waiting to break loose on their heels. The beam of the electric flash-light flickered weirdly, lighting a face here, blocking out a figure there. Forms moved silently like spirits moving. At last the three came down from the altar, stumbling in the thick dark, and went to the door at the side. There was more delay while they fumbled to find the knob, passed through the low opening, ducking their heads. Then, with the click of the latch they were gone. The church was black, darker than any dark Miguel had known before, laden, heavy with potency, which pressed against him, throttled him with the feeling of being smothered. It was as he imagined it would be to fall into a well, to breathe the solid darkness of water at the bottom of a well. The panic-sensation of being trapped was split apart in a moment by the lines of tired men in the centre of the church, who suddenly broke into a madness of noise. Miguel hadn't time to be frightened now. Wave upon wave of sensation rolled over him as the men, vivified into fiends, cracked the silence with their shrieks and whistles, shattered the gloom with their sparks of lightning. Now they *were* the damned, and the church was their hell. They produced chains out of nowhere and beat the floor with them; they stamped on the boards with their feet, made a hideous clatter with their shoes and raised a choking dust from the ancient floor, while from their throats came inhuman volleys of yells and sounds. The deafening whir of *matracas*, the glittering sparks of the flints, and the chains thundering. . . .

Sad, silent, weary men transformed, no longer sad or silent, but devils leaping and beating the air. The noise seemed to rise slowly to a peak of fiendishness, and to die down, shot through with the pattern of a hellish symphony, accidental, but formidably recurring like the rhythms of a flood. When it ended and lights were brought back, Miguel was limp, exhausted, but thrilled to the bottom of his soul. As he came out of his enchantment, he found himself clutching his mother's leg with one whole arm, while his other hand gripped his cap, rolled into a ball. Feeling ashamed, he released his mother's leg gradually, hoping that in her own excitement she might not have noticed his. He tried to remember how long the din had lasted; it might have been a minute—or an hour—but time had gone out of him. There was nothing left to gauge it by. The whole thing could have been a nightmare, lasting from sundown to dawn; he only knew that he was sorry and immeasurably relieved to have it over, and he watched while the three men came in again with the flash-light, saw how one lighted the candles on the altar until it was ablaze with flames once more. Finding his voice, he whispered to his mother: " Will they do it again ? "

" Not to-night, Miguel."

" When ? "

" Next year, maybe."

He sat still with all his vitality gone. It was much worse, he discovered, in anticipation; little remained in memory, save the feeling of being drained of everything. The sensations could not be recaptured. He tried closing his eyes, and forcing his imagination backward, but it was a disappointment; it didn't work, however hard he fought his way back over the ground. He opened his eyes and looked at the men who, a moment ago, had been creatures of dread, and they were the same, too, tired and drooping, unchanged. This was mystifying. They were men grown from boys like himself—some of them sat back on their heels, some were kneeling, all were listless, disinterested. How could they . . . ?

He turned his wide, incredulous eyes to his mother. She showed no signs of having passed through terror, either. Her face was composed, disturbed only by a slight frown which wrinkled the skin between her brows, nothing more; so it occurred to him that it was a dream, and one which had taken place long ago, in a world now closed to him. He sat motionless beside his mother, trying to figure the thing out. In a little while, at a signal from the *Hermano Mayor*, the men who were disposed in lines in the centre of the church stood up, turned about and shuffled towards the door; as they came to the portal, they lined up two abreast and passed out in that formation. Miguel, sitting near, watched their faces as they passed, searching for a clue to the transfiguration which had made them fiends for the span of his dream, or whatever it was that had happened to him. The inescapable truth was that they were ordinary men, for the most part familiar to him—many of them were cousins or uncles, some of whom were little older than he. And he was seized with a sudden resentment and envy, to think that they should be such men of the world, while he was a snivelling spectator still, cringing at his mother's knee. But he shrank from them as they passed, for there was something awful about them even now, not yet altogether of the known and familiar world of which Hormiga and the dark mountains were the compass. He edged away from their shuffling progress through the door, fearful lest one of them touch him by mistake and turn him into stone or, worse, strike him blind, like the people in the stories his mother used to tell when he was younger. It would be all right to-morrow; to-morrow he would meet some of them on the street and it would be a natural thing, without wonder, but now they were not yet men, and he made himself small. They heeded him no more than the floor they walked on, but stared straight ahead of them with their eyes fixed on the moonlit space beyond the open doors. One whom he knew well, his Uncle Tomas, looked him in the eye, and Miguel, meeting the blank beam of his gaze, shivered, for there was no recognition in it; the uncle's stare was vacant, sightless, and his eyes were those of a ghost. Miguel turned away, cold with a new fear. What was the spell on these men? It was no good asking his mother; he had asked her questions about the *Penitentes* before, and she always put him off with a shrug or a word, as if they were men beyond the understanding of ordinary people. He would have to find out for himself. Then he saw his father, his own father, marching to the door with a lighted candle in his hands. The flame, held just below his chin, cast a pale illumination along his features, filled them with a weird light which, accentuating hollows and elevations, gave him the look of a death's-head. Miguel shivered, and coughed, hoping to convince himself that it was his father by making him smile or nod or give a sign that he knew his son. But there was no change on the face which, looking down upon the candle flame, appeared reversed, its sight directed inwards upon the region of the soul.

" Father. Papa," Miguel whispered, but the father's terrible concentration held. And then, in a moment, he was gone through the door and Miguel gave up hope of understanding, was left to his own trembling isolation.

Eliseo, the father, had been among the last of the *Penitentes* to go out. Only the *Hermano Mayor* and the two men who had sat at the altar with him remained behind to put out the candles when the crowd had gone. A silence fell upon the church. No one moved, or seemed to breathe. And then after a long interval a rustling began as, singly at first and then in a wave of rising movement, people got to their feet and tiptoed out of the place. Miguel, dragged to his feet by a pull of his mother's strong arm, rubbed his eyes as if waking from sleep. They went outside. His mother stopped to talk with friends and the boy wandered off alone.

The hour was late for working people. The moon rode high and the snowy mountains glowed under it like stage mountains whitened by floodlights. The April frost turned Hormiga's muddy streets into ridges and gullies of brittle earth. Miguel strolled along, lost in remembrances and, kicking at what he took to be a clod of dirt in the road, lying beside its shadow in the moonlight, cried out at the pain in his toes when

BM

the clod turned out to be frozen earth, hard as stone.
The air didn't feel so cold, but you never could tell in
the thin and lofty air of the mountains, overlooking
the gulf of valley which the town fronted on the west,
and into which the sun began to dip every day soon
after lunch. Sometimes, with a blue mist in it and
evening purple shadows, it appeared to be filled with
water—and always there were the blue mountains
on the other shore. He couldn't imagine a body of
water as big as that; there was the lake behind the
irrigation dam at Borregos, below Hormiga—but the
shores were not far apart. It was only about a mile
long.

Miguel, checking himself in the midst of such
speculations, marvelled at his easy ability to forget
so quickly the experience he had just been through.
And for the rest of the way home he drove himself to
think how it could all have been so terrible and so
wonderful. He thought with all his might about the
noise, and there came a slight quickening of his heart,
but no more. And soon he was distracted again by
small things—the barking of a coyote, the answering
wail of an Hormiga dog. He was carried from one
thought to the next, to the coyote he had shot himself
not long ago, to the vivid picture of the slinking animal
stealing away from him through the sagebrush. It
was a pretty good shot for a kid; that was what they
said about it, his brother and his father, and he remembered feeling how they were holding back just
praise for fear of making a braggart of him. He knew
how good a shot it was, though; they didn't have to
tell him. And he knew they couldn't do much better

themselves. Not Pablo, anyway—although it was an unspeakable thought, he admitted to himself sometimes that he didn't really like Pablo. He instinctively distrusted him. Benito, the eldest brother, was different, and so much older that he was more like an uncle, but Pablo was near to him and yet far away. He couldn't explain the feeling but it was a very real one.

There now, he had gone and forgotten the *Tinieblas* again ! And this annoyed him; he wanted to remember. He wanted never to forget those sensations which were so terrible, for the memory of them quivered in his mind like a landscape seen through shimmering waves of heat—as on summer days the valley appeared to dance in the wavering air. He actually made the comparison as he walked along, for he was wont to think in terms of images; so much so that his mother was often mystified by him and unable to trace the connection between two things spoken by Miguel in the same breath. But to the boy they were perfectly clear.

Still in the maze of his thought, Miguel came to the Lopez house, entered and, finding no one at home, went to the room where he slept in a spreading white iron bed with Pablo.

Miguel, his mother thought, was her own proper son. The other two, Pablo and Benito, the eldest, were their father's boys, and she had no need of them now because they no longer needed her. They found everything in their father, although God knew there was little enough to find there. Her illusions about that man had fled so long ago that she had forgotten them, their nature and their existence. But with Miguel it was different. There was a passion of love between them,

mother and son; she would have died to preserve him
for her own, or to save him from becoming his father's,
for that would mean following him in his way, and his
way was a blind acceptance of all things, with never
a thought of changing them.

Left to itself, Eliseo's lot would have been a downward progress from bad to worse; everything that had
been done to better the family's position in the village,
she secretly believed, had sprung directly from her
initiative, not his. More often than not he was given
the credit, but such was a woman's expectancy. No
good crying against that. It was right to have it so,
for when her schemes entailed unpleasantness, it fell
to Eliseo to meet it. And thus she was satisfied, on the
whole, to let well enough alone.

Although her fears for Miguel were needless—he was
not a weak lad who identified himself easily with his
elders—she dreaded taking him to see the *Tinieblas*,
for the ceremony represented one of the dangers to
which she fancied him exposed in Hormiga. It con-
stituted, in a blurred, indistinct manner, one angle of
the father's way. If she could have put it into words
she would have said that the boy's participation (for
no one could see it without participating) in the *Tinieblas*
was a dangerous lead to membership in the order of
Penitentes, and that, also for a reason which was dim and
intuitive, she would have him escape. It wasn't his
fear she minded, it was the fascination; and because
she herself felt in her vitals the grip of its power, she
was able to understand how the boy could be taken
in by the thing, and still be terrified. After thirty years
and more of seeing the ceremony, she still wanted to go

every year, to be stunned and exalted by it. Everybody
—all the women, at any rate—felt the same about it.
They ridiculed it between times, called it a childish
piece of make-believe in which their men had to be
humoured, but every Holy Week found the women
waiting at the church doors for the *Tinieblas* to begin.

They made sacrifices, too, in order to see it. Many of
them brought their tiniest infants because they couldn't
be left at home. Like it or not, Concepcion had to
admit that the *Tinieblas* ceremony was the year's high
point of entertainment in the bleak cycle of months
which was life in Hormiga. Nothing, not even a crime
of passion, contained such dramatic stuff. Of course,
it was not intended for entertainment; nobody would
dare to give it such a name. Culminating the annual
retreat of the *Penitentes*, the *Tinieblas* was no show, but a
solemn religious observance and for many a profound
religious experience. He was a poor creature who could
witness the slow accumulation of fervour through the
psalms, ending in the frenzied release of noise at last,
without emotion. No wonder Miguel was moved.
He was no lout. He had something in him.

No wonder. It was in a few concentrated moments
the whole of Christ's passion and death, and something
of its melancholy power lasted through the procession
of days until Holy Week came around again, to renew
the spring. Concepcion, as she turned away from her
friends in front of the church, knew well that her being
was refreshed, filled with a new vitality whose pulse
would throb in her long after she had forgotten the
whole affair. She turned her face homewards into the
moon, taking the road Miguel had taken. It was cold.

She covered as much of her shoulders as her black shawl would include and hurried along with quick, short steps. She could see her breath in the moonlight, and she remembered how, last year, the same season had been warm and bright—like summer. But so it went up there in the sky. Almost every year the young crops which the men planted were blasted by untimely frosts from the snowfields. What kept people going in the face of such discouragements? God and the might of His power in their hearts, she thought, from first to last, year after year. She sighed. The struggle was a hard one. Suddenly she felt old, old and tired. She was over forty, and in a life of toil forty was the beginning of age, especially for a woman. Nothing was left of her figure, but her skin was still fresh and firm and her manner was resolute. A fire danced and sparkled in her eyes. And although she complained endlessly of the struggle her life was, of the lazy fellow her husband was, she would have hated peace and ease, would have created strife for its own sake. With her husband—had he been other than he was—she would have moved heaven and earth to create a row. As it was, there was no need to move anything. Rows sprang ready-made, from the daily rub.

She stepped into her house and her accustomed eyes detected Miguel's cap flung into a chair. He was home, then, and in bed. She picked up the cap and hung it where it belonged, on a peg behind the door. Next she put her own shawl there, then stirred the fire in the stove, put more wood on it. The boy should have brought in an armful of wood before going to bed; two things she charged herself to remember and reproach him with in the morning: his cap and the wood. She sat down for a moment to warm her feet beside the stove. Eliseo, her husband, would be in presently—not that she expected anything of him. He never did anything until he was driven to it, but Miguel usually remembered things. It was her own fault for taking him to the *Tinieblas*. He'd be useless for a week.

Up to now she had been able to keep him away, but this time he had won in the end. They always do, she reflected. You take care of them, protect them, then sooner or later they go poking into everything— have to see for themselves—learn that way. It does no good to tell them. Well, it was right, she guessed; she liked them to have something in them. It was no good raising dummies. She got up to peer into a dingy mirror hanging by the door, holding an oil-lamp to light her face. Her hair was a fright. She poked loose strands of it into the misshapen bundle at the back of her head, drew it tight away from her forehead. So. That wasn't bad. Her brow was fine, high with some remote strain of nobility which had come from Spain long, long ago. She was rather proud of her features, her straight, classical nose, the low arch of her eye- brows. Her physical pride had necessarily moved up with years, for it could no longer rightly include any- thing but her face.

Yes, she had made a bargain with fate, or whatever the powers were which formed a woman's destiny. He could have the older boys if Miguel were left for her. They could grow up like their father, farm a rocky acre or two behind the town and live from day to day as he would have done, but for her. And let them join the *Penitentes*, too, and beat their backs in Holy Week. Let them do it. What else was there for them to do? Nothing ever happened in Hormiga. It wasn't like the valley towns where there were moving pictures every night, band concerts in the *plaza* and more *bailes* than you could count. When they had a dance here, it was an event. She sat down again. Miguel would have to leave Hormiga, she guessed, if he were to escape the fate of mountain men, and that gave her a pang of dread, too, to think of the dangers awaiting an innocent lad from the hills. Some girl might get hold of him before he was ready for it—before he found himself—and yet such a thing might happen right here in Hormiga, under her eye. It had happened with Benito, her eldest boy. Before she even knew he was interested in anybody he had a girl six months gone with his child. Concepcion smiled to remember the day he brought the girl home and told them all that he wanted to marry her. A short laugh escaped her as she thought how the girl had looked, how she herself had said to Benito, " Is it your child? " When he nodded she had only grunted and left the room. That had been her assent. But if the same thing should happen to Miguel, she would storm and cry and move mountains.

She opened the door of the stove and looked inside. The red glow suffused her face, as she bathed in its hot breath for a moment, then put in a few more sticks, and banged the door to. The room smelled now of hot metal, dry, pungent, not unpleasant on a cold night, but she closed a damper to cool the chimney-pipe. No good setting the house afire. And then she leaned

back and closed her eyes. She thought comfortably
what it would be like to have daughters instead of three
sons. In some ways they required more looking after
than boys. But the vision of a slim, dark-eyed girl
swam before her eyes, a girl with a high forehead and
a fine straight nose, lips that easily smiled, shining
eyes. Herself, as a girl? No. Herself—in a daughter.
The vision did a foolish little dance, a coy turn of the
hips, and faded away. . . .

What remained of the relation between Concepcion
and her husband was so deeply laid away in their hearts
that it never came to the surface except in emergencies.
Often in bitterness, Concepcion thought it would be
better if Eliseo should die; but when he fell ill, or hurt
himself at the farm, she was overwhelmed with grief
and remorse and discovered in her secret heart that she
wanted him still. He was a trial to her. He was a small
man, and this, added to his life of toil, made him
defensively cocky, blustery of temper and surly of
manner. His assertion of importance was trying at
times, but in Mexican families such as theirs the
woman's position was defined by custom, and Concepcion was content to conform in appearances. It left her
free to manage the household from below. And deep
in Eliseo there lived a sentimental love for his family
which was equal to any sacrifice and which, on occasion, could become surprisingly articulate. She had the
final assurance that he was the father, knew it, and
would never forsake them. This knowledge, whether
she admitted it or not, was a comfort to her, and a
consolation.

Through the years Eliseo remained a spare little man,

but full of strength and courage. Concepcion, growing dumpier every year, saw with envy the husband's trim little body; now she was twice his size. It fostered a new kind of rivalry between them. On his part, he resented and hated being her physical inferior—on her part she felt that if there were any justice in the world she would be the one to stay thin, because she was a woman, and looks meant more to her. The men had it all their own way. He was kept slender by his work on the farm, but she did work enough, too, washing and cooking and scrubbing and cleaning.

Let them try having five children and see what happened to their figures—and yet, perhaps, nature made up for it in other ways. Eliseo slaved himself to the bone trying to make his farm yield. She could bring the children into the world, but he had to feed them, provide for them, and in fairness she had to admit that his was a worrying task, too. And the small general store which they had made out of the corner room in the house, although it had never done well, was another of his responsibilities. It had been Concepcion's idea in the first place, but if it didn't go well it was not her fault.

Eliseo didn't know much—had had no schooling. He could write his name in an awkward scrawl and do simple sums with infinite labour. Pablo helped him in the store now, because the boy had been to school and knew how to write in a beautiful script. But what Eliseo did best he did least: he was a fine hunter and fisherman. He could guide parties of sportsmen in the wilderness of mountains and lead them without fail to the game. Concepcion always told him that he could make more money this way than with his farm and store put together, but Eliseo was a farmer and the soil was his home; everything else was incidental and subordinate.

It was Concepcion's idea that, having conceived the store and procured it for them, it was up to Eliseo and the boys to run it. For even after her children were grown a woman's time was taken in a thousand ways. As it happened, however, it was she who did most of the work in the store, until she wished the thing in hell and hated the moment when the idea had occurred to her.

She was the more resentful, therefore, of the time the men lavished on the Order of *Penitentes*. It was not that she disapproved of them—far from it. She accepted the Order in the same spirit as she accepted the Church, as one of the facts of life, but she felt that it took more than its rightful share of a man's time and energies. In Eliseo's case there was a reason, however, deeply secreted in the past; for in the beginning, after their passion waned, and the world seemed to be cooling for her, Concepcion's children, two of whom had died in infancy, grew and became beings whose love warmed her and made her world live again. Little by little she discarded Eliseo, turning to her children for her life, and Eliseo, seeing it happen, yielded his place to the young ones because he saw nothing else to do; and driven thus to find new outlets, he turned to the *Penitentes*. He plunged into the affairs of the *Sociedad*, in a short time became its *Hermano Mayor*, and ever since had taken an active part in one way or another. By being so identified with the Order he brought it into his home and made it a part of life which Concepcion could not ignore, even if she wanted to ignore it, which she did not.

She feared God and sin and hell, directly for herself, vicariously for her children, and because the Brotherhood was older than anyone's memory, something established and solid as the Church itself, she could not think to question it, or find the courage in her heart to condemn. Yet its presence there, the *morada*—the meeting-house of the Brotherhood—a stone's throw from her house, was a constant reminder to her of the dangers which that innocent little building, with its mud walls and crooked tin chimney, contained for her sons. Dangers? Did she actually think of it in terms of danger? Probably not. But she had seen her husband year after year go to the *Penitente* retreat in Holy Week, in that same small-windowed place, and for three days he was gone from the face of the earth. What happened to him in the interval she never dared to ask, for they surrounded themselves with mystery, and only surmised from his condition when he returned with his back often a bleeding, beaten wreck, lame, exhausted, useless, with a terrible cough and pains in his chest. Even then she had given it a minimum of thought, accepted it as a part of life in Hormiga, and she knew nothing of life elsewhere; but slowly it came in upon her, as her sons grew up, that they, too, were exposed to the same things, and thus gradually an opposition was born. It was a felt opposition, however, never, up to now, put into words.

Even in her dreams, in these later days, she saw them marching. With whips lashing bared backs she saw them, dragging heavy crosses over the ground. When she saw Miguel, her beloved, with the shadow of the cross along his slim shoulders—those were her nightmares. . . .

It seemed to her, when she awoke from her sleep in the chair before the stove, that she was waking from such a dream. But it was only Eliseo, stamping his feet outside the door.

" You're up late," he said, and hung his hat on a peg behind the door, rubbed his hands together. " What's the matter ? "

" Nothing. I fell asleep here in the chair."

He knocked the ashes from his pipe against the stove. " Well, how'd you like the *Tinieblas* ? "

" All right. It wasn't as long as last year."

She watched him as he re-loaded his pipe, lighted it, heard it gurgle and bubble as he drew on it. She used to mind that, but it was so long ago.

" Are you through over there ? " she said, meaning in the *morada*.

" Just about."

" Where's Pablo ? "

" I don't know—haven't seen him."

She closed her eyes and he smoked his pipe. " Miguel in bed ? " Eliseo asked at last.

" Long ago."

" Well "—he stood up—" I think I'll go to bed, too. You coming ? "

" Yes." She, too, stood up, pushed her chair back. " Fix the stove so it'll burn as long as it can," she said.

She had to go through the kitchen to get to the bedroom. The house was very old, built by Eliseo's great-great-grandfather, and had been extended without plan so many times that one of the rooms had been completely enclosed by others and now had no windows. Here Concepcion kept her best things, opening the room only to special visitors, forbidding its use by her family under dire penalties. All objects close to her heart were there, the old chairs her grandfather had brought to Hormiga on the backs of *burros* from the valley, a few precious pieces of Mexican silver, hammered into spoons, plates, the mail-order table from Denver. Now and then she made ritualistic inspections of the room and gave herself to sentimental dreams and memories.

She heard Eliseo clanging the stove door and making a great noise over fixing it for the night; then she heard the knock, knock of his pipe as he rapped it on the edge of the stove, letting the day's foul accumulation of dregs fall into the tin the stove stood on. She would have to clean it up to-morrow. *Por Dios*, why were men such dirty creatures?

In a moment Eliseo came into the bedroom. Thousands of times he had entered that door; he used to come in as her lover. Looking at him now, her mind darted back to that time and drew a comparison which caused a smile to appear on the lips which had easily smiled.

" What's funny? " said Eliseo, seeing her smile.

" Oh, nothing, I was only thinking——" She turned away from him, continuing, " Thinking of Miguel." She undid her hair, letting it fall to her knees. " He was so scared at the *Tinieblas*."

"Was Miguel there? I didn't see him."

"You walked right by him. He was sitting on the floor beside me, near the back."

"I didn't see him," Eliseo repeated.

"He had hold of my legs most of the time."

Eliseo chuckled. "He'll get used to it. That was the first time he saw it, no?"

"Yes," said the mother strangely, "the first time."

It was cold in the bedroom. A tiny fireplace was built into the corner, but there was no fire in it. Eliseo was ready for bed first, having undressed modestly behind her back; she had seen his body, though, out of a corner of her eye. Still the body of a boy—but hard, hard as iron, astonishing power in it still, and endurance. He could work a horse and plough all day, tirelessly, doggedly; he could outlast the horse. There was something like an animal in the way he worked, plodding, yet it never seemed to carry him anywhere—up and down, up and down, furrow after furrow—nothing more. All his strength ploughing a field. That was purpose, wasn't it? But what was the good? The beans froze or were eaten by insects; the alfalfa froze or withered because the irrigation water failed. There never was enough water. Never. Most of his land was dry-farming land, anyway, and what could be more disheartening in a desert country? He complained bitterly when the rains failed, but went right on planting, hoping year after year, calling upon his vengeful God for rain. A little wheat, some strings of chili, many sacks of undersized potatoes—these were his perennial rewards.

Now if he would use that perseverance of his, Concepcion thought, in trying to make something of the store, or in using his knowledge of hunting and fishing, he might make some money, for money was, after all, the greatest need. More than once, she remembered, in the lean years which came so often, she had been thankful enough for what the farm provided. At least there had been less hunger—and hunger had been far from unknown in Hormiga.

Eliseo had crawled into the big bed and was breathing heavily. In a moment he would begin to snore. Concepcion waited for his snoring, as if it were the signal for the release of her innermost, secret thoughts. Night was her time for thinking, lying along her husband's spare, habitual body with all her passion turned inward, feeding the inward flame. And it was usually of Miguel she thought, picturing him in a thousand future situations in all of which he was triumphant. Now he was governor of the state, perhaps, luxuriating in tiled bathroom; again, she imagined his heroic return to Hormiga after winning fame and fortune elsewhere. She saw the women who were now her equals bowing down before her achievement of having raised such a son, awed by him. Most often he was a brilliant success in politics, because this was a career still open to Mexicans—or Spanish-Americans, as they were called by vote-hungry politicians. Within the fallow field of her experience her imagining ranged up and down, for ever planting Miguel here, now there, and watching him grow magically. Probably she had done the same with the older boys, when they were young. It is a mother's way. But not for long, nor with such a devotion of certainty. It was a pleasant way to go to sleep, if some ugly thought didn't intrude to spoil it.

But it was late to-night and sleep overtook her before she had time to think of anyone except Pablo. Pablo wasn't home yet. . . .

Pablo, in fact, was seldom at home. Although he was supposed to help in the store, his presence there was scarce. A dozen times a day Concepcion had to drop what she was doing and rush in there to wait on some customer who probably didn't want to buy anything anyway. Finally she put an old cowbell on the counter nearest the door for people to ring if no one was there to care for them. They had been slow to use it at first, but now the thing seemed to be clattering all day long. It showed how well Pablo was attending to business, too. She didn't know what he did, but he was off most of the time, passing the time of day *en la resolana* with other loafers like himself. It drove his mother frantic sometimes, and she scolded until she was beside herself, but it did no good.

Pablo was a loss to her already. The love she had for him was beaten down by continuous exasperation, but at unpredictable times it surged hotly and made her forgive, always forgive. She couldn't deny her blood. Nor could Pablo, either; he loved his mother in a dutiful way which may have been respect rather than love. He never tried to understand her, or to think beforehand how she might behave. He was invariably puzzled when her actions or reactions were other than what he expected. Their relation, therefore, proceeded in a series of hops, rebounds from the impact of their wills. When she scolded him, upbraided him as she had to do many times a day, he stood before her with his mouth hanging open, utterly surprised and baffled,

CM

until, stopped by the sheer inertia of his confusion, she had to put him out of her sight and mind with the mental comment that he was a stupid dolt. But Pablo was not stupid. He discovered at a tender age that many a difficulty was best met by a crafty ignorance.

II

Concepcion did not know how darkly the shadow of the *Penitente* cross lay along Miguel's shoulders. He never displayed more than a healthy, boyish curiosity about the Order, and she told herself repeatedly that her fears were groundless.

Why shouldn't a boy join the *Penitentes* if he wanted to ? When she came to answer that question for herself, she found she could not. The *Sociedad* was an institution in Hormiga, so old that its origins, extending to Spain, were lost in the distance like the tail of an incredibly long procession. And membership in it was good, a mark of superior piety, something over and above a man's simple duty to the Church and his soul. Benefits derived from it, also. The *Penitentes* helped one another in times of need and, together with chapters of the Order in other towns, formed a body not without force and influence.

Among poor people this was a good thing. They needed to band together. People talked against the *Penitentes* all the time, even the priest was always saying —and from the pulpit, too—that their ways were wrong. But she couldn't see much wrong in them, except the hurt; and yet Eliseo, who had belonged since he was fourteen, had never hurt himself very badly. Her son Benito had already been through it, and he was the same Benito, as far as she could see.

It did seem like a strange God they worshipped,

sometimes, a God who demanded pain and agony for His sign. No, it was only their way.

Pablo was coming of age. He would soon be joining. But Miguel . . .

Pablo was four years older than Miguel. He had been an unself-conscious lad from the beginning and now approached a manhood not unlike his father's. Benito, on his own, with a wife and growing family, was out of the scene, and they saw little of him except on occasional Sunday afternoons when they came trooping over to the Lopez house, or left the babies for Concepcion to look after while they went down to the city to see the motion pictures and to hear the band concert in the *plaza*.

Concepcion liked having the babies; they brought back the past and some of its warmest memories. Although she had, as a rule, had her babies easily, she hadn't had as many as most Hormiga women—one after another until they were exhausted. The two who had died—one was a girl—were quite forgotten by Eliseo, but she carried their images graven in her heart. And when Benito married, the mother rejoiced in Rosa, the wife, as if she were the reincarnation of her lost girl-child. But now that was over with. Rosa had no life, no spirit. She was starting out just like many another Hormiga woman, two babies already and a third on the way. She and Benito lived in a part of her father's house at the upper end of the village where the adobe buildings gave place to fields, cut in two by the road which ambled unevenly towards the mountains. He supported his family by working the little farm which had been Rosa's dowry, and little enough support it was. Often he had to take jobs in the valley through the winter, to make ends meet. Like his father, Benito required little, though in looks he was the pride of the Lopez boys. He was a *Penitente*, already an officer of the local Brotherhood, and this was a matter of which his father was enormously proud.

On Saturday morning after the *Tinieblas*, Eliseo paraded and strutted before his wife so extravagantly that she had to notice him at last, and ask him what was making him strut like a fresh rooster.

" They made me the *Hermano Mayor* again," he said. " Last night, in the *morada*."

" Oh," said Concepcion unenthusiastically.

" And Benito, they made him the *Celador*."

" *Celador?* " said Concepcion absent-mindedly, busy peeling potatoes. " What's he—the *Celador*? " She knew perfectly well what he was.

" Oh, he's pretty important, all right. After me, I guess he's the most important man."

" I know, but what does he do? "

" Why, he's the treasurer of the chapter," Eliseo said reproachfully, as if she ought to know such things. " He looks after the novices—sees about them—that they get in all right. He's pretty important."

Concepcion pretended to be preoccupied while she thought how to answer him. " Well," she said, " that's good—if you like it."

" Like it? Don't you like it? "

" I guess so. It takes too much of your time. I don't like that."

" Oh, not so much. Once in a while, when we have meetings——"

" Once in a while," she repeated with scorn.

Eliseo filled his pipe with fresh tobacco, lighted it, puffed it contentedly, seated in a straight kitchen chair. Most of the family conversations, councils and meetings took place in the kitchen, where Concepcion spent more than half her time. Miguel entered presently and sat down quietly on another chair beside the range. Eliseo seemed not to notice the boy, but Concepcion was instantly and acutely aware of him. When Miguel was by, she hated to have anybody mention the *Penitentes*, for no reason except the instinctive wish to protect him. She hoped he hadn't heard his father blowing off about being the new *Hermano Mayor*, but at once Eliseo spoke again, with the same boastful tone, " Yes, sir, Benito's coming right along—probably be *Hermano Mayor* some day, just like his father."

Concepcion winced and Miguel listened without speaking; she began to make a noise, slamming things down on the table where she was working, dropping the pot with a bang. A less insensitive man than her husband would have understood, but Eliseo, duly satisfied with himself, saw Miguel and spoke directly to him.

" Well, boy, how'd you like the *Tinieblas*, eh ? Pretty scary, no ? "

Miguel frowned, hesitated. " I liked it all right," he said.

" Good. That's good. Pretty fine thing. Were you scared a little ? *Que ruidoso !* "

The boy nodded, and Eliseo laughed. He was amused ; when he could laugh at Miguel he loved him, but he had little real feeling for the boy. Miguel had none for his father, either, except the filial respect which tradition implanted. The father could not understand the son. He was a queer boy—that was the word most often used to describe Miguel, not alone by his father. Eliseo used it freely, not knowing exactly what he meant, except that it suggested his inability to get near Miguel, to get inside him and see the world through his eyes. He could, with the other boys. They almost always behaved as he expected, as he himself would behave in the same circumstances. But Miguel was always saying some incomprehensible thing, or acting in ways which baffled his father and cut his patience short. So the boy really made his father uncomfortable, and Eliseo avoided close contact with him when he could. Sometimes he seemed to know what the father was thinking, without being told. It was an uncanny thing, and made Eliseo wonder if by some mischance the boy could have the evil eye. He kept the wonderment to himself, wisely; to speak such a thought would bring down the wrath of heaven and his wife. Eliseo sat there in silence, doubtless turning over some such ruminations in his mind, and finally he stood up. " I'm going over to see if everything's all right in the *morada*," he said.

Miguel sat still beside the stove. He saw that his mother was ablaze with some kind of wrath, and it made him angry, too.

" Why does he make you so mad ? " he said.

" Who said I was mad ? " Concepcion snapped. " The stupid *burro*—talking like that, in front of you," she muttered to herself.

" Oh," said Miguel with relief, " I thought he did something."

Concepcion couldn't say what was in her mind. It would sound foolish, spoken aloud. But she shook a paring knife at Miguel, saying, " Do you go listening to everything you hear—all this stuff about the *Penitentes*—you hear ? They aren't everything. You've got something better than that coming to you ! "

Concepcion bit her lip, amazed at herself. It was the first time she had ever spoken her thought. She had over-stepped herself. Luckily, the cow-bell sounded in the store, and she grasped the escape. " Go in there and see what they want," she said. " The Lord knows where that Pablo is."

Miguel ducked out, also glad to get away.

When he had sold a packet of chewing tobacco to a man with a battered *sombrero*, Miguel stepped out of the store on to the loading platform which abutted the principal street of Hormiga. The cold of the night before was swiftly leaving the air under the hot sun. He sat on the edge of the platform without hat or coat, dangling his short legs. Evidently his mother had no idea how much he knew about the *Penitentes*—he could probably tell her a few things. Because it was secret and mysterious, the Brotherhood was one of the first things to attract the curiosity of boys in the village, and each one had his ears pricked to catch every odd bit of information. Miguel, for example, knew well what the *Celador* was and what his duties were, and he had known that Benito would be the new one for the coming year almost as soon as Eliseo knew it.

He got down from the loading platform and walked to the *plaza*. What he could see from any flat roof around the square was as much as Miguel knew of the world beyond the town. It was a grand sight from the roof, or from the western edge of the *plaza* where the ground fell off steeply into a canyon. A ragged rim of *corrales* and hay barns obstructed the view from the ground, but a boy could easily climb to the top of a house and see right down into the canyon, where the tips of pine trees swayed, sweeping downward in an undulating blanket of dark green almost a thousand feet to the bottom of the canyon. Beyond lay the valley, changeless and ever changing. Miguel walked to the nearest roof, where two boys had already preceded him, shouting and playing some impromptu game. The sheds were skeletons of buildings, tipping and leaning towards the chasm, ever on the point of slipping, tumbling down the rocky slope—their crazy roofs were great for climbing.

With boys of his own age, Miguel was apt to be self-conscious. He always joined a group unobtrusively, sliding into their midst and saying hello to each one separately as his presence was discovered. They liked him, but thought him a little queer, because it was a boy's usual way to yell from afar off and dash up with all flags flying. Miguel, however, rather enjoyed the feeling of being discovered.

" Oh, hello, Miguel. I didn't see you."

This time he climbed up the opposite side of the shed and sat down on the peak of the roof before the other boys saw him; from there his eye was above the highest tree-tops and he could see beyond into the shimmering valley. The two who had been there quickly joined him. " You can see the sun shining on the roof of the church at Santa Rosa," he said abruptly.

" Where ? " The boys shaded their eyes and looked along his outstretched arm. " I don't see it. Where ? "

" Right there, where I'm pointing. Don't you see that bright spot shining ? "

" That's the river. That's no roof."

" Yes it is," Miguel insisted. " That church has got a tin roof on it, and the sun hits it every day in the morning. I know." As he always examined things before he spoke, Miguel was certain. " I know it's the church."

The others looked and looked and at last guessed he was right. " Let's go down in the canyon," one of them suggested after a trying spell of inactivity. " I know where there's a good place to build a dam in the creek."

" All right." The assent was tentative, however, half-hearted. They sat on where they were with the sun beating down on them. Somehow, the prospect of building a dam failed to fit their still unformed desires. In a few minutes Miguel saw, when he happened to look over there, that the door of the *morada* was open. A fantastic plan occurred to him, one which would make a hero of him if it worked, for he remembered his father saying that he was going over to see if everything was all right in the *morada*. As casually as he could, he turned to the other boys and said: " Let's go over to the *morada*."

Their jaws dropped. " The *morada* ? We can't do that. They won't let us in——"

" I think we can go in all right," Miguel said easily. " I think they'll let *me* in."

" Well, anybody can go into the chapel part, but not the other room—the meeting-room."

" I mean the meeting-room," Miguel said impressively, with one eye on the door. " My father's the *Hermano Mayor* now. He'll let us go in." He started to climb down, paused half way to the ground. " Don't you want to come ? "

The two boys looked at each other doubtfully, frightened even at the idea, but they followed Miguel at a safe distance. They felt, and Miguel did, too, that all the eyes of Hormiga were on them as they crossed the *plaza*, headed obliquely for the *morada*. At the gate in the wire fence which enclosed the place, Miguel's friends stopped, not daring to come farther, while Miguel, with a theatrical toss of his head, marched through the gate confidently, and stopped on the inside. " Aren't you coming ? "

They started to follow, but lost their courage in a moment and refused to budge. Miguel laughed shortly and moved to the step below the open door, peered inside. It was dark in there—he couldn't see at first. His nerve was holding up well; he was surprised at himself. Over in a corner he saw a figure of a man stooping over. In the gloom, it might have been his father or anybody else. The boy made a sound in his throat, still confident that the man was Eliseo, and waited with his heartbeats beginning to pound in his ears. When he made another sound, louder, the man stood up and turned around. And to Miguel's horror it was not Eliseo. It was a man he didn't know—never saw before. He stepped back off the step, choking with confusion and fear. " I—I was looking for my father," he faltered. The man stepped quickly outside into the bright sunlight, closing the door behind him. Miguel almost fell over backward in his fright, ready to run.

" Your father's not here. You're Miguel Lopez, no ? "

" *Si, si, señor*. I thought he was here all right. He said——"

Miguel didn't wait for more, but turned and flew from the yard, not stopping until he was out of sight behind a shed, where he found the two boys, breathless and pop-eyed. Until he discovered that he was something of a hero notwithstanding, Miguel felt embarrassed and shamed, for the thing had not gone the way he hoped. They fired questions at him, however, and cowered before the magnitude of his bravery. " Did you get in ? What was it like inside ? Did you see the whips ? The *matracas* ? Were there any skulls ? I heard they had skulls in there—a whole pile of them."

Miguel's confidence flowed back, but for the life of him he couldn't remember having seen anything beyond the door except the strange man in a corner. " No," he said vaguely, " there's nothing there—much —some chairs—a table—I didn't see any skulls."

" That man—he wasn't your father, was he ? "

" No. I thought my father was in there," said Miguel. " I don't know who that man was."

Evidently they hadn't waited for a second look at the man, nor to see Miguel's inglorious retreat. He was pretty brave in their eyes, and he saw no reason to spoil it all by admitting that he was scared to death. Instead of feeling ashamed he ended by being pleased with himself.

And when he got home he told his mother about it,

but experimentally, to see how she would take it. He was afraid she might become angry. Partly, too, he wanted to tell her because she needed reminding that he wasn't the child she thought he was.

She looked at her son, after he had poured the story into her ears, long and so intently that Miguel had time, before she spoke, to interpret what he saw in her eyes and to sound what was to come. That he had erred in telling her was evident, for he could see that, in addition to being angry, she was hurt by it. But he always told her what he had been doing—at least the things he thought would interest her; it was a part of their relation, to his mother it was a prized privilege, a dear unfolding of his life, day by day. She encouraged him in it, too, sensing that it would end soon, not wanting it to end, when his life should become too personal for her to share.

To his surprise, however, she turned away from him without speaking. He could not tell what she was thinking—only that she was sad, and he was beginning to be sorry.

He could hardly know that a large part of her sadness was intuitive, resulting from her feeling that he was at last slipping away from her, sliding out of his complete dependence upon her. She was a natural, a realistic woman. She never did or could impose her will upon her children; her own life and duties absorbed her utterly, so many things required looking after. While she remained his refuge and his sanctuary, she was happy to have it so; but when he should find another, younger, more contemporary, she would have to accept that, too.

Miguel waited in silence for his mother to cool and for the fire he had kindled in her to leave her eyes. They were in the front room where the stove was. She was sweeping in there. It was almost lunch-time. She was finishing up, collecting the sweepings in a dust-pan. His eyes were on her constantly. He liked to watch her at work, to admire the strength and competence of her movements, her fine solid arms. Her sleeves were rolled up above her elbows, and her skin was smooth, showing the muscles rippling underneath. It was good to have such a dependable, constant mother.

"You know that boy—that Rodriguez boy?" Miguel said with a dying flicker of perversity.

"Yes, I know who you mean—he's older than you are. What about him?"

"He says his father was the *Cristo* the last time the *Penitentes* had a crucifixion. Is that true?"

Concepcion stood up and leaned on her broom-handle. This time her anger was quick, for she caught his mischief. "So!" she exclaimed. "Still talking *Penitentes*, are you? Well, I don't know anything about it, and you get out of here and stop thinking about such things. You're still a baby and you ought to be outside playing like the other boys do." She made a swing at him with the broom. "Go on, get out of here!"

He jumped to his feet, surprised, and she, regretful, smiled through her anger to show him that all was well. He went out then, not quite understanding, but content with her.

Wandering into the store, he found his brother Pablo and his father. He went to them where they bent their heads together over some papers behind a counter. "What are you doing ? " he said.

"Counting up," said Pablo. It was the usual thing on Saturdays to compute the week's sales, a rite which Eliseo, before Pablo's superior knowledge of arithmetic, was an onlooker.

"Let me see," Miguel said, pushing in between them. Pablo growled at him, but let the boy peer under his arm, for he was much taller than Miguel. The younger boy studied the figures on the sheet and quickly, aggravatingly, said : "You've made a mistake."

"Where ? "

Miguel pointed out the error with a dirty finger, much to the father's delight. "The boy is quick," he said, patting Miguel on the head. "He adds better than you, Pablo." And Eliseo laughed.

Pablo was hot with anger instantly. "I just made a little mistake," he said. "Anybody does that. You get away from here ! " He snarled at Miguel, giving him a push that sent him sprawling.

Miguel picked himself up, so pleased to have humiliated Pablo that he forgot to resent the push. He amused himself by reading labels on canned goods, where Eliseo, tiring of figures, presently joined him.

"Maybe you'd like to tend the store, no ? " he said, leaning one elbow on the counter and looking down at Miguel.

"Sure," said Miguel thoughtlessly. "You give me a piece of gum, no ? " There was a brand of pink chewing gum which was popular with the boys and girls just then because it was rubbery and lasted a whole day and could be blown out in bubbles between the two rows of teeth. Everywhere it was in evidence, blobs of pink protoplasmic stuff sticking out of the mouths of children. It sold for a penny a stick.

" Where's your penny ? " said Eliseo, teasing.

" I got no penny."

" Then how do you expect to buy gum ? "

Miguel grinned, humouring his father in his little joke, and waited for the gum. Eliseo brought him a piece from another part of the store. " Thanks," Miguel said, and shoved the stuff into his mouth.

" I think you could tend store good enough, don't you ? " Eliseo persisted. " As good as Pablo, here. He's out half the time."

" Sure," Miguel agreed. " But I've got to go to school."

" Oh, that's right. That's right. I forgot about the school." For a time Eliseo could think of nothing more to say to his son. It looked as if their conversation might collapse, and he didn't want that to happen just yet. He was in a mood to talk to the boy. " I've got to go up to the farm this afternoon," he went on. " Would you like to come with me ? We might see another coyote, or a turkey."

Miguel turned his wide, black eyes upward in enthusiasm. " Yes, I'd like to come."

" All right. Better bring your rifle. I'll find a horse for you."

The times when Miguel appreciated his father and liked being with him were these, when they went off together to the farm or into the high pine-forests of the mountains where there was little undergrowth and the great trees soared austerely from the park-like carpet of needles on the ground. Eliseo was a different man up there. His whole body and being changed, grew tense, alert and keen. He was able to transmit some of his awareness to Miguel, pointing out to him tracks and signs in the forest which the boy would never have seen; and the son, in his turn, gave something to the father, too, something of his own special observation of things. He made his father notice flowers, the beauty of clouds, the stark, brittle splendour of a white summit against the blue. Thus there flowed between them a companionship and an interchange. To Eliseo, the forest was all one, a place for hunting, fishing, or cutting wood; to Miguel it was an exciting, various macrocosm, full of wonder. And he would see the bright mountain.

One summit, far back and to the north, mighty and shouldering above lesser ones, was perpetually covered with snow. This mountain Miguel had first seen as a child when all the others were dark with sombre green of pines, and it had then forged a memory in his mind and had become a symbol of all mountains, of all beauty and of life among them. It had a name, but he never used it. It was his mountain—the bright mountain— and it could not be seen from Hormiga.

Concepcion heard of their plan at lunch-time. " What are you going up there for ? " she said to Eliseo. " There's probably snow up there still."

" No, I don't think so. It's not much higher than this, and it's sheltered. I want to see what the ground is like. If it's wet enough I'll start ploughing next week." He filled his mouth with the stew she had made for lunch, and talked with his cheeks bulging. They all
DM

dipped into the dish of beans, soaked up the juice in bread, alternating mouthfuls. They ate to live—and for no other reason.

" Don't eat so fast, Miguel. You'll choke yourself all up with food."

" I want to go," he said. " We're going to hunt, too. Maybe I'll kill a coyote."

" Maybe you will, and maybe you won't," Pablo said. " And you'd better not shoot any birds—you'll have the game-warden after you."

Miguel grunted his contempt of game-wardens.

" What are you doing this afternoon, Pablo ? "

" Me ? Oh, I don't know. They asked me to go down and help bring the musicians from Santa Rosa. Maybe I'll do that."

" For the *baile* to-night ? "

" Yes."

Concepcion sighed, for she knew what they would bring in addition to the musicians—an especially fiery brand of raw whiskey which was made in the river towns. There would be plenty of it flowing at the dance in the evening. " Well, you be careful," she warned Pablo, who pretended not to know what she meant.

Miguel and his father, later, rode out of Hormiga, side by side. Eliseo had on his knee-laced boots over a pair of grimy riding-breeches, Miguel wore the usual pair of tattered overalls and rode bare-back. His father's saddle, ancient but proud, was covered with florid designs and had a silver horn. It was Eliseo's dearest possession. A coil of rope hung from the pommel and a rifle rode in a scabbard, tied to the side. Miguel held his own ·22 calibre gun in his hand, his pockets were heavy with extra cartridges.

Low, flat-roofed adobe houses straggled along both sides of the street in diminishing numbers as they moved out of town; chickens, pigs and children scrambled from underfoot. The sun was high and hot, and Miguel was happy.

They passed, in a few minutes, a tiny, square building perched on a bank above the road. " That's a gristmill," Eliseo said. " It was built by my grandfather. Your aunt Maria owns it now."

" Does it still work ? " Miguel asked, quickly interested.

" She makes a little flour there every year."

" I didn't know that," said Miguel. " What makes it go ? "

" You know what makes it go. Water. There's a ditch up on that bank."

Eliseo stopped his horse. " See where the water falls under the mill ? It turns that big wheel underneath, and the wheel turns the millstone inside. Haven't you ever seen a grist-mill working ? "

" No."

Eliseo shook his head. " Times change," he said, moving on. " When I was a boy, all the flour we had was made that way."

The irrigation ditch which turned the mill now ran along the road beside them. Grass was green on its banks, and Miguel kept his eyes on those two strips of green as he rode, searching for the minute starry flowers which grew there in the spring. He saw none, and guessed that it was too early in the year. The little mare he was riding, a sturdy, stunted beast raised in Eliseo's corral, saw the grass, too, and kept edging over to it as she walked, trying to snatch a quick bite. And once, while the boy stared absently into the sky, she ducked her head and almost pitched Miguel over her neck. He jerked her head up with a savage yank of the bridle; she had a mouthful of sod for her pains.

"You've got to watch her," Eliseo warned. "She hasn't been ridden all winter."

At the farm they tied their horses to trees and advanced on foot. Eliseo walked out to the middle of a brown field and examined the soil, letting it run through his fingers. It was still moist from the snows, and it seemed to please him. He was in a high good humour when he rejoined Miguel, and they hunted for squirrels in the pines which bordered the cleared land. They were chattering all about, and the more he shot at them the more they scolded.

"Let's see you get one, boy," Eliseo chided gently. "There's one—there's one—quick, now, while he's looking at you!"

Miguel aimed and fired, and the squirrel was off in a burst of chittering.

"I missed him," the boy said grimly.

"There's lots of them. You'll get one. Look, hold your gun close to your cheek—like this," Eliseo showed him. "There, that's right. Keep your eye down close."

They walked deeper into the forest, climbing steadily; when they came into a clearing, suddenly, on top of a ridge, the snow-capped mountains which could be seen from the town were right there in front of them, blinding-white in the sunlight—and far beyond, the bright mountain.

" Oh ! " said Miguel, his breath taken by the sight. " I didn't know we were so near."

" We're not so near. It's a good four miles over to the base of that first one."

" Have you ever been on top ? " Miguel asked, still entranced in the beauty of them.

" Oh, yes."

" Is it—what's it like ? "

" Oh, it's pretty. There's nothing up there."

" Can you see far ? "

" Yes, you can see Arizona—Colorado—it's pretty high up there. I've seen snow belly-deep on a horse in July."

" Can you see the Rio Grande, down in the valley ? "

" Sure, easy. It looks like—like a little silver snake from up there."

" Silver snake," Miguel repeated, pleased with it. " What's on the other side ? "

" More mountains. Pretty rough country on the other side—headwaters of the Pecos. There's some lakes, too."

" I'd like to go over there some day," said Miguel. " I'd like to climb to the top of that big one, the bright one."

On their way back Miguel shot a squirrel and a chipmunk, and later, when they reached the farm, his father showed him how to skin them. The boy watched intently the delicate process of slitting them up their bellies, disembowelling and beheading; but what fascinated him most was the way Eliseo neatly cut the

skin from their legs, leaving the little feet intact. Then
they found some nails and stretched the pelts on the
door of a shed.

" Now. By the time you come up here again they'll
be dried out and you can take them home."

When they had to leave, Miguel found it hardest to
part with his crucified squirrel and chipmunk.

Meanwhile, Pablo and two of his friends bought four
gallons of petrol with a part of their pooled resources
and started for the valley in an old sedan. Save for a
few precious dollars earmarked for another purpose,
the purchase left them penniless. Cash, never plentiful
in Hormiga, was at its lowest in April, for few people
worked for wages, and business was largely a matter of
exchange and barter. They took in a few dollars at the
Lopez store, most of which were in Pablo's pocket while
in his mind was the promise to replace them—another
reason why the Lopez store didn't do very much.

The road from Hormiga to the river country tra-
versed, in the space of fifteen miles, a whole zone of
climate, for it descended three thousand feet. As they
went down, the land increased in aridity, the hills
became bad lands, bare, gashed and cruelly cut by
erosion. The trees, starting with the great pines of
Hormiga, dwindled, became low-growing junipers and
piñon, trees which for unnumbered generations of
Mexicans supplied wood for their fires and rich little
nuts to eat.

As they passed through Borregos, lying at the head
of a long tributary valley, the fragrance of burning

piñon was in the air, and the hills changed in colour, to warm tones of buff and coral, brightening the world. Water sang in the ditches at Borregos, and green showed on the fruit trees. Cottonwoods, giants of the river-bottoms, were clouds of pale green against the sky. It was a kindlier land along the stream, the same waters which flowed in Hormiga's grim canyon, and it made the heart lighter, the body easier, it caused the spirit to rejoice. Pablo and his friends heeded these signs in spite of themselves and their hurry to pass the remaining ten miles to the Rio Grande and the urgency of the business in their minds. They had far to go, and there was some doubt that the four gallons of petrol would be enough; so they pressed their car to its utmost, as if speed would spare the petrol.

At Santa Rosa they picked up three musicians, a fiddle and a big bass drum. With six passengers in the car and the drum tied to the fender, they turned southwards towards the city of Gabaldon, which was one of the three largest towns in the state. On the glistening, oiled highway the world changed again, from mediævalism to modernity. Every now and then low, humming motor-cars streaked past them as if their little sedan were standing still, although the poor thing was chugging along bravely enough. In Hormiga it was a king's carriage—here it seemed to be an obstruction on the highway. This change may have caused a sudden depression of the boys' spirits—something did, for a while. No one spoke. Faces were dour. Pablo, who was driving, watched the fuel gauge anxiously, tapping the glass frequently with his finger to make sure it was registering. It sank slowly but ominously.

But their depression was short-lived. After five or six miles they came to another village which was their destination. They turned off the highway and drove their car up to a certain squat, adobe house on the outskirts of the settlement, where the groaning motor was switched off and the boys extricated themselves.

Pablo knocked at the door. An old Mexican woman answered, with a corn-husk cigarette dangling from her lips. " *Quien es ?* " she growled. " What do you want ? "

" Señor Trujillo," said Pablo. " Is he here ? "

The old woman examined the boys with a sharp, appraising eye. " *Si*," she said at last, and pointed with her chin over her shoulder. " In back. You'll find him back there."

" *Gracias, señora.* "

Señor Trujillo's name was Felix. He was found, and the bargaining began at once. " How much for a gallon of whiskey ? " Pablo asked to start the thing going.

" Three dollars, my friend."

" No, no, to us how much ? We're not rich Americans."

" To you ? " said Felix, pushing back his hat and scratching his head. " To you I make it for two dollars."

The boys closed in and made a ring around Felix. They shook their heads. " Too much, too much."

" It's good whiskey, *primo*," he protested, speaking to Pablo. " You taste it, no ? It's old, too—it's been buried under the ground, in a burned keg, you know ? "

" All right, we'll taste it. We'll see if it's any good."

" *Bueno*. This way, boys." And Felix led them into the windowless interior where a hole in the roof admitted light and the air reeked of raw liquor. Felix lifted a jug from a shelf, produced a glass and filled it half full of a colourless liquid.

Pablo, taking it first, held the glass against the light from above. " It's white," he said. " If it's old, it ought to have more colour than that."

" Oh, that takes time, my friend," Felix explained. " I have some here "—he tapped another jug—" that's real good. The Americans in Gabaldon pay me five dollars a gallon for it."

Pablo took a long swallow of the stuff in his glass, paused as if he were listening for its effect, then winced. " It's strong, all right," he said.

" *Si, si*," said Felix. " I don't cheat my customers. They get what they pay for. I treat 'em right, then they treat me right. Understan' ? " Some of the time Felix talked in English.

The boys all nodded gravely, impressed by his declaration of policy. Pablo passed the glass along and it quickly wanted re-filling. It was handed back to Felix, who put somewhat less in it this time. Finally everybody had sampled it. With a flourish, Pablo handed the glass to Felix. " Now you have a drink," he said, clapping the man on the shoulder. " Go on, have a drink. We'll pay." Whereupon Felix's eyes brightened, and he swallowed half a tumbler of the liquor.

They talked for a while. Presently the fire began to glow in their heads and Felix unlimbered the jug of five-dollar stuff. " You're my friends," he explained. "You try some of this, no? This is my finest wheeskey," he finished in English.

They tried some of it. When the six boys reeled out

of Felix's place and climbed into their car, each of the three Hormiga boys carried a jug. Felix, propped against the door frame with a silly grin, waved the empty jug of five-dollar whiskey. "I treat my customers right," he bawled as they drove away.

The road weaved and danced before Pablo's eyes as he drove back towards Santa Rosa. The others in the car were singing and shouting, oblivious of their peril, while Pablo strove to keep his senses mustered and his car in the highway. Hills miraculously rose up to threaten him, or fell away to let him down. Culverts appeared and vanished, the sedan sailed over them as if it had wings. Luckily, the dangerous part of the road came at the end of the trip; by the time they came to Borregos, Pablo was sober enough to steer, but his teeth were still clenched, his knuckles white from their grip on the wheel. But at last, at the top of the final hill, their chariot languished and died.

The boys flopped out into the road and stood beside the car, staring at it stupidly. Pablo remained behind the wheel. " Guess we've got to push," somebody said.

" She's out of petrol," said Pablo, noticing the gauge for the first time. He began to laugh, and they all laughed. Then they pushed. Pablo steering, they shoved and hauled the dead sedan over the stony road into Hormiga, past the church, and finally stopped in front of the big square hall where the *baile* was to be. There they unloaded.

Pablo didn't come home to supper. Eliseo and Miguel returned at sundown, and the comradeship between father and son ended. While she was fixing the supper Concepcion heard all about the afternoon from Miguel, about the mountains and the squirrel and the skinning, about the pine trees and the gaunt, naked branches of aspen and how they drew a lacy veil across the sky.

Everybody was going to the *baile* in the evening. In anticipation—preparation—foreboding, life speeded up. Store dresses were got out, blue suits brushed; in every house where there was a young man, in many where they were not so young, the excitement of the women was tinged with dread. For they knew their men; they knew there would be liquor, and they knew what liquor led to.

The whole Lopez family was going to the *baile*. Benito's Rosa was going, carrying her babies in a basket which would be set beside her on the bench along the wall. Eliseo cleaned some spots from his blue suit with petrol. Pablo had not appeared at all. Concepcion would wear a new silk dress and her black shawl; Miguel would drift in and out in a newer, cleaner pair of overalls. Most of the men would wear blue coats over their usual denims, blue work-shirts open at the collar, or stiffly buttoned at the neck without a necktie. One couple could be counted upon to appear in style—the Romeros, Vicente and Teresita. He would wear a grey suit with a stiff, turn-over collar and black tie; she would have on a black silk dress. Vicente's gold watch-chain would bounce up and down on his paunch when he danced. . . .

Concepcion liked Teresita, but she was jealous of her and she hated the woman's superior air. What if they were the richest family in Hormiga and owned the best store with a red petrol pump in front of it? She needn't be so snippy with her friends.

By eight o'clock, long after the supper dishes were put away, the crowd began to gather at the hall. The musicians, who had been kept on the edge of drunkenness, had set up the drum beside the old upright piano which had been there for many years—a few of the old people remembered when it came, three days out of Gabaldon in a wagon. It had been one of the town's few co-operative efforts. The fiddler sat in his chair bravely trying to hold his head up. And at half past eight, perfectly timed, the Romeros made their entrance, dressed precisely as everybody expected, and advanced, nodding right and left, straight across the hall to the chairs at the far end, opposite the door.

Concepcion, having arranged to arrive a trifle earlier, had already taken the best chairs for herself and Eliseo, and now greeted them with a haughty smile. Miguel used the arm of her chair for a horizontal bar, wriggled and squirmed and asked a stream of questions. Rosa and Benito were next and then the basketful of babies. The arrival of the Romeros was the signal for the steady married people to come in and array themselves on the continuous bench which encircled the room along the walls. The music began; it was long before a couple intrepid enough to face the crowd alone dared to dance, but at last two couples started together, and the *baile* was on.

There were none of the stately steps of old Spain, nor of old Mexico, either. They danced the adaptations of American dances, with improvised leaps and bounds, whirls and gyrations. The music was squeaky, sour, but sufficient rhythm emerged; the drum alone would have been enough.

Concepcion searched the crowd of boys, smothering the door, for Pablo. She was aware of a growing anxiety for him, which annoyed her, for she had come to have a good time. " I wonder where Pablo could be ? " she kept saying to Eliseo, and to Miguel, " Go and see if you can find Pablo anywhere."

And Miguel, returning from one of his searching expeditions, reported that he had found Pablo, standing outside talking to some boys.

" How is he ? "

" He's all right, I guess," Miguel said. " Why, what should be the matter with him ? "

" Nothing," said the mother nervously. " Nothing."

Miguel knew, well enough, but his brother had seemed sober. It was hard to tell, though, when he was standing still in a group.

In a few minutes Concepcion chanced to glance in the direction of the Romeros, and she saw that they were talking to each other and Vicente was half out of his chair. They were about to dance ! She turned and pinched Eliseo so hard that he almost cried out. " Quick, dance with me, dance with me ! " she hissed.

" What's the matter ? " he said when they were launched and dancing almost as if they enjoyed it. " Why did you pinch me ? "

" Don't you see ? The Romeros are dancing. I didn't want her to think that we were dancing just because they were."

Dancing with his wife was painful to Eliseo. It had to happen once at every *baile*, and he couldn't enjoy himself until it was done. For, more than once, he had caught sniggers on the faces of ill-mannered young, as he marched his big wife twice around the room and sat down. When it was over, Eliseo's duty for the evening was finished; now he could mix with his friends outside, a thing which he vastly preferred, and talk about farming and the weather.

Having planted his wife in her chair, he walked out of the hall, ostentatiously picking his teeth with the toothpick left over from supper. Miguel took his father's chair and sat there with his black eyes trying to follow everything at once. An hour became two hours. Vicente tried to cover a series of yawns with the back of his hand, Miguel's head drooped and Concepcion, motionless, looked over the dancing couples with seeming indifference. She was, however, intensely aware of each one. She was watching especially a group of boys over in a corner of the room, one of whom was Pablo, and he wasn't as sober as he might be. None of them were. When one of the boys broke away and tried to dance she was sure they were drunk.

She roused Miguel. " Go and find your father, Miguel. Tell him I want him to come in here."

And Miguel, tottering with drowsiness, obeyed. He was gone a long time, and when he returned at last he was alone.

" Where is he ? Couldn't you find him ? "

" Sure, I found him."

" Well, where is he ? "

"He said to tell you to wait—he'll come after a while."

This was a bad sign; he was only defiant when he had liquor in him. Concepcion swallowed her wrath and kept her eyes on the boys. Occasionally one of them left the pack to dance with a girl whose powdered face made her skin look lavender, the colour of some poisonous, horrible death. She could not understand why they used the stuff, or if they must use it why they didn't choose a better colour. Pablo was dancing now; he gripped his girl with both arms, and she was limp in them. The clasp suggested an embrace more than a dance, and a passionate one at that. Concepcion turned her face away, embarrassed, and stole a glance at Teresita. A prim, disapproving frown. The mother squirmed uneasily in her chair. And presently Pablo, too, succumbed to the suggestion and took his girl outside, butting his way through the choked doorway drunkenly. It looked like trouble. For a long time she didn't see him again. Then there were shouts and yells outside, meaning but one thing—a fight. Everybody heard the commotion—Miguel was off like a shot, squeezed through the forest of milling legs at the door and vanished. Within, the long row of women on the bench stiffened, sat up straight; the air instantly became tense, expectant. Concepcion, sitting on the edge of her chair, pitched her ears to catch each new sound. Then came the sound of blows—more yells— silence. After a little, Miguel came back, his eyes ablaze with excitement. "It was Pablo," he whispered. "He had a fight out there!"

"What happened?"

" Pablo knocked him down. They took the other boy away."

" Oh." Concepcion made an angry sound in her throat. " Why must they always be fighting ? " she said.

" They're all pretty drunk," Miguel volunteered.

" What makes you think so ? How do you know so much ? "

" Well, I can see. They can hardly stand up."

She told him to sit down and be quiet. With the worry lifted from her heart something gave way, and Concepcion wanted to cry. She hated herself for the impulse—better to go out there and take the brat by the scruff of the neck and beat some sense into him—and here she sat, ready to cry. Then Eliseo came into the hall. His eyes, circling the room once, found Concepcion; fastening the beam of his gaze upon her, the rest of him attempted to approach along it with only fair success. She watched his ungainly advance. In spite of her will to stop them, two great tears swelled from her eyes and rolled down her cheeks. He was drunk. Right there in front of the Romeros ! Every time this happened she suffered anew. She never would get used to it. It seemed that her body would dissolve—her nerves trembled on the brink of the final, absolute dissolution.

He flopped into the chair vacated by Miguel and gave himself over to a shaking, idiotic chortle. " My son ! " he was saying, and then he raised his voice so that all the room could hear: " Ho ! How he hit that boy ! "

Miguel, seeing his mother's tears, felt a wave of hate for his father sweep him; he had to strain against the impulse to fly at him, a small, maniacal fury.

As the first crucial minutes passed, Concepcion recovered her composure, but nothing remained inside her except a white heat of outrage. She moved her chair into a position which shielded her husband from the lifted Romero eyebrows—and resumed her calm appraisal of the dancers.

Two hours became three hours. The Romeros went home. Eliseo slept fitfully in his chair. Miguel had been gone for a half-hour, she guessed to bed. She was thinking of going home herself, and she nudged Eliseo savagely.

" What's the matter ? What do you want ? " he said, opening his eyes.

" I'm going home. And you're coming with me."

" All right, all right. That's good. I'm tired." He had been afraid she wanted to dance again.

And as she searched the hall for a final check of Pablo, she saw him dancing with the same girl who had caused the trouble before. She saw two boys go up to him and separate him roughly from the girl and, taking him by the arms, lead him outside. Her heart contracted. " Look ! " she whispered, clutching her husband's hand. " There's going to be more trouble. Go and see——"

Eliseo blinked. " What ? What is it ? Where ? "

" Pablo," she said. " They just took him out."

" Who did ? " said Eliseo, bristling. " Who took him out."

" Some boys—they came in and——" She was stopped by the crack of two pistol shots in quick succession. Concepcion opened her mouth to scream, but no scream came. Eliseo leapt to his feet and dashed across

EM

the hall like mad, flinging people out of his way as he ran. There were two more shots while he crossed the room.

When he reached the street Eliseo at first saw no one, for the crowd had melted to the shelter of walls and shadows. Then in the darkness beside a building across the street he saw a figure on the ground. Something told him it was Pablo, but he didn't go over to it. He ran to the corner of the *baile* hall instead, and there, full in the moonlight, not twenty feet away from him, he saw the boy who had done the shooting, swaying, with the pistol still in his hand.

" Give me that gun," Eliseo said slowly, steadily.

" *Chingadero !* Stand back or I'll give it to you, too."

" Give me that gun," Eliseo repeated, and began to advance towards the boy slowly. " Give me that gun."

" Stop ! Stay where you are or I'll shoot."

Eliseo had moved half the distance separating him from the boy; he continued to move forward, walking deliberately, but very slowly, repeating, " Give me that gun."

" Stop, I tell you ! " the boy cried hysterically. " Stop or I'll shoot you just like him ! " He pulled the trigger—the hammer clicked, but failed to fire the cartridge, and in the same instant Eliseo bounded forward, snatched the pistol out of the boy's hand, and brought the butt end of it down smartly on his head. The youth folded at the middle and fell to the ground. And Eliseo went over to Pablo.

" Are you hurt, Pablo ? "

" Not much—scratched my arm once. I thought if I fell down he'd stop shooting."

" Good boy," said Eliseo. " Did you have a gun ? "

" No."

" Good boy."

Eliseo put the pistol in his pocket and went back into the hall, fearful of what his wife would have to say.

III

WHEN Miguel was fifteen years old he had finished
all the schooling available in Hormiga. He could read
easily in English or Spanish, and write in the former
with labour but fair success. He could add sums,
multiply, subtract, and divide; moreover—miracle of
irrelevancy !—he could figure compound interest.

" Well, boy," Eliseo said to him one day, " now you
go to work, no ? Your mother and father, they grow
old, and then the boys come along and take care of
them. That's the way it goes."

Miguel nodded gravely, aware of his great respon-
sibility. He had grown quieter. The two years had made
changes in him. Now it seemed, as he left his boyhood,
taller and stronger, that he would become studious also;
for he was always reading in the evenings, even reading
aloud to his mother sometimes. She loved this, but
opportunities for it were scarce, for Eliseo disliked it
as much as she liked it. He was made restless by it,
merely, and couldn't hold his attention on it. Nor was
he prompted to listen by any great love for the boy.
Miguel had grown no closer to his father—more away
from him, rather; their trips to the farm were no
longer devoted to hunting and walking in the forest,
but to work, man's work, ploughing and seeding
and harvesting. All interchange had ceased between
them, save the necessary, superficial exchange of two
workers.

" Yes," Miguel answered his father, " but it's hard to know what to do."

" Well, we'll find something for you. I've been thinking maybe it would be a good thing to put in a petrol pump here. Then you could manage that and run the store—make something pretty good out of it."

" Yes," said Miguel again, knowing well that it was his mother who had been thinking.

" You have a good head for figures," Eliseo added, slapping him manfully on the shoulder and walking away picking his teeth.

It did seem at last that Eliseo's tough little body was beginning to decline; he could still work all day, but at the end of it he was tired out. While nine or ten hours of ploughing exhausted him now, two years ago he was ready to walk down the hill to Borregos and back again after a day's work. Miguel thought about it often and realised that it was his duty to contribute to the family's support, especially since the other boys helped so little. In the back of his mind he cherished a wish to go down to Gabaldon for a while. There was a parochial school and college down there and it beckoned to a dawning ambition which the local priest, a Frenchman who served Hormiga's church once in a fortnight and had always been a force in Miguel's growing up, had nourished in him with some care.

Father Aloysius called the boy, even in his presence, a promising lad and took a special interest in him. That he was different from his brothers, Miguel felt, himself, now; he could see their thoughtlessness, their indifference, their lack of ambition. And ever since the shooting of Pablo, which he had witnessed when his

mother thought he was in bed, he had grown away from
their habit of acceptance and pondered more and more
about the future—his own future in particular. The
incident had served, also, to make him shy of liquor,
to turn his young energies to introspection, to a strange
and very personal religiousness. It was the latter which
drew him to the priest, doubtless, for he sought the
company of the man when he came to town, and because he was a robust, pioneering priest, who scorned
the outward show of saintliness, he was a proper
influence. He spoke Spanish easily, was genial, understanding, and kind, and Miguel grew to love him and to
talk to him as he used to talk to his mother, telling the
priest of his deepest hopes, frustrations, intentions. In
fact the priest's twinkling eyes, beneficent face, and
rotund figure, his greying beard, came to represent
divinity in the boy's imagination. Concepcion was
glad of the relationship, for it flattered her a little,
and comforted her with the knowledge that the
priest would lead the lad away from the *Penitentes* if
he could.

Through the mist of striving consciousness Miguel
examined Hormiga, saw poverty, savage passion, and
a curious mixture of gaiety and melancholy. Aided by
his habit of observation, he tried bravely to find his
own way; aided by the priest, he sought to thread his
path in the confusion of forces which pulled him this
way and that; the man attempted to show him what
his choices would ultimately be, with especial reference
to his religious life. He must one day decide whether he
should be guided by the Church authority, or take some
of his atonement upon himself, as the *Penitentes* did, and

he tried to make the decision easier without actually dictating it.

Full of the need for anchorage, Miguel awaited the approach of the next Holy Week with eagerness, as if it might resolve some of the hazy doubts which tormented him; for the rites of the *Penitentes*, the sad, wailing voices, the bleat of the flute to which their ceremonies were inseparably bound, had become both the theme and the refrain of his spiritual life, regardless of the words of the *padre*. Although the man told him that the Church had banned public flagellation more than two centuries ago, that it was therefore contrary to regular law, Miguel could not escape the conviction, deep inside him, that it was good. It *must* be good. He could see no other way by which the souls around him could be saved. For it seemed to him that Hormiga was full of wickedness and that the Brotherhood of *Penitentes*, in their annual penitential retreat, thoroughly and spectacularly atoned for it.

"Atonement is right and good," the priest used to say to him, "but it should be done by prayer and confession and the penances the Church provides. You must remember, Miguel, the Church is older and wiser than you or I or the *Penitentes*. I am only her servant, here in the wilderness. I don't ask you to believe me, but to believe the Church."

Miguel never tried to argue. He listened, and tried to believe, and carried the argument with him from day to day. Concepcion could make neither head nor tail of it when it popped up in her presence; long unused to reason, she quickly lost herself in the blankness of ignorance. She had let her instinct be her guide so long that when Miguel talked to her now it was her turn to listen, and be cheered or saddened by what he said. She could no longer be his advocate; she feared it was the end of the intimacy she had known with him when he was younger, and perhaps it was the end. She knew, however, with her heart if not with her head, that it was another beginning for the boy, and she was consoled. Her instinct was more often right than wrong.

Miguel, in the interval between finishing his schooling and launching into work, was restless, idle. County funds were so low that there were only six months of school, and he was released by the first of April. There was not enough trade in the store to keep him busy, farming had not begun because it had been a dry winter and there was not a trace of moisture in the soil. He thought much about going to the college in Gabaldon, but, if the dryness held, such a plan would be out of the question. It would mean a hard winter, and he would be needed at home. Moreover, the priest told him that times were bad in the city and it would be impossible for a boy to find work to support himself. They could not realise in Hormiga, he said, where there was little need for money, how desperate the conditions were. " It seems," he said dolefully, " that wherever the Americans are—a blight descends upon the place."

So it was no good hoping for this year. Miguel would have to stay at home. " He's young," Concepcion thought. " Perhaps later on——"

And day after day Eliseo came out of the house in the morning after breakfast to scan the sky, shake his head, and frown. " No rain to-day. No rain to-day."

Miguel stood beside him one day when he came out

to meet the sun, and he said, " How is it that everybody seems to find something to do here in Hormiga ? For so many years every man has two—three—four sons, and they all seem to find something to do—they get married and have more sons. I should think the jobs would have run out long ago."

" They do run out, boy," Eliseo said. " Sometimes whole families of boys have to go away and find work somewhere else. Always somebody is going away. Hormiga isn't any bigger now than it was a hundred years ago."

" Where do they go ? "

" Oh, most of them go down to Gabaldon to start with—from there they drift to Colorado, to Arizona —everywhere. Many of the Hormiga boys have gone to the mines up in Colorado. The trouble is, there's always enough men wherever they go. They don't need any more."

They became workers, labourers with their hands and their backs. Why, then, this striving which compelled Miguel to look beyond things as they were, if his destiny were so clearly marked ? Why should he be the one to reach out, as if some larger fate awaited him ? Looking back, tracing the impulse, he could see his mother's dreams, and her dreamful talks with him about his future; in the beginning she had done it for him, and now he had caught it from her. Impatiently he wished that he might forget it and become like Pablo or Benito, content with the daily round. Sometimes in desperation he prayed to be released from his striving: " Our Father, please make me happy to be what I am ! "

Events came along to shift the burden of these days. There was the family *fiesta* on the occasion of the baptism of Benito's fourth child, a girl. It was a sickly baby. Concepcion, who knew things by their signs, said frankly that it would never live to grow up. The death of a baby was a sad thing but a common one, and there were always more to be had. Rosa herself seemed to know that the child was doomed, for her preparations for the christening were so half-hearted that Concepcion had to step in at the last minute and do it all herself.

Poor Rosa ! She hadn't been at all well since the birth, had dragged herself around. She sat moodily in a chair when she wasn't working, with blank, listless eyes. So the grandmother took charge, " borrowed " from the store the necessary pink cakes, soda-pop and delicacies, laid out the best tablecloth in the family, which happened to be the one Rosa's mother, now dead, had left her, and assembled knives and forks and spoons for the guests. Rosa's house had to be thoroughly brushed and scrubbed first, because it had been neglected, and there was a shocking pile of washing to be done, too. All the preparations had a quality of pretence; the feeling crept in despite everyone's determination to make it an especially grand *fiesta*—perhaps in the superstitious hope that, by so doing, the child's fate might be altered.

The second Sunday before Easter was the day selected. The surprise of the occasion, a magnificent layer-cake covered with green and pink frosting bordered with glittering, spangled ridge of raised sugar, with the child's name inscribed in the same stuff, arrived on Saturday. It occupied the centre of Rosa's *fiesta* table and all the next day no one had the heart to cut into it, it was so beautiful. Almost the entire congregation stayed after Mass for the baptism, and then in a chattering crowd moved up the street to Rosa's house for the *fiesta*. The baby was dressed in a new long white dress, and it wailed constantly. She went to the *fiesta*, too, in her mother's lap.

When the child died a few weeks later, the family was plunged into a whirlpool of grief, from which it emerged without a scratch. And Eliseo's morning frown deepened with a more immediate anxiety; a *fiesta* and a funeral in the space of so short a time were a financial calamity with the farms drying up and Benito penniless, anyway. True, it was Benito's affair, but he was always crying to his father about his family and his difficulty in providing for it. Now his supply of money and credit was drained utterly.

The *Penitentes* came to his rescue. The Order was benevolent as well as penitential, so they made his child's coffin for him, marched to his house and bore the baby to Holy Ground, laid her away. The *Hermano Mayor*—no longer Eliseo—read the service.

Shivering in his spine Miguel heard their sad, wailing voices singing in the funeral procession with the *velorio* drum in the lead.

It was only a short time to Holy Week. A few days before the annual retreat of the *Penitentes* began, Miguel discovered that Pablo would be a novice—would be taken in this year. And this news made the younger brother forget his troubles, for he was able to talk about it with Pablo, more, at least, than he had ever talked before. But Pablo wasn't very illuminating, with all his nineteen years. He could be eloquent about some things, such as his shooting affair two years ago, or his girl friends, but about this coming experience he was dumb.

" When will they take you in ? " Miguel asked, full of curiosity.

" Wednesday, I guess."

" How does it feel ? I mean—are you glad you're going in ? Does it make you feel good ? "

" Oh, I don't know. I don't feel any different."

" Well, what made you do it ? How—why did you decide to join ? "

Pablo shrugged. " I thought it was about time, that's all. Father—he says it's time for me to come in."

" But don't you want to—yourself? "

" Sure. I don't care."

They were sitting on a pile of logs in front of the house, along the lane that skirted the rim of Hormiga's canyon. Pablo was whittling and Miguel was looking at him searchingly, trying to learn with his eyes what Pablo's tongue could not reveal.

" I should think," Miguel said softly, " that you'd be scared."

This roused Pablo a little. " Who, me ? Scared ? " He laughed shortly. " It's nothing to be scared about. Did you ever see one of those whips they use ? They don't weigh anything. They're light—just rope fibres, loosely woven together. I don't see how it can hurt to hit yourself with one of them. You don't have to hit hard unless you want to."

" But the blood," Miguel said. " Why do they bleed so ? "

Pablo's assurance dwindled. " Yes, there is a lot of blood. I don't know——"

" I wonder why Father Aloysius is so against the *Penitentes* ? " Miguel went on, ignoring the change he had wrought in his brother. " He's always telling them to stop—doing those things."

" Oh, he just wants all the money for himself, that's all," Pablo explained, confident again. " We have dues, you see, and we have to put in a little money once in a while. The priest doesn't like that because if it didn't go to the *Penitentes* it would go to him."

This was an explanation Miguel hadn't heard before. " Do you think that's it ? " he said.

" Sure that's it. What else could it be ? "

" Well, he says it's wrong to—to whip in the streets, and to do those things——"

" Oh, it can't be wrong. They've always done it. I guess it isn't wrong."

" It's against the law of the Church," Miguel persisted.

Pablo shrugged again, and there was a silence between the brothers.

" I should think," Miguel went on presently, " that those big crosses they carry would hurt their shoulders. And the cactus, too——" He shuddered, and Pablo gave him a look, suspicious that he was being baited. But the boy was deadly serious—even Pablo could see that. " I don't see how they do it."

" They're not so heavy," said Pablo with a superior air.

Miguel fell silent. There was little satisfaction in this. He got up after a while and wandered off, his hands in the pockets of his overalls. When he stepped on stones he could feel them through the soles of his shoes, and he wondered how a boy might earn a couple of dollars in Hormiga. He was shy about asking his father for money, and a new sense of guilt had begun to trouble him since he finished school. He ought to begin to look after himself—make his own way in the world. But he didn't know how. How do you start ? What do you do ?

Across the *plaza*, Miguel walked, along a road which led across the carven foothills of the northward-running range to other mountain towns not unlike Hormiga. As he passed the store of Vicente Romero, which lay on this street some fifty feet from the *plaza* corner, Miguel had an idea. He would know—Vicente would know—how a boy might earn a few dollars to buy a pair of shoes ! It would be hard—harder, perhaps, than talking with his own father about it—but it would be better. There would be a different feeling about it, more impersonal. Miguel mounted the steps and peered through the pane of glass in the door. There was Vicente, all right, sitting alone at his old desk with his back to the light. Miguel went in, quietly.

But when he was inside, Miguel was overtaken with such a sinking of his heart that he wanted to turn and run out again. Vicente, however, had heard the click of the latch and had turned in his chair to study the boy over the rim of his spectacles. Miguel's features were invisible to him against the bright light from the street.

" Who is it ? " he said brusquely.

" It's me—Miguel."

" Miguel ? What's your name—your last name ? "
Vicente started to rise nervously, as if he had no real
faith in the security of being the richest man in Hor-
miga. But as the boy moved closer he recognised him.
" Oh," he said with a quick change of manner, "Miguel
Lopez. Come in, my boy. What can I do for you ? "

" I—I need a——" Miguel stopped, convulsed with
embarrassment, for he had almost said he needed a
new pair of shoes, and Vicente would think he was
begging. Family pride rose boiling in him, forcing
blood to his head. A close call. He choked, looked down
at the floor and began again. " I want to—my father's
farm is in bad shape—and I want to help a little if I
can." He hesitated, looking at the importance of
Vicente's desk, littered with papers, open ledgers and
pens, pencils, blotters. But having begun, he gained
some confidence at the sound of his own voice. " I
thought maybe—if I came to talk with you—you
might help me out some way, and tell me something
I could do."

" Well, now, that's fine—that's fine," Vicente said,
in a voice which seemed to rattle the goods on the
shelves. " Take a chair. Sit down. We'll talk this thing
over." He sat down again at his desk and motioned the
boy into a chair beside it. " Now then, you want to
earn some money, is that it ? "

" Yes, sir."

" Well, let me see." He rubbed his chin and the
bristles on it crackled electrically. " Do you know anything about book-keeping ? "

" N-no, I guess I don't," said Miguel.

" But you might learn. It seems to me I've heard your father say you're a bright boy—a good head for figures."

These familiar words brought on another flood of self-consciousness which almost made him dizzy. " Did he say that ? "

" Oh, yes. Now I have a hard time getting somebody to help me with the books here. I don't always have time to do it myself. If you could learn——" Vicente paused significantly.

" I could learn," Miguel said, " but how ? Where ? "

" Well, I could teach you myself. If you would come over here to the store every day, I could show you how it's done, pretty quick. Let me see, how old are you ? "

" I'll be sixteen in a little while."

" The trouble is," Vicente went on, " I have to be away so much. I've got business in the city, you know— I need someone to look after things here." He stopped and rubbed his chin again.

Miguel's hopes faded. This didn't look like two dollars right now to buy a new pair of shoes. And the whole affair was becoming more than he had bargained for when he entered Vicente's place; besides, his father would be wild if he went to work for a competing store. Escape began to seem important to him. He could feel the beginnings of a panic inside him. He'd have to stop this thing somehow—but how ? "

" I'll tell you what we'll do," Vicente was saying. " I've got to go away for a few days, but as soon as I come back you come over here and I'll show you how we keep books. How's that ? "

"That's good," said Miguel, because it seemed to be the only thing he could say. " When will you come back ? "

" Well, this is Monday—I'll be back Thursday. So. You come Thursday morning, no ? About eleven."

Miguel stood up. " All right. Thank you." And he hurried out to the street. As calm slowly returned to him he felt frightened—then jubilant—then frightened again. It would have to be kept a secret. Eliseo would fly to pieces. But why not work for Vicente ? Why not master book-keeping at Vicente's expense, then take over his father's store and make something of it ? The location was much better than Romero's—right on the corner of the *plaza*, where everybody entering Hormiga was bound to see it. He became more and more excited as he thought about the plan. The door to the future opened a crack, giving him an exhilarating glimpse. The shoes could wait—a few thicknesses of paper under his feet would keep out the stones. After all, you had to know book-keeping to be a good merchant, and that was why Pablo was such a dolt at running the store. He had never heard of book-keeping.

The idea was too good to hold altogether to himself, but Miguel kept it for the rest of the day, while he walked around with his head in the clouds; in the evening, however, it was too lonely up there. He capitulated to his mother. Seated in his old-time perch beside the kitchen range, he followed her with his eyes for many minutes after supper. Eliseo had gone, probably to the *morada*, and Pablo was outside talking to friends, sitting on the wood-pile. Concepcion was washing the dishes in a big pan of hot water.

FM

" What does Vicente Romero do ? " Miguel began obliquely.

" Oh, he has that store—you know what he does."

" But he has business in Gabaldon——"

" Yes, he thinks he has. He's a *politico*, you know. He was in the state legislature once. He never got over it."

" Is he a *Penitente* ? "

Concepcion laughed. " Of course he's a *Penitente*. Teresita pretends he isn't, but he is. Do you think he'd be a *politico* and not be a *Penitente* ? No, no. He's one, all right."

" Doesn't Teresita like the *Penitentes* ? "

" No. She came from the city, where they don't have them. She thinks they're terrible."

Miguel was thoughtfully silent for a few minutes. The mixture of religion and politics confused him slightly.

" He's pretty smart," Concepcion admitted rather ruefully. " Everybody owes him money around here."

Miguel waited a little longer before he said : " I went to see him to-day."

His mother turned to look at him with her hands poised, dripping dishwater. " *You* went to see him ? What for ? "

" Well——" He didn't know where to begin, at the shoes, or later. "—I thought he might help me find a job—something to do. We'll be needing money if—if the farm dries up."

" What's the matter with our store ? What about that ? "

" But Pablo——"

" Oh, Pablo," she cut in. " He doesn't care about it. What did he say—Vicente ? "

" He said he'd teach me book-keeping if I'd come over there every day."

Concepcion snorted. " He did, did he ? The sly coyote. You'd better not tell your father what you've done. He'll be mad, all right."

" Maybe Vicente Romero'll tell him."

" He might, but I don't think he will," said Concepcion, wisely.

" Why not ? "

" Because he probably had his reasons for wanting to help you. I tell you, he's a sly one. You've got to watch him."

" What reasons ? "

" I don't know." Concepcion returned to her dishes. " Maybe he just thinks he can get something for nothing out of you. He didn't say anything about paying you, did he ? "

" No."

She snorted again. " Well."

Miguel was temporarily deflated. She stood upon her advantage for a while, making noisy swishes over her dish-washing. The whole thing was, in fact, bitter medicine for her. " What else did he say ? " she asked at last.

" Oh, he said he had a hard time finding somebody to help him with his books over there. He's away so much——"

" Books ? What does he mean by that ? "

" His account books—where he keeps the record of what he sells—and buys, too, I guess."

" Is that such a big job ? To hear him talk you'd think he owned Hormiga."

Miguel had an idea, too, then. " He said he heard I had a good head for figures. He thought he could teach me pretty quick." And he watched her face carefully, saw the frown lighten.

Forcing back a smile, she said, " He's a slippery old goat."

Now, Miguel thought, was the moment to share his inspiration with her. " I thought I could go over there and learn book-keeping from him. Then I could work for him for a while——" He paused to see how his mother was taking it. She was still shaking her head and pushing her hair out of her eyes. " And then I could leave his store—after I'd learned all about it—and come over to ours. I'd know how to run it then, you see, and I could make our store better than his—it's a better location."

It was some time before the point of her son's device pierced her jealous disapproval. Miguel, watching her acutely, felt his spirits rise as he told her, and then, as she seemed not to respond, felt them recede as if the blood were being drained out of him through holes in the ends of his toes.

Suddenly she stopped drying dishes, turned about, and looked at him. A great smile banished all from her face except happiness. " Miguel ! " she cried, and rushing over to him, she grabbed him around the neck and danced him around the room and pressed him against her hemispheric breasts, encircled him in her fine, strong arms. Her enthusiasm was far greater than he expected. While he was being spun around the room his heart lifted him to something like bliss. He felt like a lover who has brought joy to his beloved, an entirely new sensation and one which he remembered always. And she sang a song meanwhile with a familiar tune. In a moment, having so far forgotten herself, she resumed her maternal dignity, from which only a great excitement ever made her fall.

Miguel, breathless but happy, joined her in the chorus, and he snatched up a pan with a handle on it and banged out the rhythm on the bottom of it.

" Oh ho, how smart you are, my Miguel ! " she said when the song was done. " Now listen," she whispered pantingly, " we won't tell your father at all, see ? He wouldn't understand—he'd only be mad because it's Vicente. You go over there every day and learn how to run his store." Her eyes dilated with the pleasure of it. " He knows how to run a store, all right. There's three of them here, and he gets all the business. Then you come back here and make our store the best in Hormiga, no ? " She slapped her knees and laughed, swaying her body from the waist.

Before her alarming confidence, Miguel began to feel young and unequal to the plan she was laying for him, for it was already done in her mind. Even in his own imagination he hadn't reached the climax which was so clear to her. A mere boy, beating Vicente at his own game ? It seemed a mountainous and improbable thing.

In the ensuing days of idleness, the plan was always with him, but not always foremost. Pablo's initiation approached. As the hour drew near and he became more frightened, he sought the comfort of intimacy with those who were closest to him, for it seemed more and more like a step in the dark. There was the *morada* door, and beyond—the unknown, full of shades and terrors. When, in anticipation, he wasn't cold with fear, he was dumb with dread, and Miguel suspected this, with his strange, apprehending eyes. For the first time he felt a compassionate liking for his brother, and a wish to help him through these last hours. All the blood and agony which he had seen as a child, as a boy and finally as a conscious being, in the *Penitente* exercises, now at last assumed a cloak of reality, for Pablo was one with him in kinship, and nearest him in age. Miguel had seen his father many times, then Benito, vanish behind the *morada* door, and more than once he had recognised them in the black-hooded figures who, every year, made the earth groan with their penitential pain and stained it with their blood. Heretofore, however, the gap had been too great. He had remained unconnected with them actually. They were not the father and the brother whom he knew and saw every day.

There can be no remission of sins without the shedding of blood. There can be no remission of sins without the shedding of blood.

This was the text of Pablo's waking hours and the one memorable sentence in the mass of ritual which he had to learn in preparation for his initiation. Memorising was hard for him, and he asked Miguel to help him with it; thus the young brother had a glimpse of the mysteries.

At last the day came, and then the hour. It was late in the evening, about six o'clock. Pablo was waiting inside the door of the house, pacing up and down, or sitting hollowly in a chair. Concepcion, pretending it was no affair of hers, was in the kitchen, and Miguel sat quietly, alertly, on the wood-pile which commanded a view of the *plaza* and the *morada*. In the twilight he saw a man with a lantern come out of the *morada* and walk briskly to the house where Pablo was and enter it without knocking. In a moment he reappeared, leading Pablo by the arm. And Miguel's heart throbbed as if it were he who was being led to his doom. He watched them with intense eyes, saw them stop at the *morada* door, saw it opened from within—a faint block of light —click—dark stillness again. Pablo was gone.

For many minutes Miguel sat on the wood-pile staring at the *morada* as if it might vanish at any moment before his eyes. Sparks dashed from its chimney, straight into the air. There was no sound.

On Thursday, the day after Pablo was swallowed by the unknown, the dawn was cloudy, with a chill wind blowing from the low country; as the sun rose higher, the wind mounted to a gale which blotted out the valley in dust and snatched the dried surface of Hormiga's streets in its teeth, flung it against the houses, and drove it through the cracks under doors and windows.

Everything became unreal in the storm. A weird, yellowish light, filtered through clouds of dust, sickened the world—or that patch of the world which Miguel could see through a window of his father's house. He didn't know—he couldn't have told—what he was looking at, but he saw the *morada* and thought of Pablo, saw the whirling, blinding air and thought of a kinder place he had once read about, where reaches of the sea sparkled in the sun. Then he saw a black automobile bobbing over the stones in the road; it turned where the road led on to the north, and he realised that it was Vicente Romero, returning from Gabaldon. He remembered that this was the day appointed for his first instruction in book-keeping. So much had intervened that he had quite forgotten. He found his hat and went out into the gale.

His mother was waiting for him when he came back. " Well, how did it go ? Did you see him ? "

" Yes, I saw him. He said he didn't have much time to-day. He'll have to start from the beginning. I don't know very much." Miguel was depressed, trying to conceal it. " It's pretty hard."

" Yes, I'm sure it's hard," she said gently, and with a sudden bitterness she added, " Everything's hard. It's hard to get along at all."

" It's going to be slow, too," he said. " I didn't even know what an invoice was."

" I know," the mother soothed in a softly rising tone, " but look at Pablo. He's been in the store for three years now, and I'll bet you he never heard of a—whatever the thing was you said. You'll learn, all right, Miguel. You'll learn quick, too."

" Yes, I'll learn." In spite of his doubts he was bolstered by her faith in him. " It's all in English, too. That makes it harder—so many new words."

" Oh, but you read English the best of any of us, Miguel."

" But this is different," he protested, prolonging her sympathy.

" But it won't take you long to get it. And then you'll make the rest of us look stupid—like *burros*." She laughed quietly.

Though his mother made his task easier for him with her believing love, Miguel hated coming home empty-handed; it was money they needed, not promises. Yet he dared not ask Vicente how soon he would start paying him something. He went back the next day full of determination to ask for a small wage, but as Vicente exposed his ignorance more and more he realised that he was worth nothing to the Romero store, could therefore demand nothing. So he put away the hope of earning for the present and filled the bottoms of his shoes with paper. And on Saturday, Pablo returned from his first penitential retreat.

He was haggard and silent. His cheeks were hollow and his eyes had gone deeper into his skull, leaving caverns under his brows. Although he came alone, he could not have gone much farther. He flung himself on to his bed—the great white bed with the immaculate coverlet—and lay there face down, eyes closed, breathing heavily. Concepcion, in the kitchen, heard him lie down on his bed, heard the springs creak. Then she knew, as she often did, without being told, and went in to see him. She laid her hand on his back comfortingly —he started, quivered through his whole body, and groaned aloud. Of course, it was his back. She remembered and withdrew her hand, folded it with the other in her lap, and sat on the edge of his bed, looking down on him.

Slowly at first, and then in a crescendo of feeling, she hated everything in her life in Hormiga; the poverty, the blindness, the ancient compulsions bulked into one vast, blank passion of hatred which, at the last, made her throw back her head and raise her powerless hands above it. She came to herself quickly, opened her eyes, and looked again at the boy on the bed. He was moaning softly, regularly, with each breath. She lowered herself gently to her knees on the floor beside him and held the palm of her hand against his forehead. Hot. Hot with fever. Feeling the anger rising in her again, she brushed it aside with her will. There was no time for it now. " Pablo," she said. " Pablo ! "

He heard, but did not speak. There was only a change in the rhythm of his moaning.

" What is it, my son ? What have they done to you ? "

" *Nada*," he murmured. " It isn't anything. I'm— tired."

" Ah, *por Dios, por Dios*," she lamented, and then in anger, " *Aburridos !* The fools ! The blasphemers ! It's your back, isn't it ? "

Under the force of her compassion Pablo nodded and became the boy returning to his mother, all his maturity and selfhood flowing back into her.

Then she drove herself to action. " You must get up, Pablo. Get your clothes off—get into the bed. Come "—she pulled on his arm—" I'll help you."

Pablo stirred weakly and she lifted him with her own strength to a sitting position on the edge of the bed. She took off his coat, then his trousers, his shirt. He was facing her so she didn't see his back, but she saw the blood on his clothes and was glad she couldn't see it. As it was, she gasped when she held up his shirt and saw the condition of it. But she would have to look at it—she would have to wash his back.

" Wait," she commanded. " Wait, while I get some water." When she came back, Pablo was still sitting there, his head held in his two hands. " Lie down on the bed," she said, and he obeyed like a child. Gently, then, she washed the blood from his back, biting her lip to keep from crying out at the sight of it; but it wasn't as bad as it seemed, after it was bathed. There were six long scratches in the skin, three on either side of his spine, deep enough to make the blood flow, and inflamed. Pablo meanwhile gave unrestrained expression to his pain. This she expected and understood. It was better. Silent suffering was the hardest to look upon. Miguel was a silent sufferer, and it tore her heart to pieces, for it seemed to her an inhuman, crushing way to take a hurt.

When she had washed him, she laid a clean night-shirt over him and left him to sleep—left his fever to God.

Eliseo made light of the matter when he heard of it. He was annoyed to see Pablo surrender to his mother's sympathy and let her put him to bed like a baby. The *Penitente* was expected to bear his pain in the silences of his soul, and not share it with women. He was disgusted—Pablo had failed his first major test. " Yes, it's too bad," he said. " Leave him alone. He'll get all right in a day or two."

Miguel continued to sleep with his brother. He would awake many times during the nights and hear Pablo's restless tossing; sometimes he heard him speak, and answered him, but Pablo must have talked in his dreams. The *Enfermero*, an officer of the Brotherhood whose duty it was to look after the sick, came once a day to bathe Pablo's back in Romero water, a herbal tea which they always used for the purpose. And one morning he took Eliseo outside with him when he left the house.

" The boy is bad," he said gravely. " Maybe you better get the doctor from Santa Rosa."

" You think so ? What's the matter ? "

" I don't know. It isn't the cutting—that's healing all right. But he still has the fever. I think maybe he's sick in here." He tapped his chest with his fingertips. " That day the wind was blowing, you know ? I think he got sick in here."

Eliseo nodded. " It costs money to have the doctor. You don't think you can fix him up ? "

" No."

" All right, *hermano*. I'll get the doctor."

In the afternoon Pablo was delirious, and his mother was frantic with fear. She sat in the room where he lay with the madness on him, and she shut the windows, kept the doors closed. When Miguel came home from Vicente's store, he went into the room and sat with her. Once he had to hold Pablo in his bed, had to use all his strength to hold his brother down, while Concepcion bathed his face with cold cloths. Rosa and others, hearing of Pablo's delirium, came and sat in the sick-room, came with their rosaries, and spoke silent prayers with their eyes cast down. A constant procession of friends came and went; only Concepcion and Miguel stayed there, watching, watching. One came with an infant in her arms and nursed it when it cried, pulling a great breast from within her dress, like a bag of salt. The delirium was personified into a fiend, and they silently told their beads to drive the devil out.

When Eliseo returned with the doctor the boy was quieter, but his room was full of people. As he entered, the doctor shook his head a little; he had known what he would find and was prepared. He spoke in Spanish to them, kindly, without showing the impatience which he felt, and told them all to go—even Miguel was sent into the other room. Then the doctor opened the window.

This man of medicine was a magician, who was called only in the extremity of illness; like the priest, he was summoned to administer to the dying. Sometimes his magic worked, and then it was good. More often it failed, and it was bad. He had worked long and unselfishly for the people; he had grown old in their service, and thin and tired, until now he usually looked worse than the patient. He was a scrawny man with hidden springs of vitality. Whenever he was sent for, he urged people to call him sooner, and sometimes, now, they did, but for the most part his function in the mountain villages was a matter of signing death certificates.

He came out of the Lopez house with Eliseo and Miguel at his heels. The boy was wide-eyed with alarm. The father, outwardly calm, was baffled, disturbed. For the death of a grown son was a bad thing for a man. "Well," he said in his cocky manner, which seemed hollower than ever now, " what do you say ? Can you fix him up ? "

The doctor frowned and glared at Eliseo. " If he

isn't better by to-morrow night—I think your boy will die." And he waited after that for the words to sink in. " If you take care of him the way I told you—he may be better by to-morrow night." And without saying more, the doctor turned and walked to his car.

Eliseo stood where he was, nodding his head slowly. Miguel, hearing death in the doctor's words, trembled and felt dizzy. Yet it didn't mean anything to him. Death ? What was that ? Pablo couldn't die—he was much too young. He tried to think what it would be like for Pablo to die, and he couldn't imagine it. His mind refused to take it in, even as a possibility—and yet he trembled.

All the next day Miguel watched for a sign that Pablo was getting better, fearful, remembering the doctor's warning, that at nightfall the light which kept his brother alive would go out, promptly. He didn't stay at Vicente's store—only ran over there to tell him that Pablo, his brother, was very ill.

" What happened to him ? " Vicente asked in his thundering voice. " I heard he was sick."

" He's been very bad ever since he—got back."

" Got back ? Got back from where ? "

Miguel shrank before the necessity of speaking the words. " From—from—over there," he stammered, making a faint gesture in the direction of the *morada*.

" Oh," said Vicente, hurrying over it. " Oh, yes. Yes. Well, I'm sorry. Tell your mother. And come back when he's better."

" *Gracias*," Miguel whispered, and ran out of the place.

He was in and out of Pablo's room all day. It was

his duty now, since the doctor's visit, to meet callers
at the door and keep them out of the sick-room, and
he was faithful in it, meeting people with a long,
scared face, saying, " Oh, no, you can't see him. He's
still pretty bad—you can't see him."

And nothing would have induced him to let anyone
through the door. He would have defended it with his
life. At half past four, Teresita, wife of Vicente Romero,
arrived, and Miguel, faced with such a dilemma, paled.
For he didn't see how he could refuse her. He asked
her to wait while he called his mother. In the room
where Pablo was he told Concepcion to go out and see
Teresita while he stayed in her place.

She nodded. " I think he's better," she whispered
as she passed, and Miguel was glad.

Meetings between these two women always had the
same quality, of intimacy overlaid with a jealous
restraint. They liked each other, but something which
neither could name lay between them. They were
alike, too, in many ways, both forceful women with
a flair for ruling their families while seeming not to,
and with strong wills—perhaps the clash arose from
them. In appearance, Concepcion far surpassed the
other, for Teresita was a small woman whose teeth
were concentrated in front with astonishing promin-
ence, thick eye-glasses and a beak of a nose.

In the stress of crisis they forgot some of their reserve.
Teresita went to her friend and took both her hands.
" How *is* the boy ? " she said, so earnestly that Con-
cepcion was disarmed.

" I think he's going to get better," she said, and then,
in the company of this fellow creature, sympathetic,

sincere, she felt her will begin to dissolve, and she knew that sooner or later she would have to cry. And Teresita, of all people, would be the one to free the impounded tears.

" Sit down," Concepcion said, her voice already breaking. " He's better now," she tried to go on, biting her lip and making the absurd face of a woman trying to keep from crying. " The doctor said if he wasn't better by to-night——" She had to stop, and in another moment it was too late to continue. She buried her face in her hands and gave herself completely to weeping, all the strain of the days and nights of watching breaking her down in the instant, making her helpless against the flood. Teresita put one too-short arm around her shoulders and patted her gently with her hand. " I know how it is," she said. " When the danger's over, then you let go. It's all right. It's good for you to cry—let it come. Then you should sleep afterward. I'll stay with the boy."

When the mother had her fill of crying, Teresita led her into her own room and made her lie down. In a second she was asleep. The small, fiery Teresita took off her shawl and set to work in Concepcion's house. She built up the fire in the kitchen stove, put water on, and searched the place for food, was shocked to see how little of it there was in the house. " It's a wonder they're not all sick," she muttered aloud, finding nothing but a sack of beans and a stale loaf of bread. " I wonder where Eliseo is ? "

She set some beans on the stove to boil. Then she put on her shawl and went out, returning in a few minutes stealthily with her arms full of food from her

own house, cans of vegetables, some soup and a few
fresh eggs. Miguel, sitting by the window in the
darkened room, surprised her when he stood up,
looming like a ghost out of the gloom.

" Oh ! Oh, it's you, Miguel. You scared me. I went
over to get some things for your supper. Your mother's
sleeping. How is Pablo now ? "

" He's asleep, too. I think he's better."

She stood still, looking at him. By the failing light
from the windows Miguel thought he could see a softness in her eyes.

" You're a good boy, Miguel," she said, starting for
the kitchen. " I hope you'll stay away from that
place." When Miguel didn't answer, she paused at
the door. " You will, won't you ? "

He didn't know what to say, although he knew well
enough what she meant. Any answer would be the
wrong one, so he stood there looking at his feet. " I
don't know," he said at last because she was waiting
for him to say something.

Teresita sighed, and went out of the room.

When he came home, Eliseo treated Teresita deferen-
tially, without approaching her or allowing himself to
be approached. " I had to go to the farm," he said to
explain his absence.

She disapproved, and made it plain to him. She
was smart, but not smart enough to see that it was the
only thing for Eliseo to do, to go away, get out of the
house and stay out. The only reality greater than his
desire to help his son was his powerlessness to do so;
this he felt without understanding. In addition, his
wife had so completely taken over Pablo and his need

GM

that there was no room for Eliseo in her heart, and his presence could only be a hindrance. This, too, he felt, and it was this which finally drove him away. He had gone up to the farm, but only as a place to go. He had not even looked at the soil, nor gone out to the middle of the potato field and let the earth run through his fingers. Instead he had trudged sightlessly through the forest, his heart a leaden weight in him, while his mind advanced far into the future and saw Pablo, his son, in a thousand new ways.

Now, when it seemed that the danger might be passed, the father slipped effortlessly back to the present and became the man he was. His manner with Teresita became more officious, he began to strut again, and to crow.

" I guess we fixed him up all right. Pretty close call."

Pablo was long in mending. They turned the room over to him and fixed a bed for Miguel in the front room near the stove. As Pablo improved, life improved also. It even rained one day, a dense torrent of rain which, lasting half an hour, submerged the earth and turned the streets to rivers and roared in the canyon below the town. Water fell so fast that it tore up Eliseo's fields in running off, leaving them scarred like a battlefield. But he rejoiced, and ploughed them. And Miguel went back to work for Vicente Romero, and learned from him slowly, painfully.

He learned a little more than book-keeping. He discovered that Vicente's place was as much a pawn-shop as a store. He saw the collection of valued objects which the poorest people had been forced to leave there in exchange for food. Vicente kept them out of respect for the owner's hope of redeeming them with cash, should cash ever come their way, but he knew well that they were his for ever. And Miguel felt a stab of pity for the people who had been forced to part with their treasures, of anger for the man who had taken them. He saw, however, that Vicente's position was unassailable; if people had need and no money, he was right to exchange what they needed for what they had. It was better than letting them starve. The collection contained old silver, old jewellery, even some old pieces of furniture and lace. It made him hated. This was why the man was the arch-villain of Hormiga —but he was less a villain than an opportunist.

" These things," he said to Miguel, " have been here for a long time. I don't sell them until I have to. I always lose money on them. If I can, I trade things I can use, like flour or potatoes or chili." He picked up a spoon of hand-worked silver. " Stuff like this is no good to me—I can't get half what I allowed on it. Do you understand that ? "

" Yes," said Miguel.

" If I sold any of this stuff now, I'd lose about fifty cents on the dollar."

" Do you still take things like these, instead of money ? "

Vicente shook his head. " I haven't for a long time. But this winter I'll have to again. I'm afraid it's going to be a hard winter in Hormiga."

Miguel, remembering his mother's closed, dark room, and how she loved the things in it, thought how it must hurt the people to give them up to Vicente Romero.

" I'll tell you something, Miguel," Vicente said when they returned to the store. " You won't understand all of it, but some day after I am dead you may remember it. The people here in Hormiga have only begun to have bad times. . . ."

And he gave the boy a lecture on the economics of the town as he, Vicente, understood it from experience and observation. He told how the farms had been divided and re-divided, through centuries of inheritances, into such small individual holdings that few of them could support a single family; he explained how more and more people had been driven to work for wages, how this would force upon the people all the evils of the American system and would cause, in the end, wage-slavery and even starvation.

" If people would only co-operate, under strong leadership," he said as if he were finishing a political speech, " they could do something for themselves. They could stop this foolish cutting up of land and farm it together as the Indians do, share for share in the work and the harvest——" He stopped and rubbed his chin, looking narrowly at Miguel. " A boy like you," he said thoughtfully, " could do a lot for this place—if he worked hard and learned a few things."

Miguel listened attentively, trying hard to follow. " I don't see," he said; " land costs so much—how did the people get it in the first place ? "

" The first settlers here were colonists," Vicente told him, " and the land was granted to them by the King of Spain."

" Oh. They never had to pay for it."

" No. The titles have come down unchanged. First the Mexican Government recognised them, and then the American—just as they were."

Miguel went away that day with a cloudy impression of what he had heard, but with a new feeling in his heart, a kind of swelling elation and a will to do as Vicente had suggested—to work hard and learn a few things.

IV

Lucinda Romero was Vicente's daughter, and she was sixteen when Miguel was seventeen. For months he had worked in the store without ever seeing Lucinda. Her mother was strict with her and kept her closely guarded; for the rest, she was secluded by her religion, which created the world wherein she lived, aloof. It was not that they didn't know each other; they had been neighbours all their lives, had met at Mass and as children on the streets and at the Lenten services in the chapel of the *morada*. Lucinda, however, had been sent away early to the Protestant mission school at Borregos—a school whose unorthodoxy was abhorred by all the good Catholics of Hormiga—and she lived there, boarded there. And now she was going to the high school run by the Sisters at Gabaldon, and she was at home only through the summer. There was talk of Lucinda's entering a convent—she was such a mystical, pious girl. Certain it was that *la Virgen* was profoundly real to her, the idol and centre of her soul.

Miguel had hardly noticed her before. She had been no more to him than dozens of other little girls; less, really, because Lucinda had never roamed with the boys or joined in their games. He had paused to wonder, perhaps, what kind of being she was beneath her stony exterior, but he had never learned anything about her. When she began to appear in the store, it was long before he had anything to do with her, although she had to speak to him often enough because Miguel was familiar with the place now and knew the prices of everything, and how the purchases should be handled. He was a better salesman, too. She had a take-it-or-leave-it attitude, while the boy could persuade a customer to accept a substitute for something which was out of stock.

An easy surface intimacy grew between them after a time; Miguel could joke with her, and chat, but always against their familiarity was a tenseness, a negation, which denied them any closer relationship. At least Miguel felt it, and together with it he felt dissatisfaction and a desire to beat down the barrier which intervened. When for an instant he thought he caught a glimpse of the girl she really was, when she smiled in a certain, special way or said a thing which seemed to share a bit of herself, he was thrilled beyond measure, as if God had smiled upon him. It was a kind of ravishment and gave him a suffocating increase around his heart. For she was supple and slender and full of a frail beauty.

Thus without knowing, Miguel began to woo Lucinda and to court these favours from her which filled him with wonder. It was doubtful that she knew, either, what was happening. She was elaborately cautious with Miguel, but she found herself thinking about him often, and studying him to discover if there might be anything in him which could threaten or despoil her mystical world, anything from which she must flee. But a force she could not fathom drew her to him.

They sometimes slipped away secretly and walked

together in the evening before going home to supper, down the long street past the *morada* to the top of the hill where the road dropped sharply to Borregos and the valley. From a point there, like a promontory jutting into the sea, they could sit and watch the day change into twilight, watch the purple darkness invade the valley, slowly filling its gigantic hollows and crevices like flooding water. On some evenings the sun turned the sky to eddies and pools of colour; again, it sank, a clear, golden globe in a silver-green sky.

" Do you like to watch the sun go down ? " he asked her one evening.

" Yes. It's beautiful, I think."

" Beautiful——" He repeated the word after her as if he were charmed by it. Yet it seemed a chaste and cheerless word as she used it. He sat beside her for a long time without speaking. " I've heard," he ventured, " that you'll go into a convent. Is it true ? "

" I don't know. It would be nice, don't you think ? "

" No."

Startled, she looked at him with her big dark eyes opened wide. " Why not ? "

" Well," he explained, improvising recklessly, " if you were old and ugly and—sick, it would be all right. But you're not. You're—you're beautiful ! "

She turned away. The compliment filled her with pleasure, but she tried to deny it. " I don't think I am," she said.

" Yes, you are——" Miguel pressed, and then stopped, unable to pursue the point. Her purity, militant, forced him to accept her on her own terms. He could think of her, at least in her presence, in no way other than a fragile, destructible thing to be admired remotely. " And you know a lot," he added lamely. " You'd be better here, more useful, than in a convent."

" Oh, I wouldn't like to stay here," she said quickly.

" Why not ? " he returned, just as quickly. " Why shouldn't you stay here ? As soon as anybody gets to know something—goes to school for a while—then they want to leave Hormiga. That's the trouble with the place. We need people like you here." He was fired by a remembered zeal, but he was afraid she might have heard this line of talk already, from her father. And while he waited for her reply, which was slow in coming, he was keyed to a high excitement. She knew more than he did. He had to be alert all the time, or she would best him, and then his shame was a painful thing and he hated it. " I think it would be selfish of you to enter a convent," he added.

" Selfish ? How could it be selfish to do that ? "

" Because you could do so much more here."

" I don't see what there is here for me——"

" There are poor people here, and sick people," he interposed.

" Yes, but——"

" And there are good people and bad people. You should marry a good man, and try to do something for the poor ones and the bad ones."

" Are you one of the good ones, Miguel ? "

" Yes. Perhaps you should marry me."

Lucinda was sitting primly upright, Miguel was lying on his side, looking up into her face. She laughed lightly when he said this, and Miguel, meanwhile, thought it over swiftly and put it away in his heart as one of the things he might do some day. Marry Lucinda. He watched her laughing. No, he didn't know what kind of a creature she was. He wanted to touch her, so he put out his hand and touched her arm. It was warm and soft. His fingers encircled her forearm, and her laughter stopped.

" You and I together," he said, chilled by the sudden fear in her eyes, " could do a lot for Hormiga. We could be like your father and mother, only better, because your mother doesn't really like it here. She doesn't know the people. You do. You were born here, and so you know it, even if you don't think you do."

And he left her that time with dissatisfaction still uppermost. This passionless contact left out something necessary. It was too much like a relation, not enough of the soul. Perhaps she was already selfish, he thought. She would take, but she wouldn't give. No convent would have her in that spirit—why should he? In such a mood he went home, and in the evening his mother surprised him by speaking about the girl: " You were out a long time with Lucinda Romero."

" Yes," he admitted, on the defensive at once.

" I should think you'd have enough of her in the store all day."

" I like her. I don't see much of her in the store." He began to be angry at her displeasure. " You don't like Lucinda," he accused.

" No, I don't like her very much. I don't know what you see in her."

" I like to talk to her, that's all," Miguel said. " It's easy to talk to her. And she knows a lot."

Concepcion teased. " She thinks she does. She thinks she's too good for Hormiga, too."

" Oh, that's only her mother. Her mother never liked it here."

" She never tried to like it very hard."

" Lucinda's not really like that," Miguel defended bravely. " She needs somebody to show her, that's all."

" Well, I don't see why it should be you."

" Because I like her," Miguel flared, and ended the matter by leaving the kitchen angrily. Concepcion's amused smile lingered.

By his efforts to know Lucinda and to show her what he was learning about her, Miguel gained insight. He was alternately warmed by a great love for her, or slashed by anger. He hated her supplication, her wide, dilated eyes when he reproached her for being superior, and he loved her when she forgot to be superior and talked naturally with him about people and places she had seen. She was desirable, also—always desirable. At the root of everything, perhaps, was her young body, inviting, tender.

The summer was full of idle, hot days, and these in turn were filled with work. Saturdays and Sundays were the days for social matters. A man was tired and ready for bed after a full work-day, and the women, too. Even Lucinda helped her mother with the housework—there was no leisure in that family, either, until the end of the week. And then a *baile*, or some kind of *fiesta*. Groups of boys often went fishing in the summer, far back into the mountains behind Hormiga, to streams unfrequented by the fishermen from the valley towns. It was a wilderness of hills broken only by a few trails leading over the range, and its streams were for fishing, its trees for wood, and its mountains for game. Everything in it was considered in terms of human needs or human uses, but Miguel and perhaps a few others derived something more from it. He was the exception, however. When a man digs his living from the soil, it becomes his servant, or he its slave, who cannot see the earth as beauty then, but only as a battlefield.

Miguel saw more in the mountains than the others because he was slightly removed from the farm, in Vicente's store; he felt more, and what he felt he tried to give to Lucinda. He evoked feelings in her and made ordinary things live for her in a way they had not before. For this she came to love him. It worked a change in her, but the wrong change. In place of her religion, beautiful sunsets, trees, mountains, a white cloud flying, became companion and lover for her, and these she substituted for the passion which Miguel was ready to give her, while he became the high priest of her new gods.

She loved him for this. And Miguel in his inexperience was content for a while. It was not easy for him, either, to make a close relation with anyone, and so this bodiless thing grew between them, and seemed real. He listened with wonder and envy to the talk of other boys, heard of their exploits with girls in Gabaldon, their descriptions in lurid outspokenness of this girl's capacity, that girl's readiness; then, for a while, he would want Lucinda in their way, and his desire would endure until he saw her again and her chastity would cool the fire in his bowels. Often he thought it was his fault: she wanted taking, ravishment, and he was afraid.

The conversations of his friends, in which virgins were always being seduced, or persuaded to yield by the might of their prowess, strengthened this doubt in him, flooded him with discontent; yet, in Lucinda's presence, he felt physical desire ebb away, leaving him powerless to make the first move, even if he knew what it was. Meanwhile, he saw the love of nature which he had awakened in her become a passion. He saw her waste her sighs and kisses on a buttercup, and the sight infuriated him.

" *Por Dios*, how can you kiss a flower ? " he would say to her, and her eyes would open wide to him, brimming with injury, and he would turn away in anger.

Pablo was off this summer. The previous winter had been such a time of suffering and deprivation that he had been forced to search elsewhere for the mere food to keep him alive. Eliseo managed to cut enough wood —he and a friend hauled it all the way to Gabaldon to sell—to keep the family in the simplest necessities of food, although it barely paid the costs of getting it there, and the labour of swinging his axe all day in the snow had told deeply on him. He was down with bronchitis finally, the result of alternately sweating and chilling.

He had been very sick—almost as bad as Pablo after his initiation. That had been before Pablo went away, and it was the winter's peak of desperation. If they hadn't eaten the stock of canned goods in the store, they might have starved. On top of that, two pieces of old silver from Concepcion's dark, sealed room had to go to Vicente Romero in exchange for food, and this was harder for her than living on beans for a month. It had been a time of changeless, unmitigated worry. They were lucky to have come through in good health, for many families did not. In the spring, Pablo's money began to come in, and they were saved. He had enrolled in a government camp and his wages were sent home every month. It was a great thing. They hadn't seen so much cash in a year, because Eliseo had not been hired as a guide, and Miguel still worked for nothing in Vicente's store.

From the moment he heard of Miguel's work there, Eliseo had been coldly hostile. Concepcion had managed to keep him quiet about it, making him take the ultimate view; but, as the boy worked on and on and still received nothing for it, the father's impatience threatened to boil over, and Concepcion had her hands full trying to keep him down. She had her eye on the day when Miguel would triumphantly return and make the Lopez store the best in town. She had even selected a name for their place—the *Lopez Mercantile Company*. And when Miguel, whose own enthusiasm had long since waned, talked idly to please her, about incorporating and issuing stock, she listened with glistening, prideful eyes, and her dreams opened new horizons. Eliseo valued it all slightly. He was wary of visions, and top-lofty ideas.

Now for the hundredth time he began a tirade about it, this time with really alarming earnestness. " I think you better quit working for Vicente," he said one evening after supper when they were all outside on the wood-pile. It was a night of stars which gave almost as much light as a new moon. " If he won't pay you, why should you work for him ? It's no way for a man to do—work for nothing."

Nobody answered him. Miguel and his mother waited for him to say something that would yield a better grip.

Eliseo went on, gaining confidence from their silence. " He'll never pay you anything. He thinks he can fool you—just a kid. You should tell him, Miguel——" The father raised his voice and turned to look at his son. " He should give you something—a sack of flour now and then, or some goods of some kind. You can't go on like this. I'll tell him myself. He can't work my son like that for nothing ! "

" I think he'll begin to pay something pretty soon," Concepcion said smoothly.

" How soon ? "

" In the fall, maybe." Miguel entered the discussion.

" No," said Eliseo, " he's got to pay you right now. How long have you worked there ? "

Miguel thought. " More than a year."

" You see ? It's too long already." Eliseo stood up. " I'm going to see him," he said. " I'm going to see him now. I'll tell him ! " And he marched off into the night. They could see the sparks rising from his pipe as he blew on it angrily all the way across the *plaza*. He took long, deliberate steps with his short legs.

" He'll spoil everything." Concepcion sighed sorrowfully.

Vicente's house had a porch enclosed by a white picket railing. His home adjoined his store, and it had a sloping roof of corrugated iron, painted red. If they could afford it, everybody in Hormiga would have a roof like his, for it didn't leak and it never needed repair. The usual flat, earthen roof was a treacherous thing, for rain came through, and snow, melting, turned the earth to mud which leaked in a constant dripping until the mud dried. So Vicente's tin roof was the envy of the town, and its worst ugliness.

When Eliseo, having fumbled nervously with the latch on the gate in the fence which kept stray cattle, horses, pigs, chickens, and children out of Vicente's yard, advanced upon the porch, the owner was sitting there smoking a cigar with his feet on the railing.

" Good evening, Vicente," Eliseo said, seeing him with a start. " You busy ? "

" No, no, *primo*. Come in." His manner was cordial enough. " What can I do for you ? "

Eliseo didn't like this. Vicente couldn't do anything for him—that wasn't the point, and he didn't want it put that way. " Nice night," Eliseo said. " I was passing—thought I'd come in for a minute."

Darkness concealed Vicente's knowing smile.

" How's Teresita ? " Eliseo inquired, squatting on his heels on the edge of the porch.

" She's well, thanks. How's your family? How's Pablo getting on ? "

" He's doing pretty good. He's a work foreman, now."

" That's fine. That's good. Those boys are doing good work. Pretty good pay, too, isn't it ? "

" Pretty good," said Eliseo. " A dollar a day."

Some moments of silence between them were filled

by Eliseo loading his pipe, a routine matter of tapping, loading, tamping.

" Will you have a good harvest this year ? " Vicente asked.

" Maybe. It looks all right now. If the rains keep up it should be a pretty good harvest." Eliseo watched the red glow of Vicente's cigar. He never smoked cigars himself. " That smells like a pretty good cigar you've got there," he said.

" Yes, this is a good one. Will you have one ? "

" No. No, thanks. I smoke my pipe." He puffed on it demonstratively. " No, sir, I guess next winter won't be like the last one."

" It was bad, last winter," Vicente agreed. " I never saw a worse one. Some of the people didn't have enough to eat. It was hard times, I tell you."

" People owe you lots of money ? "

Vicente made light of such a matter with a shrug. " Oh, yes. But when they got no money, they can't pay."

" I owe you some myself."

Vicente, with an air of getting down to business, said, " You mean that silver of Concepcion's ? "

Eliseo nodded.

" I'll hold that for you until you can pay," he said, leaning back and blowing a cloud of cigar smoke. " There's a woman down in Gabaldon who's interested in old Mexican silver—an American woman—but I told her I couldn't sell those pieces just yet. Of course " —he waved his cigar—" there'll be a little interest to pay, too."

Eliseo was scalded by a wave of anger, but he held
HM

his tongue. " Maybe my boy, Miguel, can work for you until he pays the debt," he said evenly.

Vicente didn't speak for a minute. He was taken by surprise that time, Eliseo thought, and felt a counter-balance for his anger. " He's worked for you for a long time, now, and it's time you paid him something."

" I've been teaching the boy," Vicente said, slightly flustered. " He's not worth anything to me until he learns——"

" Yes, he is. He tends store for you. That's something. If he didn't do it you'd have to hire somebody. I think you better pay him wages, or he'll quit. He said he'll work for nothing until the silver is paid for, and then he stops."

Vicente was angered by Eliseo's brusqueness, but he covered it with a tone of injury. " I've done a lot for Miguel," he wailed. " I've taught him everything he knows about a store. I can't pay him now—I'm pretty hard up myself."

" He's not going to work any more for nothing," Eliseo said firmly. " It isn't right. He needs the money —we need him to help—I need him on the farm, too."

Vicente thought about it in silence for a long time. Eliseo, having delivered his message, sat back at ease and puffed on his pipe. At last Vicente said, " All right. If he works for another month, I'll allow him a dollar a day and give back the silver at the end of that time. How's that ? "

" That's all right," Eliseo agreed after some hesita-tion. " That's good. I'll tell him." He was proud of himself, eager to get home with the news of his triumph, but he didn't rush rudely off. He delayed there talking to Vicente long to preserve their cordial relations, discussing anything, talking around and around the point, and when he went away at last, all was serene on the surface.

"Well, I fixed it up all right," he said when he found Concepcion and Miguel exactly where he had left them. "I told him you wouldn't work for nothing any more."

"What did he say?" Concepcion gasped.

"He said he'd pay him. A dollar a day for a month." An inspiration of the moment prompted him to keep the real bargain, about the silver, a secret from Concepcion. He told Miguel about it later. "It'll make your mother happy," he said. "It'll surprise her."

Frantic efforts were made through the summer to restore the family's cash after the black winter. In season Eliseo furnished horses and pack outfits for parties of fishermen and guided them himself when they asked it, doing double duty to keep up the farm between trips. They were all American, these men, and Miguel especially stared at them as if they were a race from another world, but he shied at talking with them. He helped when he could, too, but since he had been working for money, Vicente had tightened up on his hours and made him earn his wages. It was a new kind of harness which he didn't fancy particularly because, among other reasons, it gave him much less time to pass with Lucinda. It was no good trying to talk to her in the store.

On the proud afternoon when Vicente handed over Concepcion's silver, Miguel took the two pieces at the end of the day and made a bundle of them and asked

Lucinda to take a walk with him before supper. They had to be careful about these walks. Teresita would never have allowed them, had she known, and the gossips would have had it on everybody's tongue. They usually left the village separately and met quietly at some agreed place.

In spite of having the silver, Miguel felt depressed and morose as he set off alone on the lane that passed the store. Where the road dipped into the dry bed of a canyon he sat down to wait for Lucinda under a great pine tree. In a few minutes the girl joined him and he unwrapped the silver, to show it to her.

"She'll be happy," he said, "because she loves these pieces. It's funny that we never seem to get things as nice as these any more." When he followed his words with a glance into her eyes, he saw them shining not with admiration of the silver but with love for him. "Do you suppose," he went on trying to ignore it, "that our great-grandchildren will love things we have now and pass on to them as much as my mother loves these?"

Lucinda tried to answer him. "I think they will."

"But why should they? And what will they love? We have nothing like it. We buy the cheapest things we can because we're poor—ugly things from mail-order stores. Can you think of anybody loving a tin cup, or a steel coffee-pot, and loving it so much that they'll cry when it's gone, or taken away?"

Lucinda smiled with singular vacancy and looked at Miguel in that new way of hers. It was almost a religious adoration in her eyes. She had never known anybody who could talk as Miguel did, who could see so much and hear the singing of the angels; she was spellbound and could only listen. "Talk some more like that, Miguel," she said softly.

"Like what?"

"Like that—about things that other people don't think about."

"Don't think about?" he questioned. "But they do. It isn't anything—I just wonder why it is, that's all. We never get things as nice as these old pieces of silver, do we?"

"No, I suppose we don't. Silver was cheap in those days, I guess. Everything must have been cheaper than it is now."

He looked away from her, letting his eyes roam over the landscape, brilliant in the sunlight, dark in the shadows. "Yes," he said, "but everything was better, too, and more beautiful."

"I wonder why?" she said.

"Maybe it was because they made everything themselves—with their hands. You can't make a plate as nice as this with a machine." He held up the hammered silver dish, richer for its purity and imperfection.

"If we had money enough," Lucinda observed, "we could still buy beautiful things."

"But we have as much money as they had," Miguel objected, "and yet they could buy them." He sighed. "No, something's different—something's changed."

He was sad and she wanted to comfort him. "People who like beautiful things should be able to have them. You're right, Miguel."

"I think our people were better then, too," Miguel continued, speaking his thoughts aloud. "I think they

must have been better people, with more—more "—
he groped for the words—" more ambition, or—something. They did great things in the beginning, settling
a new country, making new farms out of nothing."

Lucinda's whole purpose now was to keep him
talking, not to heed what he said; when he paused she
put in anything that would start him again.

" It was all different, then," he went on. " The
people were soldiers—men of Coronado." His eyes
brightened as he spoke of those days. " Think of how
brave they were ! Marching into a new country—no
water—enemies everywhere. Then came the *paysanos*
—the farmers who made these farms. Oh, it was brave
work. Brave work. We still own the land—the same
land "—he lowered his head and ran his fingers through
some sand—"but it doesn't do us much good."

" We're independent, though," Lucinda said, hoping
he'd have an answer for it. " Nobody can tell us what
to do."

" No. We're Spanish-Americans. But what does that
mean ? Have we gained anything by that ? "

Lucinda again was dumb. She only looked at him,
and he grew impatient with her. " Don't you ever think
about such things ? " he asked her with a shadow of
bitterness.

" No, I guess not."

" What *do* you think about ? "

This evoked an enigmatic smile which he saw and,
unable to interpret, became more annoyed than before.
It struck him as nothing more than a smug, female
smile, to humour him. He picked up a handful of
pebbles and flung them one by one at a stump, aiming

each one carefully. If he had been a little older, a little more experienced, he might have known that she was thinking about him—that she had to think about anything through him, through some human being or through *la Virgen*. Now he wondered if all women were like Lucinda, enigmatic, elusive, hard to get at like this. She had hardly moved since they sat down under the pine tree. She was motionless, her hands idle in her lap, her lids shielding her eyes. She had long, black lashes, and as he watched them a consciousness of her beauty swept over him and made him forget the questions he had been asking. For a moment this angered him slightly, for it occurred to him that it might be the effect she was hoping for, and he was falling in with her design. Could she be so full of guile?

" Do you pray? " he asked suddenly.

She opened her eyes to him again. " Yes, of course I pray. Don't you? "

" What do you pray for most? "

She hesitated shyly. " For you, I think."

" For me? " Miguel's surprise was genuine. " Why do you pray for me? "

" Oh—I pray for you to be the kind of man you want to be—strong, smart—able to do the things you want to do."

Thinking this over, Miguel found it vague. " Is that all? "

" No."

" What else, then? "

" I pray for you to love me."

He was silent for a time, and embarrassed. Then he said : " But you don't need to do that. I *do* love you."

"I know," Lucinda said. "And I love you. You know that?"

"Yes."

Miguel felt that his heart was beating slightly faster, but not fast enough. For he had imagined such an annunciation differently; not, certainly, coolly sitting under a tree, inches separated from her. After a time he turned to Lucinda with an almost ludicrous deliberateness. "Kiss me, then," he said.

She stirred closer to him. Self-consciousness scorched both of them. Miguel, biting his lip, made a heroic effort to put his arms around her shoulders; his left hand he placed at the back of her head, feeling the silken richness of her hair. The warmth of it, of her body beginning to come through to him, lifted him out of the commonplace and gave him the courage of hot blood. With his hand he pressed her head forward, her lips towards his, pausing when they were close to look at them. Her lips were shut and dry, and it chilled him to see them—again it was not as he imagined it—and he hurriedly touched his lips to hers. He kept them there, while the pressure increased. She held her mouth shut, but she arched her back in the instinct of love, and something deep within him impelled Miguel to lay his hand on her breasts.

She shivered and drew back. "No," she whispered.

Miguel ignored her protest, the fire hot in him, and drew her closer, pressing his lips against hers. Gradually he released his embrace, watching her.

Lucinda didn't speak, but resumed her stiff position, her head a little lower, her eyes cast down.

"Is it—the first time?" Miguel said at last.

" Yes."

" Did you like it ? "

She nodded, plainly reluctant to talk about it.

" I liked it," he said earnestly, " but I think—I think we should do more."

" No." She raised quick, frightened eyes to him.

" Why not ? "

" No."

After a long, difficult silence he said, " When, then ? When will you—love me ? "

" Well, you must go to the high school, for one thing —and I've got to finish," she answered, glad to leave the topic.

" How can I ? There's no high school here. I've finished the school we have."

" Yes, but you must go to the school in the city—in Gabaldon."

" Oh," said Miguel disappointedly. Again he had the sensation of being whipped by her will. Was she using her new power over him to re-make him into something she wanted him to be, other than he was ? Instinctively he resisted her. " There's no way to manage that," he said. " My mother wants me to go down there, too, and the priest has talked about it, but I don't see how I can."

" There must be a way," she said quietly. " I'm sure there is."

" Maybe there is," Miguel admitted, slipping back into his original mood. " But I don't think I'd like it very much. I'd be a stranger—I wouldn't feel right."

" You're not happy to-day," Lucinda complained. " Why ? "

" I don't know. Everything seems hopeless. I want
to learn, all right—I want to study, get to know something. But there's no way I can see. There's no going
ahead. You can always go back, that's all."

She laid her hand on his arm to soothe him, but it
didn't soothe him. It only increased his discontent. Her
eyes were wide with pity—there was more passion in
them now than when he kissed her. It angered him,
but it passed, and he felt calm with her. The early
feelings of striving in her presence were gone now; they
had reached a level—an equilibrium. She might have
more knowledge than he, but he was the wiser, and
somewhere between knowledge and wisdom they were
coming to rest.

" I think we should have done more," he said after
a long interval, but it was only his discontent speaking
now, their unfulfilment. " We shouldn't just sit and
talk all the time."

" I like to hear you talk."

He scoffed at her.

" And we mustn't sin, Miguel."

" Oh, sin——" Miguel cried impatiently. " I don't
think it's a sin." He faced her again fiercely. " Didn't
you like it—the kissing ? "

" Yes, but——" She stopped, confused, baffled by
the attempt to see beyond her feelings. Her brows
wrinkled with perplexity. " I don't know—I know I
love you the way you are—I'm afraid if we went on,
you'd be different—we'd both be different. I might not
like you then, and—and you might not like me."

" It doesn't change anything, I think," Miguel said
positively, " only makes it better. You can see that, in

other people. It couldn't be a sin if it makes people better. I don't believe it's a sin."

" Please, Miguel—can't we keep it as something ahead of us? Something to hope for and—dream about ? "

He shrugged his resignation. " All right, then. We'd better go back now—it's getting dark."

When they stood up, Lucinda went to Miguel voluntarily and pressed herself to him, putting her arms around his neck, and held her lips against his. When he recovered from his surprise, he held her tightly in his arms; for long he was to remember her moist lips and how her young breasts felt against him.

In the end, however, it only disturbed him the more; after all her talk, why had she done this, just when he thought he was beginning to understand her. Did it mean that she was sorry for what she had said ? Long after they had parted he wondered, and got no nearer an answer; at last he put the mystery aside and turned homewards, where, as he had his hand on the door-knob, he discovered that he had left his bundle behind. He must have dropped it in that last embrace and for-gotten it altogether; there was nothing for it—he would have to go back and get it. Trudging over the long way he had come, he took stock of himself. He felt older—something about which he had been restlessly curious was less of a mystery now, but still a mystery because it was unconsummated. At least he could go further in his imagination. Love was revealing itself little by little. He thought it might be better to let it unfold slowly this way, better than having it burst into full bloom all at once. Perhaps Lucinda was right in holding some of it back. But it was hard to be content with only a beginning when the end was in sight. And he wasn't sure that it was right, or a fair deprivation. They loved each other. Why shouldn't they—— ?

The pieces of silver were there on the ground, but they were hard to find in the failing light. It was late. He would have to hurry. His mother would suspect where he had been, that Lucinda had delayed him, and she would be mad. She always was angry when he stayed too long with the girl, though she tried not to show it. She didn't like her, and that was the end of it. She wouldn't like her if she were an angel. To-night Miguel relied on the silver to appease his mother.

" She even makes you forget to eat, does she ? " Concepcion said when he came in. " Well, it would be better if you ate more and forgot her. What have you got there ? Does she give you presents now ? What is it ? "

" Oh, it's nothing," said Miguel, tossing the package carelessly into a chair, but being careful to choose an upholstered one. " It's just something she sent for you."

" For me ? Oh, no. Lucinda wouldn't send me anything."

" Open it, then, and see for yourself."

Concepcion picked up the package. " It's heavy." Then she dropped it. " I don't believe you."

" All right, I'll open it for you." Miguel undid the string, loosened the paper, and handed it back to his mother. " There. That's for you, isn't it ? "

Concepcion, seeing what it was, let out a cry of joy. " My silver ! Miguel ! *Hijo !* " She stopped suddenly,

and her face grew severe. " You say Lucinda sent
them ? "

" No, no, mother. I was teasing you. I earned them
for you. Vicente said he'd give them back to me if I
worked for a month—well, to-day is a month."

" To-day is a month," she repeated tearfully. " Oh,
oh, I'm so glad to have it back again. Thank you, thank
you, Miguel." She turned her face away, wiping her
eyes on her apron. " I didn't think I'd ever see it
again," she wailed, as if she were deep in grief, and
then with a sudden sad shift she said, " Now he's got
a girl—pretty soon he'll be getting married, too,
and——"

" No, not pretty soon, mother," Miguel said gently.
" Not for a long time."

" No ? " She smiled again and looked at him.
" That's good, Miguel. You wait, no ? There's lots of
time."

He nodded, and she hurried happily to the windowless little room to put her silver away.

It was a bitter confidence which permitted Miguel to
say with such certainty that it would be long before he
and Lucinda married. It may have been the thing
which persistently stirred him to dissatisfaction. This
dedication of hers, this consecration to some ideal of
purity—it was all too spiritual and bodiless. And he
soon discovered the mistake of having kissed her as he
did. Whenever they were together thereafter they had
to fight to subdue the desire which that first kiss had
brought them, and the calm which had marked their
early companionship could scarcely be recaptured. It
was as if, now, when they came together, their hearts

were held fluttering above them, beating the air. Miguel didn't like it, yet it charmed him and gave excitement to the time he passed with her which lingered afterward. Gradually his whole existence became charged with this strange, suspended affair with Lucinda—and then Vicente told him one day that his services were no longer needed at the store.

" There isn't enough business," he explained. " I won't need an extra man in the store through the winter."

Miguel received the news stoically, while he tried to discover within himself whether it was a blow or a relief. It should have been a disappointment; it should throw all his plans out of joint. Yet, searching for the signs of distress he could find only a pleasant lifting of his heart which tokened something quite different. He was glad.

Now, why should he be glad? The thing puzzled him. His mother and father would be sorry and full of anger at Vicente; Eliseo would say he knew it all the time, that as soon as he had to pay Miguel he would let him go. The villain had succeeded again. The mother would take it hardest; her castles would crash, for days she would be crushed, and ashen with the dust of them. And here was he, standing before his doom with a lightened heart, ready to shout for joy !

" All right," he said. " I—I guess I'll go now, then." And he started to leave the place. It was mid-morning.

" Wait," Vicente called. " Don't you want your money ? "

" Money ? "

" Your wages," Vicente explained, looking as if he regretted having spoken of it.

" Oh, yes, my wages. How much ? "

Vicente shook his head. " You're a queer one. You don't seem to care whether you get paid or not."

" I forgot," Miguel said, embarrassed. " I worked here so long without money. It was a dollar a day, wasn't it ? "

" Yes. Fifteen days at a dollar a day." He was counting out the sum in dirty bills. " Here you are."

" *Gracias, señor*," Miguel said, stuffing the money into the pocket of his overalls. " Well——"

" You ought to have a pocket-book," Vicente advised. " You'll lose your money if you carry it like that."

" No, I never lose it," Miguel said. " Well—*adois, señor*."

" Good-bye, Miguel," Vicente said, still shaking his head.

This was an abrupt, unexpected ending of things. The money in his pocket made up for the slight annoyance he felt—so slight that it evaporated under the hot sun of the street where Miguel paused to consider this new freedom and to decide what immediately to do with it. He looked around him, seeming to observe Hormiga for the first time in months. On the mountains the aspen leaves were golden as if buckets of gold had been poured over them. And how blue the sky above the golden summits. White sunlight—purple shadows. Even the houses celebrated the spectacular death of summer, with vermilion strings of chili hanging from their eaves. Colour, colour ! God, the world was

beautiful, after all ! Miguel entered the *plaza* and, as he
walked, his exhilaration grew until he couldn't contain
it all. He flung his hands above his head and ran, leaping now and then into the air. Free ! " Oh, God—
thank God ! " He ran to his father's corral and bridled
the little mare, and rode her without a saddle, hard,
towards the mountains. He didn't stop until he
mingled with the golden aspen leaves and, looking up,
could see their pattern against the astounding blue.

" But what—what will you do now, Miguel ? "
It was the question he expected, and he couldn't
answer it. " I don't know," he said. " I haven't thought
about it." For days he was content to drift in a lazy
haze of aimlessness. He turned over his earnings to his
father, to help settle the debt at the wholesaler's, from
re-stocking the store, and he was penniless, his normal
condition. Until he had exhausted his capacity for
idleness he put off thinking, even, and let life sweep
over him, have its way with him. If it had been
Vicente's intention to break up the romance between
Miguel and his daughter, it failed. He saw Lucinda
every day, and took walks with her as often as they
could slip away without being seen. His easy acceptance
of the loss of his job shocked her somewhat, but she
came at last to think of it as a release, designed by God,
to permit the working of Miguel's greater destiny. He
was willing to let it go at that, too, although he knew
in his heart that he had been bored to death at Vicente's store and was only glad to be out of it. They
talked much, inspired by her habit of mysticism, of

God and His ways with men, until Miguel began to sicken of this odour of piety and to yearn for a relation he could lay his hands on. Here he brought up against Lucinda's reluctance, and the wearying cycle of negation began again.

It was Lucinda's slow urging, however, which broke the spell of laziness and inertia which had him in its grip ever since Vicente had let him go. She wanted Miguel to go to the Catholic school in Gabaldon and she saw in his new freedom an opportunity to bring it about. Miguel admitted that the financial position of his family was much improved now; Eliseo had done well on the farm, and had orders for his services as guide in the hunting season. And the priest who had been Miguel's friend when he was younger reported that conditions were better in the city and it might be possible for a boy to find work there, to support himself while he went to school. Miguel still had great respect for the priest, although he had outgrown him in a way.

In his young search for new outlets, he had found the priest ready with a helping hand; when Lucinda came into his life, he found much in her that he had sought in the priest, and maturity had taken the keenness out of his old religiousness. He was guided more and more by his own groping intellectual efforts to solve moral problems by the evidence his life afforded, and as this was a habit which was foreign to most of his people it was met with surprise and disapproval by those who were able to recognise it. To Lucinda it was dangerous, and in itself a wickedness; to his mother it was a sadness, and to the priest, chagrin. Eliseo didn't know of its existence.

IM

For most people in Hormiga, right and wrong were for ever separated and written down; they sinned, to be sure, but when they sinned they knew it, and called it by no other name. The priest was probably the only one who identified the symptoms as intellectual striving in Miguel; and in order to prolong the Church's influence during the process, he quietly made it his task to get the boy into the school in Gabaldon. He set in motion certain influences of his own.

Lucinda, meanwhile, succeeded in rekindling some forgotten fires of ambition in Miguel when they met in their rendezvous, a shed which clung precariously to the canyon-side, tipping over the brink in a frozen collapse. There they met in the autumnal evenings, cold, now, and shortened by the earlier darkness. Their time together was getting short, also, for soon she would have to return to the academy in the city, and this she used for one of her arguments. It would be nice for them to see each other occasionally through the winter, if Miguel went down to the school. It may have been this thought, or almost any other, which solidified his determination. In any case, he bravely advanced upon his father, armed with Lucinda's arguments.

For this he chose an evening when he had not been with the girl, for when he came from her an involuntary mood of opposition to all his doings was induced in Concepcion, and he wanted her support. His father was free enough of this kind of opposition, but he was prejudiced traditionally against such things as schools in Gabaldon. " You waste your time down there," he said as Miguel expected, " for two, maybe three years. When you get through you come back here—you try to find work—it won't be any easier then than it is now. What's the good of it ? "

" I want to learn," Miguel said without quite enough confidence. " I want to learn more, so I can do better."

" Learn what ? I had only four years of school— your grandfather, he had none. If they could see you now, as you are, they'd think you're a wise man. They'd say you know too much already."

" Lucinda goes to school down there, doesn't she ? " Concepcion interjected.

" Yes, she does," Miguel had to admit.

" Um-hm," she added significantly.

" She says they're very strict with the girls—I probably wouldn't even see her," Miguel told them quickly to get his mother on his side.

" What'll you do about money ? " Eliseo went on. " I can't give you any. You should stay here and help us, anyway. I'm against the whole thing. Pretty soon we can't work any more, and we'll be needing our boys."

" Maybe if he goes to school down there he can make more money when he gets through," Concepcion, pacified, exclaimed. " Then he can help us all the more in the end."

Miguel smiled gratefully to her. He knew now that he was going, for with his mother's help it was as good as decided. His father's consent was merely a form which had to be secured for the sake of propriety, and it would be forthcoming.

Eliseo drew noisily on his pipe for some minutes. Miguel sat down to wait. " We'll go down there, then,"

Eliseo said shortly, with an air of having made the decision himself. " We'll look things over down there. I'm thinking of putting in a petrol pump—I'll go down and see about that, too, at the same time. If I can get one cheap enough, maybe you better stay here and look after it," he added. " If you can find work down there—enough to pay your own way——" And thus, in the end, he left his decision dangling.

The idea of going to school in the city was now distantly pleasing to Miguel, but a thing so remote that he could not imagine it or think beforehand how he would get along without any money of his own. His fancy was taken by the prospect—the details would have to take care of themselves.

It was, however, the priest who took care of the details. When Miguel and his father made their trip to Gabaldon, they found much of their way smoothed ahead of them. Their first stop was on the *plaza* in the heart of the town; as it was Miguel's first visit in three years, everything looked new to him. So many strange faces filled him with discomfort, a feeling of insignificance and lost identity. He was nobody here—Miguel Lopez was a name without a body or a face. Although the same drowsy sunshine poured out of the sky, shadow-spattered under the trees in the *plaza*, there was a commotion, a restlessness in the air after Hormiga's peace which induced a feeling of agitation, a need to escape. It was imponderable, a mental restiveness, like the invisible stirring of a quiet pool. Motor-cars circled the square in an intermittent stream, occasionally blasting the atmosphere with the sound of their horns—nowhere could he hear the comforting sound of people talking.

On the east he could see the great mountains, almost as close as in Hormiga, yet far more distant and unreal, like painted mountains. They could have no part in the lives of people here as they had in Hormiga. And Miguel began to have the feeling that he wanted to go home at once, that he was being encircled by the tentacles of a monster. All his first enthusiasm vanished, and he became a child lost in a wilderness. Sitting in the battered cab of Eliseo's truck, he repulsed his feelings and tried to stamp them out, and he succeeded so far as to drive them deeper, out of his way for the present.

" Where do we go now ? " he asked his father.

" You wait here, watch the truck. I'm going to see a friend—find out about my pump."

When Eliseo had gone, loneliness settled over Miguel completely; soon he was not content to sit quietly in the truck, and he got down to wander into the square of grass where cement walks criss-crossed and green park benches carried each a load of people—Mexicans like himself, wearing overalls, blue work-shirts. A few, he noticed, were dressed in store clothes, suits and trim hats and haberdashery, and Miguel wondered what these did for a living which allowed them to dress for every day with such elegance. He had a suit himself, it was true, but only for weddings, funerals, and *fiestas*.

Here he heard the familiar sounds of his own tongue being spoken, and he felt less lonely as he listened, trying to catch a passage of conversation here and there. Finding a place on a bench, he sat down. The stores which lined the *plaza* on all four sides carried their signs in both languages, and this, too, comforted him: *boticas* on the drug-stores, *groceterias* on the grocery, *barberia* on the barber-shop. They gave him a nice glow of warmth and nostalgia, for the use of Spanish on the signs seemed a kind of recognition of himself and his people.

Something else he noticed, also. The girls who passed walked with a self-assurance which seemed brazen to him. The shyness and humility of Hormiga girls was not in them. Possibly, he thought, they were no different underneath, for, judging by what he heard, those virtues were not deep even in Hormiga. These Gabaldon girls fascinated him. He watched one after another, some dressed in American clothes, some shabby, some luxurious, a few in black shawls, Mexican-fashion. The latter didn't interest him at all; the others filled him with an inner trembling and excitement.

While he sat there, warmed by the sun and the friendly sights and sounds of his own people, his enthusiasm returned. It would be good to come here, to discover new things and to share for a while the tempo of city life, the stirring of which he already felt in his blood, the same, perhaps, which had frightened him at first. When Eliseo appeared, very dejected, Miguel was deep in his thoughts and didn't see his father; Eliseo had to come to the bench and shake him by the shoulder.

" Come on, boy. We'll go now and find the school."

" What did they say? What about the pump? "

" Oh, they want all the money. It's no good. I don't think we sell enough petrol in Hormiga, anyhow."

They found the school. It was not particularly inviting, with grey stone buildings, formidable, utilitarian. The brother who met them had on a long, black robe with a little white collar such as Miguel had never seen before, which flapped as he walked. He was very grave, and spoke to them in English. " Yes, Father Aloysius had made arrangements——"

It was all so easy and pre-arranged that Eliseo was instantly suspicious, but powerless to object. The whole affair was a conspiracy, engineered by his wife, like Miguel's job at Vicente's store. He agreed to everything and realised with sadness at the last that Miguel was actually slipping away from him, under his eyes. This city, with ten thousand strange people in it, was to swallow him like Jonah in the whale. He was to live in its checkered darkness. He might never see this son again. He could find no sense or reason in such fears, but he was moodily silent all the way back to Hormiga and hardly spoke to Miguel at all.

V

To leave Hormiga for a long time was a new experience for Miguel. It put new compulsions upon him to weigh and judge those things he was departing from. It had not been necessary before because he was always coming back in a little while, and there was no need to charge his memory with this and that.

For the week remaining before he would have to go, he noticed everything. He noticed, for example, the manifold ways in which he would remember his mother, how she differed from other women, how certain of her characteristics were remarkable, memorable. He observed and catalogued objects in the house of which he had never been aware, which he could not have foretold—chairs, carpets, oil-lamps, pieces of furniture swam into his vision as if for the first time.

Outside the house he walked in a new consciousness of his surroundings, and his mind became a map of the town showing how the church was here in relation to the *morada*, and the house was there in relation to the rest. One day he walked completely around the village on a crooked lane which threaded among squat, adobe houses, an ancient road, manure-laden, uneven, intimate. He had not realised this way until now, nor felt its peculiar humanness as if it knew all persons who lived along it and was familiar with their private lives. It seemed to him, about to leave, like the patriarch of

Hormiga's streets, for it enclosed the town and encom-
passed its history, and, as far as he knew, it had no
name. It led him at last along the north side of Vicente
Romero's house and store; and he was obliged to think
of that interlude in his life, when he had been a clerk
in Vicente's hire. He could hardly remember what it
had been like, or how it had felt in there, but a misty
certainty enveloped him, as he passed the place, that
he was glad he was not working there now. He
thought he saw Lucinda through a window—there was
some woman in there—but flashing reflections of sunlight opaqued the glass. He walked by without pausing
to make sure. They would meet later, in the evening,
anyway, if she could slip away.

They would meet later in the evening ! There should
have been more excitement in it than there was. It
didn't seem right that a coming meeting with Lucinda,
the girl he was going to marry some day, should be so
ordinary. What was the matter ? He liked Lucinda—
loved her, didn't he ? Yes, they would marry, and
Vicente and Teresita would be his . . .

Teresita embodied for Miguel the words which her
name suggested—terror, terrible. Since his earliest
childhood he had been aware of the similitude, and
every mention of her name evoked it, and always
would. And more than once it had seemed a perilous
thing to bind himself to that fierce little woman by
means of her daughter. It had been, he recalled, one
of the first thoughts to enter his head when marriage
with Lucinda had appeared on his horizon. He had
ignored it successfully until now—or had he ? Had it
not crept with the stealth of a cat into his feelings about

the whole affair? Who would wilfully join himself to
a family like that? There was no real sympathy anywhere. Concepcion hated Lucinda, distrusted Teresita.
Eliseo made no secret of his dislike for Vicente. Even if
he married her, he would never be able to bring his
mother and the girl together. In view of all this, Miguel
began to wonder at his temerity in choosing Lucinda
for his love. Or had he chosen her? Had she not, actually, chosen him? With his brows troubled he tried to
remember just how aggressive he had been—he couldn't
recall having asked her to marry him. . . .

Oh, these were doubts, merely—inevitable doubts.
Qualms. And yet—what was there of any substance
between them? Searching, he couldn't put his finger
on anything. The kiss? Perhaps. But otherwise it was
talk—much talk, without much meaning.

Now, going away, he felt the need of a more solid
bond with Lucinda. He made up his mind to talk about
this with her later, when they met in the shed, and
instantly he rebelled at his own thought. Talk, again—
nothing but talk! What did married people do? How
did they establish their companionship? Was it all
begun and ended with talk? There could be no
answering such questions yet. He would have to wait
and see.

Miguel was left to ruminate and make his recordings
alone, for Pablo returned during the week, and the
family attention was transferred to him. He had tales
to tell. He looked better. He was heavier, his biceps
bulged through the sleeves of his shirt and he grinned
at everything, at his mother, his father, even at Miguel.
Concepcion felt strange with him at first, he had been

gone so long. She discovered that it was hard to regain in a moment the old intimacy with a son who has been away, and it bewildered her. She couldn't even scold him for a while—he was a visitor, a guest in the house, and she was ill at ease. Eliseo, however, had no such difficulty: from the first moment, he pressed Pablo to declare his plans, which was like trying to press juice out of a dried fruit. Pablo had no plans. He was just another mouth to feed.

" Well, you come home to work, no ? " Eliseo would say nervously. " We need you here, all right. I've got nobody to help me, with Miguel going away."

" Miguel ? Where's he going ? "

" He's going down to the school in Gabaldon."

Pablo's guffaw was not endearing to Miguel. His immediate reaction was a mixture of anger and hurt, and an unbroken silence thereafter.

" The money you sent home," Eliseo continued blandly, " that was a good thing. It was all we had last winter. But we don't need it so much now. I'm glad to have you here again."

Pablo made no reply to these leads of his father. He wasn't at all sure that he was glad to be back, for life in the camp had been easy, and the work light, but he had been bothered by the scarcity of girls and money, two of his necessities. A man couldn't buy much with five dollars a month, and that was all they gave him after sending the rest of his money home; he never even got his hands on the bulk of it. If he had, the family would never have seen it. On the whole, therefore, he thought he'd prefer his freedom. A man could scare up more than five dollars a month in Hormiga, and he

could do as he pleased. Yes, it was good to be home
again—but as for the future, that could take care of
itself. He put his father off with shrugs and silences, for
it was quite evident to Pablo that nothing would be
different. He would resume his life where it had left off,
he'd work a little in the fields, in the store, help with
the chores and loaf on the wood-pile, boast, love as
much as he felt inclined. His father could be relied on
to forget his notions of a plan for the future and all that
—give him two or three days and all would be as before.

But it took him a week. Eliseo went on in a diminishing key, mouthing his expectancies until they expired
naturally, like the wind in a leaky balloon.

It was the mere fact of Pablo's return, the change it
made in the house and the life that went on inside it,
that set up these strange ideas in Eliseo. It happened
whenever anyone close to him returned after a long
absence, as if, during their sojourn away from Hormiga,
they had been dosed with some mysterious medicine
which injected change, ambition, plan into them.
Concepcion felt it, too, but she got over it sooner. In
a short time she was at ease with Pablo again, his home-
coming was forgotten and he slipped into his old
groove without the least friction, proving that he was
the same Pablo who had gone away.

Before he left Hormiga for the camp, he had made a
promise in the *morada* to do an exercise upon his safe
return, and this obligation occupied him for a while,
trying to think up means of escaping it. It was the
usual thing, however, and there was no escape. A good
Penitente always made a promise to his favourite saint
before a journey, against his safe return and the sins

which might accumulate in his absence. And Pablo, having been gone six months and having sinned much in that time, had a consciousness of guilt in him which wanted a purge, and the want was even greater than the repugnance he felt just now for any kind of discomfort. He would have to go through with it. The occasion was arranged, therefore, by the *Hermano Mayor*, and fell out on the first Friday night after his return. Miguel, still wandering about in a state of idleness and keener observation than usual, detected the impending ceremony in ways of his own, mainly by watching his brother's quite apparent uneasiness. Fortified by his coming departure he asked to be allowed to see the exercise, and was of course refused.

" Then tell me," he said to Pablo, " what will they do to you ? "

Pablo eyed him suspiciously. " What do you want to know for ? Why don't you join the *Penitentes* and find out for yourself ? They don't do it to me, anyway—I do it to myself."

" I will join," Miguel said, " but I can't this year— or next. I'll be down at the school. But I'd like to know something more about it before I go." He knew Pablo had no sympathy with his going, and so expected nothing of this argument.

" Why ? "

" Well, so I can—think about it and decide if I want to join or not——"

Pablo laughed contemptuously. " Oh, I see," he said with a sneer. " Well, nobody ever told me anything about it before I went in. I had to find out for myself. I guess it won't hurt you——"

" Maybe you wouldn't have joined, if you'd known something about it first," Miguel suggested with mock gentleness.

Pablo stared at him frowning, uncertain whether to be angry or not. " Maybe not," he said. " Nobody asked me whether I wanted to join or not, either."

" Why did you, then ? "

Pablo shrugged. " Oh, my father, he came to me and said he thought it was about time I did. I thought maybe it was, too, and——" He lifted his hands in a gesture of resignation, his mouth drooped at the corners. " So I went in, that's all."

Miguel didn't reply for some moments, then he said decisively, " Well, I don't think you should join that way. I think you should think about it yourself first— then if you don't want to go in, don't. That's why I want to know something about it, see ? "

A spark of appreciation gleamed in Pablo's eye for an instant, and then went out. " What's the difference," he said, " if you know or you don't know? You'll go in anyway. You know what it is—all the boys around town know pretty much what it is. And everybody joins, all your friends. It's all the same."

" Yes, I know that," Miguel insisted, " but I want to know if it's the right thing to do."

" Of course it's right," Pablo said. " They say the Order is four hundred years old. It wouldn't last so long if it was wrong."

" Some don't think it's right," Miguel went on. " The priest, Father Aloysius—Teresita——"

" The priest is jealous—Teresita's a woman— scared, that's all. You can't believe people like that."

Still Miguel plied his argument. " But you don't know why you joined. Because father and his father did —that's no reason."

" It's reason enough for me," said Pablo.

" What will happen over there on Friday ? " Miguel asked, veering from one vain inquiry to another. " What will you do ? Will they come outside, or—— ? "

" Oh, I'll whip a little, I guess. I don't think they'll come out of the *morada*. There won't be anybody else. I'll whip alone."

The words gave Miguel a shudder. He didn't know whether this casualness of Pablo's was bravery or just brutish indifference, but it impressed him none the less. To whip with the whole Brotherhood looking on seemed a terrific thing, a violation of a man's privacy. He couldn't understand it. " I wouldn't like that," he said.

" No, I don't like it much."

" Will they cut your back ? "

" Sure. They always do that."

" You were sick the last time," Miguel reminded him.

Pablo winced. " That wasn't from the cutting. I got too cold. I got excited, and——"

" Excited ? " said Miguel, interested again. " That's funny. What—why did you get excited ? "

" I don't know. It's exciting—so much blood everywhere."

And suddenly Pablo chose to reveal no more of his secrets. He stood up and walked off, leaving his brother seated on the wood-pile, skimming chips thoughtfully away from him.

Nothing of the conversation remained in his memory

except this thing about being excited. He had never been able to understand how a man could hurt himself —but if he could get excited, so that he didn't think about it, then it might be explained.

Well, some day he might find out for himself. It was no good trying to get anything out of Pablo. But Miguel was still curious, and when Pablo and his father slipped out on Friday night, Miguel was watching them from the wood-pile. Was it a feeling of guilt which made them steal away so silently? He shivered. Guilt of what? No, it was something else. He watched until they entered the innocent-appearing building, and the *morada* door closed after them. As the light faded, sparks became visible, dashing from the tin chimney, and the old wooden door was a barrier to the world outside as grim and thick as stone. They had guarded their secrets well through the years, for even Miguel, who had pried as much as anyone, did not know what happened behind that door.

Damn their secrets! What was wrong with it, that they must walk in stealth?

There can be no remission of sins without the shedding of blood.

Was this the answer? Was this the beginning and the end?

He got down from the wood-pile, still nursing the wrath of being thwarted, and thrusting his hands into his pockets he wandered aimlessly across the *plaza*. Only half aware of his intent, he allowed his steps to take him near the *morada*, while his thoughts sped afar, alighting like birds upon the hint Pablo had accidentally given him. " I got excited . . . so much blood everywhere. . . ." It meant something, but what?

Evidently a man either took these things as they came, like the seasons, or sickness, or death—or he thought about them. And if he thought about them he had to think of everything else, including death. Miguel liked to think of death. There was a melancholy fascination about it—he often thought about his own death, with glad agony. It was a force pulling a man along to his grave, like a ten-cent magnet.

Right now Miguel was held in such a grip of thoughtfulness that his supper-time came and passed while he was still strolling up and down near the *morada*, with his hands deep in his pockets, his brain plunged in speculation. This was why, he guessed, he wanted to go away for more schooling, so he could think about things with a better chance of finding answers to the demands life was already making. As it was, he felt impotent in his head. He couldn't see beyond, to the truth which must underlie all things. Father Aloysius could, or seemed able to see most often to where appearances fell away and truth lay bare. He went over some of his own, personal questions which wanted answering: Why did the *Penitentes* chastise themselves with no more compulsion than their own desires? Or was that the force behind them? Was it perhaps some other he didn't even suspect? Why did the love he felt for Lucinda seem at times unreal and unconnected with him? And again, so strong that it gripped his heart until it bled? Why did this thing which Pablo hinted at—this pain and exaltation of suffering—attract him like—like—*por Dios*, like the love of a woman?

At this thought, he stopped in the street and felt his heart give a twist which caused him pain. There was

KM

some additional connection here, some dim and deep alliance between his yearning for Lucinda—and his desire to experience the thrill of Pablo's initiation ! Somewhere, far beneath any possibility of his knowing, the two were joined. He started moving again suddenly, as if he had seen a shape in the darkness, alarmed, frightened by an apparition. And quickly the aperture through which he had peeped closed, and he couldn't find it again, but he trembled in his soul as if he had seen death.

Under the need of breaking free from his frightening thoughts Miguel sought a release, but he did not go home. He went to Lucinda's house. They were just finishing their supper. " Come in, Miguel," Teresita said. " Have you had your supper ? "

" No," he said in a distant way that made them wonder.

" No ? "

" No. I didn't—I haven't had my supper yet."

" Well, have some of ours," Teresita said, and got up to get him a plate. She shoved a platter of meat and chili to his place at the table. " Help yourself."

He took some, mumbling thanks, and ate deliberately, wondering meanwhile what his mother would say if she knew what he was doing.

" Where have you been ? " Lucinda spoke to him for the second time, guardedly, as if she were fearful of exposing a secret.

Miguel looked up from his plate. " Oh, just walking around. There's something doing in the *morada* tonight." He knew this was the wrong thing to say in front of Teresita, and said it with sullen mischief.

" Is that why you missed your supper ? " she flared.
And Miguel, raising his eyes again, noticed that
Vicente was absent, was probably in the *morada* with
the rest of them, and he realised that his remark was
even less timely than usual. A scared look came into
his eyes.

" Oh, no," he said. " I was just walking and—and
thinking.'"

" Were you expected at home ? "

" Yes, I guess so."

" And your mother doesn't know you're here ? "

" No, I don't think so," Miguel admitted meekly.
Teresita—terror—terrible.

" Well, you get right out of here and go over and
tell her where you are. She's probably worried to
death about you. Then if you want to you can come
back and have your supper here."

She even reached over and snatched his plate away.
There was nothing for it but to go as she commanded.
He hated the little woman just then with all his being.
He stood up and looked at her, then at Lucinda.

" Please come back," she said so softly that Teresita,
whose back was turned, didn't hear.

But for Lucinda's gentle invitation he thought he
would never go back—never enter that house again,
but his mood moderated as he crossed the *plaza*. After
all, it didn't matter about her mother—one scolding
more or less . . .

Concepcion was ready for him with another tongue-
lashing, and it was no less than he expected. She
finished by saying, " You can go without your supper,
too ! "

Thus it worked out better than he expected. He merely walked out of his own house and back to the Romeros', where he finished his meat and chili while Lucinda sat warmly at his side.

" Thank you, *Doña* Teresita," he said when he had finished. " My mother was so mad she wouldn't give me any supper." He grinned.

" Well, she had a good right to be mad. I wouldn't have given you any, either, if I had known."

" Thank you," he repeated, not meaning to be insolent, but she gave him a look that brought the blood to his face. He turned to Lucinda when Teresita left the room for a moment. " Do you want to take a walk ? "

" For a little while," she agreed.

" Lucinda ! Lucinda ! " the mother called shrilly from the kitchen, " I want you to help me with the dishes ! "

" Yes, mother."

Miguel waited, not liking any of this. She was a shrew, that woman, a yapping she-goat. He hoped Lucinda wouldn't turn out like her. She was mild enough now, but who could tell what a girl would be like in twenty years ? Teresita didn't seem to realise that he wasn't a child any more. She had no right to order him around like a child. " I'll meet you in the shed," he whispered.

When Lucinda could elude her mother she joined him. The evening was still and dark—there was no moon. " Where shall we go ? " Miguel said rather gruffly. Some of his anger with the mother was transferred to the daughter, inevitably.

"Oh, let's walk a little, nobody will see us if we go down into the canyon."

Without saying more they started. In a moment he felt Lucinda groping for his arm, and for an instant he felt like repulsing her, pushing her away, but he didn't.

"What's the matter with you to-night?" she said, sensing his reluctance. "Your mother—or mine?"

"Both."

"Well, what do you expect if you stay away from supper without any reason?"

"There was a reason," he said sourly.

She put a slight pressure on his arm. "I thought probably there was. What was it? What's the trouble?" And when Miguel hesitated, with boyish sullenness, she added, "You can tell me, can't you?"

"I don't know whether I can or not."

She knew how to handle him now. He was sulking, like the child he thought he was not. "Oh, yes, you can," she said, silkily coaxing. "Come, tell me about it."

They came to the *plaza*, deserted and filled with a profusion of starlight. From the *morada* chimney, sparks shot upward, and Miguel, reminded of his original perplexities, returned to them, and blurted them out in response to her urging: "It's Pablo."

"Pablo? Isn't he all right? What's the matter with him?"

"Nothing's the matter with him." They walked in silence, Lucinda waiting, until they passed the *morada* on their left. "He's in there," Miguel said, pointing over his shoulder with his thumb.

"Oh." She didn't see anything particularly disturbing in that, but she waited instead of saying more, hoping Miguel would explain without being urged. It was a long time before he spoke again.

"I had a talk with Pablo to-day," he said at last. "About the *Penitentes*. I tried to make him tell me what they do, and why he joined."

"Did he tell you?"

"No. He doesn't know. He knows what they do, but he doesn't know why he joined—or why they do it. Or why he does it." In a moment, then, he turned on her, full of a strange intensity. "That's what I want to know! Why? *Why* do they do those things? Why do they whip themselves, and carry crosses and tie cactus to their backs? Why?"

As Miguel lapsed into his restive silence, Lucinda wished passionately for a ready answer, and one which would elevate her in his esteem. But she found none, and had to say, as she said so often, "I don't know."

Miguel seemed not to hear her, and she was glad. "There's something there that we don't know about," he went on presently out of the depths of his silence. "If we did know—if you knew—if your mother knew —she couldn't say they were doing wrong. Nobody could. Even if they knew what Pablo knows, they couldn't."

"If Pablo knows so much, why can't he tell you?" Lucinda risked the question timidly.

"Because he can't say it in words. He—he—feels it." He looked at the girl and saw her dark hair blacker than the night. He felt a little sorry for his earlier brusqueness. "But to-day Pablo gave me an idea——"

he said in a softer tone. "He didn't mean to—he didn't know he was doing it."

"What was it, Miguel?"

"I don't think I can tell you."

"Oh," she breathed, and there was such disappointment in the word that Miguel was sorry again.

"I could tell you if—if things were different between us," he tried to explain. "But there's so much we've never said—never done."

She knew then what he meant. Tears filled her eyes, but she drove them back. She was afraid the whole question was coming up again now, and she didn't want it to. It was decently buried. Since then their relation had been happy enough, and safe; she had felt safe with Miguel lately, as if a deep understanding was between them, and now this was being threatened. "But what has it got to do with Pablo, and the *Penitentes*?" she said.

"I'm not sure," Miguel replied mysteriously. "Maybe nothing, maybe everything." Then, abruptly, he changed the subject. "We'll both be in Gabaldon this winter. Will we see each other?"

"Yes, but only on Sundays and—a few other days."

"Will we ever see each other—alone?"

"Maybe," Lucinda said, fearful that she was lying.

"I love you, Lucinda."

Her heart began to beat fast. His even, impassive voice—what did it mean? What was coming now? "I love *you*, Miguel." What a queer boy! She wished she could follow his thoughts through their darting changes. Never more than half expressed, they left her groping, guessing, and she disliked it. Why couldn't

he be more like other people? There were no handles
to hold him by. What was coming now? She waited,
almost trembling.

"Before I go away," he said, stopping and holding
her by her shoulders, "I want to know more about—
us."

She looked into his face as long as she could and then
lowered her eyes. "Is there more to know, Miguel?
We love each other, and——"

"And what? How do we know we love each other?
We've never *tried*. What will you think of me in six
months? How will I think of you? What will I remember? Lucinda—oh, yes, she's the girl I kissed once—
twice—and talked to in the moonlight. Talk. Will it
be like that, do you think? Is that the way I'll remember you?"

"It's enough—for me, Miguel," she said so softly
that he had to bend low to hear. "Isn't it enough for
you?"

It was his turn to say, "I don't know."

"Kiss me, then, Miguel."

He kissed her, but he was careful to keep a hold on
himself, for it availed nothing to let himself go. And
she, being kissed, knew that he would stop before it
was too late; and she thought, "If he shouldn't stop—
if he didn't always believe me—if he were not so gentle
—I couldn't stop him—I couldn't stop him."

So it wasn't altogether Lucinda's blame that they
never had tried loving each other. His errant spirit was
too diffuse for seduction, and it lacked direction.

Miguel felt something of this vaguely, when he left,
and was walking home across the *plaza*. He felt the

lack in himself instead of in Lucinda and it didn't serve
to quell his discontent—nor did the sound, as he passed
the *morada*, of men's voices singing in unnatural, nasal
tones. He stopped and stared at the darkened building.
But nothing, he told himself, was to be gained by standing there and looking at it. Memorising the outward
appearance of the place had nothing to do with what
went on inside. Yes, he really wanted to know, this
time. Before, it had been a boy's curiosity to learn about
something his elders knew and he did not, but now
there was a need in his soul, in the tangled roots of him.

He hoped he might learn in Gabaldon to separate
these sources and label them conveniently. Then he
would be able to say, " I want this—I don't want that.
I want Lucinda—I don't want the *Penitentes*." Or the
other way round. He walked on. Perhaps it was
something new that he wanted; perhaps he was like a
fiddle—when you sound one string, it makes the others
hum a little, too.

As the time for leaving Hormiga approached, he
came to look upon the school in Gabaldon as the opening door which would lead him to the answers for all
his questioning. He was eager to be off. And his mother,
as the hour drew nearer, became dumb, unable to talk
about it at all. Pablo's going away had been nothing
like this—but there was an adequacy about Pablo, a
tough, indestructible quality which made him seem
secure. He could take care of himself in any situation:
he knew what to do in a fight or in anything else. If he
came to something he didn't understand, he accepted
it, or went around it; there was nothing quixotic in
him; life was easy for him. The mother knew this about

Pablo as well as she knew that Miguel was one to charge and charge again, that he was stubborn, and in danger of beating his head against walls. Even now, grown as he was, and escaped from her protection, she kept an eye on him and knew more about him than he ever suspected.

And when she saw him lingering about the wood-pile with his eyes for ever on the *morada* she guessed somewhat of his thoughts, and was almost glad that he was going away. Down there he would be far from all his mystifying over the *Penitentes*, and freed of the invisible net in which she was sure Lucinda was trapping him. Oh, she knew well enough what was going on there—the little she-devil ! There was nothing to it, but the girl kept him in a turmoil and fuddled his brain so he couldn't see through her. Concepcion knew all about that kind of thing. Lucinda might catch him for good, though, if he weren't careful—if he didn't get away from her pretty soon. It had been done before. He'd escape all right, by going away—only to be grabbed by some other scheming female. How a boy ever grew up at all in Hormiga, with the *Penitentes* and the grasping maidens . . .

If they were grasping, Pablo appeared to have eluded them—at least he seemed to be free. Concepcion was still awake when Miguel came in, awake when Pablo came home from the *morada*, but she didn't see either of them. She listened to Pablo for a while, but he was all right. He talked naturally to his father, and there was no groaning or tossing when he lay down to sleep. Why should he be a *Penitente* ? A boy of his age couldn't have sinned so much that he had to go whipping his back. And as she thought about it, she felt a surge of anger speed her blood, and if Eliseo had come in just then she might have let it loose on him, for she couldn't hold anger back with any comfort. He entered her room a few minutes later, when she was off on a calmer track. In the darkness he fumbled for the chair.

" It's all right—I'm awake," she said.

He grunted. She heard him breathing, could tell by it whether he was as sober as he ought to be. He was not. She knew every motion he was making in the dark, out of long habit.

" What happened over there to-night ? " she said.

" Just a meeting. Pablo whipped a little. He'd made a promise, you know."

" Why don't you bring a lamp in here ? "

" Don't need it. I'll be in bed in a minute. I'm tired."

No more was said. In another minute Eliseo was asleep beside her, before she could ask about Pablo, if he was unhurt. He was already so confirmed in the ways of the Order that he could whip his back and forget it—after his first terrible sickness, too. *Por Dios*, what creatures men were !

But on the day of Miguel's going, Concepcion pulled her wits together and had a talk with him about the present and the future and a little of the past. She felt that this new adventure of his would be a turning-point whose nature she could not foretell; she was both saddened and thrilled by it. At first, all was submerged in the past. She couldn't separate herself from Miguel, or think of him and herself severally, as units of self-conscious being. Tradition, sentiment, surged up and blotted out their individualities. She wept, and was the primitive mother, he the archetypal son. He was going away; she was staying at home—from time immemorial. Gradually as they talked there was a slow emergence.

"You won't forget about us—up here?" she was saying to him.

"No, I won't forget." He could see that she was still striving to control her sadness at his going. "I couldn't forget that," he added awkwardly. And anxious to stem her sorrow he went on blindly, "It isn't so far away and maybe they'll let me come home once in a while to see you. I think they let boys go home for Sundays sometimes if they can get a ride. Sometimes, maybe, I'll find a boy who's coming up this way—to Borregos on Sunday for Mass, and then I can come with him—and maybe Pablo could meet me there in the truck and bring me here—or I could walk from there, it isn't very far——" Breathless, he stopped to see if she was still on the edge of crying. No, she was better now.

"Yes, I think somebody could do that," she agreed, and then she smiled. "You don't want me to cry, do you?" He lowered his eyes from hers. "Why are boys so afraid of crying? It doesn't hurt—anything. It feels good to cry. You used to cry yourself—every time you got hurt, or—thought you got hurt." Her voice was rich with tenderness. "Don't you remember? Have you forgotten how you used to cry when you were little? Your father used to get mad, and say you'd never stop crying—you'd never get over it." She laughed gently. "But I don't see anything wrong in it."

"No, I—I guess there's no harm in it," he said

bashfully. " Only I don't like to see you cry. It—it makes me sad, too."

" I know. You're ashamed to let the tears come. I know. But it isn't anything to be ashamed of."

After that there was a hard silence between them which they both strove to break, feeling its hardness.

" But you'll write to me, won't you ? " Concepcion spoke first. " You'll write when you get the chance ? "

" Yes." He was gazing at his shoes. " Yes, I'll write as often as I can."

" Do you think they'll keep you pretty busy all the time ? "

" I don't know. I'm afraid I'll be pretty busy."

" What kind of a job is it that Father Aloysius found for you ? "

" I'm not sure. I think I'll work in the school—in the kitchen. And then I've got a job outside, too."

" In the kitchen," the mother repeated absently, for she was thinking about something else, now. She was wondering why it was so hard to talk naturally with her son; this was more like a conversation between neighbours, over a fence. What was the matter ? If she had something to do with her hands it would be easier, so she picked up her sewing basket and started to work on one of Eliseo's shirts that needed mending. Miguel, perhaps aware of the restraint, too, sat down in a chair near by. She stole a glance at him now and then and could see the little muscles along his cheeks move and ripple under the skin, and then she knew he was feeling the same kind of embarrassment that she felt.

" Will you—not like Hormiga afterwards ? " she

asked, putting a quick thought into words. " Like everybody else who goes away, will you never want to come back here ? "

This roused Miguel. " I'll always like Hormiga," he said. " One reason I want to go is so I can come back here and—and——" Somewhat to his surprise he couldn't finish what he started to say. Come back and what ? He didn't know well enough to say it in words; he wanted to say " do something for the people," but it sounded false, ambiguous, and it still had a cloudy meaning.

" Lucinda doesn't like it here, does she ? " Concepcion asked with some archness.

" Well—no. But it's her mother," he was quick to explain. " I tell her she's wrong, and she ought to come back here and do something for the people——" There, it came out after all.

Concepcion looked up, startled. " You mean—— ? "

" Yes, maybe teach in the school here, or help the people when they're sick. A man should run the kind of a store that would give the farmers the right place to sell their crops—help them instead of trying to beat them every time."

The mother was amazed, and stared at him; at the same time a great expanding pride began to dim her eyes. This was no ordinary boy, this Miguel !

" Everybody's trying to beat and cheat everybody else," Miguel went on ruefully. " Somebody ought to show the people how foolish that is."

" Vicente Romero——" Concepcion suggested and waited for Miguel to enlarge upon it.

" He's the worst of all," the boy said with heat. " He

thinks only about Vicente Romero. He could help the poor people more than everybody—if he would."

Concepcion gasped to hear him talk of the poor people so glibly—as if there were many poorer than the Lopez family. With her heart full of pride to hear him preaching like a man, she fed fuel to his fire: " He's a *Penitente*, though——"

" Yes. But he shouldn't be. They shouldn't let him be a *Penitente*. Why is he one ? "

" Oh, I don't know. I suppose because he's a *politico*. He gets votes."

Miguel snorted his disgust, and returned to silence.

" Maybe you won't want to be a *Penitente* after you've been down to Gabaldon to school," she said cautiously.

" I don't know, I don't see why that should change anything."

" I think it will."

" No. I think it's all right to be a *Penitente*—if you do it because you feel like it. If you think you need to belong because—because of sin, or—something."

And thus their conversation came to an end, negative, indefinite. These were his words which the mother would remember, her words which he would carry away with him in the afternoon. Miguel stood up, stretched, yawned. His mother watched him over her sewing. He was still young and shy and avoided her direct gaze where a great tenderness was shining for him to see. For a fugitive moment he did see it, and felt the powerful, inarticulate love for his mother swell in him and ebb away. He hoped he hadn't hurt her by anything he had said. He thought about that afterwards when it was sometimes too late. Now as he moved about the room in an aimless fashion he could feel her eyes boring into him; she knew all about him really—what was the use of trying to impress her or hold anything back? She trapped him every time with her boring eyes. "Well," he said, becoming uneasy beneath her wise, clairvoyant stare, "I think I'll go and see some people before lunch." He went to the door. "I'll be back in a little while."

"All right, Miguel. Don't be long, will you? It's soon time to eat. If you see Lucinda, don't let her keep you too long."

"No."

How did she know he wanted to see Lucinda? Just for that he wouldn't go to see her. He went instead down the road which led to the valley, and he was soon lost to his surroundings in a cloud of undirected thoughts—an easy, comfortable thoughtlessness, rather. At the top of the hill where the road took its first plunge he encountered a man, an American, looking into the eye of a surveyor's glass, mounted on a tripod. As Miguel stood there staring, the man straightened and pushed his hat back on his forehead. "Well, are you going to stand there all day, or am I going to use this glass?"

Miguel jumped aside as if he had stepped on a snake. From a little distance he examined the stranger. He wore breeches and boots, dirty, and a tan shirt open at the collar; his hat had four neat dents in the crown; he was sweating, he was powerfully built and aggressive in a way which Miguel had already sensed in all Americans, and his movements were quick, his contours angular. And the boy's thoughts moved at once to the months ahead which he would spend in the company of people like this man who seemed so cold and brittle even at this first instant of contact after the warmth and languid tempers of the people he knew best—his own people. It didn't seem that he would like it very much. He felt an immediate dislike for this surveyor, something like his reaction to all Americans, but more severe, more poignant. From his position to one side he watched, and followed the direction of the glass with his eyes. Far off he saw, then, another man holding an upright bar painted in red and white stripes.

" What are you doing ? " Miguel said, trying to make his voice sound friendly.

" Surveying," the man said shortly, squinting into the eye-piece.

" What for ? "

Much more squinting and signal-waving before Miguel's question was even heeded; then the man took off his four-dented hat and spoke to Miguel. " What did you say, sonny ? What am I doing this for ? Not for my health, by God. It's a hot country you got up here. You'd oughta try this some time if you think it ain't hot."

" I'd like to," Miguel replied seriously.

" You would, would you ? " The man had an amused, slightly contemptuous look. " You're pretty ambitious for a Mex, ain't you ? Most of your *compadres* want to sit around on their tails all day." He turned again to his glass.

Miguel winced; hate threatened his calm detachment. Why couldn't they be friendly ? Why did they have to talk in insults ? He didn't answer the surveyor.

LM

He had an instinct for courtesy, and it had been violated; he was angry and hurt at once. In a moment he moved away, shuffling his feet in the dust, walking in the pool of his own shadow. For a long time he was deeply troubled by this small incident and tried to account for it. Why didn't he answer the insult with blows ? That was what another American would do. If Mexicans had the money, the power, the control of everything, would Americans still dare to insult them and be so aggesssive ?

He didn't think they would. He walked along the level table-land from which the road descended; below him he could see the tiers of similar abutments falling in giant steps to the valley floor, fifteen miles away, on the topmost of which he and Hormiga stood. Immediately below, a light truck stood beside the road. It looked hardly bigger than a toy, but in the crystal air he could make out an official-looking seal painted on its door. It was the surveyor's car, doubtless, and he quelled an impulse to drop a rock on it. Then he followed with his eyes the dwindling thread of road, appearing and vanishing in the folds of the hills, down to the low country around Borregos. Until the Americans had come, he realised, there had been nothing but a wagon track to the valley, a treacherous, winding thing of discomfort; the Americans had built the present road even within Miguel's memory. It wasn't much, but it had seemed a titanic endeavour to him, with their dynamite and engines.

Why did they never cease ? The existing road was the third they had built and now they were at it again. What sort of people were they who had to build and rebuild their own work, over and over? He shook his head in bafflement. Why couldn't they leave well enough alone? Why should he even think of patterning himself after such people? Why not stay in Hormiga, and be what God intended him to be, a farmer and a *Penitente* and a father of a family? Did anything make him different from the rest, from his father, his brothers? He shook off these troublous matters and turned his face homewards—it must be nearing time for lunch. And he had to pass the surveyor again. " Are you surveying for a road? " he said without any attempt at friendliness this time.

" Yes, we are, sonny. Didn't you know we're putting a new road up here this year? "

" No, I didn't know it."

" Christ, what's the good of putting roads up here in the sticks. You never drive anything but wagons over 'em, anyhow."

Miguel again made no reply, but gazed at him with plain hostility. The man spat and turned away. " Who asked for the road? " Miguel said. " The old one was good enough."

" Yes, what's good enough for your grandfather's good enough for you, ain't that it? You'll never get anywhere that way, sonny." The man dismantled the instrument and folded the tripod, and then lifted his voice in a bellow that startled Miguel. " Come on, it's time to eat," he yelled, and waved at the man beyond. While he waited for the other man to come up he spoke again to Miguel: " You live in the town here? "

" Yes."

" What do you do for a living? Farm? "

" Yes. Farm, and run a little store."

" Keep a store, eh ? Well, I guess you're lucky at that —the farming don't look so good up here. Nothing but rocks."

" No, it's not very good," Miguel agreed.

When the other man came up, the surveyor shouldered his tripod, and the two started down the hill together towards the truck. He waved a jaunty farewell to Miguel. " Be seein' ya."

The boy acknowledged it with a nod which had his inevitable dignity in it. He was thinking now that the man might not be as bad as he seemed; under his buoyant, rather contemptuous manner might be a brotherhood, after all. Miguel wandered slowly back to town after watching the two men until they disappeared. And gradually under the stupefying heat of the sun his mood mellowed and a challenge grew. Why not show these Americans what a Mexican has in him ? When he got home, Miguel was full of determination again, to show the Americans, to expose them in their childishness—their foolishness.

" Did you know," he said at lunch, " that they're going to build a new road to Hormiga ? "

" Sure, didn't you know that before ? " Pablo answered. " They've been talking about it for a long time."

" Yes, I heard something about it," Eliseo said. " I didn't know it was so soon."

Miguel, slightly deflated, added, " I just saw the surveyor down the road. I didn't see anything wrong with the road we have now."

" It's bad for autos," Pablo explained. " Muddy in

wet weather—rough all the time—too many turns. It's a very bad road."

" It's a good thing," Eliseo agreed. " It means jobs for many men this year."

" It means trouble, too," Pablo said mysteriously.

" Why trouble ? "

" Because they put these new roads anywhere they want. If somebody's house is in the way, they put it right through his house—or his barn—anywhere. People aren't going to like that."

" They pay them for it," Eliseo protested.

" Yes, but not half what it's worth. It makes a lot of trouble, too. How would you like it if they come to you and say, ' Here's a hundred dollars. We put our road through the middle of your house ' ? You'd tell them to put their road somewhere else, wouldn't you ? "

" Sure," said Eliseo. " They can't do a thing like that."

Pablo shrugged knowingly. " But they can. They do. That's the trouble."

Eliseo began to get excited. " You mean I can't stop them from tearing down my house ? " He chuckled boastfully. " Huh. I can shoot. I've got guns."

"Yes, and you land in the penitentiary," Pablo finished. " I don't know how they can, but they go through anything that's in the way. I know. I did it all last winter, in the camp."

" Where was that ? " Eliseo demanded.

" Up in Delgado county, where the camp was."

Eliseo snorted angrily. " Well, I bet I stop them." He filled his mouth with food, and waved his knife at Pablo.

This discussion which Miguel had started served to keep the family off the subject of his going away until after lunch, Eliseo suddenly remembered then and put his arm on Miguel's shoulder. " Well, boy, you all packed and ready to go ? "

" Yes," Miguel said.

" All right. We'll go pretty soon, then. What will you carry your things in ? "

" I've got a box."

" He ought to have a nice valise," Concepcion said. " Vicente has some made of straw in his store——"

" They cost a lot of money," Eliseo objected automatically.

" He has one that's made to look like leather," Miguel added, merely to back up his mother, " with straps on it."

" He'd better send it back—he'll never sell it in Hormiga," Eliseo said with finality. " When will you be ready to start ? "

" Any time."

Eliseo stood up. " I've got a few things to do first——" He took out his watch, an ancient, inch-thick heirloom. " Say three o'clock—that all right ? "

" Yes, any time."

" *Bueno*." And Eliseo went out, leaving Pablo and Concepcion with Miguel. The older brother was in a mood to be-devil Miguel.

" Do you still want to go ? " he asked.

" Yes, I think so."

" Do you think you'll speak to the rest of us when you come back ? Maybe you'll be too full of learning. Maybe you won't like us then. Maybe you'll want to stay down in Gabaldon and be a big *politico*, like Vicente, no? And cheat all the people."

" I don't think so," Miguel replied, holding on to his temper.

" What do you want to go for, then? What do you think you'll get from it? "

" I don't know," said Miguel, speaking closer to the truth than Pablo would ever know. " I want to see what it's like down there, and—and meet some of the people——" He couldn't tell Pablo what he felt, when he could hardly express to himself the kind of wishes which were drawing him away from home. His brother's hostile manner repelled him, anyway.

Concepcion came to his rescue. " He wants to go so he can get a better job afterward. Don't you, Miguel? "

Miguel nodded half-heartedly, and Pablo sniffed his contempt.

" Now you stop, Pablo," Concepcion ordered, and carried a handful of plates over to the dish-pan. " I wish one of you boys would get me a bucket of water from the well." She glanced at Pablo, but he, after the immemorial custom of older brothers, passed the task to Miguel with a nod. Miguel fetched the bucket and went outside. They heard the well-rope screaming. When he came back, Pablo had gone.

" You don't mind him, do you, Miguel? "

" No."

The actual departure was a simple thing, without a great amount of wailing or emotion. When all preparations were made, and Eliseo's truck was chugging at the gate, Concepcion stopped the work with which she had been filling the last minutes and turned with resigned equanimity to face the boy. She stood inside the door, Miguel on the threshold, Eliseo impatiently beside his truck.

"Well," the boy said, "I guess that's all." He stepped to his mother, then, and knelt on one knee before her, taking one of her hands and holding it to his lips. "Give me your blessing, mother."

She laid her other hand on his head, raised her moist eyes. "Go with God, Miguel—and come back safe. God bless you!"

"*Gracias!*" He stood, and kissed her again, on the lips. "*Adios!*"

To cover the rising pain of this farewell, he dashed out, then, and jumped into the truck. Once he looked back and saw his mother in the doorway, waving something white.

He waved his hand in return, choked and blinded by the sadness of parting.

VI

THE CITY to which Miguel retired for his further
education was not in fact more than a large town. There
were, as Eliseo had surmised, about ten thousand people
in it, and this, compared to Hormiga's five hundred,
was an astonishing number. More than half of its
population, however, were Catholic Mexicans like
Miguel, who differed from him only in their overlayer
of citification. But the American influence was so strong
in this place that the greater number of Mexican people
could only give the town its tone, a certain colour, and
picturesqueness which rescued it from the bleak fate of
other American towns of the same size. Most of the
business was done by Americans, which consisted in
luring, by one means or another, more Americans and
more to the place, and to make them spend their money
while they basked in the atmosphere which Miguel's
people helped to create and which was hardly more
than a resistance which nullified all American attempts
to plant their material civilisation amid the inviolable
desert and mountains.

To be sure, there were converts to the alien philoso-
phy—men such as Vicente Romero in Hormiga—but
they, too, were lost in the torpid temper of the land
and its bronze-skinned, dark-eyed people, who had
remained, after four centuries and much interbreeding
with the even more ancient Indians, a volatile, passionate race, less indolent than inert, melancholy, gay,

hospitable. The Spanish in their ancestry was Andalusian, peasants for the most part, turned into soldiers and colonists by the fire of adventure and Cortez; the other strain which was in them—the Indian—gave them, perhaps, the stolid childishness, their habit of acceptance, or a blunt savagery which protruded suddenly, surprisingly, like the rock at the core of a mountain.

The opposition of two forces so fantastically various might have produced a greater conflict between the Americans and these docile, relatively satisfied people, but there never was any doubt of the outcome. The Americans were destined to prevail from the beginning. In this town, in fact, the Mexicans had fared better than in other places where they had often been driven out altogether and confined within the limits of a " Mexican quarter " which ever after remained the one redeeming, colourful aspect of the place. Here in Gabaldon they lived side by side with Americans, and were good neighbours.

The Indian was no factor: he lived disdainfully in his own tragically tiny, but autonomous domains.

The abruptness with which Miguel was dumped and abandoned in this strange environment reduced him to insensibility for a day; little by little he emerged from numbness and began to see things selectively. His fellow students were far more sophisticated than he, for they came mainly from the larger towns, or villages near them. There were none from far and primitive hamlets like Hormiga, and this discovery was painful to Miguel.

Furthermore, he was subjected to the more or less

organised scourging of all newcomers to a school for
boys; when they discovered that he had never seen a
shower-bath before, they were merciless in their
ridicule, inventive in finding ways to torment him.
And Miguel made the mistake of taking them seriously;
unused to their ways, and serious-minded by nature,
he was unable to throw off their attacks. They sank
in, with the result that at the end of two days he
was ready to run away—anything for the peace of
Hormiga. It seemed to him that the whole school
conspired to persecute him alone, and there was no
defence against it; by losing his temper he lost the last
frayed semblance of defence, and laid himself hope-
lessly open. If he had been a fighter, he might have
beaten his way to their respect, but he was no fighter;
he had no instinct for it. When he got mad his hands
and brain would not work together, and, separately,
were useless.

On one occasion when a blindness of rage had made
a fury of him, he lunged at a boy twice his size with
his hands flying crazily and the taste of blood in his
mouth, and it had been a simple thing for his enemy
to knock him down with one timely blow. Of course,
Miguel lost station by this, for he had been knocked
breathless, unable to come back. Such losses were hard
to regain, and they were frequent.

One who was kindest to him and sensed the torment
in his soul was an American boy whom they called
Pat, a minor hero in the school; and from Miguel's
gratitude to Pat was born a kindly feeling for a certain
type of American which withstood time and change.
He was bothered to discover, also, that it was not the

Americans, but boys of his own people who tortured him most; and this was not what he would have expected, had he been able to anticipate any of it. They reminded him of a pack of coyotes, devouring their fallen comrade; and Pat alone came to his aid.

At last he learned, when he stopped responding as they expected, that they soon lost interest in baiting him, and left him in peace. And his next discovery, no less puzzling, was that few of the boys were at the school for the reason which had brought him down from Hormiga. As nearly as he could judge, they were there for the fun of it, or to play games, the first of which in their minds just now was football, one which Miguel had never seen before, and heard of only vaguely. His best efforts to comprehend it, and like it, were failures; he saw no sense in it and certainly no pleasure in rushing about on a bare, rock-strewn field crashing into other boys and hurting yourself—all over an odd-shaped ball. The transports of enthusiasm the game induced simply left him cold. And this, it soon developed, was unfortunate, for it left him quite alone and isolated from the others who appeared to thrill to the game without stint, and to have it on their minds the whole time, to the exclusion of all else. It was hard for him; but when he saw the first actual game, he was consoled to find that he could enjoy it a little as a contest—beyond that, however, he could not go.

Perhaps his failure to enjoy football was merely another personal trait, or it may have been deeper; he had never taken pride in muscles, and there had been no occasion for it in his life. His soul belonged to the Church; his body, as the temple of his soul, had to be respected, but not glorified; in any case, his body was a private affair. Thus when they gave him his physical examination and he stood with half a hundred new boys in the gymnasium with nothing on but his drawers, he was self-conscious and embarrassed. And after he had pulled weights, blown into a bottomless tank, had all his measurements taken and recorded, his eyes, ears, nose, throat and teeth inspected—when the man had said, " Well, your feet are pretty good, any-·way," he felt like a bad bargain at a horse trade. And he had cause to envy, momentarily, the bulging biceps and expanded chests all about him, while he remained at heart impassive to it all. They had taken shocking liberties with his person, with their feeling and poking and probing, and he felt robbed for ever of his privacy; he hated every moment of it.

In the confusion of interests, studies seemed to be the least important thing; until one day at an assembly of students it was announced that the time had come for the examining and grading of the new boys. A Brother in a black robe and one of those flapping white collars spoke to them in English, and Miguel had such difficulty in following his words that he had to go up to the desk after it was over and admit that he hadn't understood much of what had been said. Whereupon he was turned over to a Spanish-speaking teacher who led him like a blind man through the rites of matriculation. And he found himself at last in what they called the junior college, taking on the side two subjects in which he was deficient, English and Latin. In addition, he had classes every day in Spanish, history and mathematics.

Religious instruction was taken for granted, and he had to go to chapel twice a day.

As the days passed and merged one into the next with diminishing dread, Miguel saw order come out of confusion. By waiting on tables in the dining-room, washing dishes afterward, by tending three furnaces in the neighbourhood (these duties were arranged by Father Aloysius, too) Miguel was able to support himself. Gabaldon was a lofty town and the winters were almost as severe as in Hormiga, but the sun was warm in the middle of the day, and it shone most of the time, tempering the cold. He was busy; there was no leisure left to him. It meant hard work all day, every day.

In a short time he began to wonder, what about Lucinda ?

There had been no opportunities at first even to think about Lucinda. When he inquired, now, about the academy for girls he was told that it was not far away, but as far as the boys in the school were concerned it might as well be in another city. Perhaps on Saturday afternoons, when the girls were allowed to come to the football games . . .

When he thought about Hormiga, his home up there and the freedom of living beside the brooding mountains, his heart still contracted with homesickness. After three weeks of this new life he could find nothing to bind him to the past; what he was now was severed from what he had been like cut string. All was absolute newness, and no one he saw seemed to think or feel exactly as he did. Even their speech was different. The Spanish spoken by these low-country boys had a clipped swiftness that made it hard to understand although his ear was growing accustomed to it.

And hardest of all, after the torture of the first days, was living in close contact with many boys, sleeping, bathing (in three weeks he took more baths than he had taken in his whole life before), eating with them in such inescapable intimacy; it made him feel like one of many animals in a pen. To this he was afraid he would never be reconciled. He had not realised until now how solitary and private his life had been at home. When he had wanted to be alone, he could walk half a mile and have limitless wilderness for his own, trees and the bright mountain for his companions. Here he was restricted, and the restriction served without his knowing it to keep him stirred by a hidden discontent. Here his feet fell upon cement and stone—too rarely upon the earth or pine-needles; his eye beheld motor-cars and buildings—the mountains, though near, were far, far away.

The first letter from Hormiga, even before he opened it, brought a quickening like pain to his heart. It was written by his mother and, although it betrayed the poverty of her schooling, it was a prize, a treasure, which he concealed even from his room-mate. From the look of it, it was the first letter she had written in her life, though it could not have been—the formation of the letters was crude, the spelling grotesque. It was in Spanish. " Dear Miguel," it said. " I can't write very good. When will you write to us ? We miss you like anything. Did you see the snow in the mountains ? It's here, too. Just a little in Hormiga. Pablo has a job with the road. Pretty soon Christmas."

It was only a glimpse, a tantalising taste—but it savoured and brought a lump to his throat. He sat still in his room for a long time viewing the pictures which the letter called forth : Eliseo was going up to the farm early in the mornings—frosty breath from the horses' noses; his wagon was coming home in the evenings loaded with potatoes in queer, lumpy sacks that he used to sit on. Perhaps Pablo went with him now—but no, Pablo had a job. Then the father was complaining about having nobody to help him on the farm. There was Benito—he might be up there helping him, for a share in the crop. One of them might come to town soon to sell the surplus—there was always a market for them, for not many people raised potatoes in this part of the country. Yes, he might see somebody from home, unless Vicente Romero bought the whole crop, as he did sometimes. It would be good, good to see someone—even if it had to be Pablo !

And after thinking hard about them in Hormiga, Miguel sat down at once to answer the letter, for he had half an hour to spare. He was greatly tempted, when he had the pen in his hand, to pour on to the page all the dismal things he had been feeling; with his pen poised, all his suffering and discontent stood at a point in his throat, ready to flow to his finger-tips. Should he let them go—or force them down ? No. He decided to be brave and gay in this letter, and he wrote one which fooled Eliseo and Pablo, but did not deceive his mother.

" Football ? " said the father, when the letter had been read and lay folded in Concepcion's lap. " What's football ? I never heard of it. Well, if Miguel plays it, he'll be a good player—he's a pretty good boy."

" Do you think he likes it down there ? " Concepcion said, knowing the answer.

" Sure he likes it. He says he likes it right there on the paper, doesn't he ? "

" He doesn't say anything about Lucinda," Concepcion added thoughtfully.

" Maybe he forgot about her," Eliseo chuckled.

As is the way in schools, boys sought out their friends, and, like water finding a level, came to a tentative rest after a month or six weeks. Those whose tastes corresponded banded together, while hero-worship centred about the football team. Miguel's indifference to that body excluded him for ever from the charmed, inner circle, and he was too busy to give it much thought. His first friend Pat, who turned out to be the son of a railroad engineer, continued friendly, but as a hero of the athletic field could not approach the heretic closely. Miguel's friends, therefore, were restricted to boys more or less like himself, who had come to school for a single purpose, or who came from places where football was a stranger.

His room-mate, a lad named Merijildo Quintana, was raised on a farm in an irrigated section of the lower Rio Grande Valley, and he, too, was slow to catch the appeal of such an organised game. But he had lived near a city and knew far more about the world than Miguel did—its sins as well as its virtues. He was a quiet, robust youth with healthy appetites, and his principal aim was to keep these appeased. Although only a year older than Miguel, he knew all about women, and

MM

talked of his conquests in a matter-of-fact way which soon became the secret envy of Miguel. Merijildo was never boastful—always simple, sometimes crude, like a breeder discussing his brood-mares. And Miguel's awe was such that he never betrayed his own virginity, but listened in silence when the topic was in the air, and tried to give Merijildo the impression, by his knowing manner, that none of this was news to him. They became friends. And Miguel determined to be virginal no longer.

There were three hours in the afternoons when the students who had nothing else to do were accustomed to move out to the athletic field and watch the practice of their football team—or to wander foot-loose over the town. For Miguel, however, these hours were taken by his jobs. Until furnace fires were lighted in November, his employers found work for him to do in their gardens, spreading fertiliser, covering plants and the like.

In this way he earned two dollars a day and came in contact with a class of Americans which was quite new to him. The people called them *ricos*—rich ones. They had so much money that it was never counted. They were people who had big houses, automobiles, servants; people who tapped by hidden channels the magic country to the east, were thus mysteriously allied to the rulers of the earth. In olden times, the rich man who employed Mexicans was their *patron*; the term was rapidly dying the death of democracy, however, and boys of Miguel's generation thought of them only as employers, the source of wages, impersonal, irresponsible.

It did not often occur to Miguel to wonder about these rich ones; except in the case of one young couple for whom he worked, envy was not in his heart. They were not much older than he, yet the source of their money was both mysterious and inexhaustible; their name was Fayerweather, and he never learned to pronounce it correctly, slurred over it when it was necessary to speak it. The man was exceptionally kind to him without being patronising; the woman, his wife, was always smiling, and was the most beautiful human creature Miguel had ever beheld. He hardly dared to look at her, as if she were a perishable kind of angel. He grew fond of them. Whenever he needed anything in his work—a new rake, or a shovel—Mr. Fayerweather went down town in his car and brought it back, brand-new, and he always bought the most expensive kinds. Miguel knew, because the price-marks were still on them. He would pay three dollars for a shovel, six dollars for a roll of hose, and buy something every day if Miguel asked him to. Money in such abundance was beyond belief, and sometimes he wondered, with a rebellious spark in his heart, why a young couple should have so much when other couples—Benito and Rosa, for instance—should have so little. But they were so fine and good to him that such thoughts really troubled him little. He was glad to work for them. And it was the way of the world, he guessed. Some people were born to have much—some things in life were above questioning. And as long as he got along, there was enough to worry about. Furthermore, they were Catholics.

They had a maid working for them, too—a handsome,

spirited Mexican girl who was older than he was. Although she had a reserved and quiet manner, he could see that she was a fire-brand underneath. He was slightly afraid of Maria, and approached her as if she were explosive.

" They've got a girl up there at that house where I work," he said cautiously to Merijildo, his room-mate. " Her name's Maria. She's pretty——" and he tried to leer.

" Young ? " said Merijildo.

" Well, not very."

" How young ? "

" Oh, I don't know. Maybe twenty-two or three."

"That's dangerous," Merijildo pronounced promptly. " Be careful you don't get into trouble. A lot of people don't think about that until afterward."

" I don't think I'll get into trouble."

" Well, be careful."

And Miguel decided to be careful—whatever that meant. For him it meant to treat Maria with even more circumspection. It wasn't difficult at all—one can easily be careful with a volcano. But he couldn't deny the warm beginnings of an interest in Maria. For long she was out of his reach. His timidity made him unequal to her. But still prodding him was his determination to end his virginal purity, and a need for the companionship of a girl.

Merijildo seemed to have no trouble keeping himself supplied with this sort of thing. On the few occasions Miguel accompanied him on his foraging expeditions he was amazed at his room-mate's audacity, and embarrassed at his success. For Merijildo's method was old.

He and Miguel would fall in behind a pair of girls—Miguel burning meanwhile with the fear of offending them—and from a slight distance he would start a series of remarks loud enough to carry forward to the girls and designed to make them laugh. If they smiled and looked around, his boldness increased and he advanced to their sides, Miguel trailing—if they ignored him, so be it. Try again. When he was a party to such doings Miguel suffered an anguish of dread, lest they should mistakenly insult nice girls, but once a conquest was made and they walked off arm in arm with girls, his fear vanished, but his self-consciousness remained.

For he didn't know what to say, or how to handle girls like these. Sometimes they were pretty, and merely adventurous, more often they were professionals, brash, crude, and business-like. In the latter event, a deep revulsion made him recoil and desire to escape from them as quickly as he could. This strange fastidiousness worried him. It never seemed to bother Merijildo, why should it trouble him? Many a time he walked back to the school alone, after ridding himself of the girl in one way or another, and wondered what Merijildo was doing, knowing full well, envious in his heart. When the girl didn't offend him, he walked with her down to the south end of the town beyond the street lights, into the flat land below the railroad tracks where there was nothing but sand and rubbish heaps—a tree growing forlornly in the river-bottom.

These episodes were infrequent, and never came to anything more than laconic conversations, ended by Miguel walking to the girl's home and leaving her there with a self-conscious grin and a shy lift of his hat.

Furthermore, he was likely to be too busy in the evenings to go with Merijildo at all. His room-mate never discussed their expeditions when he came in, much later, tired and silent.

" Well, I can't do any more than give you a start," was as much as he would ever say.

Meanwhile, Miguel became more dissatisfied with himself. Merijildo admitted but one purpose and accomplished it. Why couldn't he be like that? He began to suspect defects in himself, and to worry and to long to talk about it with Merijildo; but to talk would betray the whole fabric of the false impression of himself he had tried, from the beginning, to build for his room-mate to see. It might, too, destroy his friend's respect for him, and that would be too hard to bear in a place where friends were scarce. No, he would have to work it out himself, in solitude.

The scramble of work he had to do, combined with his studies, kept these matters in a subordinate place. There was no danger yet of their turning him inwards too much upon himself. One day he saw Lucinda. On Saturday afternoons the students gathered to watch the football games, and the girls from the academy were allowed to come and sit in the grandstands near the boys. They were flanked and guarded on all sides by Sisters who looked like great black crows in their winged headdresses, but Lucinda slipped out of line as they were marching in and spoke to Miguel. " How are you getting along? " she said. " How do you like it? "

" Pretty good. Why don't I ever see you? Don't they let you out at all over there? "

" Not very much. You can come to the school, though—they let us have visitors on Sundays."

" Where ? "

" At the school. There's a room where we can see people."

" Alone ? "

" Well—no. There may be others there—and always one of the Sisters."

Miguel shook his head decisively. " Couldn't we go out alone ? Couldn't I take you to the movies, or——"

" Oh, no," she interrupted him. " They wouldn't let us do that ! "

And before either of them noticed her, a Sister had come up and taken Lucinda by the arm. " Come Lucinda—over here." And as she spoke she gave Miguel a look that made him feel like a criminal.

Lucinda smiled as she was led away, but Miguel couldn't return it. Rebellion rose in him hotly, as it had done so often since coming to this place. She didn't seem to care whether she saw him or not—those restrictions she talked about as if they were the most natural thing in the world. He picked up a stone and flung it with all his might into the middle of the field. To hell with her ! If she didn't care any more than that, then by God he was through with her ! Love ? How could her cold, precious aloofness be love ? He kicked angrily at the ground and gritted his teeth. Love ! Somewhere, by God, love must live in warmth, in passion—in union, not in separation. " I'll find it," he muttered. " I'll find it if I never find anything else ! "

He found a seat in the grandstand and sat grimly through two hours of play, surrounded by yelling, waving maniacs, untouched by them. The girls' shrill screams coming through the deeper tumult of the boys' voices impinged on his remoteness like needle-pricks, roused him from time to time.

He was plunged in a dour mood. What *had* he thought to gain from all this ? Advancement ? But what sort of advancement ? Was it not surrender he saw all about, a cringing imitativeness of these low-country Mexicans, a rush to wipe out the stain of being Mexican ? Weren't they hurrying, hurrying to make themselves into young Americans, to take over everything American as their model ? Wasn't that one of the reasons for his isolation, that he was too Mexican ? And for the first time he saw Lucinda infected with the same disease—the girl who loved him, the girl he was supposed to marry. She struck him now in afterthought as more American than Mexican, and long weeks of self-restraint swelled up to condemn what he saw. Even Merijildo, his friend, was more American than Mexican, was bent solely upon obliterating his Mexicanness. All of them were doing the same thing—nothing remained but their darker skins. They hurried to marry the lighter people when they could, to bleach even that vestige of the past ! And his heart leapt to think—wasn't his own exposure to Americans—Pat, the Fayerweathers and his other employers—wasn't it beginning to affect him, too ? Wasn't it because he felt less than they were that he was down here trying to transform himself ?

He clenched his fists and closed his eyes, and with lowered head said fervently to himself, " Oh, God, make me happy to be what I am ! "

Miguel left the grandstand when the game ended,

without knowing what had happened except that the home team had won. No one could escape that. The walls of the surrounding buildings knew it—the earth itself must know it, the stones of the field where the battle was fought. He didn't try to see Lucinda again, but turned his back on the whole scene as if for the last time, for revolt was still seething in him. And he liked some of the things he was doing, he reflected, as he made his way to his room. The studies were interesting, except the arithmetic and algebra. The chapel was undefiled, comforting, and made him feel close to God. The Brothers who were teachers were hardly people to him; impersonal, they were none of them Mexican. He didn't know what they were—they didn't seem American either. They were superior beings who gave him a sense of lowliness in himself. What did it mean? Why were those in authority, in the Church and out of it, so rarely Mexican? In Hormiga all authority in his life except Father Aloysius, who was French, had been Mexican. And now the world changed. He was homeless in it, vagrant.

That night he started for the picture show with Merijildo. They were supposed to be in their rooms by nine o'clock, but they got special permission to be out a little later because the picture lasted until after nine. That Merijildo had plans for the evening Miguel could tell now by the air of expectancy which came over his room-mate. Doubtless it was the thrill of the chase in anticipation, and it began to invade Miguel too, as they walked down the street together.

" What's at the movies, do you know? " Merijildo was saying.

" No, I don't know."

" If it doesn't look good, I don't think I'll go."

Miguel had been expecting this, had only wondered how Merijildo would make known his intentions. " There's nothing else to do," he said, giving a bigger opening.

" Oh, I'll find something to do."

" Do you know her, or will you pick her up ? "

Merijildo smiled; his pupil was learning. " No, I don't know anybody. How do you like those two across the street ? "

Marvellous, how Merijildo kept his eye peeled all the time ! Miguel glanced to the other sidewalk with trembling starting in him; the girls didn't look like the kind who could be had by Merijildo's crude methods, but he couldn't really tell. He had to admit that his judgment was worthless. " Do you think they'd like it ? " he said cautiously. " They look like nice girls— are they Spanish ? " He had learned to say Spanish instead of Mexican down here.

" Sure, they're Spanish girls. Shall we give them a try ? "

" Let's wait," Miguel said quickly. " Let's wait until we see what's at the movie."

" O.K.," Merijildo said easily. " I hope they don't get away from us. They look pretty hot." He spoke in English, using all the slang and cusswords and Miguel rather liked it, for it was a chance to learn the words from Merijildo, who used them more easily than Spanish. He turned suddenly to Miguel and flashed a broad smile.

" What's the matter ? What are you smiling at ? "

"I was just thinking—if it wasn't for me, you'd never speak to a girl, would you?"

"I don't know," Miguel said. "Maybe not to ones I don't know."

Merijildo laughed softly. "You won't get anywhere that way."

They strolled along side by side, but far apart in spirit. For nothing had yet succeeded in dimming the clear fire of Miguel's idealism which he strangely brought with him from the mountains; the barren realism of these low-country *paysanos* remained detached from him and probably always would. They seemed to accept everything about which he most bitterly complained in his heart—without thought, without rebellion. He only knew that he was impatient with it now; much later, when he could look back upon all this from the pinnacle of his own regeneration, he saw that it was only their feverish desire to outstrip their Mexicanness, that they were living contradictions of themselves. "What do you expect to do when you get through school?" he asked Merijildo.

"I don't know for sure. Maybe I'll go back to farming. But I don't think I want to be a farmer all my life. My father wants me to go to agricultural school, but it takes too much time. I don't want to wait that long."

"Wait?" said Miguel. "Wait for what?"

"Well, haven't you got any ambition? I want to get ahead—be somebody—make money. Right now."

Miguel had to pause to ponder this. He was both impressed and puzzled, feeling a disagreement, but unable to put his finger on it, isolate it. Perhaps it was the hurry—"What's your hurry?" he said. "If you went to school it would take longer, but—you'd be a better farmer, I guess, wouldn't you ? "

" No, it's a waste of time. Anyway, I want to get through with going to school. Here's your movie."

It was a " western." Miguel loved this kind more than any other; Merijildo did, too, but he was beginning to be superior about them. And there were other things he liked still more. " I don't think I want to see that," he said.

This also was what Miguel expected. He looked at the pictures from the reels posted outside, and at last decided to go in alone.

" All right," Merijildo said. " I'll see you later. Sure you don't want to come with me ? "

Miguel wasn't at all sure. And Merijildo, seeing his hesitation, added, " They're out to-night. We've got two hours." He had a way of putting such suggestion in his voice when he was feeling predatory that Miguel was often warmed to his idea against his will. Now his skin began to prickle. And he changed his mind.

" All right—I'll come with you."

It was cold, and Miguel had little heart for the thing at all. As usual, he was left with the girl Merijildo found for him—he had made up to a pair within five minutes, merely by falling in beside them and remarking that the night was cool—and now he found that his fickle thoughts were moving in the direction of Hormiga, that the girl had no power to change their direction. Looking at her out of the tail of his eye (he never could look at them squarely) he saw that she was pretty, but dressed in a shabby imitation of elegance. He walked with her down an unlighted street, and his dislike of the whole affair grew upon him; he didn't feel very well, either. " I don't think I feel very good," he said to her. "Where do you live?"

" Oh, I live a long way from here—'way up on the hill."

Miguel's heart sank. It was a good two-mile walk. " Where do you live ? " she said.

" I go to school here. I live in Hormiga."

" Oh, I've been to Hormiga. I've got a friend up there. That's where they have those *Penitentes*, isn't it?"

Miguel looked at her in astonishment. " That's one place," he said, disturbed by her air. " They're in lots of towns—Hormiga isn't the only place. What's your friend's name ? "

" His name's Lopez."

This time he was startled. " That's my name," he objected, as if he had sole right to it.

" Well, what of it ? His name's Lopez, too. Pablo Lopez."

For some reason, finding this girl who knew his brother—it must be Pablo she knew—filled him with confusion. He was resentful and yet warmed by the contact where it was least expected. He looked at her suspiciously. " Where did you know him ? "

" Do you know him, then ? "

" Pablo Lopez is my brother."

She gave a little squeal of delight. " Oh, he's *nice*," she cried, drawing out the word to its fullest length. " I knew him last winter—I was living up near the camp where he was. He's a nice boy, Pablo is ! " And she stroked his arm suggestively.

Miguel inched away from her. " Have you ever been

to Hormiga?" he asked her, recoiling from the invitation.

"Yes, I've been there—once."

"Did you like it?"

"Well, I think it's pretty, but I wouldn't like to live there."

"Why not?"

"Oh, it's too far away from everything. I shouldn't think you'd have any fun up there."

"Fun," he repeated, examining her meaning. He'd have to get rid of this one, too, Pablo or no Pablo. "Who else do you know?"

"I know a girl—Lucinda Romero."

Once more his heart jumped; Pablo was possible, but this seemed incredible. "How did you know her?"

She caught his inference and pouted. "Why shouldn't I know her? She's here now at the academy."

"I know she is. Did you know her in Hormiga, or—?"

"No. I used to go to the academy myself."

"You?"

She stood off and struck a pose, hands on her hips. "Say, what's the matter with me. Why shouldn't I go to the academy? Why shouldn't I know Lucinda Romero? Is she a friend of yours, too? The damned snippy little brat!" She lapsed into English for emphasis.

Miguel was rather sorry for his implications, which had slipped out unwittingly. He tried to smooth her ruffled feathers. "No, no, I was only a little surprised to find anyone here who knows people at home. Do you know anyone else?"

The girl's revolt was quelled. "Well, there's Cosme——" she began.

"Cosme?"

"Yes, Cosme Martinez. She lives 'way out on the edge of Hormiga, in a little house towards the mountain. They're awfully poor people, but she's pretty. Oh, she's pretty. Nice, too. Not grand, like Lucinda."

"I don't know her. There are lots of families up there named Martinez. I guess she's one of them. Is she there now?"

"Yes, I think so."

"What's she like?"

"Oh, she's quiet—doesn't say much—she's sort of good and strong, you know? She makes you feel good inside. She makes you feel—well, have you ever felt all upset inside and gone out alone to the hills and lain down and looked straight up into the sky? You know how it makes you feel better, and makes you forget all your troubles? Well, that's the way Cosme is—always quiet, simple—and far away, like the sky."

Miguel was touched by this unexpected reverence for another human being, and surprised to see this girl— he didn't even know her name—leave her character and become for a moment real. For she *was* real when she talked of this Cosme—he sensed it so deeply that he couldn't say anything for some time, could only stand like some stranger before an alien, but completely holy, altar. Presently he shook off the mood. "Well, I think I've got to go back," he said.

"Oh——" the girl was herself again instantly. "Must you go?" She began to stroke his arm as before. "Aren't you even going to—kiss me?"

Miguel shivered. " Not to-night," he said quickly before his senses played him false. " Can I take you home ? "

" No," she pouted. " I'll walk back with you as far as the movie theatre."

She did her best to beguile him on the way, but without success. Miguel was far away from her already. When they parted he said good-night politely, but she refused to return it, turned her back on him angrily. He shrugged and walked away.

There was some elation in him to know that he had caught Pablo at last, but it soon left him. What he remembered, and would long remember, was the girl's strange mention of Cosme Martinez, and the description of her clung in his memory. He would like to know a girl like that. He charged himself to remember the name—he would look her up when he went home. Stupid of him not to get the other girl's name—what good was the joke on Pablo without it ? Oh, well—it was only a joke, anyway. But Pablo thought he was so smart. . . .

It was getting colder. Looking up, Miguel saw clouds, low-flying on the night wind. Over the *plaza* they were tinged with rosy light from the electric signs on the stores. It might snow before morning; and snow reminded him of home, brought back even the hot, metallic smell of the stove in the room where they all spent their winter evenings. And he remembered how pieces of wood roared in it, how its sides sometimes grew red-hot and how those fiery slabs of iron used to fascinate him as a child. He would hold a stick of *piñon* wood against them and watch the smoke curl away from the point where wood and metal met, filling the room with fragrance. When they caught him at it they scolded him, for it was dangerous; they said, " Do you want to burn the house down ? "

There was nothing home-like or comforting in the steamy coils of radiators that kept the school warm— too warm; nothing comparable to a ticking wood stove, whose fuel you cut yourself in the forest.

Back in his room, Miguel switched on the light, flooding the place instantly in a white glare. What a wonderful thing, to make night into day by pushing a button ! These were the things by which the Americans conquered, and no man could say they were not marvellous. He was beginning to learn, however, that not all the wonders they brought with them were new wonders; only yesterday in a textbook he had read that the ancient Romans, who spoke the Latin which was so like Spanish, had carried water in pipes and had fountains and buildings far grander than anything the Americans had brought to New Mexico.

He opened the book again now, and ran through the leaves. There were pictures of marble buildings, of heavy-set men in flowing robes, of spears, axes and coins. He tried to imagine all this vanished from the face of the earth, as they assured him it was, but it was hard to believe that nowhere could the men who created these things be found alive. In another book which he took up next were more pictures, of New York City, the magic source of the wealth which was tapped by people like the Fayerweathers. He stared and stared at the pictures—the streets ought to be lined in gold, but he saw no glitter there. And he had to admit

Nᴍ

that some of these buildings dwarfed the work of the Romans.

He shut the books. Yes, perhaps they were right, Merijildo and the others; perhaps it was good to make themselves into Americans as fast as they could. For three centuries the Mexicans—his people—had stood still. There was not one foot of water-pipe in all Hormiga. . . .

Damn ! He picked up a book and slammed it down again on the table. Wasn't there more to it than electric lights and water-pipes ? He put his elbows on the edge of the table and held his head in his hands, and tried to force his brain to open his eyes, cudgelling it like a lazy *burro*. " I am eighteen," he said to himself. " Most of the boys are no older—but they all know more than I do. Any one of them would know what to do if a girl said, ' Aren't you even going to kiss me ? ' "

Miguel heaved a great sigh, infinitely displeased with himself. He beat down an impulse to run away, knowing that he couldn't escape by running away. Perhaps a year of this, or a winter of studying here, would teach him other things than Latin or history; but what would he be by that time, Mexican or American ? Why not go on, then, and make a good job of it, go to the university, learn to play football, learn to *like* it ? No, there never would be money or time enough. The cycle of good times and bad in Hormiga was short. They were certain to need him up there next year. He should be thankful for this much—it would be stupid and ungrateful to run away.

When the proctor of the dormitory made his rounds

at nine o'clock, Merijildo was still out. " I guess he's still at the movies," Miguel said. " I didn't go."

" Hm. Tell him to report to me when he comes in."

" Yes, sir."

He hoped Merijildo wouldn't be too late, and get into trouble. It was a wonder that he kept out of trouble as well as he did, for he was always breaking some rule. Miguel couldn't seem to break even the least regulation without getting caught, and he hated getting caught, because no amount of indifference or will-power could quell the shaking of his knees when he was brought up for reprimanding. It was never very serious, but they made him understand that his was a rather special case and he'd better behave himself. Just how his case differed from others he couldn't see, and this threat they put upon him added to his discontent, to his feeling of not belonging. Was it because he had to work to pay his way ?

As time passed, and Merijildo didn't return, he began to get nervous; and when at last he did come in, Miguel was pale with the premonition of what would happen to his room-mate. " You'd better go and see Brother Adolph—he was looking for you."

" Was he ? " said Merijildo casually. " All right. What time is it ? "

" It's after ten."

" Oh, that's not so bad." He went out, and was back in ten minutes.

Wide-eyed, Miguel asked, " What did he say ? "

" Oh, nothing. He was a little sore, but I kidded him out of it," said Merijildo in English.

Miguel gasped. " I thought he'd put you out for sure this time."

Merijildo laughed. " Hell, they won't fire you for a little thing like that. You've got to talk to 'em, you know—kid 'em along a little—make 'em laugh and forget about it. It's not hard to do."

" No," said Miguel, " I guess not—if you know how. I can't do it."

" Well, you let 'em see how scared you are—then it's hopeless."

" Were you scared ? "

" Of course I was. If I get kicked out of here my father'll kill me. What time did you get in ? "

" I guess it was about eight-thirty."

" Eight-thirty ? " He shook his head. " You're hopeless," he said, and went to bed.

Another letter came from Hormiga early in December. " Dear Miguel," it read, " are you coming home for Christmas ? Will they let you out ? We think we have a good Christmas this year. Your father says we have wild turkey, and he made money with the hunters this fall. So come home for Christmas pretty soon now."

But Miguel didn't see how he could get away—he couldn't just let all the furnaces go out. They were burning all the time now because the winter was cold in Gabaldon, and fireplaces were not enough. Then one day he met Lucinda again, on the street this time, with three other girls. They had another of those tense, hasty conversations, as if they were talking against time and punishment.

" Hello, Lucinda."

" Hello, Miguel. Are you going home for Christmas ? "

" I'd like to, but I can't leave my work here. Are you going ? "

" No, my mother and father are coming down here to stay with my auntie. It's too cold in Hormiga."

" Too cold——" Miguel repeated. " But——"

" Yes, they think it would be nicer if they come down here. It's too bad you can't go home. Maybe I'll see you, though, if you stay here."

Miguel suddenly sensed a change in Lucinda, but he couldn't tell what kind of a change. " Yes—maybe," he said vaguely. " Well, I'll look for you."

" The house is on Onorio Street—number twenty-one."

" All right, I'll remember. Good-bye."

" Good-bye, Miguel."

Reluctantly he wrote his mother that unless the people he was working for gave him a day or two off, he didn't see how he could come home for Christmas. Her disappointment would be great, he knew; she might even cry. But what could he do ?

Merijildo, as usual, told him what he might do. " Why don't you hire somebody who lives here to do your work for you while you're gone ? Just turn over your wages to him."

" But he wouldn't know how to do it—or where to go," Miguel objected.

" Take him around with you once or twice before you go. I'd do it myself, only I'm going home, too." Then Merijildo laughed. " You know, if I didn't know you better, I'd think you didn't have a brain in your head."

" It's a good idea," Miguel said, grinning sheepishly. " Maybe I can work it that way."

" You'll learn, some day—maybe." He smiled good-naturedly. For Merijildo liked Miguel, and respected the qualities in him which were solid and incorruptible. His small inadequacies which were always cropping out he laid to Hormiga and inexperience. In fact, this respect of Merijildo's was a greater thing than either of them realised. The truth was that the low-country lad was plastic, viscous at the depths of him, where Miguel was firm and secure. Their friendship, which seemed lop-sided, was actually counter-balanced. Despite doubts and reaching-out, Merijildo sensed that Miguel was Mexican and nothing else, while he, with all his self-confidence, was constantly borrowing from what he was not, until the borrower and the lender were confused. And he was lonely in the midst of it. He played a lone hand, had no other friends in the school, and came to rely on Miguel for his soul's need.

Before telling his mother of the plan to hire a sub-stitute for a few days, Miguel thought he had better tell his employers about it. And he learned that the Fayerweathers were going away for a month and were leaving the maid, Maria, in the house to look after it. They had no objection to his plan; but for the first time Maria paid him more than passing notice.

" Are you going away, too ? " she said. " That's too bad."

" Yes," Miguel said, at once doubting and hoping

for what her voice seemed to contain. " But only for a few days around Christmas."

" You come every day just the same, to see the furnace ? "

" Twice a day—morning and evening."

" Oh, that's good. I'm glad, because I'll be all alone here and maybe I'll be a little scared."

" Yes——" He began to be self-conscious. " Haven't you any relatives in town ? "

" No, I come from Tapiacito, you know ? 'Way down by Socorro."

" Oh, so far ? " There was an awkward pause; Miguel turned his hat over and over. " You're not—married or—anything ? "

" No." She sighed. " I was married, but——" She finished with a shrug.

" Oh—I see," he breathed, while his eyes searched the kitchen for relief. " What kind of a stove is that ? " he blurted.

" That's an electric range. It's wonderful. See——" She went over to it and faced him radiantly. " You just turn the switches."

He joined her and pretended to examine it; stood there, turning the switches. " Do you like working for —these people ? "

" Yes, they're nice, both of them. They treat me very good." She was standing close to him. " They're funny, though. All Americans are funny."

" Are they ? How ? "

" Well, they're awfully kind and nice, but they're funny about other things." She laughed lightly. " They don't like me to have men come here to see me—here in the house, in my room. I have a little room there, off the kitchen." She pointed to a closed door, and Miguel glanced at it shyly.

" Oh. I wonder why ? "

" I don't know. Mr. Fayerweather, he says he's afraid there might be fights and things. He says he doesn't care what I do, but he wanted me to be careful who I bring into the house."

" Oh, I see."

She lowered her eyes. " He knows you, though—he doesn't mind if you come into the house."

Miguel had the sensation of being sucked into something, like water into a drain ; he began to edge towards the back door.

" So I don't bring people here at all," Maria hastened to say when she saw his alarm. " I like the Fayer-weathers, and I try to treat them like they treat me, see ? "

Miguel nodded.

She came up to him and patted his arm. " You're a nice boy. Never mind. I'll keep you from being too lonely when all the boys go home."

And with that he fled. When all the boys went home Miguel found time heavy and superfluous for a while. The Fayerweathers left for " the east "—he felt home-sick and homeless. They let him keep his room in the school, let him come and go without supervision, and no bells rang. This he enjoyed. It was like a liberation from a cell. For a time he was occupied with teaching his substitute how to tend furnaces—he found a boy among his fellow students who was glad for the job— and showing him where the three houses were. And he wrote to his family telling them that he would come home the day before Christmas and stay until the day after. Each time, meanwhile, he went to the Fayerweathers he stayed longer talking to Maria, for he felt sorry for her—she never seemed to see anyone, and she became a warm haven of friendliness in a deserted world. Gradually he grew to feel at ease with her; she mothered him and surmounted his tremendous shyness while he thought he was doing it himself. Finally he arranged his rounds so that he came to the Fayerweather house last, morning and evening.

She watched his clothes and made him wear warm things when it was cold, rubbers on his feet when the snow melted and mud was underfoot. And he began to wonder about his feelings for Maria, for her motherliness disarmed him, yet a force emanated from her of a strength beyond his reckoning. He had never felt such power before, or such comfort, like the cool shadow of a pine tree on a hot day—or a bed in which to lay his weariness, his tedium. And plainly, in addition to all this, she made him want her in the simple, physical way. And yet, perhaps because she reminded him, by her solicitude, of Concepcion, he had a feeling of respect for her and a sense of guilt when his skin prickled and he thought of going with her into that closed room that opened off the kitchen. This confused his feelings beyond explaining.

One day she said to him: " But I'm not your mother, Miguel. I'm not old enough to be your mother. I'm just someone who likes you—*very much* ! "

Oh, what she put into those last two words ! His heart beat wildly, insanely—and after that his sense of guilt never reappeared. In its place came confidence. He felt himself growing older, not slowly with the years, but hour by hour, as if every moment passed with Maria were a year's worth of living. At last he could talk with a girl—a woman—as a friend and equal, not as a son to his mother, full of respect and remoteness. He didn't know whether Maria had done it with design in her heart, or whether he had at last conquered himself. He only knew that it happened, and in his joy he forgot Hormiga, Concepcion, the bright mountain and the whole copious discontent of the early days when he felt so much alone.

When it seemed that they were as close to each other as could be, something would happen to draw them closer; Maria gave him all his meals, now, and they went out together as often as their work allowed, usually to walk among the rocky, coral-coloured hills studded with emerald *piñons* and junipers. The shadows on their shaded sides were as dark as the midnight sky, and sometimes when the sun was high and hot, this shade was comfortable to lie in. Often he mentioned to Maria his astonishment to feel such warmth in the middle of winter with snow lying on all the northerly slopes.

It was usually like this, just wandering aimlessly together. They seldom went into town, for he had no money to spend. Miguel complained about it a little, for he was beginning to want to give things to Maria. " I have no money," he would say. " I've saved a little to get my mother something for Christmas, but I have none to spend."

" Never mind, Miguel. I have some money. They

pay me pretty well, and I don't spend much."

So when they went to see the "westerns" at the theatre, Maria paid for the tickets. And she discovered everything about him. She probed and ferreted facts with a tenderness which easily conquered his old defences. And when she learned that he was eighteen, she said, " Do you know anything about love, Miguel?"

" Well—a little, I guess."

" But have you never loved a girl ? Really loved her, I mean ? "

Miguel thought of extending the lie he had lived with Merijildo—but the words would not pass his lips. " N-no. No, I don't think I ever have."

" Oh, that's too bad ! I think you should know something about it." They were walking hand in hand along a wagon-track in the hills ; now she stopped and looked up into his eyes in which a swimming softness shone. " I'll teach you, Miguel. I'm a little older—I know— I can teach you. Would you like that ? "

" Yes," he said fervently, while everything within him seemed to break down and flow into her for her keeping. " I'd like that ! "

" It would be nice for you—if you loved me a little, though," she said.

" I *do* love you ! Maria——" Suddenly he realised how much he loved her, and the realisation choked him. " I think you're the most wonderful girl in the world," he fumbled. " I'm not afraid, at all, any more. You make me feel—easy—right—inside. Oh, I *do* love you, Maria ! I didn't know ! "

" There's a lot you didn't know." She started to walk on.

He ran after her. " Yes," he cried in abject surrender, feeling not shame but a vast swelling of his heart, relief as if a stone had been rolled from it. At last he was in the open, concealing nothing, unconcealed, and she would manage everything. He felt himself expanding, joyfully, like the loving unfolding of a bud.

Maria stopped again. " But first you must kiss me. You haven't done that yet. Have you ever kissed a girl ? "

" Yes. Yes, I have——"

" Perhaps she didn't know how to kiss you. See——"

She drew his head down, and pressed her moist, parted lips against his. Miguel left the earth. Oh, this was not like Lucinda ! No chaste, tight lips were these ! He closed his arms about her and all his senses focused upon one barely tolerable yearning.

She broke away at last with a gay, nervous little laugh. " No, not here, Miguel. No, no, wait. To-night, maybe—no ? You'll stay—after dinner ? "

" Yes, yes, I'll stay. I'll stay for ever, Maria. Oh, God, you're beautiful ! I've been a fool ! "

" Look, Miguel, how low the sun is. You'll be late— your fires will go out. We'll have to go."

" Oh, the fires——" But he faced about, although his heart was bursting, and put his arm about her waist as they walked, holding her pressed against him all the way into town.

" I'm cold," she said suddenly. " Come on, let's run a little."

And Miguel, running behind her, thought he never saw a creature so beautiful, running with the slender

grace of an animal. While she went home to start their
supper, he raced like a madman through the part of
town where his employers lived, dodging into the houses
and out again quickly for fear of being caught and
given some extra work to do. And he approached the
last one—the Fayerweathers'—with his heart pounding
like a tired engine.

" You're back quickly," she said, giving him a smile
full of love. " Your supper isn't ready yet. I didn't think
you'd be back so soon."

" I hurried."

" Why ? "

" Why do you think ? "

" Hungry ? "

" Yes," said Miguel, taking her in his arms.
" Hungry ! "

She laughed while he tried to kiss her. " Sit down
there by the table. Can you peel potatoes ? "

" Of course I can peel potatoes."

" All right." She gave him three potatoes and a
paring knife. " Get to work, then."

He held her wrist and looked up into her eyes from
the chair. " I've never been so happy, Maria. I didn't
know anybody could be as happy as I am ! "

" Are you ? " She ran her fingers through his hair.
" I'm glad."

The silent Miguel was talkative; the shy Miguel was
bold. All through the preparations for their supper, all
through the meal, he kept the talk going gaily, for his
heart was singing and his spirit was on the wing. The
dishes were washed and put away, they went into the
Fayerweathers' living-room and lighted a fire, put out

all the lights and sat together on the sofa in the warmth and the glow. As the hour grew later, Miguel felt a return of his shyness; but Maria managed that, too.

Her room off the kitchen was cheerful and warm.

" Do you think they'd mind this—if they knew ? " Miguel was saying.

" No. Not if they knew. But pull down the shades— we don't have to tell anybody."

With a pounding heart Miguel obeyed. His pulses dashed spurts of flame. But most happy, he was un- afraid ! No sense of guilt, no fear—no reluctance !

" You go out now, Miguel," Maria said. " I'll call you when you can come in."

And Miguel left the room regretfully. In the kitchen he couldn't sit still, so he roamed over the house, listen- ing for her call. Then he heard it ! Oh, God !

She was lying in the bed, covered by a sheet. He stood beside her looking down, his face full of wonder, eager reverence. Then he knelt suddenly, as if his knees had given way, and pressed his lips against her breast, feeling her warmth through the sheet. She saw the worship in his eyes, and had no misgivings. " Did you put out the lights in there ? "

" Yes. Maria ! How beautiful you are ! "

Quite naturally, without too much shame, he took off his clothes and stood again looking down at her.

" You're strong, Miguel—I thought you would be. Come. . . ."

VII

First DAYS REMAINED of the week before Christmas. Except for his work, Miguel was never parted from Maria. The intense proud manhood which he had found banished his doubts about himself; his happiness in Maria ended his longing to be happy in Miguel. He walked in confidence, laughed and smiled; he looked back over the road he had travelled, the saturnine mode he had cast off, with contempt and wonder. He felt new strength in his bones, the stature of a man. And his worship of the woman who had worked the change was boundless and mystical, for she was everything to him; mother, beloved, companion—even divinity. When he felt impelled to pray and give thanks to God, it seemed logical to pray to her, who contained God; he laid himself body and soul before the altar of Maria, with utter sacrifice.

He laughed at his old attempts to love; and when he thought of Lucinda, he couldn't hold her image in his mind—it evaporated, like a cloud consumed by the sun. Maria included and surpassed all other women. Lucinda was in her, that attribute which went to Mass with him on Sundays and lost itself in the ritual; all the girls he had touched with Merijildo were in her, absorbed in her gaiety and passion. All that he loved in the past was contained in her, even pine trees and mountains, even the shimmering immensity of the coloured desert.

He gave no thought to the reality of these feelings; his only purpose was to continue them. He revelled in his right to be with her always, rejoiced in the rightness of being beside her when she went shopping in the town, or calling on some friends whom she revealed now, hospitable Mexican people living in their own houses lovingly made of adobe bricks with their own hands, as in Hormiga. Here at last was the feeling of belonging, too long a stranger to him; this completed such happiness that he didn't see how life could continue, now that he had reached its pinnacle.

Everywhere they went they encountered preparations for Christmas which stirred what remained of the boy in him, made him think of home. Even more it made him think of buying a present for Maria. But what could a mortal buy to please a goddess? She had nothing and everything. He did buy her a silver bracelet, however, with a part of the money he had saved for his mother's present, and although it wasn't much, he knew that she would adore it. And it would be beautiful on Maria's wrist; the turquoise would be like a prisoned piece of the sky against her luminous skin !

On the day when they were to come for him from Hormiga, he gave it to her. " I've got to go in a little while," he said to her with the whole world's sorrow in his voice.

" But you mustn't be so sad, Miguel—it's only for a little while."

" Three days," he moaned, for it seemed like years.

" Well, what's three days ? It's nothing."

" I brought you this—for Christmas." He handed

her the bracelet in a white box, and he was overcome by a sudden bashfulness.

"What is it?" She straightened and looked at him with shining eyes; he had been following her around as she worked with a dust-mop in the living-room. Now she took the box from him and opened it, saying, "But you shouldn't spend your money on me—— Oh! Miguel, how pretty it is! See how nice it looks!" She held out her arm with the bracelet on it. "Thank you, Miguel—my beloved!"

To hear her use that endearing word made his head dizzy with love of her. He kissed her, and then said, "I wish I could buy you more. I want to buy you everything in the world."

She laughed. "But I don't want everything in the world. I only want a few things—and I've got most of them now."

They kissed again.

"I've got to go now," he said, choking over it. "They're coming for me at eleven."

"But they haven't come yet——"

"Oh, they're not coming here. They'll be at the school. They don't know about—us."

"No," she said. "Will you tell them?"

"I don't know. Should I?"

"No. Let's keep it a secret!"

"All right. It's nicer that way, isn't it?" He sighed bitterly. "Oh, I don't want to go. I don't want to leave you, Maria!" His eyes brightened. "I wanted to go to Midnight Mass with you to-night. It's Christmas Eve."

"I'll go alone, Miguel. And I'll pray for you."

Oм

" Will you? I'll go in Hormiga—and I'll pray for you, too."

" It'll be—almost like being together, Miguel."

" Almost." He had to turn away from her then, overwhelmed by this parting; his throat closed, and the pain of it filled his whole body, dimmed his eyes. And then he rebelled. He began to rage up and down, words falling from his lips crazily, hands, arms waving. " I'm not going ! Why should I leave you just because they want me up there for Christmas—just because my mother thinks I ought to come home ? It's no good, anyhow, going up there for three days—I'd just have to come right back again, and she'll feel worse about it than if I didn't go at all ! I'm not going ! I'm not going ! I won't go ! I'll go down to the school and tell him I can't come—then we can go to Mass together " —he stopped and looked at the clock. It was just eleven. " He'll be there now—waiting," he said in a strange hush.

Maria, calm, touched his arm gently. " No, you must go, Miguel. She's expecting you. You can't disappoint her. She's your mother—now go on, Miguel." She turned him around and gave a weak push towards the door while her eyes filled with tears. " Don't act like a baby." He leaned against the slight pressure of her hands, as if her touch alone was happiness. At the door he turned and took her in his arms, closed her lips with his kiss.

" All right, my darling, I'll go."

The sight of his father's truck, waiting beside the school, brought no joy to his heart—it remained cold

and heavy as a stone even when Eliseo, in one of his
rare onsets of such emotion, put his arms around Miguel
and touched his cheek to his, lightly. " You're looking
pretty good, boy. Feel all right ? "

" Yes, I feel all right. Wait a minute. I've got some
things inside to take up. Have you been here long ? "

" No. Five minutes."

" I'll be right down."

They started as soon as he returned, carrying his
bundle. He had nothing to say to his father, and his
thoughts refused to accompany the wheezing old truck
in its flight. But Eliseo asked so many questions that
Miguel was kept constantly answering them and
dragged into the bitter present, out of the nostalgic
past.

He sat half-turned about in the truck, watching the
road shooting out behind like water out of a pipe,
and he saw again how the snow lay on the north slopes
of the hills which in winter were robbed of the sun.
Looking ahead, he saw the south slopes clear of snow
and shining with a summer brightness. In front of him
it was summer—behind him, winter. He smiled. It
was the other way around, in fact. For once nature
was not in accord with him. Nothing was in accord
with him. He was rushing away from everything he
wanted, all that life contained for him. His heart sank,
grew heavier, with every mile. As they dropped down
into the low country along the Rio Grande the heat
became apparent and the brilliance of the land, reflecting the sun from pink-yellow surfaces, hurt his eyes.
The contrasts of deep shadows, in themselves a relief
from the glare, made the glitter no easier to behold.

It was good, however, to see the familiar land again, for this was what he used to see from the roof-tops of Hormiga, and from any unobstructed point along its shelf. It brought him such a flood of memories that for a time Maria was crowded out of his thoughts.

But the cloudless sky was the colour of the bit of turquoise in the bracelet he had given her, and that was enough, thus the whole world sang of Maria. . . .

On the long, twisted climb to Hormiga's *mesa* they had to stop often to let the truck cool; and as they mounted the flanks of the mountains, winter closed in on them, the land darkened and the sun's heat diminished. First they ascended the wide arm of a tributary valley, walled near its beginning by cathedral cliffs, pink in the sunlight, where Borregos was hidden in the creases; from there, they rose into a clutter of *piñon*-stippled hills—the same as the trees which dotted the slopes around Gabaldon, where his love was born. And at last, with a great throbbing of the motor, they emerged on the plateau, the final elevation, where Hormiga perched in wintry, beautiful isolation.

It took his breath away. Deep in snow, the mountains smiled down upon the town, their white brows shining. Perhaps because they were dark in summer they seemed less friendly then than now, in all their austere frigidity. For even the pines which covered their sides were whitened as if a giant had breathed a frosty vapour over them.

Miguel and his father bounced along the rocky road to the truck's medley of complaint; they passed, one after another, the adobe houses strung along one side of the way. Then came the *morada*, and the past enveloped Miguel when he saw it, jealously closed out everything and reminded him by constricting his heart that Hormiga had dominion over all who lived there. The *morada* was only a short distance from the house—in another moment the truck drew up to the gate, and Concepcion, hearing its expiring clatter, rushed into the yard, throwing a shawl over her shoulders as she came.

He had almost forgotten the grateful comfort of being smothered against her bosom, though now he was too tall for it—so she took his head in her hands and pressed it against her heart, as if he were still a boy. They were all there to meet him, Pablo, Benito, even Rosa, big with a new child. He didn't think they all loved him enough to come to his home-coming, but it seemed that they did; and it became evident soon that they were all in awe of him, too. They expected him to show signs of his learning at once, studied him covertly, as if it might show in his face or his hands or in some new thing about him. He began to feel uncomfortable under their examination.

Finally Rosa said, " He don't look any different "— and stopped there, expecting to be contradicted.

" No," said Eliseo, " he's just the same, aren't you, Miguel ? "

" I think so. I don't feel any different "—and he glanced at his mother to see if she detected the lie.

" He looks older," she said, squinting at him.

" Well, he *is* older," Benito laughed.

" But not as much older as he looks——"

Miguel winced, fearful that she might pursue the objection; but she let it go for now. How sharp she was ! In a little while she'd know everything, without his telling her.

" How do you like the school? " This was Pablo, always challenging.

" Oh, I like it all right. How do you like your job on the road ? "

Pablo shrugged. " Got to do something."

" Are they building the road ? I didn't see any of it, coming up."

" Sure they're building it. The new one's a mile north of the old one. It won't be up this far until spring."

" What are you doing ? What's your job ? "

" I'm working a Fresno," said Pablo in a voice which was meant to be natural, but showed pride.

Miguel felt that he should know what a Fresno was, so he didn't ask. He nodded understandingly. " Will they work all winter ? "

" They will if they can— if there isn't too much snow. We've been laid off only a week all winter, so far."

" That's pretty good."

" Snow melts fast down below," Eliseo put in, eager to share some of the talk. The mother looked on silently. " We've had lots of snow up here, but we've had some warm days, too. Snow's mostly gone on the level."

" It looks like a good snow on the mountains," Miguel said. " That's a good thing for next summer."

" You bet. That means water in the ditches."

One by one they left the conversation. Rosa, Benito, Pablo retired, and just sat staring heavily at Miguel. Concepcion, who had said little, was still squinting at him, and Eliseo was beginning to falter. In a moment

the silence was complete. Nobody could think of anything more to say, and Miguel, nervous, thought this
might be the moment to chide Pablo about the girl
who had known him at the camp. But he didn't know
her name—it was stupid of him not to know her name,
and the thing would fall flat without it.

"Well," Concepcion stood up, "maybe the rest of
you have got nothing to do, but I have. Lunch is
almost ready. Will you stay, Benito—Rosa?"

"No, thanks. We got to go now, too." Rosa turned
to Miguel. "It's good to see you again, Miguel. Will
you stay long?"

"No. I'm afraid I've got to go back the day after
Christmas."

"Oh, so soon? It's too bad."

Those who were going shook hands and departed.
Miguel noticed how Benito's handsome face was
beginning to droop at the jowls; and Rosa—what a
sight Rosa was! Not a sign of a figure. The image of his
fine, slender, strong Maria intruded as he watched
Rosa waddle to the door. *Por Dios!*

The household slipped into its accustomed way.
Eliseo, with nothing to do, found something to do;
Pablo went out presently on unannounced business.
And Miguel sat down and tried to recover the feeling
of home. After a moment he wandered into the kitchen.
How dingy it was, after the white, sparkling kitchen
where Maria worked. A bitter gall oppressed his
spirits as he looked around the house. No progress—
three hundred years the same. The cold discomfort of
the out-house, after three months of miraculous bath-
rooms; the room where he was sitting—was it as nice

as the Fayerweathers' living-room? It was hard to make a comparison, for it was home. The religious prints, gaudily framed, which hung on the walls seemed now for the first time a little too gaudy—yet they flashed their colours and told their stories in a language they could all understand. He still liked them, he decided. The oil paintings in the Fayerweathers' house seemed flat and dull in comparison; he had to work to like them. Here, too, the furniture was familiar, used; there it was cold, placed, immovable. Oh, but there was Maria!

In the afternoon he helped set up the little stacks of wood which would be bonfires at twilight. Nearly every householder in Hormiga did the same, so that the village was aglow with red spots of fire on Christmas Eve, in the door-yards and sometimes at the corners of the earthen roofs. In the churchyard, bigger fires were kindled. Miguel had warm memories of the way the whole front of the building glimmered in their light. It was a waste of wood, perhaps, but it was a custom and a rivalry to see which house had the best and most fires. The Romeros usually won the contest, but they were counted out beforehand because they were rich.

Candles were set in the windows and lighted as soon as the sun set—and Concepcion decided at the last minute that she wanted a tree to put in the parlour, so the men went back to where the timber began and cut a small spruce for her. This was pleasure for Miguel, and helped him to get into the spirit of his home, but all the while, in his heart, was an undiminishing ache for Maria. She should be here to share with him the joy of being loved, and of having this place, these things, to love. Visioning her loneliness in Gabaldon, her solitary march at Midnight Mass and back again to the deserted house, filled him with an agony of longing and tarnished his joy. He called himself a coward for not leaving Hormiga now, and dashing back to her side.

When all the work was done he went into the kitchen and sat on his old chair beside the stove. The place was warm, and full of fragrances. His poor contesting heart was soothed by the sight of his mother, busy over her endless tasks, and the balm of her presence. It was plain that she was happy to see him there. This was a comfort.

" What's a Fresno ? " he said, after a long time of watching her in silence.

" A Fresno ? It's the thing Pablo says he's working on the road."

" I know, but what is it ? "

" I thought it was some kind of a scoop, you know ? Pulled by horses. Something they use to scoop up dirt."

" Oh, yes—one of those things. I've seen them."

Maria was more like his mother—the same competence, not bossy, but sure, certain. And Concepcion said, " You know, Miguel, I'm afraid for Pablo and this road."

" Afraid ? Why ? What do you mean ? "

" Well, there's some bad men in this town, you know."

" Yes." He thought there were always good and bad.

" And down at Borregos, too," she said.

" You mean the Chacon boys ? Yes, they're bad ones, all right."

" And there's a lot of talk here—and down there, too

—about stopping this road. The people don't really want it, and it's got to go through some houses between here and Borregos, the way they've laid it out. I'm afraid there's going to be trouble."

" Do you think so ? What's that got to do with the Chacon boys—and Pablo ? "

" Well, don't you see ? The people will try to fight the road, and those boys won't wait for the law. They'll start shooting. They stole some dynamite from the road people last week."

" How do you know it was them ? "

" Oh, everybody knows who it was—except the road people. Those things get out. They're all *Penitentes*, you know, and they won't tell on each other—the Chacon boys and—the others, I mean."

" Are they ? " said Miguel, beginning to understand. This obviously included Pablo.

" And Pablo's working for the road—and I'm afraid for what he'll do. You know how he is—he gets mad quick, and goes crazy over nothing."

" Do you think Pablo had anything to do with— stealing the dynamite ? "

Concepcion flared like a rocket. " Of course he didn't ! Who said so ? "

" Nobody," Miguel replied quietly. " I was only asking."

" Well, he didn't. And anybody who says he did is lying ! "

This denial was too violent. Sometimes, Miguel thought, his mother was sharper than necessary. . . .

" But they've got a detective in town asking questions," she added fearfully.

" Have you seen him ? "

" Yes. He was in the house yesterday and talked to your father for almost two hours."

" What did he think about it ? "

" Who ? "

" My father."

" Oh, he doesn't say much about it. He's trying to help the detective."

Miguel understood her implication, knowing his father; in his simplicity, Eliseo might easily blunder into a betrayal. He felt a pang of pity for his mother, in her dread, and he wanted to say something to ease her mind. It was a ticklish matter, though. He said, " Why are they building the road, anyhow ? Who asked for it ? "

" I don't know. I suppose Vicente Romero had something to do with it. I've heard him say that a new road to Hormiga would bring more people here, and be good for the stores. He means his store, of course. I think the one we have is plenty good enough."

" Yes, I do, too." Miguel was silent for a time. " Well," he remarked at last, " if Pablo has any sense he'll stay out of fights."

" He won't, though. Did you ever see him stay out of a fight ? " She put the matter aside with a sigh. " Tell me something about the school. Do you like it ? Are you learning lots of things ? "

" I like it all right. I guess I'm learning some-thing——" He had to smile at the double meaning; it must have been a guilty smile, for she caught it immediately.

" Why do you smile that way ? "

Fairly trapped, he stammered, " Well, it seems—it's funny to be here after—it's so different from——"

" Is it so different? What do you do all the time? Have you seen anything of Lucinda? "

" I've seen her twice—I don't have much time for it. You see, I work in the dining-room, and afterwards in the kitchen. And then I have three furnaces to look after, and if there's any other work they want me to do, I have to do that, too." He talked fast, nervously, for she was on the scent.

" Who wants you to do work? "

" The people I work for—the people whose furnaces I keep."

" Who are they? "

" Oh, they're all Americans—rich people who live in Gabaldon."

" What are they like? Are they nice to you? "

" They're all right. I like the Fayerweathers the best. They're rich, too, but they're very nice. They don't show it off the way some of them do. They're Catholics."

" Hmm. What do they teach you at the school? "

" Well, I'm studying English and Latin and history and arithmetic. After Christmas I'll start algebra."

" What's that—algebra? "

" It's like arithmetic, only there's letters in it, too, besides numbers."

She rattled a stove-lid impatiently. " What good is it? "

" I don't know." Thinking, he couldn't find an answer to this one. He saw that she was not satisfied with what he was studying, and he didn't feel especially

satisfied himself, now that he looked back on it. There
was no concrete addition to his equipment, nothing
useful, like learning how to shoe a horse or mend a
broken wagon. She expected him to wield his Latin
and his algebra like a hammer and pick-axe—or
weapons to confound his enemies.

" Will it help you to make speeches ? " she asked
ambiguously.

" Make speeches ? " said Miguel. " I don't think it
will. But I'm not going to make any speeches."

" You might." She crammed a piece of wood into
the stove. " Vicente Romero does."

He laughed shortly, but she ignored it. " I thought
maybe you'd be learning something useful," she told
him. " " Like how to keep books and things."

" Oh, that comes into it. We've been studying
those things."

" Have you ? " she beamed, relieved at last. " That's
good. I hope you study hard."

" I do. I have to."

" They make you ? "

" They'll put me out if I don't."

" Put you out ? " She was stern again. " They can't
put you out. You pay them to teach you, don't you ?
How can they put you out ? "

" I'm not paying them as much as most of the boys."

She was displeased, and pricked in her pride, but
she said no more about it.

" Is Lucinda here ? " Miguel asked after a time.

" Yes, she came home a week ago."

" That's funny. She told me they were all going to
Gabaldon for Christmas."

Concepcion scoffed knowingly. "That was just talk."

"That school she goes to—it's like a convent. They never let the girls out."

Concepcion smiled. "So you don't see much of her. You've forgotten Lucinda, no?"

"No," Miguel protested weakly. "Not exactly."

"No? What, then? It's somebody else, no?"

Miguel's hesitation was signal enough for Concepcion, who began to laugh; he acted like an embarrassed child, losing an easy battle with his desire to keep it all a secret. When she said, "I thought that was it, all the time," and laughed louder, he hung his head and laughed with her.

It was, after all, a joy to share it with her. When they were alone together after that he talked of nothing but Maria; and his mother was faithful, keeping the news from the others, knowing that Pablo could make him miserable if he knew.

Miguel and his mother walked together up the moon-lit street in the night, on their way to Mass, and talked about Maria. The mother was gay and sorrowful by turns, glad of his happiness, sad for her loss. She warned him not to be distracted too much from his work, and not to tell the girl he loved her. For she might believe him, she said, and get him into all kinds of trouble. He didn't want to be burdened with a wife, did he, right at the start of his manhood?

Miguel made no reply to these warnings. He was thinking, recalling, how he had taken marriage with Maria for granted, when the time came for it, remembering that it had never been mentioned between them.

She had never mentioned it. Perhaps she didn't want to marry him—but she must have taken it for granted too. How else could she give herself to him? As he walked to the church, thoughts of Maria became confused and mingled with thoughts of piety. Father Aloysius, his old confessor, would be there; to-morrow he would find an opportunity to put it all up to him, and get it straightened out.

The Mass was a long remembering. Maria was in a church, too, praying, and thinking of him. It brought them together marvellously—it was almost like being with her. He could imagine that his mother, kneeling on the opposite side of the bare, benchless church, was Maria, and his heart pulled towards her. He gave himself utterly to the service, rejoicing meanwhile that separation from Maria brought no forgetfulness, no diminishing of his love and longing for her, but only increased them and gilded the shining of her virtues. The Mass was a long praying and giving thanks.

Christmas Day brought brightness, warmth, and a feeling of festival in which the world was one. There was some drunkenness in Hormiga because a few could never dissociate liquor from any festival. Pablo was among them, and when Pablo was drunk he was a hateful, pugnacious fool. For the most part they banded together and formed a noisy, contentious group on the south side of the *plaza* where the sun was warm against adobe walls. Most people had sense enough to leave them alone and to hope that the day would pass

without any knife-work or other blood-letting, realising
in their doubting hearts that it was almost too much
to hope for. The Lopez family, gathering for dining
upon Eliseo's wild turkey, tried to rise above their
disappointment and apprehension—but the gaping
vacancy of Pablo's chair was too much for them. The
dinner passed, shadowed over by a tense air of listening
and expectancy.

By four in the afternoon the suspense was over, and
Pablo was safe in his bed, dragged there by Miguel and
his father, himself slightly tipsy, but able to stand.
From the porch where they were sitting in the still,
warm afternoon sun they saw Pablo go down under a
pile of yelling, thrashing young men. They ran over
there, and seizing their opportunity, hauled him out
and home with little consciousness left in him, and a
bloody nose.

Miguel noticed how, even in this tough and rowdy
company, Eliseo was not without some authority, and
until he realised that they were all *Penitentes* he wondered why. They didn't stop to learn the cause of the
fight, but yanked Pablo out of it before he got hurt;
and it was well they did, for two of the boys finally
resorted to knives, and carved each other in the usual
thorough manner.

Within a few minutes the incident was on everybody's
lips, spreading through the town like a conflagration.
The savagery of it was nothing new; when these boys
fought there was generally a bloody sequel, but this
time someone was really hurt. They said his name was
Martinez, but Miguel didn't know him, and thought
little of it.

To lie through the night, however, beside a reeking, groaning Pablo was an unpleasant conclusion to his Christmas visit. When it was time to leave in the morning, Pablo was still asleep, and Miguel's vividest memory was his talk with Father Aloysius, who had told him that of course he would have to marry Maria now—there was nothing else for him to do. He had said that Miguel had sinned, also, but this he could scarcely believe, for he felt no guilt—no guilt at all.

Concepcion had little to say. It was plain that she was ashamed and grieved over Pablo's behaviour. And then at the last moment, when all the farewells were said, a man came running to Eliseo and begged him to take the wounded boy down to Santa Rosa to the hospital there. It was on the way; Eliseo couldn't refuse. It was the boy's father who asked it. And so with that gory load they started, and lurched over the bumps, down the hills to Borregos, down the long valley to Santa Rosa. By looking through the back window of the truck's cab, Miguel could see the boy's face. It looked like death. It fascinated him. He thought the boy would surely be dead by the time they reached the hospital. Every lunge brought agony to his face. He had five slashes in him, the father said, whose expression was of dumb, sad-eyed anxiety.

" He didn't do anything," the father complained in a hollow voice. " It was the other boy started it."

" Did they do anything to the other boy ? " Miguel asked.

" *Si, si*, that detective, he come and took him away to Gabaldon."

Shivering to think of it, Miguel realised that it might
PM

have been Pablo who had been taken away in the detective's car—or sliced to pieces like this boy here. " Who was the other boy ? "

" His name's Chacon—from Borregos."

So this was the company Pablo was keeping.

" I hope they put him in the prison," the man said, hate giving substance to his voice.

" I hope they do," Miguel agreed.

" I'm afraid they won't, though. He'll say my boy started it. He'll get witnesses to say so, too—and then they'll let him go."

" Oh, I don't think so," said Miguel without conviction, for he knew the poor man was probably right.

A great dejection enveloped Miguel after that, and he could say no more to the man, had to leave him to his solitary, crushed grief. For Miguel was not pleased with his holiday. Comparisons had been forced upon him, contrasts to which his eyes had been closed before were now crowding in upon him. Pablo, this boy—the brutality of the death which stared him in the face— the white light, the blue shadows—violence, hatred— his relief in flight from it—his mother—love—Maria.

Was there meaning in it anywhere ? Was it only Maria drawing him back to Gabaldon ? Or was he glad to get away from Hormiga because of what he had seen there. He was crushed under the weight of all that had happened, imprisoned under the burden of it. He couldn't see beyond. Where did he stand ? Had Hormiga spoiled him for Gabaldon ? Or had the school, Maria, Merijildo spoiled him for Hormiga ? Was he never to belong anywhere again ?

Questions, questions ! Instead of giving him the

means to answer them, the school had only raised a crop of new ones ! When at last they topped the final ridge which the down-thrusting arms of the mountains put across their path, and swooped into Gabaldon, Miguel was sure of only one thing—that he wanted desperately to see Maria again. She could help him with all his questions, or make him forget their existence. The memory of the wounded boy lingered, and he wanted to forget that, too; the father's dumb supplication, the shaking of heads. . . .

Eliseo left him at the school, solemnly. " Bad luck, wasn't it ? " Eliseo said.

" Will he die, do you think ? "

Eliseo nodded. " Sure. He's awful sick boy." Then he tried to shake himself free of it. " Well, come and see us again when you can. Next time maybe we'll have no fights."

" Maybe I can come at Easter," Miguel told him, trying to be cheerful. " *Adios.*"

" *Adios*, Miguel."

With nothing but coldness on his heart Miguel watched his father turn the truck about and drive away. Slowly he entered the school, and quickly, before he even reached his room, he felt the new life enclose him. Leaving his bundle of clothes in his room, he hurried to register his arrival with the Brother in charge, and went out again, sprinting up the street to the Fayerweathers' house, and a wild excitement took the place of his gloom

Did she still love him ? Had no one else taken her from him ? His breath was almost gone and his heart-beats cracked against his ribs, but he ran on. At the turn, where he took a side street, he had to sit down. It wouldn't do to appear so breathless that he couldn't speak to her ! He was dizzy from exhaustion, and it was cold; the sweat he had raised dried under his clothes and his flesh pricked like tiny stabs of icicles. He shivered. It might snow again to-night—more work to-morrow, shovelling it from entrances, roofs. Even here in Gabaldon they had to shovel it from their roofs. Standing water on a flat roof was likely to freeze and crack the surface. Well, more work meant more money.

He stood up as soon as he could and walked for a while, then increased it to a trot; and when he turned the last corner he got a full view of the house. It was still there—the same. What change he had expected he didn't know, but he felt immeasurable relief to see it safe and standing, as if it might have vanished in his absence, and Maria with it. He had to break into a run again, although it was uphill. He noticed in passing that some of the trees wanted watering—they all looked scrawny in their winter skeletons. At last, the door. She answered his knock, and when she stood there before his eyes he couldn't speak; he could only watch her expression change from cold inquiry to the joy he had been anticipating for three days.

Enclosed in her arms, he kicked the door shut behind him with a groping foot.

For a time after he returned, and the school re-convened for the winter term, Merijildo regarded his room-mate with wonder and some admiration. He didn't know—and Miguel was not telling (it was much too sacred to be told)—what event had produced the change in the shy mountain lad he had parted from when he went away. Moody silences, restlessness, discontent were ended now; Miguel went about his business and his studies with an air of confidence, his head held high.

But it was his complete disinterest in Merijildo's night work which finally gave him away. Furthermore, Merijildo had the tact to leave Miguel alone when the cause of his new aloofness came out. Perhaps this was because the low-country boy sensed love in the air, and was bound unwittingly to respect it; in any case, he envied Miguel's fortune in finding a peaceful anchorage for his passions. The terms of their relation thus were reversed, and it did them both good.

The end of the holidays brought no comfort to Miguel, however. It meant staying in his room at night, returning to the routine of which bells were the measure. But the Fayerweathers were still away. When he was in the house, he and Maria had the run of it, and this made the days tolerable.

Even this pleasure was soon to go. The Fayerweathers came home, Miguel's time with Maria was more restricted then ever. They had to be careful because her employers suspected nothing and neither Miguel nor Maria wanted them to.

As the material bond—the symbol of a happiness beyond words—she wore his bracelet always. But she saw, since his return from Hormiga, a taint upon this happiness, and her insight was not long in finding the cause of it.

" Never mind, Miguel," she told him. " It's hard, going back to Hormiga after this. But only for a little while."

He shook his head. " I was glad to come away. I never had that feeling before. Maybe it was because I wanted to come back to you."

She sat down beside him and put her hands over his. " You'll always want to go back there, Miguel," she said, looking deeply into his eyes. " But you've got to have land of your own, before you'll really be happy. You're like that. You can't work for other people." She sighed, looking away from him. " You'll always be a *Penitente*. You'll go back to your bright mountain."

" Not without you, Maria."

" Yes. No matter what you do—where you are—or who you marry—you'll always want to go back. You may not believe it, but you will."

Miguel felt a great terror grip him. Maria went on, not noticing his face. " You'll never like Americans, either. You'll never be like them." Then she looked at him again. " With land of your own—— Why, what's the matter, Miguel ? "

He was staring at her intently. " No matter who I marry, you said. Do you mean——? We're going to be married—some day—aren't we ? "

Maria turned her face away from him, but he could tell by the droop of her shoulders that she was suffering. When she turned to him again her eyes were filled with tears. " Oh, Miguel—I knew this would happen—sooner or later." She shook her head, biting her lip and fighting back her tears. " I can't marry you, Miguel. You can't marry me."

Miguel's heart seemed to stop altogether. For a wild moment he thought it would never begin again. " I can't marry you ? " he repeated incredulously. " But Maria—we *must* be married now. I'll never marry anybody but you ! " He was on his feet, holding her arms above the elbows.

She only shook her head sadly.

And Miguel's eyes hardened—he let her arms go, and took a step back. " You've been fooling me, then ? You don't love me ? "

She had to smile through her sorrow. " No, that isn't it, Miguel. I told you—long ago—that I was married before, and——"

" But I thought you meant you weren't married any more ! "

" I'll always be married, Miguel, even though he was an American—and left me two days afterward."

Then he lost his head. He raved and ranted about the kitchen until she had to remind him that the Fayerweathers were in the house; and finally she had to go up to him and put her hand over his mouth gently. " I meant that I was free to love you, Miguel. Don't you understand ? "

" No, no, no ! If you're free to love me, why aren't you free to marry me ? It's only right——"

Once more she stopped him. " It may be right, but it isn't true," she said quietly. " We'll talk about it some other time. Look at the clock, how late it is, and I've got all my work to do." She kissed him. " Don't be like this, Miguel. Don't worry. It'll be all right."

Wonderful, the balm of her sweet voice ! Who else

could calm a lad in the heat of his blood? He went away composed, but bitterly sad, a blight upon his paradise. He didn't go back to see Maria for the usual hour after his work was done at the school, but moped in his room and made the air heavy with his glooming. Of course Merijildo noticed it, and laid it to a lovers' quarrel, said nothing. But when days passed with little clearing of the atmosphere and Miguel hung to his mood of sullen, silent despondency, Merijildo, weary of it, said, " What's the matter with you, anyway? "

" Nothing."

Merijildo coaxed it out of him at last, and when he had heard the story, he laughed. It flung Miguel into a rage and made him regret having spoken at all to his room-mate. Merijildo, still good-natured, called him a damn fool.

" Do you think a woman's got to marry you," he said, " just because you sleep with her? You ought to be thankful for what you've got. If she can't marry you, she can't. What of it? You'd better get back up there and tell her you're sorry for being a fool, or you *will* lose her. She's not going to do much waiting around for you, my little friend."

Hateful as it was, it was good advice, and the push Miguel needed. He sat up under the lashing and blinked at Merijildo.

" I thought you'd grown up a little, but I see you haven't. I'm ashamed of you, Miguel! " He made a threatening movement towards him. " Go up there right now." He hauled Miguel bodily out of his chair. " Come on, get your coat and get up there, right now! "

Miguel balked at this point. " But why did she—why did she—do it, then ? "

" Because she probably likes you—God knows why ! "

Miguel stared at him for a moment, and then deliberately obeyed. He put on the leather jacket which he had bought near the beginning of the fall term and upon which, like every other student in the school, he had inked the college initials across the shoulders. As he passed sluggishly through the door, Merijildo gave him a push and slammed the door after him. With a grin he sat down, shaking his head from side to side. " *Pobrecito,*" he muttered. " Poor little fellow."

And Miguel, still reluctant, pushed his hands into his pockets and walked in a cloud of misgivings. Maybe he could persuade her to marry him, after all. Maybe she didn't want to marry him.

As he approached the Fayerweathers' house his pace increased; he wouldn't slip in and out of the basement as he had done for a week, without seeing Maria. No, the coldness was lifting from his heart. The old warmth of expectation, which he feared had gone for ever, was returning. He began to run.

Maria wasn't in the kitchen when he went in, but he knew she was in the house because pots were sizzling on the stove. He waited for her to appear, standing in the middle of the room with his hat in his hand. When he heard her coming, he hid himself behind the door; she jumped when he said, " Hello, Maria ! "

" Oh, it's you is it ? " she said coolly, giving him

a shivering stare. "Where have you been? Did you think I didn't see you sneaking into the basement to fix the furnace? Well, I don't care whether you come upstairs or not." She turned her back on him.

Miguel, discouraged, wanted to retreat—but he remembered Merijildo's warning. "I—I'm sorry, Maria. I guess I've been a fool. I wanted you to marry me. I thought, if you loved me, you could—divorce your husband, if—if that's what's the matter."

She looked at him again, and he melted like wax before a flame. Tenderness was driving the wrath out of her eyes. "Is that what's the matter?" She gave a small laugh. "Has it all been about that, Miguel?" She dropped her offended manner altogether now and came up to him. "*Pobrecito.* I'm sorry. But I told you to come back and we'd talk about it. You never did. Why didn't you?"

"I don't know," he admitted. "I thought I knew what you meant. I thought we'd be married, and——" He heaved a resigned sigh. "I guess I don't know very much about you, Maria."

She was laughing with her eyes. "But, Miguel, even if I could marry you——" She stopped, baffled by his look of unbelief. "You can't marry everybody you love," she said, lamely searching for words. "Don't you see? You don't *want* to marry everybody you love. Why," she laughed outright, "you'd be getting married all the time, and you can't do that. They don't let you have but one at a time!"

"But, you don't want more than one at a time— do you?"

" Oh, Miguel," she pleaded with him in exasperation, " don't you understand ? There's no such thing
as divorce in our Church. I liked you, and—we needed
to know each other better, and—and what we did was
—the only way we could do. Don't you see ? That's
all there is to it."

" But I want you to marry me," he protested stub-
bornly. " I want you to be my wife. I love you, Maria.
I'll never love anybody as much—again."

" Oh, yes you will. You'll forget all about me when
you go home. Can't you just be satisfied the way things
are ? "

He looked down at his shoes. " I'll try," he said.

" That's a good boy. Now kiss me."

They kissed tenderly, and Miguel felt re-born. Later,
when he could speak through laughter instead of
sorrow, he said, " I didn't understand. We can go on
as we are. I'll be here all winter, and maybe in the
summer you can come up to Hormiga, or I can get
a job here in the city. Maybe in the end something will
happen so that we can be married."

It was her turn to be sad now. " Do you really love
me so much, Miguel ? "

" Yes, I do. More than anybody in the world, Maria.
I'd do anything—go anywhere—for you."

She tried to smile, but it was crooked; pressing her
face hard against his leather jacket, she whispered,
" Hold me tight, Miguel. Why do you love me that
way ? You don't know anything about me. I may not
be the kind you think I am—at all."

" Yes, you are. I know you better now. I'll learn the
rest some day." And he kissed her again.

Peace with Maria restored, life brightened for Miguel in the school. During the winter term, the former enthusiasm over football was transferred to basket-ball, a game with which Miguel was more familiar, for the little school in Hormiga had a bottomless basket rigged on a pole in the school-yard, into which the children tossed a ball, or their books, hats, rocks or anything that came to hand. And they used to scramble for the object when it fell through, and the first one to get it tried to drop it into the basket again.

The formal game as played in Gabaldon was far from this wild tangle of Hormiga, but the idea was similar, and Miguel was able to apprehend it. He applied for a position in the team, for his relation with Maria was a smooth flowing which left him undisturbed and able to take an interest in other things. He made a few new contacts with fellow students this way, but none of them succeeded in penetrating his strange, dignified reticence.

The months of January and February were given over to basket-ball. In time, Miguel was given a place in the second team. The only thing which kept him from a position in the first was his attitude—not a conscious one, but inevitable, for he played because he enjoyed playing, and while he was fresh enough to have a good time, he played well. When he got tired, he didn't want to play any more, stopped trying, did badly, fumbled, and infuriated his team-mates. It was the way he had always played any game, and it seemed only natural. Team spirit, *esprit de corps*, were hysterics which he could not appreciate. In one game he substituted for a boy who was hurt, and for fifteen or twenty minutes dazzled the spectators by his brilliance —and then, tiring, he stopped. Presently his captain snarled at him, " What's the matter with you ? Why don't you play like you were ? "

" I'm tired," Miguel answered simply, and in a minute he was on the side-lines, pulled out of the game in disgrace. He never altogether understood this, but it didn't trouble him. Even Merijildo's thumping lectures on the subject failed to impress him; team spirit was something for ever outside his experience. He was giving too much time to it as it was, for they called him up one day and told him that his studies were being neglected, advised him to drop basket-ball for a while, which he did without regret. He gave the time to books—and Maria.

The months of January and February were warm, also, and dry. At midday the sun felt hot as summer, but you could tell by stepping into the shade that summer was far off. The nights were crisply cold and the ground froze. Miguel took a small portion of his life from Maria and gave it to the school; he looked more like his mates now. His hair was more apt to be brushed, and in place of overalls he wore dark trousers; his hands and face were always clean. He brushed his teeth. On the surface he was transformed, but his heart, as Maria predicted, belonged steadfastly to the mountains.

Trees had to be watered in February. Miguel's work for his furnace people, as he called them, doubled; even Saturday afternoons had to be given over to irrigating. The Fayerweathers' fruit trees received his most tender

attentions, for reasons which were plain enough. Sometimes Maria came out to see him during the slow work,
and it was good to have her standing beside him. She
didn't do a great deal of talking, he noticed; it seemed,
in fact, that she was quieter than usual, as if she were
brooding over something, but no amount of urging
would make her reveal it. Perhaps he only imagined
it, anyway.

It made him wonder, this remoteness which was on
her, if she loved him, or if her love could be beginning
to cool—but then she would suddenly change and become passionately interested in him.

Sundays were their days together. They met after
lunch and walked out of town into the hills, climbed to
high places, and sat down with their faces turned to the
view; these were hours of unmingled happiness, for she
never allowed an argument or a quarrel to intrude.
She treated him, he thought from time to time, like
one who is ever on the point of parting: tenderly,
lovingly—sorrowfully. He felt it in all her moods, until
it began to disturb him deeply, but as nothing appeared
to give it substance, he put off mentioning it. Ever in
her voice, or in her eyes or in something about her,
this note of lingering departure became the one remaining mystery in Maria; he couldn't approach it, for
when he did, it vanished; it made for a tantalising
incompleteness, a hidden seepage of fulfilment.

On a day in Lent, which began early in March, the
captain of the basket-ball team came to Miguel and
told him that he had been chosen to accompany the
team on a trip as a substitute in a game with an
out-of-town school. Since it appeared to be more of a

command and an honour than a request, and since
the authorities approved, Miguel dared not refuse. He
went, was gone three days, and never got into the
game. When he came back, he hurried up to the Fayerweather house to tell Maria that he was through with
basket-ball for ever—and there was a new girl in the
kitchen.

" Where's Maria ? " he asked when he had caught
his breath.

" Who ? "

" Maria—the girl who works here."

" Oh, I guess you mean the girl who was here before
I came. I don't know. I guess she's gone. I just came
to-day. I don't know."

His heart bounded and then quieted quickly. Oh,
no. There was some mistake. He stood there staring at
the new girl. She was young, her black hair was bobbed
in imitation of a movie star, and the powder on her
cheeks turned them lavender. " Where is she ? " he
said again.

" I tell you, I don't know. Maybe you better see Mrs.
Fayerweather. Are you Miguel Lopez ? "

" Yes—that's my name."

" Well, she said for me to tell you to see her when you
came."

Miguel looked around him. Was he in the right
place ? Everything looked the same. There was the
door to Maria's bedroom—maybe she was in there. He
went over and opened the door, looked inside. Bare.
Deserted. And for the first time it occurred to him that
these terrific happenings might be true. Still, unbelief
was heavy on him. He thought he had never seen a

more uninviting, barren room. And this was where they had—they had——

Mother of God !

Dismay swept over him. He returned to the kitchen and frightened the girl there with the wild look on his face. " Where's Mrs. Fayerweather ? Where is she ? "

The girl stepped back from him—it looked like murder in his eyes—covered her mouth with the back of her hand, and pointed ineffectually with her other arm towards the living-room.

" She's gone," Miguel cried at the astonished girl. " Where's she gone ? Why did she go ? When did she go ? Did *they* send her away ? " He looked darkly angry. " Did they do it—the Fayerweathers ? "

Tears of fear were standing in the girl's eyes. " I don't know anything about it," she wailed. " See the *patrona*—see the *patrona* ! "

Without another word Miguel bolted through the door and into the other part of the house, where he met Mrs. Fayerweather, attracted by the commotion. Confronted by her, he snatched his hat from his head and struggled to recover himself. " Where's Maria ? " he said tensely. " Where has she gone ? "

" She's gone, Miguel." Mrs. Fayerweather was calm, her voice was softly soothing, for she saw his suffering. " She said she had to go—she gave no reason. We were sorry. We liked Maria. She left a letter for you—I'll get it."

While she was gone Miguel passed through every shade of torment. He took the letter from her when she came back with it, and left the house without trusting himself to speak again. With the note clutched in his hand he walked down the road to the concealment of an adobe wall, and there he opened it. " Miguel," it said. " Forgive me for leaving you like this. But I had to go, because I fell in love with you, too. You must forget me. I'm going far away, so don't try to come after me. You'll never find me. Maria."

The writing blurred before his eyes. He remembered how his mother had said to him once that boys were foolish to be ashamed of crying. Well, he was crying now ! Oh, if she could see him crying now ! Tears running down his cheeks ! Maria ! Maria ! He went deeper into the orchard behind the wall where no one could see him, and gave way completely to his anguish, holding the note crumpled in his fist. He pressed his face against the cold adobe bricks, wet them with his tears, clawed them with his fingers, blind, mad in his grief. Time and again the great surge of his sorrow rose to his throat, driving tears to his eyes like blood to a wound, ebbing and flowing.

Gradually he came to his senses. He opened his clenched fist and looked at the note in it, flung it fiercely away—in a moment, he had it in his hands again, smoothing it tenderly with his fingers. Maria ! Maria ! And his grief flooded back. Slowly the savage onsets of sorrow abated, leaving him coldly hollow, as if his guts had been cut out. Dry-eyed, he emerged from behind the wall with a numbness over his whole body. His fickle mind went back to a day in the mountains long ago when his father had pulled the entrails out of a chipmunk and nailed the pelt on a door to dry. He felt like that—like the skin of a man flattened against a door. He didn't even think of pursuit for a while, so

Q M

great was the weight of his misery, and when he did, a fateful voice within a voice told him it was useless.

She didn't want him to come after her. The terrible finality of it. She would see to it that he wouldn't find her if he were foolish enough to try. He had no taste for trying, no taste for anything, least of all for living. She was gone, that was all—gone. The flow of grief threatened to choke him again, and he set his jaw. He'd fight it this time. What was the good?

His muscles, like a trained dog, were taking him back to the school. He didn't want to go there, but he didn't want to go anywhere else, so he let them go. The future without Maria in this traitorous place opened bleak as day in a prison. He could feel its chill gripping his heart, for there was nothing in the school or in the life down here to fill the gap of her going away—nothing anywhere, for that matter. He saw himself moving through life with a great hole in his heart. Could a man live with a hole in his heart? Must he not die of it?

Tapiacito, near Socorro. Even if she did come from there, she had probably gone somewhere else. That would be too easy to find. Tapiacito, near Socorro. . . .

He was in his room, taken there by his feet as if he had been lifted and set down there. On a map of New Mexico, he found no Tapiacito near Socorro. There was a town by that name up in the wilderness of the Apache Indian country, where no Mexicans were likely to be. He put the map away sadly. She must have known, then, from the beginning, that it would end this way. With awful certainty he told himself that he would never know any more about Maria—never see her again. Like a shooting star, she had come into his life, revealing nothing of herself except a bright shining. Henceforth she would become a memory. He sat down, and took the first steps towards preserving it for cherishing.

Miguel tried bravely to forget Maria. Naturally, the first sharp suffering left him, but it left, also, a wound. Days advanced in a procession of dreariness which nothing could dispel. His whole happiness now was a remembrance of loving, and it was a poor thing. It dried up his enthusiasm and nothing had the power to rouse him to a state of real, zestful living. He worked hard, raised his marks, and became once more the serious, silent fellow he was before Maria. In every way left to him he retreated into the past, discontented, dissatisfied with what he was and what he might become.

For once Merijildo had nothing to say. He was awed by the depth of Miguel's suffering, unable to understand a love which went beneath the senses. He could only watch his room-mate sink into himself; he was ready to help, but powerless, and not enough of a cynic yet to belittle the value of experience.

The winds of March blew the surface off the town. They were dry, desiccating blasts which shrivelled the soul and robbed the land of its mellowness, turning the city into a skeleton which rattled in all its bones. Miguel knew then that he had reached the end of his endurance. He would never come back here again. When the spring recess came, two weeks before Easter, his mind was made up, although he had told nobody. They were coming down from Hormiga to get him as before, and he was ready, days ahead of time.

Finally, the night before, he told Merijildo. " I'm not coming back after Easter."

" Not coming back ? Why not ? "

" I don't like it. It's no good——"

" Oh, it's all because of that girl," Merijildo said. " You shouldn't do that, Miguel. You shouldn't let it get you like that. You ought to finish the year, anyway."

" No. I'm not coming back. There's no use. I'm not learning anything that will help me with what I've got to do—and what I've got to be."

" What have you got to do ? "

" Help my father with his farm, and "—he quoted Maria with fierce bitterness—" and be a *Penitente*."

" But you can't do that all your life ! You've got to get ahead—be somebody—make money."

" Why ? "

" Well, because that's what you go to school for. That's what——"

Miguel broke in with a mirthless laugh. " You don't know why," he said. " I don't, either. So I'm not going to try to, any more. I'm going home to do what I can up there. That's where I belong. I don't like the city. I don't like any of it. I hate it ! "

Merijildo knew he meant what he said. " Have you told them—here ? "

" Yes."

" What did they say ? "

" The same things you've been saying, that I was foolish to give up now—I ought to finish the year. But they couldn't tell me why, either. It doesn't make any difference—three more months." He shrugged.

Merijildo was unhappy. Somewhere was the right thing to say, the word which would make him see his mistake. He held his breath while he searched for it. But if the Brothers couldn't find it, how could he? Seeing the sardonic smile on Miguel's lips he was discouraged and gave up the quest. " Well, I suppose that's the end of it, then. I think you're wrong, though. You're making a big mistake."

" Maybe," Miguel sighed. " I only know I don't want any more of this. They're not my friends, any of them —except you. I'm sorry to leave you, Merijildo."

" I—I'm sorry you're going. I wish you wouldn't. The others—they just don't understand you. You're quiet—don't say much—and they don't know where they stand with you, so they leave you alone. I've got used to it, so I——"

" I know," Miguel stopped him. " You've been a good friend. Maybe some day I'll see you again. Anyway, I won't forget you."

Merijildo shuddered at his sober finality, and changed his tone. " Cheer up, Miguel. You look like a ghost."

Miguel smiled then. " I will. I'll be all right as soon as I get out of here."

Eliseo came for him next day. Miguel went with him gladly this time, his heart light with a feeling of release.

VIII

FROM WHEAT which had been buried in moist sand since the harvest, and has sprouted pale yellow shoots from the kernels, a penitential food was made every year in Hormiga for use during Lent and Holy Week. Concepcion was at work on a tub of this *panocha* when Miguel and Eliseo arrived from Gabaldon, and she was so absorbed in it that she didn't hear the truck. She was humming, too, perhaps because the making of *panocha* signalised the coming of spring, and made her feel good inside. The batch she was making was destined for the *morada*, to feed the *Penitentes* through the coming retreat, and this gave her a feeling of well-being, for the work was thus in a way sanctified. When Miguel came in and she dropped her ladle to fold him to her heart, it seemed to her that her fate was noble and sufficient. She held him off at arm's length to look him up and down, to gauge how time had dealt with him. She was arrested for a moment by his eyes which contained something that hadn't been there before. But the smile on his face distracted her, and he said, " Well, everything all right ? "

" I guess so," she said. " You're thin. You need some of this *panocha*."

" How is it this year ? " he asked, dipping a finger into the golden mass and tasting it. " H'm—good, very good."

" How long will you stay this time ? " she inquired, back at work.

" A week, maybe," Miguel lied. " I got another boy to do my work down there." This much was true.

This home-coming, he thought for a while, was good. For two days he felt only relief, none of the restlessness, impatience of the Christmas visit. He had wanted to come home this time, and now he wanted to stay home and submerge himself in the comfort which was Hormiga, to bathe in it like a man too long covered with filth and to be made whole again, But it was not as simple as that, he found.

When he had listlessly lived for two days, letting the old life flow back into him, resistlessly surfeiting himself with it, he discovered with a shock that this would not suffice. Here was no magic lifting of burdens as he had supposed. With a cry of anguish, almost, Maria came insistently back to him. She would not be forgotten and dismissed like this ! She intruded more and more, he saw her lurking in the deep shadows the sun made in the corners of adobe walls, and she lived in his heart doggedly. And it was not long before he was ashamed of trying to put her out and away from himself.

And then, again, this ancient place seemed right for him, and the future here an open road. On bright days when the sun was warm and the earth quick he felt good—but let the wind blow, or clouds hide the blue, and Maria spoke to him dolefully, sighing for him in the pines, in the chimneys, in the dark shadows. And he for her, in all his moods and in all places.

By working on the farm he managed to put away

these troublous ills. And he saw that Pablo was the wise one, and Benito, too—Benito, who looked like his mother and had her fine, straight nose and archless brows, was a solid member of the community whom no frenzied wishfulness disturbed. Pablo knew what he wanted. Just now he wanted to be a road-hand, operating a Fresno—what he would be to-morrow, no man knew, least of all, Pablo. He was seldom at home, and when he was he revealed nothing of his doings, nothing of his hopes and plans. He came home to fill his belly and rest his bones. His work was near at hand, convenient, so he came home when other men slept at the camp.

Like a small army they moved over the countryside by day, leaving a straight scar behind them in the land, gnawing their way forward with their machines like an earth-eating monster. They obeyed a remote will which commanded them to advance and stop for nothing. Pablo liked the work. He liked to look back and see the long, undeviating gash he had helped to make with his Fresno, and the straighter it was, the better he liked it. When nature put a hill in the way and forced a turning, he shared a sense of defeat and was spurred to new conquests. He felt akin to his exploring ancestors who had conquered the land in the beginning, a brave, small crew. There was glory in this, too, good pay, and a kindred ruthlessness.

None of it appealed to Miguel. To him it seemed like destruction, not building. He went down to watch sometimes, and every time they felled a tree—even a stumpy old juniper or *piñon*—he felt a hurt in his side and a kind of hate in his heart. It took a long time for a tree to grow. With their mighty machines they could destroy one in a moment, and this seemed a terrific thing.

It was hard for him to take an interest in anything that was going on about him, and when he did, he found himself opposing, always opposing. Oh, why could he never acquiesce ? The schooling in Gabaldon had made it worse, it seemed. Now everything except incorruptible mountains and trees vexed him. The house seemed empty, the drudgery of carrying water, of endlessly winding the well-rope, of dumping dishwater filthily in the street—the harsh discomfort of the outhouse, of washing in cold water—innumerable small annoyances accumulated and fed his deep, deep discontent. Mother of God, what had happened to him ? This was not what he had expected of Hormiga, the sanctuary. This was to be release and haven at last, after long suffering. Who would have guessed that he would miserably miss the things which he had bitterly turned his back on ?

He laughed at himself mockingly, feeling a profound contempt for himself. It was Maria he missed, really—these other things tormented him because of her, because he was still trying to deny his need for her. Well, what could he do ? Maria was gone, and none knew where. Oh, God, it wasn't true. It wasn't true ! He had never tried to find her. Fool ! Fool, to think that he could turn his back on her like this, she who had brought life to him, had joined her life to his, making one whole. Without Maria he was only half alive, and small things matter to a man who is only half alive. But what——?

No, she had gone away, and by going away had shown him that she didn't want him any more. But he must do something ! He couldn't sit here for the rest of his life and dream about Maria. He must drive himself, drive, drive, drive himself to do something. The farm, the store, the road—anything, but never again to spend an idle day and let his dreams drive him to the edge of madness.

Hormiga was beautiful now in the spring. Wild plum bushes, robed in white blossoms, lined the *acequias* like tumultuous snow-banks. Summer clouds held captive to the earth. And life in the ground was awakening, stretching and beginning to grow. These brought joy to Miguel, and forgetfulness, and a momentary acquiescençe. Yes, Hormiga was beautiful and he loved it. It was good. Even Holy Week, and *Penitentes* bloody in the streets, gory beside wild plum flowers, could not altogether mar his pleasure in the spring—an early spring, for Holy Week almost never coincided with wild plum blossoms. It was a strange coincidence and many people remarked about it, some sorrowfully, for they knew that the spring, coming too soon, would be blasted by a later frost, and all things would have to begin again.

Which was exactly what happened. Early in May, a storm brought twelve inches of snow, and the freeze blackened the plum flowers and withered the young leaves. Miguel tried to ignore the portentous event, but frustration was so deeply imbedded in his heart that it laughed at his efforts. It was just another sign.

Idle days, perforce, were not entirely avoidable, for

you cannot plough in the snow. Miguel plunged into the store and took an inventory of all the goods, not because it was necessary, but because he had to do something.

And then an idea struck him. He could make this store serve him. It had never served anybody, had made slaves of all who looked after it. With the new road coming to town, the store might be made to amount to something, for its location on a corner of the *plaza* was prominent, advantageous. Far better than Vicente Romero's side-street. For the first time since coming home from Gabaldon, Miguel felt some real enthusiasm. Thus, long after, the experience gained in Vicente's store would prove useful. Vindication dwelt in the thought. Purposes lay hidden, then, obscurely, within the pattern of things happening. Futility, as he felt it, was man-made, perhaps, and not an inevitable concomitant of life.

Miguel said to his father one day, by way of opening a conversation and approaching the subject obliquely, " Whatever happened to that boy we took down to the hospital ? "

" He died."

" Oh. He died, did he ? That's too bad."

" Yes. Too bad."

Both shook their heads, thinking back.

" And the boy who did it—the Chacon boy—what happened to him ? " Miguel asked next.

Eliseo looked angry, glancing quickly at Miguel. " Nothing. He got off. He's working now, with Pablo, on the road. Or he was—I heard they fired him."

" But they had witnesses," Miguel said. " Half a dozen witnesses."

Eliseo sneered. " When they got them to court for the trial they all said they were drunk and couldn't remember anything." The father shrugged. " So the judge threw the case out of court. It was all he could do."

Miguel felt an old resurgence of burning hate, undirected but fierce. And lacking an object, it merely choked and oppressed him. He couldn't even find a reply to make. " That's bad," he said finally. " That's terrible—to let a man like that off."

" Yes, but what can you do? They stick together, those boys. They don't tell on each other."

" And the boy died, eh? " He shook his head again. " Are there any brothers, or——"

" I think there's a younger boy—and a girl. It's a poor family. They live up on the north edge of town. Martinez is the name. Your mother knows. She went up there to see them. They had a big *velorio*. I didn't go."

Though he didn't know for sure, he supposed that the girl was Cosme Martinez—the girl who was deep and peaceful, like the sky. He would have to find her, for a man couldn't be without a girl altogether. And he was a man, now, and he had lost a girl. Lost a girl. He sighed, from the depths of his soul. No, he must think no more about it. That was over. " I've been thinking," he said, " about the store, here. You know it has the best location in town. If the new road comes in, our store will be the first one people will see. I think we ought to make plans to enlarge it now, and—and make it look better—paint up the front—put some colour on it."

Eliseo nodded. " It would be a good thing," he agreed. " Would it take much money, do you think ? "

" Not very much."

" How much ? " Eliseo, unknowing, had come to rely upon this educated son for many things such as estimates of costs and the best ways of getting things done. For he was not inventive himself, and couldn't see his way very far ahead.

" Maybe twenty-five dollars altogether."

Eliseo shivered. " That's a lot of money."

Miguel wondered. Perhaps it was a lot of money; but, down in Gabaldon, people spoke of such a sum in half a breath. It was nothing. Yes, even among the students, twenty-five dollars was a piddling amount. " Well," he explained, " there's the paint—some adobe plaster——" They walked over to the front of the store and stared up at it critically. " You see how the plaster's fallen off there near the roof. We'll have to fix that—it won't look like anything until we do. And the planks in the loading platform are pretty bad. We'll need some new ones. But the main thing's some colour—to attract the people's attention, you know ? That's the main thing." And with a strange bitterness he added, " Nobody ever thinks of that up here. They put up any old adobe shack and forget it. They all look alike—they're all the same."

The father didn't know just how to take this. He looked at Miguel almost shyly, like a scolded child, and said nothing.

" And then we'll have to do a few things to the inside,

too," Miguel went on. " The counters are all dirty, and the glass is broken in half of them. You don't see things like that in Vicente Romero's store. It's neat inside—and clean."

This son, Eliseo was thinking, has grown up. He's a man now, with a man's head on his shoulders. " Well," he said, " you go ahead and do what you think ought to be done. Only don't spend any more money than you can help. I'm a poor man, don't forget that."

" Good," said Miguel. " I'll fix it up right. I'll go down to Gabaldon one day and look around."

Eliseo, who had started to walk away, checked himself. " Look around for what ? "

Miguel smiled. " I mean, I'll see what they do down there to make stores look like something."

Eliseo peered at him suspiciously for a moment, shrugged, saying, " Well, don't buy too much," and walked away.

Miguel was embarrassed. He had thought for a moment that his father had read his thoughts—but Eliseo was not one for mind-reading. It was only an excuse he wanted for going to Gabaldon. It had been pulling at him for weeks, this desire to go back, not because he liked it, but because there was a chance—just a chance—that Maria might have returned. And one other thing. He had never gone back to those people up on the Loma who had been her friends. They might know where she had gone.

The next day he took the truck and went to Gabaldon. In order to appease his conscience, he went to every store on the big *plaza* and examined it carefully, inside and out. Colour, that was the thing. Let people know what you've got to sell. A store-keeper can't afford to be bashful. Even if signs were ugly, they were necessary.

He found the people easily, the hospitable Mexican people he used to visit with Maria, who had seemed then to live so peaceably in houses they had built with their own hands. Now they seemed neither as peaceful nor as beautiful. They were polite to him, asking him in and offering him a chair in the usual stiff, shy way. He shook a dozen hands, limply shoved at him like wooden handles. The only thing he had to say to them he said quickly. Where is Maria ? And the rest of the talk meant nothing to him and he didn't listen. One after another nodded negative heads. Maria was gone— none knew where. They missed her, she was so gay and joyous. As if he needed to be told ! Only one old woman looked wiser than the rest, and Miguel soon fixed his attention upon her. She knew more than she would tell, and she grinned slyly at him. She was the one Maria had called " auntie," he remembered.

" Are you Maria's aunt ? " he questioned her.

" No. She only called me that."

" She loved you."

" Yes."

" And you know where she is ? "

The old one nodded.

" Will you tell me ? "

" No. She doesn't want you to know," the old hag wheezed, and Miguel wondered what Maria had seen to love in this one. She loosed a rasping laugh which infuriated him, and spoke in a thin voice, wiry as the bleat of a kid. " She told me not to tell you." Then

she winked. " But you could find her if you tried. It
isn't far away." And she doubled up in a dry laugh
which possessed her completely.

Much as he loathed the old woman, who refused to
say more, he was grateful for this first shred of hope
that had come to him. So it wasn't far away. It wasn't
impossible to find her, then. Good. He could go home
repaid—furious, but repaid.

Maria was brought vastly, infinitely nearer to him
by the words of this old woman. In Hormiga he worked
with a new purpose in the store; the world seemed a
more tolerable place, of a more friendly design. He was
working for Maria, now, building for Maria. When the
time should come, he would find her and show her
what he had done. It didn't matter that he had no
more idea where to look for her than he had before.
Something had happened in his heart to brighten the
future.

It lasted for a while—he could hardly have known
that it was only a boost—and when his old dreariness
threatened to return, he took steps to avert it. Realising
at last that he was actually no nearer to Maria than
ever, he was no longer able to side-step the truth. In
an effort to recapture forgetfulness, he accepted a leering invitation of Pablo's to go to a *baile* in Borregos
that would be a *baile*. He promised there would be
none of the stiff staleness of Hormiga dances, where the
walls were lined with censorious old women freezing
the air, and the best a man could do was to get drunk
and start a fight for the sake of a little excitement. This
would be a dance that was a dance. Wait, he'd see.

Pablo and some other boys had the remains of an

old open car which they had acquired by painful saving for more than a year. The brothers, therefore, set out in their death-trap of a car which had one dim head-light and no brakes. Miguel sat in the front seat with Pablo and told him the long delayed story about the girl in Gabaldon who had known him at the camp; this seemed to open a little-used door of intimacy be-tween them, for Pablo entered upon a long description of this girl, and women in general. Miguel thought he knew something about a woman's body, but Pablo's details made him gasp. The ultimate wonder was not this, however; it was Pablo's attitude. Miguel, who had loved Maria, had also respected her; from her he had learned to respect all women, and this was his starting point.

Pablo's lecherous attitude left no room for respect, ever. He considered girls and talked about them as creatures for his pleasure, nothing else. Any ideas of decency—of right-doing—with girls were simply left out of Pablo; a man was expected to take what he could get, that was all. This puzzled Miguel, partly because it was so alien to him and partly because he couldn't see how two brothers in one family could be so different. He kept his wonder to himself, however, and only listened to Pablo with unbelief growing in him.

The dance was evidently an outlaw affair, for it was held in an isolated house far from the village and deep in the cleft of a canyon. No light from the moon reached the spot, although one rocky rim on the canyon was aglow with moonlight, reflecting the illumination spectrally over the dark depths around the house. It was mysterious, exciting. The windows of the place

RM

were blinded, all sounds muffled; Miguel didn't know
what he was about to see, but it looked dangerous.
They were let in as soon as Pablo was recognised;
hostile glances greeted Miguel until his identity was
made known—then he was ignored. A white light revealed the single large room brutally, and all its con-
tents, with a searching brilliance from three petrol
lamps hanging from the ceiling beams. They hissed
while they gave off this awful glaring, and blinded
Miguel for a time, after the outer darkness. When one
of them began to splutter and fail, a man would take
it off its hook and pump air into its base, hang it up
again. On benches against all four walls, boys and girls
were sitting, squinting against the glare—in a corner,
a man with a fiddle, another with base and snare drums.
Tobacco smoke blued the air, in which the stale smell
of whiskey blended.

Miguel wanted to get out, found an inconspicuous
place in a corner and watched instead. Hours of this
would make him sick. Anything could happen in here,
too; the faces he saw about him were the most savage
he had ever seen gathered in one place—the tone of
the scene was scarcely human, he felt—it was more like
a congress of animals. Watching Pablo, he saw him
circulate among the people and speak to most of them,
saw him slap backs heartily and pinch girls; he could
hardly believe his eyes when he saw Pablo walk up to
one girl and fondle her breasts while he talked to her.
He didn't know such things could be done without a
sequel of fighting or objection at the least. But the girl
only laughed, twisting her crooked mouth. Nobody was
introduced to him, no names told. He sat down on a

bench, and he must have shown his misery, for a girl joined him in a moment and asked him why he looked so sour.

" Do you know Pablo Lopez ? " he asked her.

" Sure. That's him, standing there." She pointed to him.

" Who's that he's talking to ? "

" That's Romulo Chacon. Don't you know him ? I thought everybody knew Romulo."

" Is he the one who was tried for the murder of the boy in Hormiga ? "

" Yes, yes ! " The girl laughed raucously. " That's him. He's the one. Oho, they'll never get Romulo in gaol ! "

With a mixture of fear and hate Miguel beheld a murderer. He ignored the girl and stared at Romulo Chacon, trying to reconstruct the black heart of such a man. And yet, beside Pablo, no special difference was apparent in them, no clue explained why one was a brute and the other his own brother. And the next thing he knew, the girl had her arms around his neck and was pressing her wet, full lips against his mouth. She was heavy, and he struggled to get her off, finally managing to shove her away and plump her down on the bench beside him. He wanted to spit, so he did, glaring at her meanwhile with his disgust plain on his face. She was insulted.

" Oh, so you don't like to kiss girls," she snarled.

" No," said Miguel violently.

Whereupon she let out an obscene whoop and dashed off to tell anybody who would listen to her that Miguel was the kind of boy who didn't like to kiss girls.

Nobody paid much attention to her, and Miguel relaxed, glad that he wouldn't have to choke her. He watched her for a few minutes, saw her do the same thing to three other boys—and then forgot about her.

The fiddler had begun squeakily to play, the drummer to tap plaintively; couples moved on to the floor and danced according to their lights and their degree of intoxication. Not relaxation, not gaiety was the presiding deity, but passion—there could be no doubt of that, after watching the dancing for five minutes. And Miguel decided to participate, since he was here and Hormiga was a five-mile walk, uphill. But first his senses would have to be deadened. He sought Pablo, found him, told him he wanted a drink, and Pablo, leering with the delight of seeing his saintly brother's fall from grace, provided one without delay. It was a big drink, out of a big jug, and Miguel swallowed it manfully, as if it were something he did normally on the half-hour. And it worked with astonishing swiftness: girls became attractive, the music became a heavenly singing and sent its rhythm to his toes. He must dance ! Grabbing the prettiest girl he saw, he whirled her around the room until an awful dizziness attacked him and he had to stop. She laughed and laughed, and he grinned; she threw her arms around him, then, and danced him around the room, supported in her strong grip. Feeling her pressed against him, he gave himself into her keeping and let the light of reason go out in him, comforted by the knowledge that in the eyes of Pablo, at least, he was proving himself actually and surprisingly a man.

Men did these things—got drunk, broke laws,

ravished girls, or were ravished by them—which of the two he was never quite certain. He always knew that men did these things, but until now he had never done them himself. It was good, just to let yourself go—— Evidently girls did the same, and this was new to him. It was true, though; he only had to look about him to see that it was true, and it was duly interesting to him. He took another drink, and danced with a rotation of girls. Men were no more the assailants than women. Not as much, sometimes. As the evening ravelled on, one girl emerged from all the rest and attached herself to him more or less permanently; he suddenly emerged from a mist and realised it. Her name was Cosme Martinez, and she had chosen him because she liked his looks and because she, too, was behaving in this particular way for the first time. She felt a comradeship between them, and never left him thereafter. When he was sick outside from the amount of raw liquor he had swallowed, she was beside him; when he walked in the cold night air to regain his balance, she walked with him and held him steady with her arm, and Miguel talked to her incoherently, sick, dizzy, remorseful.

At last she said, " Let's get out of this. Let's go home."

" How ? "

" Walk."

" It's pretty far."

" Maybe somebody will come along and give us a ride."

" It's too late. Nobody would be on the road now. It's uphill all the way."

" I don't care," she said. " I'm not going back in there."

" Who brought you here ? " Miguel asked her. He was sobering quickly in the cold. " You're not like the other girls in there."

" I came with a boy from Hormiga. He's drunk in there now."

" Why did you come ? "

" I don't know. I didn't know it would be like this, and I was tired of—staying home."

Miguel stopped walking and stared at her. " Are you—did you know that Romulo Chacon is in there ? "

" Who ? I don't know anybody in there."

" Romulo Chacon. He's the man who——" He caught himself just in time. There was no need of telling her.

" The man who what ? "

" Nothing."

She repeated the name several times; the third time she began to breathe heavily, and Miguel could feel the muscles of her arm grow taut. " I know," she hissed. " Now I remember. He's the one who killed my brother ! I'll kill him ! "

She broke away from Miguel and started to run for the door of the house. Miguel ran after her, stumbling. He mustn't let her go back in there now. He caught her in time. " Please—let's go home. You can't do anything—it'll only start a fight, and somebody might get hurt—you might get hurt. Come on——" he pulled her away from the door. She resisted for a moment, and then gave in.

" All right. I guess you're right." She shuddered.
" If I had known——"

" Have you got a coat ? " Miguel asked.

" Only the one I have on. Where's yours ? "

" I left it in my brother's car. Let's look for it."

They searched for Pablo's borrowed car, found it at last and extracted Miguel's coat. " There," he said. " Now we can start." He looked at Cosme unsteadily. " Where's your coat ? I thought you said you had one."

" I have. This is it. I've got it on." She indicated an imitation fur jacket which came only to her waist.

" That thing ? You call that a coat ? You'll freeze."

" Not if we keep walking. Come on."

" All right."

They started. She wore slippers whose once-high heels were worn to lopsided stumps; her dress hung from her shoulders without apparent shape or design, dragged on the ground behind. Miguel didn't notice these things; he liked her spirit from the first and admired her sturdy, competent walk. She *was* strong and calm and distant, like the sky. She would have gone up to Romulo Chacon and tried to kill him with her hands—he was glad he had saved her from it. She pulled the flimsy jacket close about her throat and took long, sure steps. They had to climb out of the canyon where the house was before they struck the Hormiga road and its series of mounting hills. On top a fragrant night wind was blowing, but it contained a stinging cold which bit into their nostrils and made their ears ache. Slowly Miguel's head cleared entirely.

" You must be used to walking," he said.

" I am. We've never had anything except a wagon in

our family. And the horses are too poor to work, most of the time."

" Why don't you feed them ? "

" We do feed them—when we can."

He knew then what she meant and said no more about it; he felt a great sympathy for her growing in him. She was a fine girl, and a brave one. " Didn't you go to school in Gabaldon once ? " he said.

She laughed shortly. " Yes, for a month. I hated it. And I couldn't stay, anyway, because my mother got sick and I had to go home and take care of her. It was a crazy thing."

Oh, it was good to hear somebody talk like that at last ! Miguel took off his coat and put it over her shoulders. " You'd better wear it."

" No, you'll need it yourself.   You'll catch a cold."

" No. I've got a leather coat and a wool shirt. You've got nothing on under that coat."

" I'm not cold," she protested, but he made her wear it. " It's nice and warm," she said.

They walked on in silence, endlessly. Miguel was right, no one was on the road at this hour. They met one man on horseback, going down to Borregos.

" *Buenas noches le de Dios,*" the man mumbled with extravagant politeness, and they returned the salutation in the same words.

Their conversation lagged more and more as they grew weary, and they trudged in complete silence at last. The moon dipped and was gone, but starlight was bright in their accustomed eyes and, over all, the great white peaks watched as if the world were in their keeping, now that men had gone to sleep. An hour became two hours. Miguel, walking in a trance of weariness, saw that they were passing a building made of logs, fifty, a hundred feet off the road on the left. A great hill lay immediately, discouragingly, ahead.

" What's that ? " Miguel said, startling her in the stillness.

" What ? " She looked around, frightened.

" That building over there. Maybe we could rest there for a while. Wouldn't you like to rest before we climb this next hill ? "

Cosme looked at the forbidding slope before them. " I would," she agreed. " I'm pretty tired, aren't you ? "

" Yes. I'll go over and see what it is."

" I remember seeing it—but I never looked inside."

Miguel walked over to the log hut and tried the door; it was not locked, and he went in, reappearing in a moment. " It's open," he called to Cosme. " Come on. It's a hay-shed, and there's still a little hay in it."

" We could build a fire outside," she suggested.

" Yes, but we can lie down inside, and sleep a little if we want to. The hay will keep us warm."

" We're almost home," Cosme protested weakly. " This is the last hill."

" I know, but why not take a rest ? It's a good place."

" Yes," she agreed, going in. " I'm awfully tired."

Miguel made a bed of the remaining hay, Cosme laid his coat on it.

" No, we'll put the coat over us," he said. " You lie down first and I'll put it over you."

She obeyed. " If we lie close together it'll cover both of us," she said. " Oh, it feels good to rest, doesn't it ? "

" Yes." He crept under the coat beside her. She was asleep.

Miguel, drugged with weariness, was yet long in falling asleep. He was conscious of the girl beside him. Remembering another girl's description of her—strong and distant, like the sky—he tried to piece together his own ideas about her, gained from her furious readiness to assault Romulo Chacon, her presence at the orgy they had fled from, and that other, older impression.

And as he lay quietly it came to him. Peace flowed from her now, a starry calm. It was true, what the other girl had said. Though she could rise to fury like any girl, she was strong and distant, like the sky.

Now at last Maria was driven into the background. A love for Cosme had been born in him. Now Miguel could live within the moment again, in fair completeness and joy. He worked hard in the store, doing the work with his own hands, helped by Eliseo when the father felt that he could spare some hours from the farm. In the tight, circumscribed cosmos of Hormiga it was not easy to see Cosme alone, but they managed to come together often in secret, and their love grew. All had a right feeling because she declared a long love for Miguel from afar. She had watched him, she said, for years and had long cherished a bodiless, ideal love for him, which the Borregos *baile* had happily brought to reality. And once more Miguel had the good sensation of seeing a purpose in the pattern of events, that pattern which had seemed so cruel and purposeless, leading to futility.

And the road came up and paused a mile from town. No one knew why it stopped; some said the money for it was exhausted, some said they would begin again as soon as the Congress allotted more money for relief. Others were sure they stopped because they had reached the edge of a farm, owned by one Filemon Rodriguez, who objected to the right of way going through his barn. And roads, and the men who plan them, do not consider such things as a man's barn, nor his right to keep it intact if he wants to. They will turn aside for a hill or a mountain, but not for a barn. Miguel heeded the road talk as little as he could, but when the work stopped and Pablo was turned loose about the place, he had to hear, for Pablo was full of it. They couldn't put the road through the middle of Rodriguez' place, he said. They had no such right. And he and his friends knew what to do about it if the road people refused to listen.

The next thing to penetrate Miguel's new-found contentment was the incredible news that during a certain night soon after, one of the tractors had been disabled by a charge of dynamite. It was instantly evident to him what had happened, after Pablo's boastful talk. Pablo was now a criminal—a hunted man. He was gone, too, vanished; and with him a few of the suspicious characters with whom he had been playing. Well, it was Pablo's concern, but if they should fail to finish the road, what of the Lopez store and its new coat of paint, new counters? Here was something to worry about. Should Miguel go ahead with his plan of having a petrol pump installed?

Meanwhile, roadwork stopped and the men who had

been depending on it for their living roamed dejected in the streets or talked sadly in groups along the shaded sides of adobe walls. In summer men followed the shade around a building; in winter, the sun. This was the compass of some lives in Hormiga—of some old men and too many boys to whom the changing world gave no employment.

Although Concepcion wore a dark look of worry, Miguel could not be bothered about Pablo. For he had made up his mind to marry Cosme Martinez. That would settle Maria once and for all, and he couldn't go on living a dream. Or a wish, or a fond longing. He needed something solid and real to lay his hands on. And this was it.

Accordingly, he made known his desire, and there was a scene.

" When I was a boy," Eliseo cried, " it was right to wait until a boy could support a wife before he got one."

" But you're too young, Miguel ! " said the mother. " You've got so much to do before you settle down."

" What will you live on, what will you do, where will you live ? You've got no house, she's got nothing to bring to a marriage, they're too poor."

Like a bird waiting for a storm to pass, Miguel stood untouched, complacent in his certainty. He had the store, he said, and a room or two in the Lopez house would do for them until he could find a place of his own. And in the end it worked out as he wanted. Conversations began with the Martinez family, the usual devious formalities, the banns were read in the church at fortnightly intervals. After the third reading,

they could be married. Miguel had long since begun
the accumulation of gifts for the bride which would be
formally presented to her at the *prendorio*, or engage-
ment feast, a few days before the wedding. With his
mother's help he bought clothes for Cosme, shoes, hats,
dresses; and because she had no daughter herself,
Concepcion gave her own wedding-dress and worked
on it for days to make it fit. She would have given it
to Benito's Rosa except that she had been altogether
too small. Cosme was a strong, sturdy girl, as Concepcion had been long ago. It delighted Concepcion to do
this work, although she kept up her feigned disapproval
almost to the end for the sake of propriety. Why it was
more proper to disapprove than to approve she could
not have said, but it seemed the right thing to do.

The *prendorio* was an ordeal. Guests flocked to the
Martinez house at noon. Four rooms had been scrubbed
and prepared for their coming with chairs along the
walls and fresh cuttings of wild flowers and greens
placed attractively round about. No one would have
believed the house could be made so hospitable and
pleasant, to see its crumbling outside; but Mrs.
Martinez, squat and tiny, had worked hard and
managed well. As they entered, guests were shown to
chairs by the young Martinez son, where they sat in
aloof and courtly silence. The bride and her mother
were busy in a room closed from the others, while the
father roamed silently among his guests, nodding, or
shaking a wooden hand. " Thank you for the compliment " was all he ever said—the compliment of
honouring his house with their presence. Eyes alone
were busy, while tongues were held in check. Dark

eyes darting hither and yon, all-seeing, alive. Suddenly the door of the hitherto closed room opened and *Señora* Martinez stood in the opening. Circling among the guests she selected by a silent touch on the shoulder the first few whom she elected to come into the dining-room and partake of her food. These first ones were her most intimate friends and relations. They filed in and stood in a circle about the table, where cakes, cookies, wine, soda-pop and whiskey were laid; at a signal from the father, all reached forward and took food and drink, the men taking whiskey, the women wine, the children soda-pop. A toast was drunk to the bride and her parents, the sweets nibbled—and the guests filed out again, to resume the silent chairs.

At three o'clock, Miguel and his family appeared, laden with a shiny new trunk filled with his gifts to the bride. They were met formally in the big room, where Cosme, her parents and close relatives had quickly assembled. Sombrely, Miguel was introduced to all the Martinez clan, then his mother, his father, Benito, Rosa—and Pablo, if he had been there.

Even in this respectable gathering, there might have been a few who knew where Pablo was—in hiding from the law.

And then the wedding, on a Sunday morning, three days later. Father Aloysius married them, Miguel's old friend. He was gentle and beneficent and beaming. And he went away immediately after so as not to be a hindrance to the merrymaking. Cosme, serene, smiled all day, although Miguel's gift-shoes hurt her feet excruciatingly. Bravely, she smiled through that, too. They were not free for an instant from importuning guests, nor from the more or less ribald raillery of them. They ate hugely of the Martinez wedding-feast and posed obediently for their photographs. They went to the *baile* in the evening and sat upon two thrones draped in white sheets like a royal pair, and the longer the dance lasted the harder it became for Cosme to ignore her aching feet. Miguel, overcome with weariness, fell asleep on his throne, but Cosme, ever in demand, danced until all feeling fled.

They returned in the full light of morning to the rooms in the Lopez house which Concepcion had found time to make ready for the bridal couple. And in the moment before he fell asleep Miguel realised that he was married and that a whole new life lay before him to which Cosme was irrevocably joined. It was strange to think about. He was two people now, not one. Every thought and every deed of his belonged in part to Cosme, who must share also in the consequences of every act. He fell asleep smiling at the fantastic change which had come over his life, as if until now he had been blind.

Ensuing days settled Miguel gently upon the earth again. A man could not long remain adrift in a place like Hormiga, where all things conspired to emphasise actuality. Geraniums potted in coffee-cans, blooming on window-sills behind lace curtains, ubiquitous, lovely, reminded him by their unreality that they were real and that he was a young man with a new wife and a struggle for existence in his path. He was not dismayed. By one thing only was he frightened, and this was to see how complete and successful he had been in his blindness, in marrying Cosme to drive out apparitions of the past. Yes, they were gone. Time brought no diminishing of his surety. Cosme was a joy to Concepcion. She fitted into the Lopez scheme without a rub, helped with the cooking and the housework. Concepcion had not been so happy in many years—here at last was the daughter for whom she had longed. She was even content with Miguel. She had harboured for long—ever since he came back from the school—a secret worry about him, for she had seen his distress, had been eager to question him and talk it over with him. But she had never surmounted his silence; it had been too much for her. Now all that was gone. He was normal again, his old thoughtful self. And she even found courage to say to him one day: " Why did you never go back to the school in Gabaldon? "

" Because it was no good. I—didn't like it down there, and—and I wasn't getting much from it."

She had to be satisfied with this, for it was all she would ever know. And she risked one more question: " Whatever happened between you and Lucinda? "

Miguel's lips curled disdainfully. " She's a fool. She's a traitor. She's turned away from her people."

This, too, was all. Concepcion filled in the gaps in his explanation to please herself. " Now you'll stay here and run the store? " she said, and was happy when Miguel put his arm around her and squeezed her.

" Yes," he said. " For the rest of my life."

IX

ELISEO'S FIELD OF POTATOES looked good in the autumn. The plants were two feet high, and sturdy. But when he came to harvest them, he found the potatoes small and soft—good for nothing. This was a terrible blow, for he counted on the crop to get him out of debt. The summer had seen some reckless spending, getting Miguel married and remodelling the store, and here was a crop failure.

"What happened to them?" Miguel said. "They look so good from the ground."

"Too dry—too hot. The plants grow, but the potatoes don't."

It was like a death in the family, because it was so unexpected. Everybody mourned. And as Eliseo was the only man in Hormiga who attempted to raise potatoes, there was little sympathy about. Only lifted eyebrows.

Miguel felt bitterly for his father, for he had been the cause of his indebtedness. And now the road still lay uncompleted a mile from the town, with no sign of activity there. Even Pablo had dared to creep back into town, only to go away again without explanations. It was a strange thing about Pablo. The family had written him off, as they said of losses in the store. Whenever his name was mentioned it was met with silence, or a grim head-shaking. Concepcion was the only one who

SM

seemed to care, and she only betrayed it by a look of sadness and a veil of moisture in her eyes.

It was no surprise to anybody when, in October, they learned he had been arrested and sent to prison for his part in dynamiting the highway tractor. Thereafter his name was never mentioned at all. It was a disgrace. He might have brought more misery upon the town by his act, for many people lived on the wages paid by the road people. The Lopez family was ashamed, although it was said that the dynamiting was not the reason the road work stopped. It might well be the reason for its not beginning again, however.

It was good enough, Miguel tried to believe, to have the new road within a mile of town. They could finish the stretch well enough to encourage travellers to keep on until they came to the *plaza*, at least. After the harvesting was done he organised a crew to bring the new road over to join the old, a distance of only a few hundred yards, and there it was. Good enough. And he tried to believe that it made a difference in the amount of travel to Hormiga, that it would, in the course of time, repay him for renovating the Lopez store. He could hardly expect many visitors now that the season was over and snow threatening daily. They might as well settle down for the winter and wait.

Autumn faded slowly. From gold, the mountains changed to grey. Little by little the people sold their crimson strings of chili which earlier had framed their dwellings in colours of flame. The golden flowers of *chamisa* faded, sunflowers bowed to the setting sun for the last time. Snow appeared on the mountains again

and blew its icy breath upon the town. Miguel, responding to the seasonal change, felt his soul shrivelling,
though he didn't call it that. He didn't know what to
call it, and it filled him with fear. Fear of himself, and
distrust. For Cosme no longer made him happy when
he looked at her, nor made a warmth surge about his
heart when he thought of her. He thought and looked
beyond her, to something else. Or was it behind her?
Many times a day now he shook himself free of this
brooding and turned his hands to some activity. He
made some chairs for Cosme, and a table for their
room; he built new shelves for his mother in the
kitchen, and attended to the dribble of slow sales in the
store. He watered the geraniums in their tins and
watched over them as if they were bits of heaven caged.
No man in the Lopez family before had cared so much
about geraniums. It was a woman's province, not a
man's. But they said nothing to him about it, of course
—merely watched and wondered.

Cosme grew silent. More silent, for she was quiet to
begin with. The time came when she and Miguel could
no longer talk about themselves, not because they didn't
want to, but because, when they tried, something froze
inside them and cut off speech. And when snow came
and blocked the roads they sat in their rooms like two
volcanoes rumbling—dumb and inert seeming, but
seething in their hearts. Miguel held on to himself well,
not knowing what he wanted that he didn't have, and
hating himself for wanting it. But on the first day the
roads were open he took the truck and drove to Gabaldon alone, on the pretext of seeing about a petrol
pump for the store in the spring.

At first he thought he had only wanted to get away. As he drew near to Gabaldon the pounding of his heart told him the truth and shamed him so that he almost turned back to Hormiga without going to Gabaldon at all. But he had not strength enough for this. It would be better if he obeyed, but he could not. He wanted to see the place again and to recall its memories. This was all he needed—then he could go back to Hormiga and be content.

Few people were on the *plaza*, for it was cold and a gusty wind swirled dust along the streets. It didn't matter to Miguel. He only wanted to look, and feel the warm, nostalgic pleasure of looking. He didn't love this place—he hated it ! And he hated the warmth he felt now in seeing it. It wasn't Gabaldon he loved, it was—God and all the saints, it was Maria ! Maria !

Her name came to him like an audible cry on the wind. He cringed before it. And he drove his truck twice around the *plaza* staring at the people on the sidewalks as if he might see one there whom he recognised. He couldn't keep circling the square, so he turned and headed his truck up the street which would lead him to the Fayerweathers' house. It would be good to see them again.

The place looked bare—not as he remembered it last —with the trees all gaunt. Otherwise it was the same. The garden was brown and covered with a layer of manure. His truck made a great noise which reverberated from the house walls, and he shut off the motor quickly lest it disturb the Fayerweathers. His thoughts went to the furnace—then to the kitchen, and then flew into a thousand pieces like an exploding fire-cracker.

" It's Miguel Lopez, from Hormiga," Mrs. Fayerweather said to her husband, seeing the truck from a window. " I wonder what he wants."

" I don't know. Maybe he wants me to lend him money."

" Oh, dear—I wonder—should we tell him about Maria, do you think ? "

" What about Maria ? "

" Why, that we heard from her—that she wants to come back and work for us."

" Oh. Damned if I know. I don't know what went on between them. Do you ? I thought they had a fight, or something."

" Something was up. He acted like a maniac when he found out she had gone. It was almost a year ago. Remember ? I told you about it, but you probably don't remember. You don't remember anything unless it happens to hit you in a receptive mood."

Mr. Fayerweather smiled at his wife. " No, I don't remember."

" And then he went home soon afterwards, without finishing his year at the school. I guess I'd better not say anything about Maria."

" Oh, yes—I begin to recall, now. I'm glad he came down—maybe he can suggest a caretaker for that grant they've been hounding me about."

" Well, go out and meet him. He won't come in unless you drag him in—he's so shy. I'll join you in a minute."

Miguel was still hesitating at the door when Mr. Fayerweather opened it and asked him to come in.

"It's good to see you again, Miguel," he was saying. "Come in. Sit down. Tell me about yourself. What have you been doing?"

Miguel could tell by the heat in the house that the furnace was not being handled properly. "Oh, I been working pretty hard," he said. "I been running my father's store."

"Have you? That's good. You were lucky to have something like that to go back to."

"Yes."

"Are things pretty bad in Hormiga? Lots of people out of work?"

"Yes, it's pretty bad up there. The people are awful poor this winter. Too much snow—no feed for the horses. They lost about ten horses already this winter."

Mr. Fayerweather shook his head. "That's bad. How?"

"Well, they get poor, you know, and lie down, and then they can't get up again, and they"—Miguel shrugged—"they just freeze, or starve, that's all."

"The people get help, don't they, from the government?"

"A little bit. Some of them about fifteen dollars a month."

"And they live on that?"

Miguel shrugged again. "They have to."

Mr. Fayerweather shifted uneasily in his chair. Why did these people always have a tale of woe to tell? Something in their character—racial character? Perhaps, on the other hand, it was real desperation—

destitution. Nothing was done for them. The government poured money into the Indian reservations, gave them schools, doctors, nurses—these people, just as needful, just as deserving, got nothing. Mr. Fayerweather remembered reading somewhere some statistics about Mexican health and economic conditions. He shuddered this time and felt a kind of embarrassment, looking at Miguel. "It isn't enough," he said, half to himself. "They ought to do more for you."

And then Mrs. Fayerweather came in and rescued him.

"Well, Miguel, it's nice to see you again. What brings you to town in this kind of weather?"

Miguel, overcome with shyness, hung his head and mumbled, "Oh, I don't know. I just thought I—I'd like to come and—and see the place again." As a thought struck him, he brightened. "My father and I have been talking about putting in a petrol pump at the store. I came down to see about that, too."

"Oh, that sounds like a good idea. I suppose the oil companies put them in and give you a share in the sales. Isn't that the way they work it?"

"Yes, ma'm. I think so. Something like that."

"I think it's a very good idea. Is there a—a filling station in Hormiga?"

"Yes, ma'm. Vicente Romero has one."

"Oh. But you think it—the town's big enough for two?"

"Yes, ma'm."

A lengthening silence was a strain upon all but Miguel.

"Have you got a—is somebody working for you

now ? " he asked at last, lamely, and hung his head, sensing at once that they knew why he asked.

" Yes," Mrs. Fayerweather said. " I guess we have the same girl who was here when you left."

" Who tends furnace for you ? " he said, veering quickly from the kitchen.

" We have a boy who comes in. He isn't very good."

He wanted to ask directly about Maria, but he dared not. Perhaps he would get a chance before he left. It would be foolish not to, having come all this way. They might have news of her. They might know.

" Miguel," Mr. Fayerweather was saying, shattering a new silence, " do you know anybody in Hormiga who'd like to have a job as caretaker of a big land grant near there ? "

Miguel scratched his head. " Well, there must be lots of people who'd like the job. What sort of a job is it ? "

" The man would have to live there and watch out for fires—keep people from cutting wood—keep the fences repaired. And he could farm as much of the land as he liked, for his wages. The owners pay no wages in money. But they say it's good farming land— a part of it that isn't timbered."

" Which grant is it ? "

" It's one owned by an eastern group. It's called the Pedernal Grant."

" Oh, the Pedernal, yes, I know that grant. I've been there a lot of times. It's not far from Hormiga."

How well he knew it ! It was beside—right under— the bright mountain !

" Well, if you hear of anybody who could handle it, let me know, will you ? "

" Sure. Sure, I will. Maybe I'll find some poor people who need the work."

Poor people. Mr. Fayerweather smiled sadly to hear him say it.

During another silence Miguel mustered all his courage for the one question he wanted to ask, and at last he asked it. " Do you ever hear anything from Maria ? "

Mrs. Fayerweather glanced at her husband and got no help from him. " N-no," she hesitated, and then gave up. After all, it was no affair of hers. " Well, I did get a letter from her just the other day. She wants to come back here and work for us."

Miguel snapped to an upright position in his chair, and then relaxed, controlling himself. But he couldn't speak for a minute. His head was swimming and his heart trying to leap through his ribs. " Will she come —do you think ? "

" Well, we haven't decided. I'd like to have her back. She was a nice girl."

" Where is she now ? "

" I don't know. The letter was left here by a little girl."

This Miguel recognised as a lie. Why were they all against him ? Why shouldn't he know ? " She must be here in town," he said.

" Yes, I guess so. The little girl is coming back for an answer some day this week."

Perhaps it wasn't a lie, then. Mother of God ! He would have to get out of this house. He couldn't sit here and hold himself in.

Much as he liked and trusted the Fayerweathers, Miguel was glad to get out of their house and to feel the roaring motor of the truck under him once more. His head was still swimming with the news they had given him. Now that he knew what he had desperately wanted to know, he was thunderstruck, fleeing from it. He couldn't get out of town fast enough. And he didn't feel safe until the gleaming mountains behind Hormiga comforted him.

" You'll always be a *Penitente*, Miguel—you'll always want to go back to the mountains—you may not know it, but you will ! "

Her words ! He saw that they were true. But only partly true. He would want to go back to the mountains—or any other place on earth—with Maria. Without her—ah, that was another thing.

" Well, did you find out about the pump ? " Eliseo said, meeting him in front of the store.

" Yes."

" How much will it cost to get one ? "

" I don't know. I didn't ask them that."

" Didn't ask them ? I thought that was what you went for."

" Yes. They put it in—then they give you part of the money you take in from sales, see ? "

" Oh. Then it costs us nothing to put the pump in ? "

" That's right."

" Well, that sounds pretty good. Maybe it's a good thing to do."

"The oil company may not want to put one in for us."

" Why not ? " said Eliseo, bristling. " Why shouldn't they ? "

" Because they may think there's not enough money in it for them. With the new road, though, and our location, I think they might."

Eliseo grunted. Miguel was rather pleased with his improvising. Cosme came out and greeted him.

" Did you have a nice time, Miguel ? " she said.

" Yes, all right. Pretty cold, driving."

" Come inside and get warm. There's some coffee on the stove for you."

It wasn't until he had drunk his coffee and sat with his feet on the railing around the base of the stove that Miguel knew where he stood after the day's experience. Then in retrospect it all welled back over him in a returning wave. Peace was at an end. He cursed himself for ever going to Gabaldon, damned himself for being fool enough to see the Fayerweathers. And he had to do it all in secret, keeping an outward calm. They were nothing to him, anyway, the Fayerweathers. They lived in their world, he in his, and there was no bridge between. He hadn't gone there to see them, but only in search of Maria, Maria whom he loved and who was now returning, to damn him to everlasting pain.

They sat around him quietly, Eliseo, Concepcion and Cosme. Though each was occupied within his own four walls of consciousness, it seemed to Miguel that they were spying on him, searching into his soul, and he rose suddenly, kicked the stove-rail fiercely and left the room. He couldn't stand them any longer !

Poor Cosme ! She watched him go anxiously, her face a mask of worry. Concepcion reached out quickly and patted her hand. Eliseo, distracted from his task of repairing a bridle, looked after Miguel and said, " What's the matter with him, anyhow ? "

" It's nothing," said the mother gently. " Just the winter—not enough for a young man to do around here in the winter." She smiled at Cosme. " Sometimes I think it would be better if he had a regular job— like teaching in the school. He could do that, you know."

Cosme nodded, and tried to return the smile. But her heart was hurt, for she knew that nothing so simple was disturbing Miguel. She knew him well enough for that, though she hardly knew him at all, even now.

" There's plenty to do if he'd do it," Elisco retorted gruffly.

Outside in the dusk, Miguel stopped by the house door and looked up at the stars, beginning to show. A mongrel dog crept up to him, scraping its belly on the ground. As he reached down to pat its head, it rolled over on its back and wagged its inverted tail foolishly. " No," he muttered. " No, not like that. Stand up, like a man ! "

But the dog stopped wagging its tail and lay there. Miguel turned his back on it.

He was sorry now for his impulsive action. If he went back and told them he was sorry—no, it wouldn't help. It would make matters worse. Oh, God ! He clenched his fists and rubbed them hard into his eye-sockets. Maria was coming back. Where did that leave him ? Out of the unknown again, into the known. He shouldn't have rushed into marrying Cosme. But she was gone—Maria was gone, and he had wanted to forget. He had wanted to begin again, and rightly, too.

Why should he wait and hope, when she had deserted him? Oh, he was right in what he had done!

He began to walk on the valley road. As he passed the *morada* on his right hand he glanced at it, cold and lifeless now, its windows blinded, its tin chimney awry. Perhaps, one day, that place would contain his answer, after all. How many men—*Penitentes*—gave over their souls to God, for His keeping, in that place? There could be no telling. He could see no difference between those who were and those who were not *Penitentes*, yet there might be differences, deeply buried in the men themselves, too deep to show.

As he walked on, calmed by the quiet stars, his mind began to clear. He must be strong, and not give in to every turn and twist his heart made. Cosme was his wife—nothing could change that, and that being the case, he must stand by her and follow the road already begun. It looked easy now, for the air was cold and clear and swept through his head like a stream of snow-water. Standing on the edge of the canyon, he looked down into the valley, a bottomless, mysterious gulf by night where lights flickered and went out, and a few burned steadily. A few burned steadily. He fixed his attention upon these. Yes, he would be a steady-burning light. Come what may.

Later, when they were going to bed, Miguel even risked talking a little about himself with Cosme. He began by saying he was sorry for the way he acted before supper.

" It's all right, Miguel," Cosme said. " I'm sorry you
were so—so upset."

" Yes, I—I've been a little bit upset—by things."

" What things, Miguel ? "

" Oh, nothing much. I went to see the Fayerweathers
down in Gabaldon, and——" He found that he could
not go on.

A wave of faintness passed over Cosme and was
quickly replaced by a blinding fury which she held in
check superhumanly. Her voice was charged with
violence as she said, softly, " Was it Maria ? "

" Maria ? " said Miguel, turning on her with his eyes
flashing. " Maria ? "

" Yes. I know about Maria. Your mother told me."

For a moment Miguel tried to stare her down, but he
could not and was forced to lower his eyes. From that
instant he felt lost, his guilt poured out of him for
Cosme to see.

She began to speak quietly, but rage quickly got the
better of her—simple, jealous, female fury. " I hate
Maria ! " she cried. " Why won't she leave you alone ?
You married me—you belong to me ! Why didn't you
marry her, then, if you're so crazy about her ? Why did
you marry me ? I didn't ask you to. You wanted it."
She began to throw things about, her shoes, a dress and
at last a chair splintered into a corner of the room.
She fumed and sputtered at him, stopping in the end,
out of breath, her breasts heaving, her eyes flaming.

" I didn't see Maria to-day," Miguel said quietly.

" No, but you'll see her soon enough. You won't
leave her alone. But you can't have her, Miguel ! You
can't have her ! I won't let you ! "

" I know. I know."

And then she was sorry. Her anger cooled. She sat down on a chair and began to cry. " Oh, I didn't mean to get angry. I couldn't help it." She raised her face, wet with her tears, to Miguel. " It's because I love you, Miguel. I want you for myself. I want you to love me ! You do—don't you ? "

" Yes," he said. " Always."

" More than Maria ? "

He nodded, unable to speak because his throat had closed.

And Cosme went quietly to bed.

What would she do, he wondered, if she really had cause to be jealous ? If she really caught him in un-faithfulness ? He shuddered to think of it. He must be more careful. She was a fighter, this Cosme of his. He must watch his step. But it was all over, anyway. He had made up his mind—a steady-burning light. Maria still had the power to make his heart contract with pain, but that would pass. He would ignore it, force it away. He wouldn't think about her any more, and if he didn't think about her, how could she possibly bother him ?

Cosme was serene again, after her outburst, and no one else in the family knew that anything was amiss between them. But she watched Miguel like a jealous mother, and he, knowing he was being watched, steeled himself against betraying any of his thoughts. He felt calmer inside himself and when the school-teacher asked him to help decorate the schoolroom for the Christmas exercises, he worked there for a week, hanging bunting and spruce greens. Spruce grew far back in the mountains where the snow was too deep for horses, so he walked back there on snow-shoes. It was the most memorable day in the winter, for he went alone, carrying an axe, and the wilderness of blinding white and mighty trees cleansed him of all impurities. He lived on the memory of that day for days afterward, until Christmas itself was upon them.

Concepcion wanted some things in Gabaldon which she couldn't buy in Hormiga. A little money was left in her treasury—an old cow-hide box kept behind the bread-box in the kitchen—left from that part of the harvest which Eliseo had sold. And Miguel snapped at the chance to do her errands for her, so readily, that Cosme was made instantly suspicious. She decided that she would like to go with him to Gabaldon. And there was nothing for it—she would have to go. Miguel assured himself that it was best, but it did no good. His disappointment was bitter and lasting. Maria, if she were coming, must be there by now, working for the Fayerweathers; and his heart gave him an angry stab when he imagined it, reconstructed the whole re-membered scene. Her room would have the warmth of her presence in it again, which, when he had looked into it on that unforgettable day, had seemed so desolate and cold. And his longing became acute, like pain, enclosing him within its walls. He moved in this imprisonment, and saw without seeing. All people wore the features of Maria, all voices were the sound of hers. Intolerable, vain ache ! Why could he never shake it off, when it attacked him ?

Cosme sat beside him in the truck. She tried to be natural with him, failed, succeeded only in being stolid and aware of his resistance to her presence. While Miguel sat heavily in the truck, she did her mother-in-law's shopping, mostly in the five- and ten-cent store.

" Is there anything else ? " Miguel said when she joined him again. " Anybody you'd like to see here ? "

" No. How about you ? "

" No. Nobody."

On the way home he sank deeper into his mood. Cosme did not exist for him at all, not even as a presence to resist. And his mind dwelt ponderously upon the waste of coming all the way to Gabaldon without seeing Maria, or lifting a finger to find her, when he knew where she was, less than a mile away.

But the Christmas season lifted him out of it for a few days. Concepcion decided at the last moment that she would have a tree for the room where they all sat around the stove, so Miguel went out again on his snow-shoes, back into the white mountains. It calmed him as before—made himself and his puny thoughts and troubles seem insignificant—but it did not cure. When, in January, it became evident that Cosme would bear him a child, he came once more to something like assurance. This wonder, that God should select him out of His countless millions for the miracle of father-hood, seemed to cure him of all obsessions. Cosme was revivified by his love, and all his purposes found a new direction. He rejoiced in the new surety, and for a time was content.

This was followed by a sense of freedom. Cosme

T M

slowly became absorbed in herself and the child within her, just as the fields in spring become aloof and stir with their secret life. Miguel no longer felt any dependence from her; she was self-sufficient now, defiant, and communing with forces and feelings he knew nothing of. He was hurt at first, then indifferent—and then relieved. He could go his own way, at last. Her air was confident, she had this final hold upon him, and it was enough. She seemed to know, where she had only hoped before, and one of the things she knew was that he was hers—he might wander, but he would come home again.

All this Miguel sensed in her now; she had never uttered a word. It set off the rebellion which since childhood lay like a spark in him, but she knew better than he did the force of the powers within her.

The weather moderated as it often did in mid-winter, and Miguel's thoughts turned again to the store, what to do there, how to plan. The petrol pump came up again. After many and long conferences with Eliseo, it was decided to install one. First Miguel went out to the spot where the new, unfinished road stopped and joined the old. He watched for a whole day to see how many people were discouraged and turned back when the smooth road ended. Not many. It was no time, really, to tell, for few people were travelling merely out of curiosity. Most of the people he knew, and had reasons for coming to Hormiga, but he was encouraged, none the less, and decided in favour of the pump.

Cosme had no objection now when he said he was going down to Gabaldon to see about the pump. She only smiled at him and wished him success and a good trip—she even asked him to be careful, and not to drive too fast.

On the way down, Miguel made up his mind to see the oil company people first, and Maria afterwards, for a premonition warned him that he might not get to the oil company offices at all, otherwise. They were not as enthusiastic as he was, and they asked embarrassing questions about how many people visited Hormiga in a year, how many cars were owned in the village and whether other filling stations had been installed there. Miguel invented answers to questions he could not answer, and left the matter undecided, in the oil company's hands. They would have to go up and look over the ground.

This time he left the truck a block away and walked to the Fayerweather's house. His heart was pumping wildly. She might not be there, for all he knew. How would it be to see her again? How would she look? How would she greet him? As he approached the house, all these questions congealed to form one solid, insupportable yearning to see her, and he broke into a run. How many times he had run up that last hill to the Fayerweathers' house!

Slipping into the basement, he stole up the kitchen stairs. Somebody was moving about up there. He would make it just like old times, he would appear from the basement as if a year had not intervened. He would have to tell her about Cosme, and how he would be a father before long. That would be all right—she'd understand. Maybe it would be better not to tell her—she might take it in some unexpected way. Women do, sometimes, he thought. All a man's plans and ideas were apt to give way before a woman's eyes.

When his face reached the level of the kitchen floor he stopped to look. His heartbeats sounded in his ears. Her back was turned, but it was Maria ! Not quite as slim as before—more womanly, older. But unmistakably Maria. He feasted his senses upon her through his eyes. Almost afraid to make his presence known, he held his breath quiet and watched her. Surely she could hear his heart pounding, when he could hear it so plainly himself. She was humming softly and her voice worked its magic—he felt dizzy and held tightly to the edge of the floor with both hands. When it passed, he crept silently up the stairs until his whole body was above the floor level. And then Maria looked around.

Seeing him, she turned and gripped the table where she was working, with her hands behind her. Her mouth and eyes opened wide. She didn't smile. Miguel was waiting for her to smile. She must have known that he would appear—like this—sooner or later. They stood at opposite ends of the kitchen, staring at each other.

" Hello—Maria——" Miguel was the first to speak.

" Miguel——" Her voice was a whisper. " Oh—Miguel——"

For another long moment they stood off, looking at each other, and then Maria flew across the kitchen and he caught her in his arms.

Ecstasy ! It was long before either of them could speak.

" Where are the Fayerweathers ? " he said.

" He's working, and she's out somewhere. We're all

right. Miguel—where have you been? Why haven't you come before?"

" I've been—at home. I've had work to do up there, and—and the road has been—closed."

" I went to Midnight Mass—on Christmas Eve. And I prayed for you, Miguel. Did you go?"

" No. I didn't go."

" Oh."

The disappointment in her tone took his heart and twisted it cruelly. " I couldn't," he added. " I wanted to go, but I couldn't."

Then, at last, she smiled, and he could breathe again. But he hadn't expected to find her so open and forthright. He expected her to be shy and mysterious as she had been before, when he knew her. Something had changed her. She concealed nothing from him now. And she loved him—he could see that, from the moment she had fled to his arms.

It took some minutes for the implications of this knowledge to pierce his joy. Slowly he realised that he had not known until now just where he stood with Maria—and now he knew. She loved him as much as —once—he had loved her. He added the mental reservation—once—himself, for he could not love her now, could he? A married man, with a child on the way? She was close to him, looking up into his face and studying him keenly. When he met her eyes, he saw that she loved him in a way which swept all before it, and he was completely engulfed, and the truth was carried to him on the tide. He loved her now as much as he ever did. All else was lost. All was lost.

" What have you been doing since I went away,

Miguel ? Oh, I was mean to go away like that and leave you——"

" Why did you ? " he asked quickly. " I never knew why you did. Why did you ? "

" I had to, Miguel."

" Why ? Where did you go ? "

" Because I loved you, and—I was right here, all the time in Gabaldon."

" But you said——"

" Yes. I didn't want you to know."

" But why ? "

" Because——" she bit her lip and lowered her head. Her voice sank to the thinness of a hair. " We had a son, Miguel—you and I."

" A son——" he repeated hollowly, and threw back his head, closed his eyes, while his hands blindly sought hers and gripped them. " Oh, God, Maria——"

She looked up, then, and took his head in her hands, pulled it down to hers. " No, Miguel—you mustn't take it this way."

" Where is he—now ? " he asked without looking at her.

" He died. I tried, but—I couldn't keep him alive. They did everything they could. I wanted him to live, Miguel."

Still locked within his own suffering, Miguel said, " Who was with you ? Who helped you ? "

" I was with my friends here—those people up on the Loma. The one I called ' auntie ' helped me most."

" Oh—I see," he breathed. " I see."

" So I had to go away, Miguel, you see, because I—

I was married, and I couldn't stay here. And I was scared, too, and wanted to hide, and be alone."

In spite of all he could do, two tears escaped from under his closed eyelids. Maria, seeing them, was torn with pity.

" No, no, Miguel. It's all right now. Don't you see ? It's all over. I'm free now. I've been to a lawyer, and got a divorce. I never heard from my husband. I didn't write you because I knew you'd come back to me. Please——" she shook his shoulders gently. " Please smile, Miguel. Kiss me again."

Miguel staggered away and sat in the nearest chair, dropped his head to his arms on the kitchen table. " Oh, God ! " he mumbled in a voice wrenched with agony. " Oh, Mother of God ! " And then he began to sob, and nothing Maria could do or say had the slightest effect upon him.

At last, in utter perplexity, she sat down beside him and waited for him to come to his senses, running her fingers through his hair meanwhile, shedding hot tears of her own.

When he raised his head after timeless suffering, she was terrified by the torment on his face. " What is it, Miguel ? " she cried. " What's the matter ? Don't you see ? It's all over now, and—and everything is all right."

He took one of her hands and crushed it with his strength. " Oh, Maria, Maria——"

It was no good telling her, he thought now as he gazed with complete tenderness upon her. And if he stayed with her, he would surely tell her. He wasn't strong enough to keep it to himself always. He took a deep breath and smiled. " Yes, it's all over now," he said, biting his lip to keep back a new onslaught of pain. " I'll have to go now, for a while—I've got a lot of things to do. It was a shock, that's all. I—I'm sorry he didn't live." He stood up, swaying for a moment.

" When will you come back, Miguel ? "

The question swamped him again. Come back ? Come back to what ? " Can I come—this afternoon ? After I get through ? "

" Yes. They're going out to dinner to-night. It would be a good time. Come then, Miguel. About six ? "

" Yes. All right. About six."

And before he left he held her in his arms again and kissed her in a passion of tenderness, all other passion gone.

Groping his way along, Miguel found the truck where he had left it. He climbed into the driver's seat. Where should he go now ? What could he do until six o'clock ? How could he bear the crushing weight of sorrow until then ? He didn't want to live that long. Eternity.

He started the motor, let the truck roll idly down the hill into Gabaldon. Where to ? Oh, where to ? The *plaza*, when he came to it, was hateful to him. He couldn't endure the sight of it. He drove out of town, to the north, in the direction of Hormiga, but with no intention of going there. And presently, within a few minutes, he knew where he was going—to Father Aloysius, at Santa Rosa. It was a long way—he might have to buy petrol—but he was going to him, his first friend. And with this decided, he lost all consciousness of everything except his objective. He drove blindly, recklessly. Father Aloysius. Yes, he would tell him what to do. He would listen, and he would understand. Oh, it would be good to pour the whole thing into his ears ! Only to get it out of himself would be good ! He was bursting with it, aching, suffering, dying with it !

He ran into Father Aloysius' house like a man frantically rushing for a doctor. The priest was there, working in his study, and Miguel burst in upon him breathlessly. " Oh, Father——" he moaned. " Oh, Father——" And he collapsed in a chair.

Two hours later he emerged, stood with the priest in his doorway, blinking in the bright sun, now sharply inclined to the horizon. Miguel's face was drawn and crooked; he felt like the shell of a man, with his guts torn out. Once more his mind went back capriciously to the skin of a chipmunk, nailed against a door. Words of the priest were still sounding distantly in his ears like remembered bells. " It will take you a long time to recompense this, Miguel. Your path lies clear in one direction, and one only. See that you stick to it, and save your soul."

" I should tell her, though, you think, Father ? "

" Yes, you must tell her. It will help you to be strong."

" It will hurt her."

" Yes, but she has sinned, too. And the Church, you know, does not recognise her divorce."

Miguel nodded.

He could just get back to Maria by six o'clock. He couldn't go home. He couldn't face them all, up there. Not yet. Without looking back, he left Father Aloysius and walked unsteadily to the truck and drove away.

The lights of Gabaldon were on when he reached the top of the hill overlooking the town. It was cold, and the wind whistled through the battered cab of Eliseo's truck. Miguel did not feel the cold because his heart was colder than any wind could ever be. His hands and feet were numb, but his eyes burned two hollow borings in the frozen air, straight ahead.

With leaden feet he climbed the basement stairs. The brightness and warmth of Maria's kitchen in no way melted the icy hopelessness of his mood. And his face was immobile, even when she met him with her smile. He began at once.

"Maria—we can never be married, you and I. We can have no more sons. We must live without each other. We can do it, because we have to. I married a girl last summer. I thought—I didn't think I'd ever see you again. She's going to have my—child—in—the—spring."

Slowly Miguel, having spoken, closed his eyes, leaned back against the wall and sank to a sitting position on the floor.

At half past six, Mrs. Fayerweather looked out of a window.

"Why, there's Miguel again," she said to her husband. "Isn't that his truck?"

Mr. Fayerweather went to the window and looked out. "Looks like it. I guess he came to see Maria."

He went back to his dressing for dinner.

"I think it would be nice if they got married, don't you?" said his wife.

" Yea."

" I think she's crazy about him."

" I guess he likes her pretty well, too."

" I'd hate to lose Maria, though. I suppose she'd have to go up to Hormiga to live."

" I should think that would be the way they'd manage it."

" Maybe we could persuade Miguel to come down here and get a job."

" I hardly think so. He's got a wild look in his eye. I doubt if he'd be happy down here, away from his mountains."

" Funny——" she said raptly, "—how little we really know about them—or what's going on in their heads. I suppose we don't seem like people to them, either. Just chunks of life—who somehow move and breathe as they do."

" Yes, there's quite a gap, all right. But you can't get over that. I doubt if they really like us."

" Oh, I think they do."

" Well, it's something different," he insisted. " Something's left out of it. There's no real affection."

" I think there is."

" It's all right," he added. " I'm not complaining. It's part of their self-respect, I guess. I like it better than this dog-like devotion people sentimentalise about. It shows that they're real people, whether we realise it or not."

" Oh——" She listened. " He's going. I'm sorry we didn't see him."

" I guess he'll come again."

X

THE FALSE SPRING vanished in swirls of snow.
Hormiga was white again and the tight, small houses
comforted them they sheltered, or pressed upon them
like inquisitorial walls.

Cosme was gentle with Miguel now, for all his silent
brooding. She knew what had happened without being
told, and she was waiting for time to do its work.

Time was doing its work. Her intuition was right, in
the main, save for one thing it did not tell her of. All
pain of loss and separation was gone out of Miguel now.
When he looked at Cosme he looked at his future. This
he knew. And it was not painful. But gnawing at his
heart, threatening, it seemed, the air he breathed and
the life that kept his perverse heart at work, was a
sense of guilt. No repentance assuaged it—only made
it grow like a sore in his breast. It was driving him mad,
for it was secret, unsharable. Father Aloysius had
prescribed for it, knowing, perhaps, that it would come,
but his medicine was worthless, aggravated the disease. It was a demon in him, forcing him back to his
childhood religiousness. He went to the church for
every service held there, and when Lent began he was
in the church, or the chapel of the *morada*, for half of
every day.

What had happened to him no longer mattered at all.
He had broken the life of Maria—that was the thing !
And it grew monstrous in his idle imagination. He had

loved her, yes—that only made it worse. He had brought awful suffering upon another, and one whom he loved. It was like killing his mother—murdering *la Virgen.*

He prayed mostly to her, when he prayed alone. A picture of her hung in the church. She wore a red robe, whose colour had fought off the assaults of time which had paled all else in the painting. She burned on the dingy wall like a spot of fire. And when he spoke to the image in the painting he dared to call her not *Virgen*—but Maria.

Why not? That was her name. And she was the soul of forgiveness. Oh, Maria—the real Maria—had forgiven him, but it was not enough! This one must forgive him, too, and make him whole again.

Santa Maria! Make him whole again!

Lent grew older, approached the Resurrection and the Life. Miguel's passion mounted. Was there no repentance, anywhere? Why would she not speak to him and give him peace? Mother of God—Our Lady of the Rosary—Maria!

The *Penitentes* lighted the fire in the *morada*—sparks danced from the crooked chimney, and Miguel, seeing them one night for the first time, felt a cold wave of clarity envelop him like a bath of light, revealing him starkly in the blackness. He stared at the sparks with a fanatic gleam in his eyes.

It was settled now. He turned on his heel and went into his father's house, drew Eliseo outside, pulled him out, without giving him time to get his coat or hat.

" I want to join the *Penitentes*," he said.

Eliseo in his pleasure forgot the cold. At last the

wandering son was coming home. " Well, that's good. That's fine. I guess we can take you in all right. I thought you were an American now—I thought you didn't like the *Penitentes*."

" I hate Americans," Miguel muttered violently. " I want to join the *Penitentes*."

" All right. I'll fix it up for you."

On Wednesday of Holy Week the retreat of the *Penitentes* would begin. And at sundown of that day the *novicios* would be initiated. Miguel waited impatiently for the day and the hour, with all his hope and crying need focused there. Quickly he learned the ritual which the *Celador* had given him to memorise. And he fixed his mind and thought upon his coming entrance into the Order as if it were a transmutation from which he would emerge remade. He thought of nothing else. Nothing in the visible world existed for him, for his eyes were turned utterly inward, where dwelt the guilt which was driving him to this. As he examined it, it continued to grow, malignantly, and he feared that expiation might not come in time.

When the hour came, he was ready for it, prepared in body and mind. The single purpose of redeeming his soul from its foul sin burned in him like a clean flame. He was waiting where he had been directed to wait, on his father's doorstep, and in his hands he held two candles. In his heart was a great calm, but the quickness of intense readiness was there also.

As the rims of the sun and the western mountains met in a crimson fusion, the door of the *morada* opened, and a man came out. His shoes squeaked on the dry snow which still overlay the ground, and he made in a straight line for the door of the Lopez house.

" You are Miguel Lopez ? "

" *Si, señor.*"

" You have said you will join the Society of Our Father Jesus the Nazarene ? "

" I have."

" I am the *Maestro de novicios.*"

" *Si, señor.*"

" Repeat this vow after me : ' I solemnly swear never to reveal to anyone in any way the secrets and ceremonies of this Order.' "

Miguel repeated the oath.

" ' I believe there can be no remission of sins without the shedding of blood.' "

This also Miguel repeated.

" Light your candles—so. Now come with me."

As he turned to follow the *Maestro*, Miguel caught a glimpse of his mother watching him through a thin parting in the window curtains. He realised that he had not thought of her until now. And he was sorry he had left her out of everything. She must have been hurt by it, hurt by his solitariness and his preoccupation. Half way across the *plaza*, carrying his lighted candle, the thought of his mother stabbed him again and he turned and waved woodenly to her, and tried to smile.

She must understand, though. Everything and everybody had been left out—even Cosme, even his own material body.

The *Maestro* had gained on him. Miguel hurried after, shielding the bent flame of his candle from the wind his walking made. At the door of the *morada* the man stopped and took Miguel's candle from him.

" Go in," he said.

The *Maestro* followed him inside and shut the door. Miguel blinked. The light of one feeble oil-lamp was dim, even after the falling dusk outside. So this was the room—the mystery. And there, separated by a short, jutting partition from the rest of the room, was the source of those sparks which, darting into the air above, had filled him with wonder. A stove. An old, rusty, iron, red-hot stove. A great kettle hissed and bubbled on it.

He asked no questions, however—only stood by the door and waited silently.

" Take off your clothes."

He obeyed deliberately. The close, damp warmth of the place was good after the brittle cold. In a moment he stood naked, waiting again. The *Maestro* was bent over an old wooden chest in a corner. When he came to Miguel he carried a pair of white, knee-length drawers and a black cloth.

" Put these on," he said, handing him the drawers. " So. Now turn around and I'll tie this over your head."

When the black cloth covered his face, Miguel could see through it well enough, but he could not be recognised. Good. It fitted in with his desire. The more he could wipe out the stain on his soul the better. And it showed on his face. It must show on his face. Cover it, then. Let him search for redemption without a face.

" Follow me. Take your candle and hold it so." He put the lighted candle in both his hands and pressed his elbows to his ribs. The flame was level with his chin. " Come, then."

They had to go outside again, for there was no connection within the *morada* between the chapel and the meeting-room where they had been.

The sharp cold struck him like a blow. He began to shiver. While they paused at the door of the chapel, waiting to be admitted, his trembling increased and he could do nothing about it, neither stop nor control it. When the *Maestro* had knocked in a particular code, the door swung slowly open, moved from within—and added to his trembling. Miguel felt, for the first time, his heart begin to race. He tried to keep his mind fixed upon the ultimate thing, the repentance he would find here; but the trembling went on.

Though he could see nothing at first, he could tell by the heat and the foulness of the air that the chapel was full of people. And then, gradually, through his black hood, he began to see the pale flames of candles—and behind each little blaze a face, nothing more. Disembodied faces.

" Kneel ! " a voice commanded, and Miguel dropped to his knees like a stone.

" Come forward to the altar. No, no, on your knees. *On your knees !* "

Miguel had started to rise again, and once more he dropped to his knees. Bewildered, he hesitated, and then saw how the brothers had separated, forming an aisle up the centre of the chapel, ending at the altar, where more candles burned. Up this dimly lighted way he advanced, crawling painfully on his knees. But his heart was so filled with joy that he felt no pain.

Uм

They left him there, kneeling before the altar, for a long time—he didn't know how long, for he poured the burden of his guilt before the saints arrayed in front of him, and his heart swelled with gratitude. At last the *Maestro* was beside him again, showing him how he must adore the saints, anciently carved in wood and clothed like precious dolls in lace and robes.

" Now come back and kneel before the brothers. . . ."
Reluctantly he turned his back to the altar.

> " *Forgive him, O Lord,*
> *Who is already forgiven by me.*"

And Miguel, remembering the ritual he had learned, said in reply:

> " *Jesus Christ, Our Lord,*
> *I am the sinner*
> *Who comes to do his penance*
> *And to offer his devotion.*"

Deeply rumbling came their answer:

> " *May the Lord increase his devotions !* "

Then they greeted him solemnly one by one as he went down the arc of illumined faces, shaking their limp hands. " Know me as thy servant," he said to each.
" And I as His servitor," they replied.

Formality relaxed when this was done. The brothers talked naturally and smoked and passed outside into the cold night. Miguel moved in their midst, detached utterly from their presences. He was not attuned to men, had nothing to say to them. His spirit clamoured for more. This was only a beginning.

Lights were brought to the meeting-room, and slowly the brothers gathered there. Miguel found a place on a bench along the wall and sat still, deep in solitude, too deep even to be impatient. No one seemed to notice him, though he was the only *novicio*, and the only one clothed in nothing but white cotton drawers.

Slowly the men assembled—the door was closed at last, and a silence took possession of the room. And Miguel began to emerge from his solitude. Something was going to happen. At last the physical body would be humbled. Oh, that was what he wanted ! The spirit could writhe and suffer, but, as long as the physical body lived in gross ease and comfort, no suffering, no penance, could be complete. His eyes flashed as he waited. He almost laughed at himself for not realising this before.

A man who was not the *Hermano Mayor* assumed command.

" The brothers who intend to whip with the *novicio* will get ready," he said in a loud voice which stirred Miguel to his toes.

Four young men began to take off their clothes. In a moment they were clad as Miguel, in white cotton drawers and nothing else. Their black hoods hung from their hands. And Miguel, alive now to all that happened, asked a man beside him who it was.

" He's the *Picador*—the man who does the cutting."

Miguel nodded and watched. The *Picador* held a piece of glass in his hand—and with his fingers he tested its edge. It seemed to satisfy him, for he raised his head

and called, " Come forward, *novicio*, and receive the
Three Meditations of the Lord ! "

For an instant a gulf of horror opened before Miguel.
He sat upright, looked about him. All eyes were turned
upon him. He wavered, closed his eyes—and when he
opened them the gulf was gone. Only Maria remained,
and his guilt. He leapt to his feet and went to the
Picador.

" Bend over from your waist, *novicio*."

Miguel supported himself with his hands on his
ankles. In that position he could look up along the
front of his body and see his heart-beats coming through
his ribs like hammer blows. He waited.

Ah, the first cut—and then five more, quick, expert,
three on each side of his spine.

There was no pain, but the feel of the sharp glass on
his skin made him wince and bite his lip. He pressed
his eyes shut and bared his teeth through the last three
cuts, and then the *Picador* stopped.

" If you want more, you say, ' For the love of God,
give me the Ten Commandments.' " The *Picador's*
voice sounded in his drumming ears but Miguel was
too filled with wonder to ask for more. And the *Picador*
pushed him gently aside.

" Now the brothers," he said.

Miguel stood by and watched the cutting of the four
who were to march with him. The cuts on his back were
beginning to sting and he could feel his warm blood
trickling from them, and the feeling was nothing but
good. At last he was shedding his blood for Maria !
Santa Maria. Let her look, and see how penitent he was !

He became conscious suddenly of the silence in the

room as the men were sliced by the glass of the *Picador*. He saw the scars where the bared backs had been cut before. Happy men ! Oh, happy men ! And he watched the thin red lines on their backs grow wide, and he saw a drop of blood fall upon the earthen floor and, merging with it, turn brown. Without realising it he began to sway. His lips moved soundlessly, forming the words of a hymn he had learned. And somebody began to sing, the very words which were coursing through his brain like fire. Miguel threw back his head and sang, letting his voice come from his nose, as if the sounds came not from his throat but from his head where the frenzy was.

> " *All upon our knees*
> *Ought to implore*
> *This blood of mine*
> *That I am going to shed.*
>
> *I am the sinner*
> *Who has already sworn*
> *To praise the blood*
> *Of this discipline.*
>
> *To praise you I come,*
> *Jesus and Mary*——"

Somebody thrust a whip into Miguel's hands. He took it, without looking at it or seeing how its frayed end had been dipped in the kettle of boiling water on the stove. And as soon as he closed his hand around it he started awkwardly to swing it over his shoulders, to bring it down on his back, now sanctified to receive it. And he heard voices, faint and undirected.

" We're going now. Put on your hood. Put on your hood ! "

Somebody grabbed him, swaying and singing, and held him still while the black cloth was bound over his head—then he was pushed outside, through the door. Bare feet in the snow brought no sensation of cold:

> " *To praise you I come,*
> *Jesus and Mary,*
> *To implore the blood*
> *Of this discipline !* "

Like a rope slipping through his hands he could feel his mind deserting him, going out like a fading light. He staggered about, within a circle of men, bareheaded, clothed and nasally singing by the light of lanterns and the moon. Crazily he belaboured his back and felt his hot blood run.

As the procession got under way, Miguel was brought into line by two brothers who walked on either side of him. And he swung his whip, rhythmically now, as if he had done it for years, first over one shoulder, then over the other. His singing stopped, caught in his throat; he gave everything to his whipping, in silence. His eyes rolled up under his black hood—he raised his head and held it lifted—he saw nothing except a far, rose-coloured light. This was what God required—the way to redemption—this was what God required—what God required—God required. . . .

On Friday night, when the retreat would be over in a few hours, the *Hermano Mayor* took Eliseo aside in the

dooryard of the *morada*. " Your boy—Miguel—what's
the matter with him ? "

" I don't know, *Hermano*," said Eliseo. " He acts like
he was crazy, no ? "

The *Hermano Mayor* nodded gravely. " I don't know
what to do with him. He's whipped three times, and
now he says he wants to carry a cross to *Tinieblas*
to-night. I don't think I should let him do it."

" No," said the father, shaking his head. " I think
he's done enough. I'm afraid he'll get sick like my
other boy—Pablo. Remember ? "

" It's cold, too—looks like more snow." The leader
shrugged. " He's wild—he's got a crazy look in his
eyes. I don't know. Maybe I should let him do it and
—and get it out of him."

" Maybe," said Eliseo, for whom it was much easier
to agree than disagree. " Maybe he just needs to wear
himself out."

Miguel sat on the floor, waiting. As he had been
throughout the retreat, he was enclosed in a strange
solitude. In order to get his attention it was necessary
to speak two or three times to him. It was noticeable,
now ; many were talking about it, in whispered conversations.

" That *novicio*—that Miguel Lopez—he's gone a little
crazy. Look at him now."

When the flute piped, or men began to sing a hymn,
he came back to earth, and his eyes burned with fervid
intensity. He marched in every procession, sometimes
only as a guardian, sometimes as a penitent himself.
Now, as the retreat was nearly over, his zeal reached

its height, and so great was it that the brothers shunned him, as if some fiery emanations came from him in his solitude.

He carried a cross to *Tinieblas*. When the time came, the *Hermano Mayor* had not dared to refuse. And he knelt with his eyes closed through the service—through the darkness and the light. How a man could bear what Miguel had been through, no brother knew.

Cosme was waiting for him when the retreat ended. She was anxious for him, for word had gone about and reached the women. He came home at four in the morning and lay down on their bed without taking off his clothes. She tried to help him tenderly.

" How are you, Miguel ? How do you feel ? "

" I'm all right. I'm tired."

Cosme hardly knew what to say to him. His strange, mystical solitude still enveloped him. Once as he lay on the bed he said, " I'm a *Penitente* now. I'll always be a *Penitente*. But I'll never go to a retreat again. I—I'm clean—now."

" No ? " said Cosme softly. " Why ? "

" Because a man needs it only once. I'll never feel that way—the way I felt—again."

And those were the last words he spoke for three days.

They were all afraid. Miguel lay on his bed utterly lost to them. Concepcion and Cosme took turns watching him, but he seemed not to be sick—no delirium, no fever. At least none that they could see. He tossed for a day, and then quieted, but he never opened his eyes, nor spoke a single word. They bathed his back with Romero water, a herbal tea the *Penitentes* always used for the purpose, and it began to heal. No mortification. And yet he lay like a dead man.

On the fourth day when Cosme awoke in the morning, she looked at Miguel as she had done for three anxious mornings previous. And she saw that his eyes were open, staring at the ceiling.

" What is it, Miguel ? Are you all right ? "

" Yes. I've—been asleep, I guess."

" Yes."

" Cosme——" He didn't turn his head to look at her.

" Yes, Miguel ? "

" I've decided something."

" Yes ? "

" We're going away—you and I. We're not going to stay in Hormiga."

" Why not, Miguel ? We have the store here, and——"

" No," he cut her short. " I won't have anything to do with Americans. They'll be coming here, more and more. I don't want to see them. I don't want to depend on them."

" But Miguel—what will you do, then ? Where will we go ? "

" I've decided that, too. I'll go to Mr. Fayerweather and tell him that I am the man to take care of the Pedernal Grant."

Cosme was bewildered by this. " What ? "

" He told me that he was looking for a man to look after the grant—to go up there and live on it—and farm it. The land will be as good as ours. Well, I'm the man. I'm going. We're going. I want—land of my own."

After that, Miguel got up and, as nearly as anyone could tell, was normal again. It was as if his body and his spirit had been sifted of all it had contained of strife and contest. He wrote to Mr. Fayerweather about the Pedernal Grant and received a letter authorising him to go ahead and take the job. Henceforward, he lived and planned for nothing else.

When Eliseo and Concepcion heard of it, they were hostile.

To Cosme, she said, " You girls make me sick. You don't want to go up there, do you ? "

" No, but I want to do what is best for Miguel."

" Ah, nonsense. When you're young, you let your man do anything he wants with you—and you spend your old age being sorry and mad that you did. It's too late, then. When a man's young and in love with you, he'll listen. When he gets old and stubborn you can talk all day at him and he won't hear a word of it. Where is the Pedernal Grant, anyway ? "

" It's up north—about ten miles."

" Is there a road ? Or do you have to walk ? "

" I think there's a wagon road."

She looked at Cosme and saw that she was smiling. Whereupon she threw up her hands and left the room.

Miguel waited until the baby was born. Then he set out in an old wagon alone, to prepare the land for his family. It was a hard journey. Time and again he had to clear the way of rocks and boulders before the wagon could pass, or cut down seedlings which had grown since the last one had passed. With all the labour of it, and the danger of upsetting his load, Miguel was happier than he remembered being. Untouched beauty was all around him, and his heart sang. He was a man at last, and a whole man. His imagination flew ahead to the time when he should bring his wife and new-born son over this road, to take possession of the land he would wrench from the wilderness.

It was not impossible that some day he might own the Pedernal Grant; the timber alone on it was worth half a million dollars, Mr. Fayerweather had said. It was a sum beyond his power of apprehension, but it sounded mighty on the tongue ! At least they might sell him the piece he intended to farm. And then at last he'd be a man, a proper man.

The road led north across the wrinkles in the mountains' flanks; he crossed a succession of dry *arroyos*, some shallow, some as deep as canyons. By mid-afternoon the horses were tired, walking with angry reluctance and looking around reproachfully at Miguel perched and whistling and singing on the driver's seat. It was hard going, and he spared them as much as he could, letting them rest frequently and walking beside the wagon on the level places, but his own impatience to see his new home made him drive them harder than he would ordinarily.

He came at last to an even, park-like upland, clear of undergrowth and studded with great pines—then a fence with a broken gate to let the road through. The south boundary of the grant ! His heart skipped. It couldn't be far from here to the cabin ! The horses, sensing the end of the journey, moved at a faster pace; Miguel shouted to them, told them the end was near and asked them if they didn't think the land was fair ! He sang aloud, tried the echoes, and exulted in the greatness of his fortune.

He wasn't sure, when he saw it first through the trees in the failing twilight, whether the cabin was a cabin or just a cubical formation of rocks and earth. Like a good farmer, he attended to his animals before himself, or the place he was to live; he found the remains of a corral, which he made secure with some rusty wire and turned his horses into it, laying a good feed of alfalfa on the ground inside.

It was almost dark when he finished. Out of the stuff in the wagon he dug a lantern, and entered his castle. Filth. Dung of a dozen different sources lay on the floor, ruin claimed the bunk and the old iron stove. Through holes in the roof he could see the stars; a dank smell of decay and mildew filled the place, and the door hung crazily on one hinge. Instantly he saw that he had not brought enough materials to repair the house. He had no extra hinges, no boards; a few nails were in the wagon and a roll of tarred paper, for he had expected to find the roof collapsed. And he had a shovel, to clean the floor. Well, if he could proof it against the coming rains he could finish the job later.

For to-night, he preferred to sleep out of doors and leave that foul interior to the pack-rats and chipmunks. Having laid his bed at the foot of a pine tree he stretched out on it before thinking of a fire or food and gazed upwards through the mighty branches to the sky.

Peace—this was peace. And oh, God, how good it was !
How still ! He could hear the horses—their teeth grind-
ing the sweet hay, the swish of their tails, and no
other sound but the elfin humming of a breeze in the
pine-needles. Until the cold came through to chill him,
he lay there too happy to stir; but having moved, he
realised how hungry he was, and how tired.

With all the trees, he could find little dead wood for
a fire; he had to chop the branches from a fallen titan
before he could build a blaze. His supper of beans and
canned beef finished, he sat still beside the fire, watching
the flying sparks until sleep overpowered his eyes.

Those who came to populate his fancies before he
fell asleep were not Cosme, not his mother nor his
father, nor anyone whom he knew now and had seen
every day. In the darkened starlight among pine trunks
he saw his sons and daughters without number, heard
their cries, heard their mother calling. But whose
voice ? Not Cosme's—whose, then ? Maria's. Maria's !
He sat up with a start—and smiled at himself—and
relaxed again. How tired he was ! Yes, it might have
been different if he had married Maria; but only if she
could be here with him now, lying in his narrow bed.

Land of his own ! How right Maria had always been !

In his great contentment, his thoughts went back to
the only other time when his happiness had been as
complete as this—to the first days with Maria. Yes—
Cosme was good and fine, but Maria—she was
beautiful !

The days were clear and Miguel worked like a slave.
Under the litter on the floor, he found a good, solid
base made in the ancient manner, of earth mixed with

ox-blood. It was hard as stone. With a leather thong, he devised a hinge for the door; he repaired the fireplace set across one corner of the room, remade the bunk, cleaned out the mess and burned quantities of sweet-smelling juniper branches to drive out the odours.

He examined the land around the house and decided that he dared to hobble the horses and turn them loose: not knowing the condition or location of the fences, he was afraid to let them graze unhobbled. But what delighted him most was the great cleared expanse of good, dark soil west of the house, sloping gently towards the valley; it looked to be at least a hundred acres in extent. Who ever heard of one man having a farm as big as that? But what labour, before it could be made to yield!

No plough had touched it for years—its old scars showed faintly, but had mainly healed and been reclaimed by the tough grasses which grew elsewhere. Patches of tumbleweed grew on it, but he could burn that now, for it was dry and right for burning. As if to heap him with blessings, fate disclosed a stream about a mile east of the house, towards the high mountains, which could be ditched—with what terrific labour—to the fields below. The water would have to be lifted out of its bed and brought circuitously around hills, but it could be done. Knowledge of how to do it was almost an instinct in Miguel and all the mountain men; many an American surveyor, with instruments and tables to guide him, laid out a ditch with less success than a Mexican with nothing but a pick and shovel.

But he would need help for this; alone, it would take him a year. Benito, perhaps, and some of his cousins would come up later on and help him with it. And he hoped for an open spring so they could come early and get it finished in time for planting. Evidently the man who had tried to farm the land before had been too lazy to build the ditch, and he hardly blamed him. It would be a huge task, especially if he had to do it alone.

Fixing the roof was the hardest of all his jobs, for he had to rip the whole of it away and begin from the beginning, using green boughs of pine trees for his base. Over this he laid his tarred paper, then six inches of earth, then another layer of paper. It was a flat roof on a log house, and he didn't know how to manage. But his work was tested one day when it rained so hard for half an hour that he didn't think anything could stand under the downpour. He sat under his roof beside the fireplace, where a feeble blaze fought the deluge of raindrops coming down the flue and quickly lost. But the roof held.

His triumph was boundless, but so, also, was the cost of it in labour. Eliseo could have done everything in half the time. Miguel saw now how the years passed in going to school and keeping his father's store availed him nothing in practical things. The right way of doing everything, from driving a nail to building a house, had to be discovered, after much wasteful trying and failing. Finding the right way, however, gave him a sense of achievement such as he had never known before.

Until he had to go back to Hormiga for more supplies, he lived and worked more like an animal than a man. His brain had no time for any but useful functioning— no dreams, or flights or reveries. At night he was so tired that he almost fell asleep over his supper, and awoke in the morning refreshed and eager for the day. Reluctantly at last he hitched the horses to the wagon and turned his back on his land. His heart was heavy at leaving, but he was lifted up by the certainty of returning—with Cosme and his son.

They made a *fiesta* of the departure from Hormiga. They were gay to hide the grief which underlay their feelings. Concepcion's tears hid close beneath her laughter, and Eliseo smiled through a mask of sorrow. Only Miguel felt nothing but hope. Three wagons formed the sparkling caravan—for such his fancy made it—and six men to help him plough his fields and bring the water to the farm.

Suddenly confusion ended. A silence fell upon the crowd of friends and relatives waiting to see them off.

All was ready—the drivers of the wagons sat with their whips poised. And then Miguel gave a shout and brought his whip down on his horses' flanks. Concepcion loosed the weeping which had been choking her, the crowd waved and shouted. As Miguel's wagon, in the lead, moved to a creaking start, he turned and waved his arm.

Cosme—bright-eyed and smiling—sat on the seat beside him, holding her son in her arms. At the first lurch of the wagon, she turned her face forward. She swayed as he swayed, to the dipping of the wheels, and did not look behind.

THE END